THE SMALL RAIN

THE

SMALL RAIN

by

MADELEINE L'ENGLE

New York

FARRAR STRAUS GIROUX

To my father,

CHARLES WADSWORTH CAMP

Western wind, when wilt thou blow,
The small rain down can rain?
Christ, if my love were in my arms
And I in my bed again!

*T*HE SMALL RAIN is very much a first novel. It was begun in college, and then worked on more single-mindedly after I graduated and went to New York, sharing an apartment in the Village with three other girls—two aspiring actresses, an aspiring pianist, and myself, an aspiring writer.

A writer of fiction does not earn a living by writing novels, at least at first, so, with less naïveté than it might seem, I decided to try to earn my living in the theater. I'd had a couple of summers of stock, and had spent most of my extracurricular time at Smith working in plays. I knew I was a good actress. I also knew that I was much too tall and clumsy to become a star, and anyhow, what I wanted to be was a writer. So I was willing to take any kind of job whatsoever in the theater—general understudy, assistant stage manager, anything.

It so happened that Eva Le Gallienne, Joseph Schildkraut, and Margaret Webster were offering auditions, that winter, to any aspiring young actor or actress who wanted to apply. So of course I applied. I did have the sense to use my own material, geared to a gawky, still-adolescent young woman. Most of the girls were doing Shakespeare for Miss Webster, Chekhov or other familiar playwrights for Miss Le Gallienne and Mr. Schildkraut, and there I was, anything but the glamorous young actress, saying lines they had not heard before. So they listened.

And that led to my first job, in *Uncle Harry*, the play in which Eva Le Gallienne and Joseph Schildkraut were then appearing. The understudy was leaving, and I was given the job. I also played the matron of the prison in the last scene, and I had two lines to say: "But it might be important, sir." "But it can't do any harm."

And I wrote. I wrote backstage. I wrote, after the play closed on Broadway and went on tour, on trains, in hotel rooms I shared with other girls, in dressing rooms. And I sent out, mostly to little magazines and university quarterlies, stories I had written in college, and I began to get acceptances. To my surprise, I received letters of inquiry from several publishers who had seen my stories and wanted to know if I had a novel in mind. Of course I did. I had a novel almost finished, in longhand.

When we came back from the tour of *Uncle Harry*, I typed up the manuscript and sent it off to the first publisher who had written to me.

It was my good fortune that there was at that time at Vanguard Press a young editor named Bernard Perry. Bernard was able to make me know how to take my shapeless manuscript and turn it into a book. I was given a hundred-dollar option, and I spent that summer rewriting my novel. I had a deadline, not set by the publishers. In the autumn I was going to be general understudy, assistant stage manager, and play several bit parts in Chekhov's *The Cherry Orchard*, produced and directed by Margaret Webster, with Eva Le Gallienne and Joseph Schildkraut as stars. I wanted to have the book done before we went into rehearsal.

I had left the apartment I shared with three other girls, and moved into a smaller one of my own where there were no interruptions. I had more to pay out in rent, but I had managed to save a good bit out of the $65-a-week Equity-minimum salary, and I had that hundred dollars option money, and I lived frugally. And wrote.

I was not unaware of the world around me. The United States was at war, after the bombing of Pearl Harbor. I was corresponding with school friends in England who were spending nights in bomb shelters, or were nursing at the front lines. In France, I had cousins who were fighting with the Maquis, going to Africa with de Gaulle. The streets of New York were full of soldiers and sailors.

And yet the pages of that first novel make no mention of war at all. The story is set in those years of precarious peace between the First and Second World War—still, I find it strange that my personal preoccupation with war is in no way reflected in the book.

Most first novels are a mishmash of the writer's experience. *The Small Rain* is not autobiographical, but my theater experience is on the first page. I am not Katherine, though we share much in common. I was a slow developer, Katherine a quick one. I was a writer, Katherine a pianist; but she approached her work with the same determination and single-mindedness with which I approached mine. Katherine's mother died when she was fourteen, and I was blessed in having my own mother live to be ninety. But my father had died when I was seventeen, and I worked out some of my grief in the death of Katherine's mother.

No fictional character can come only from the author's imagination. Our subconscious minds store up millions of impressions for us. But I do not deliberately write from anyone I know, and until a fictional character becomes as real for me as my family and friends, I can't write about that person. So Katherine and the people surrounding her —Julie, her mother; Manya, her stepmother; Justin, her piano teacher; Felix, Sarah, Pete, her friends—became vividly alive for me. Like Katherine I went to a boarding school in Switzerland, and like Katherine I was lonely and unhappy. I had a piano teacher I loved, a gentle Frenchwoman who encouraged me. I did not have a special friend like Sarah during those years; my second year at school I had some good friends, but no one with whom I was able to talk as Katherine was able to talk with Sarah. I did not share with anyone my grief about my father until after high school.

My Greenwich Village experience was not unlike Katherine's, but it was mine, and Katherine's was hers. The deeper I got into the novel, the more Katherine became Katherine and the less Madeleine. But we are sisters, there's no doubt about that.

The Small Rain was a surprise success, and did well enough so that I could live comfortably for a couple of years, and I thought I was on my way. In a sense I was, though the way was more roundabout and far more bumpy than I expected. I worked on my second novel, met my husband, Hugh Franklin, in *The Cherry Orchard*, and married him in *The Joyous Season*. We had our first child; I published a third book, and a fourth while I was again pregnant, and we had left the theater and moved to the country, where we ran a general store, and finally, after a near decade, returned to the city, and Hugh to the theater.

That was a rough decade. There were babies, and washing machines which froze when full of diapers, and the deaths of friends, and hard work building up a store, and rejection slips for me, hundreds of rejection slips.

I did some of the growing and hurting and living I knew I needed to go through before I could write another book about Katherine—for, ever since the publication of *The Small Rain*, I had known I was going to find out what happened to her. There are twenty-nine books and thirty-seven years between the publication of *The Small Rain* and that of *A Severed Wasp*.

After that desolate decade my books began to sell. When Farrar, Straus and Giroux accepted *A Wrinkle in Time*, I had finally found my publishing home. There, I am given a freedom seldom available to writers, to write whatever I want and need to write, moving from fiction to non-fiction to poetry to drama, to books marketed for children to books marketed for adults.

Finally I began to get hints in the creative subconscious mind of what kinds of things might have happened to Katherine in the intervening years, very different from the things which had happened to me, and yet nevertheless within the context of my own being, for Katherine and I are still sisters, especially in our attitude toward our work.

In *A Severed Wasp* I returned not only to Katherine but to other characters from *The Small Rain*. Characters continue to grow when the writer is not looking. I was surprised indeed to have Felix a retired bishop; I never thought he'd turn out that way! The war which was not in *The Small Rain* had its drastic effects on Katherine and Justin, as it had on all of us who were young during those dark years. I was surprised to find Mimi Oppenheimer, a character from a much older novel, *A Winter's Love*, be both friend and foil for Katherine, and I became very fond of Mimi.

I hope that I will be able to move into old age as realistically and graciously as Katherine did. I hope that I will continue to serve my writing as she served her music. Because she was the protagonist of my first novel, I feel a special closeness to her, and that closeness deepened and strengthened as I wrote *A Severed Wasp*. I am pleased *The Small Rain* is back in print, for it completes a circle.

MADELEINE L'ENGLE
New York   1984

THE SMALL RAIN

ATHERINE knew, before the first act was half over, that something was wrong with Manya. She stood in the wings, waiting for her entrance, a good ten minutes early, because she could hear no cues from her dressing room. Manya's voice, coming from the stage, was rich and vibrant, as usual, but there was a break a fraction of a second long in the middle of one of her speeches, and the child knew, without seeing, that Manya had pressed the palm of her hand against her forehead to collect herself before she went on. Katherine turned to Mac, the property man, who was arranging the tea tray on his small table in the corner.

"Mac, what's the matter with Aunt Manya?"

Mac put his hand behind his ear, and she repeated her question in a louder whisper, but he just shook his head and stirred the tea in the teapot, cut two slices in the loaf of bread and fitted the pieces together again. Katherine left him and went to stand by the fire inspector, who had watched the play from his post in the wings every night for six months, and every night for six months had confiscated Manya's cigarettes only when she had smoked them down to the end. He put his arm around Katherine when she came up to him but didn't take his eyes off Manya on the stage. The child stayed leaning against him in the shadow for a moment, then wandered over to where Pete Burns, the assistant stage manager and general understudy, was holding the book. When he saw her he beckoned.

"It's kind of slow tonight, kitten. See if you can pick up the pace."

Katherine loved Pete because he treated her as though she were an adult. "What's the matter with Aunt Manya?" she whispered.

"With Madame Sergeievna? Nothing, kitten. The whole act's just dragging. It's almost time for your entrance."

Katherine left him, tiptoeing across the back of the stage, running her forefinger softly over the mass of radiator pipes that lined the back wall higher than organ pipes, radiators that were never very warm, because Manya could not bear to have the backstage or her dressing room too hot. Katherine was glad because she disliked heat, too. She climbed the wooden stairs with the inadequate railing that had given way once at an understudy rehearsal when Pete Burns leaned too heavily against it, and stood on the platform, waiting for her cue. She ran her fingers through her heavy, dark hair to make sure that it fell down her back in a shaggy mane, peered through the peephole until Manya crossed slowly to the fireplace and sat down beside it, and waited until Manya leaned down and pulled off one jeweled shoe; then she ran down the stairs. The scene went easily, quickly. She did not have to worry about picking up the pace. But sitting at Manya's feet, looking up at her, speaking her lines with unaffected sincerity, she still felt that something was wrong, and she was not surprised when Manya did not come in on cue. In the silence that followed, a silence that seemed gigantic but in reality lasted only a second, Katherine saw Pete in the wings, his lips half opened, ready to throw Manya the cue if he had to, saw Manya push against her forehead again with the palm of her hand, saw the dark, Slavic eyes suddenly go blank. Manya's line was not an important one, and Katherine came in with her own next one. The expression came back

4

to Manya's eyes, she picked up her cue, in the wings Pete Burns relaxed, the scene continued without difficulty, and certainly no one in the audience knew that anything had happened.

Pete Burns came into Katherine's dressing room while she was taking off her make-up. Because the cast was so small, she had a dressing room to herself, and Pete sat down in a straight chair, tipped it back, and leaned his fair head against the cream-colored plaster of the wall, watching her smear cold cream onto her face.

"That was nice work, Miss Forrester, covering Madame Sergeievna like that."

"Was it all right?" she asked, a little anxiously. "I didn't think her line mattered right there."

"It was the best thing you could have done. You've an amazing instinct, kitten. You ought to be a very fine actress someday."

"I don't think I want to be an actress."

"Oh," he said. "I suppose you want to be a policewoman or get married and have eleven children."

"No. I want to be a pianist like my mother."

His face lost its teasing look and became almost reverent. "I heard your mother play once," he said. "I think it was the last concert she gave at Carnegie. She was soloist with the Philharmonic. I remember it very clearly, because it was my seventeenth birthday and I'd just been given my first job, a bit part in a musical that closed out of town. I was awfully excited about it at the time, though, and I went to the concert to celebrate. I did what I always wanted to do in the theater, bought a seat in the front row, even though I knew that wasn't what you're supposed to do for music, but I'm glad I did, because I could really look at your mother. I certainly fell for her. Baby, I dreamed about her for months. I

5

don't know what it was, her music or something about her, but I fell."

"Yes," Katherine said, wiping off a layer of cold cream and putting on another. "People always did."

Pete untilted his chair so that all its four feet stood on the floor. "It wasn't that she was beautiful. Manya Sergeievna, now, is what I call beautiful. But there was something about her, I don't know, a magnetism, something that certainly got me. It's funny how you can fall in love with someone you don't know. I never did with actresses or movie stars. I thought it was crazy. I thought I was above that kind of stuff." He paused, and Katherine knew he wanted to ask her something, but when he spoke, all he said was, "Look, kitten, how old are you?"

"Ten. I was ten in October. I haven't seen Mother for three years. I wish I could see her. I want so awfully to see her. It's so hard to have a mother and not be able to see her." This was something she had never said; not to Aunt Manya, with whom she lived; not to her father, with whom she had dinner every Sunday, but with whom she didn't live because he was a composer and much too vague and preoccupied with his music to be any good at taking care of Katherine. Manya could go from one play to another, entertain lavishly, work on innumerable charities, and still find time for Katherine, who was really no relation at all, just the daughter of Julie and Tom Forrester, her closest friends.

Katherine's lip trembled. "It's not that I don't love Aunt Manya, you know," she said. "She's wonderful to me. It's just that I need my own mother."

Pete didn't say anything, but he smiled at her, and she felt that she could talk to Pete, although she had never been able to talk to anybody else, because he loved her mother.

6

There was a knock on the door, and Irina, Manya's maid, stuck her head in. "Miss Katherine?"

"Yes, Irina, come in."

"Mme Sergeievna will be a little late tonight. She has visitors, so she says just to wait."

"Oh. All right."

"Does she want me to take the baby home?" Pete asked. He sometimes took Katherine home when Manya was going out and her nurse couldn't come for her.

"No, thank you, Mr. Burns. She's going right home. She just has—someone—in her dressing room. And a dozen people waiting to see her tonight, when she's so tired. So she says will you just wait for her, please, Miss Katherine."

"All right. Thank you, Irina."

When Irina had gone Katherine turned back to Pete. "Aunt Manya said as soon as Mother was well I could see her. I should think a person could get well of almost anything in three years, wouldn't you?"

"Well," Pete said, "I guess she was hurt pretty badly." He looked embarrassed, as though he weren't sure how much he should say.

Katherine got up, her face shiny with cold cream, some of her blue grease paint still smeared about her eyes, and stood in front of Pete. "Pete," she said solemnly, "if you know anything about Mother, please tell me. It isn't fair that I shouldn't be told things. I'm old enough. I ought to know."

"Well, kitten," Pete said slowly, "tell me what you know."

"I don't know anything," Katherine said, "except it was the day before my seventh birthday and Mother was driving out to Aunt Manya's place in Connecticut and she had an accident. I know her left shoulder and arm were badly crushed, and I guess it means she can't play any more. I don't know. I woke up on my birthday and nobody was there but Nanny and she was crying and I knew something awful must have happened because Nanny never cries and she never lets me cry, and then Dr. Bradley and Father and Aunt Manya came in and Dr. Bradley told me Mother had hurt herself and I wouldn't be able to see her for a few days until she was better, and I was naughty because it was my birthday and I didn't want my birthday to be spoiled and I wanted God to take back everything that had happened. And Father and Aunt Manya couldn't do anything with me, and then Dr. Bradley took me off and talked to me, and he said he'd lend me half his birthday. His birthday was in July. And he did, too. I went to his house and he gave me strawberries and cream and he was lovely to me and talked and talked. I guess he loved Mother sort of like you. I haven't seen him much since then because he and Aunt Manya fight, and anyhow I think he's mad with Aunt Manya about something." She was talking rapidly, letting her thoughts tumble out in any order they came to her. "And I remember the afternoon of my birthday Nanny took me to the park and I played with a little girl called Sarah Courtmont and she said I ought to find out what hospital Mother was in and sneak out after I went to bed and go see her. And I tried. I got to the hospital; I found out which one it was from Aunt Manya; but they wouldn't let me see Mother, and Aunt Manya came and got me, and then a few days later I went to live with her. Nanny came, too. You know Nanny."

"Um-hum," Pete nodded.

"Father never would tell me anything. Aunt Manya told me that her shoulder had been crushed and bones in her arm broken and her face and neck were cut, too. I kept thinking I'd see her in just a little while. But I never have. And this year when I've asked Father about her he's been mad at me, and Aunt Manya's acted funny. Sometimes I've wondered if

Mother's been at Aunt Manya's place in Connecticut, because Aunt Manya drives out almost every week end, and she never takes me and I think that's sort of funny. And that's all I know, Pete."

"That's about all I know, too, kitten," Pete said. "My show was in Boston when she had the accident, but it was in all the papers, of course. But they didn't say much, except that she'd been badly injured and probably wouldn't be able to play again. I didn't know anybody at the time who knew your mother or who could give me any information, so I just had to take what the papers said. And lately there've been only rumors, and you know what theatrical rumors are, kitten, completely not to be trusted."

"Well, what were the rumors?" Katherine demanded.

She knew Pete was sorry he had spoken, but he went on. "There was one that she came to the opening night."

"Pete!"

"It's just a rumor. There's probably not an ounce of truth in it. Remember that time when everyone said Madame Sergeievna was going to marry that dreadful creature, and she'd never even met him? I shouldn't have mentioned it."

"Yes, you should, Pete. It's not right that I should be treated like a baby."

Pete smiled, but all he said was, "Look, kitten, maybe you'd better not tell anyone about this little talk."

"Of course not, Pete. Pete, what was the matter with Aunt Manya tonight?"

"Oh, I don't think anything was, baby. Everybody has an off performance once in a while."

"Aunt Manya doesn't unless there's something the matter."

"Well, she's probably just tired. She's been doing a lot."

From downstairs a voice shouted. "Pete! Pete Burns!"

9

"I guess my girl's here," Pete said. "Good night, kitten. Don't worry your little head." He pushed the chair back against the wall, looked in the mirror to smooth down his hair and see that his tie was straight, and left.

Katherine finished taking off her make-up, wiped her face with witch hazel, and dressed. She locked her dressing-room door, went downstairs, hung her key on the board, and wandered across the stage toward Manya's dressing room. Irina was sitting outside the door, reading a newspaper, and she looked worried when she saw Katherine.

"You'd better wait upstairs, Miss Katherine," she said. "Madame Sergeievna isn't ready yet."

"I'll wait here with you."

Irina looked anxiously toward the dressing-room door. "I want to read my paper. You'll be more comfortable upstairs."

Suddenly a man's voice, loud and excited, was heard through the closed dressing-room door. "I know you want to talk to Julie alone, Manya, but really, I—"

And then Manya's voice, gentle, soothing, the words indistinct.

"That was my father," Katherine said.

Irina stood up. "I'll tell Madame Sergeievna you're here."

"Oh, no, don't. I'll go upstairs." She turned, grabbed her key, and almost ran back toward her dressing room. On the iron stairs she bumped into Pete Burns coming down with his girl, and she wanted to catch hold of him, to say, "Pete, Father's in Aunt Manya's dressing room and something's the matter and they were talking about Mother," but he wasn't alone, so all she said was, "Good night, Pete."

"Good night, kitten. You know Rosa, don't you?"

"Yes. Hello. Good night."

"Is anything the matter?" Pete asked.

"No. Aunt Manya isn't ready for me yet. That's all. Good

night." And she ran the rest of the way upstairs and to her dressing room.

It was almost an hour before Manya was ready. In the taxi on the way home she put her arm around Katherine, drew her close, and said, "Baby, I didn't dream I'd be so long. I should have had Nanny come for you or let Pete take you home."

"It's all right," Katherine said. "Pete had a date with his girl and anyhow I'm not sleepy."

Manya fingered one of Katherine's smooth heavy braids for a while before she spoke. Then she said, "Would you like to drive out to the country with me tomorrow night?"

"Yes."

"Good. I'll get Nanny to pack your little bag for you, then." The taxi drew up in front of the apartment house, and Manya asked Katherine, "What does the meter say?"

"Fifty-five," Katherine answered.

She was always allowed to have some supper and stay up an hour after the theater. Tonight she wandered into Manya's study, pulled *The Oxford Book of English Verse* off the shelf, and curled up in the big red-plush chair. Nanny brought her a bowl of vegetable soup and went to draw her bath. She ate the soup quickly and began leafing through the book, reading a poem here and there, reading the verses aloud, half singing them to little tunes of her own making.

After a while Manya came in and sat down opposite her. Katherine put the book down and watched her aunt, watched her pull off all her rings and shake them in her hands like dice, as she always did when she was nervous. And Katherine noticed that she was speaking with practically no accent. On-stage Manya had only a slight musical inflection in her speech to mark it as being foreign, but in private life she almost always spoke with a heavy Russian accent, saying that it helped her to keep her identity. Only when she was particularly distraught did the accent go.

—I mustn't ask her anything, Katherine thought.—I'll find out more if I wait till she's ready to talk.

After a while Manya slipped her rings back onto her fingers, reached over to Katherine, and took the book out of her lap. Katherine, watching her, noticed that there were deep circles under her eyes and that her hands trembled a little as she turned the pages until she found her place. Then she sat staring down at the page for a long time. Finally she got up and walked hurriedly out of the room. Katherine could see that she was crying.

She gazed after her, and when Manya had disappeared through the door and down the hall and around the corner, Katherine kept staring at the bright rectangle of light the door made of the hall. After a while she got up, and picked up the book from the sofa, where Manya had flung it, its leaves all crumpled. She smoothed the pages down very carefully, and when she came to one that still had little wet spots on it like rain, left there by Manya's tears, she knew that the short verses with the title heavily underscored were what had made Manya cry. Softly she read to herself:

> *Western wind, when wilt thou blow,*
> *The small rain down can rain?*
> *Christ, if my love were in my arms*
> *And I in my bed again!*

For some reason her tears mingled on the crumpled page with Manya's. She put her head down on the book and sobbed in a sudden outburst of agony.

Nanny came in and picked her up, asking with anxiety, "Whatever's the matter?"

"Nothing."

12

"What are you crying about?"

"Nothing. I—I don't know."

"I've never heard such nonsense. It's all those books your Aunt Manya lets you read. Your bath's ready. Come along to bed." Nanny's voice was sharp, but her hands were gentle as she stroked Katherine's head.

TWO

AFTER the play the next night, Manya had her car brought around to the stage door. Katherine said good night to Pete, followed Manya out, and climbed into the car beside her. They started off in silence. Manya headed west to the river to get up on the drive that would lead them to the Merritt Parkway. She drove silently, smoking constantly. Katherine looked out the window, but she kept watching Manya out of the corner of her eye, watching her carefully when she lit her cigarettes and wondering why she was so silent. They had driven for an hour when Manya said abruptly, staring ahead through the windshield, "Katherine."

"Yes?" Manya never called her Katherine. Always Katya or Katyusha or baby.

"You will see your mother tonight."

Katherine began to tremble. "Oh—" she said, and she, too, stared ahead through the windshield.

They drove on for about fifteen minutes. Then Manya spoke again. "You'll find her a little changed." And after a long pause, "But not really."

Katherine didn't say anything. She sat very tense, staring into the blackness, until Manya turned off the Parkway and headed down a small road.

"Are we nearly there?"

"About fifteen minutes."

Again Katherine sat silent. She ventured a quick glance and saw that Manya's lips were set and that her hands were

14

tight on the steering wheel. In the small rear-view mirror she could see Manya's eyes, clouded, unhappy, unveiled.

They turned off on a dirt road, and Manya said, "Here we are." She drove up a steep hill and stopped in front of a small white gate. Someone was standing at the gate, waiting. Katherine opened the door, tumbled out of the car, and fell into her mother's arms.

"Oh, Mother—" she gasped. "Mother—"

Julie's arms were tight around her, Julie's cheek close to hers. Katherine nestled against her, trembling. It was a long time before Julie said anything. Then she whispered, "Darling, you're trembling, you're shaking." She kept Katherine pressed tightly to her, holding her close when Katherine tried once to pull away. She, too, was trembling.

"Let's go inside." Katherine felt Manya's hand on her shoulder and felt her mother stiffen.

"Not yet, Manya, not yet," her mother said.

"Julie." Manya's voice was sharp. "Stop being a fool. Come along."

"I'll put the car in."

"Charlot will put the car in."

"But he's—"

"Julie. Charlot will put the car in. Come along." Manya took Julie's hand. "Come along, Katyusha, and Julie and I'll show you the house. Sleepy?"

"No." Katherine put her arm around her. mother and whispered, "Oh, Mother."

Manya led the way into the house. They entered into a small hall, lighted by a kerosene lamp on a round mahogany table. Three doors opened off the hall, and a stairway. Manya opened the center door, and they went into a large dark Victorian room filled with books and photographs of

15

theater people and comfortable chairs and two grand pianos. Manya began turning on the lamps.

"Oh, Manya," Julie said.

"You've got to stop being an idiot." Manya bent down and put a match to the fire that was laid in the fireplace.

Julie pushed Katherine away from her and said, "Let me look at you, my darling."

Katherine stared up at her mother. It was the same beautiful face, in spite of a deep scar that ran across one cheek and down onto her neck, the same beautiful face, in spite of the lines that pain and agony had left on it. It was her mother, her mother, and she was safe once more.

"You've grown," Julie said slowly. "You aren't a baby any more. You're grown up. Even your braids are longer. You're thin. You're still much too thin. But you're still my Katherine."

Katherine gazed at her hungrily, mutely, until Julie said, brusquely, "Well? How about me? Do you still know me?" Katherine nodded. "Have I changed too much?"

"You're not changed. You're not changed."

Julie raised a hand to her face and traced the scar with one finger. Katherine reached up and caught hold of her hands and shouted over and over, "You're not changed! You're not changed!"

After a moment Julie broke away and almost bumped into Manya coming in with a tray laden with a bottle of white wine and three glasses. Julie took the bottle, which was already uncorked, and poured herself a glassful. Manya put the tray down on a long table in front of the bookshelves and stood watching while Julie finished her drink and poured another, then filled a glass for Manya and put a little in the third glass for Katherine.

"Do you want some, baby?"

16

"Yes, please." Katherine took the glass and held it tightly. The wine felt warm and comforting as she swallowed it. Julie curled up in a big blue chair, pulling Katherine down beside her. Katherine leaned her head on her mother's shoulder and sipped at her wine. After a little while Julie turned her face around so she could see it.

"Sleepy, baby?"

"I don't think so."

"Tomorrow we'll have a long talk, shall we?"

"Yes."

"I'd better take you up to bed now. Coming, Manya?"

Manya crossed to her desk. "Not quite yet. I want to write a letter."

"All right. I'll be down. Come on, baby."

Katherine stood up, and Julie put an arm around her and led her into the hall and up the stairs. The wine made her a little dizzy, and it was good to have the wine making her brain feel funny because she knew it would have felt that way anyhow, and knowing that it was partly the wine made everything seem less confusing. She felt her mother's arm close around her and felt drowsy and happy—the kind of happiness she had felt on the opening night of the play when she had taken a curtain call all by herself.

Julie took her into a small room paneled in blue, where there was just room for a bed, a chair, and a low chest of drawers. Katherine stood still while Julie undressed her, and she realized that her mother's left arm was stiff and gave her a good deal of pain, although she tried to hide it.

"I practiced two hours every day."

"Did you, baby?"

"Every day. Sunday, too."

"You shall play for me tomorrow."

17

"All right. Will you—I'm all undressed and it's cold! My pajamas are downstairs!"

"Get into bed quickly and I'll get them."

Katherine slipped her naked body in between the cold sheets and watched her mother go out of the room. Julie, in her blue tweed suit, was still the most erect person Katherine had ever seen, but she was very thin. As thin as Katherine. It was cold between the sheets with nothing on, and she shivered, but Julie was back in a few minutes with flannel pajamas, and she climbed into them quickly.

"Tired, darling?" Julie asked.

"A little. There's still lots of snow here, even if it is April, isn't there, Mother?"

"Yes."

"There isn't much snow in New York."

"Isn't there?" Julie switched off the lamp and the moonlight came in the window and hit down against the snow and its reflection came in the window again. Julie went over to the window and pushed it open wide. She stood there, looking out.

"There's one side of the moon nobody ever sees," Katherine said.

Julie didn't answer.

"We turn around, I mean the world does, around the sun and around on our own axis, and the moon turns around us but we both turn so that we only see one side of the moon and the moon only sees one side of us," Katherine said. "That's interesting, isn't it, Mother?"

"Yes. Manya tells me you read a lot."

"Yes."

"Do you like to read?"

"Yes."

"Do you like to practice?"

18

"Yes."

"Do you want to be a pianist?"

"Yes."

"You don't want to be an actress?"

"I don't think so."

"Not sure?"

"Not quite."

"Well, you've still got a long time to decide."

"Yes."

"It isn't because of me you want to be a pianist, is it?"

"No."

"Because a decision like that must never be because of somebody else. It's got to be for you, yourself, alone."

"I know, Mother."

"You're sure?"

"Yes. Oh, Mother!"

"What, my darling?"

"Oh, Mother . . . it's so good . . . to be able to say 'Oh, Mother' and have you hear it."

"Baby!"

"Why couldn't I have been with you? Where have you been?"

"It's too late to talk now, darling. We'll have a long talk tomorrow."

"But I won't have to leave you now, will I? Can't we all go home?"

"I don't know."

Katherine sat up excitedly. "But I don't want to leave you. I won't!"

"You won't have to leave me."

"Then can't we go home? Can't we, Mother?"

"I'm not sure."

"But I won't have to leave you?"

"No."

"Have you been here at Aunt Manya's all the time?"

"No. Only the past week."

"Where have you been?"

"Baby, I said we'd talk tomorrow."

"Couldn't we talk now?"

"It's too late."

"But I'm not sleepy."

"Tomorrow morning we'll go for a long walk all by ourselves and we'll talk and talk and talk. You go to sleep now."

"Where are you sleeping?"

"Just across the hall."

"Will you sing to me?"

"Yes."

"Tickle behind my ears?"

Julie tweaked Katherine's nose in the old familiar way. "If you're a good girl."

"I'm a good girl."

Julie bent down and began to kiss her, little loving kisses that made her feel like a baby again, completely secure and protected. Then Julie began to sing, softly, in the low, rather husky voice Katherine had tried so often to hear in her mind, and had never quite been able to. And she was sleepy. And she was asleep.

She woke up the next morning to see the sun flashing in on her from the mirror of the snow and a huge tiger-striped cat sitting on the foot of the bed. She jumped out of bed quickly and ran across the hall. The door to her mother's room was open, and the bed empty. Katherine ran back to the small blue-paneled room and dressed. Then she hurried downstairs and stood in the hall for a moment. The door into the library where they had been the night before was open and she went in. A very thin young boy, about fourteen years

20

old, was putting logs in the basket by the fireplace. He grinned up at her as she came in.

"Hello. You are Katherine?" He spoke fluent English, with a slight French accent.

"Yes."

"I'm Charles Bejart. I live with your aunt. I work for her."

"Do you know where Mother is?"

"Maybe she's in the kitchen. Aunt Manya's still asleep. They talked extremely late last night."

"What time is it?"

"Twelve-ten."

"Where's the kitchen?"

Then her mother's voice came from behind her. "All dressed, my baby?"

"Mother!"

"Darling! Whoa! You'll knock me down! Well!" Julie sat down in the big blue chair and pulled Katherine down with her. "This is Katherine, Charlot."

"Yes, I know."

"Do you think she looks like me?"

"No. Not a bit."

"Good. You still look like your grandmother, darling. I hope you'll grow up to be like her. I married your father because of your grandmother. Are you hungry?"

"Sort of."

"Charlot, would you be an angel and bring Katherine's breakfast tray in? I don't want to bother Masha. She's cooking a very special something for lunch."

Charlot was off like a streak. He moved with a wild sort of grace that made Katherine follow him with her eyes, even though she wanted to watch her mother.

Julie was looking at him, too. "I've only seen one other

person move the way Charlot does. Sarah Bernhardt. You slept well, didn't you, baby?"

"Yes. I meant to wake up early. I'm mad."

"I'm glad you slept. You looked so tired last night. You shouldn't have circles under your eyes. I don't like to see you with circles under your eyes."

"I'm not tired."

"What time do you get to bed at night?"

"Twelve-thirty, usually. But I sleep till ten-thirty every morning."

"Have you been happy with Manya?"

"Yes. But I'd rather be with you."

"She loves you very much."

"I'd rather be with you."

"You're going to be with me, my darling."

Charlot floated in with a breakfast tray, which he put on a small table by the fire—orange juice and a soft-boiled egg and toast and apricot jam and a big glass of milk. Julie pushed Katherine gently off her lap and toward the breakfast table.

"I'm going to see how the rooster is getting on with the new hens," Charlot said. "You'll let me know if I can do anything for you, Mrs. Forrester?"

"I'll let you know, Charlot."

He left slowly, draggingly, unwilling, this time, to leave, turning back at the door to look at Julie. She smiled at him, then said to Katherine, "Eat your breakfast, baby."

"I am. Mother, why haven't I been with you? Where have you been?"

"I was very ill and in the hospital for a long time."

"I know."

"I had to have a lot of operations. Things didn't work out the way they should have and after one operation I had pneumonia and they thought I was going to die."

22

"Nobody told me. Nobody told me anything."

"I didn't want you to know, my dear. You're sad and melancholy enough as it is."

"I should have known."

"It wasn't only my body that was ill, darling. It was mostly my mind. I was all bitter and eaten up with self-pity inside, and I didn't want you to see that. I knew I'd never be able to play the piano again—and I knew that my scars, my deformity, made a difference to your father. I was a great deal worse to look at for the first two years and a half than I am now. There were several operations and I wasn't strong, so they had to wait quite a while between them. And I didn't want you to see what I was like during that period. Not my body. Me inside. It would have been dreadful for you. I'm very much ashamed of myself now. I try to excuse myself by saying that it's because I'm still very young. I was only twenty-seven when the accident happened. I'm only thirty now. But that seems ancient to you, doesn't it, my baby?— and it's no excuse for having become the nagging, jealous, bitter, small person that I was. I drank too much, too. It eased the pain, both the inside and the outside pain. Sometimes I still drink too much. You'll have to help me with that. But anything that's happened to me *since* the accident I've deserved. *That* I didn't deserve."

Katherine made no response. She went on eating her breakfast slowly. After a moment Julie began to speak again.

"I'm all right most of the time now. I'm strong and myself again. I'm adjusted to the prospect of never playing again, really playing, adjusted enough to be able to go on living. I'm strong enough to be your mother again and not hurt you. I didn't behave very well at first, last night. I was afraid that you might be changed, or that you might hate me be-

23

cause I'm changed. But that's all right now. We're ourselves again, aren't we?"

"Yes. Oh, yes, Mother, we are."

"Finished your breakfast?"

"Yes."

"Shall we go for our walk now?"

"Yes."

"Where's your coat?"

"Upstairs, I guess."

"Your shoes are good and strong, aren't they?"

"Oh, yes, they're waterproof."

"Hurry up and get your coat, then."

"Mother, if you haven't been here with Aunt Manya, where were you?"

"I was in the hospital a lot of the time. The rest of the time I was on a small farm in Upper New York State. It was quiet and beautiful, and I found peace there again. Go and get your coat and hat now."

Katherine went upstairs. Manya was in the blue-paneled room stroking the big tiger-striped cat. She kissed Katherine and held her close, and the cat jumped up on Katherine's shoulder and licked behind her ear with a strong, rough tongue.

"That's Catherine of Russia," Manya said. "But I'll bet she's had more lovers than the old Empress ever hoped to have. Your mother says she's going to get you a dog. I told her to wait till Lyuba has puppies." She paused, then said abruptly. "I'll miss having you with me."

"Oh."

"But we'll see each other every night at the play, won't we, Katya?"

"Yes."

"Katya."

"What, Aunt Manya?"

"I love your mother more than I would my own sister, and the last thing I want in the world is to hurt her."

"Oh."

"If you grow up to be anything like your mother, you'll be a very wonderful person."

"I know."

"And I love you very much, too."

"You've been so good to me—I—I'm very grateful."

"Don't be silly. I love you as I would my own child. I'm going to miss you like hell. Don't pick up swearing from your mother. Sometimes your mother swears too much."

"I haven't heard her."

"She's being careful. But she'll start slipping soon. Don't worry about her if she gets frightfully depressed—she'll be all right—she's stronger than everybody else I know put together. No matter what happens, she—" Manya broke off and stroked the cat, who began to purr loudly. From downstairs Julie called, "Katherine!"

"I—I'd better hurry," Katherine said. "Mother's waiting for me."

"All right. I guess I've said what I wanted to say. Just don't ever forget that I love you both."

"I won't." Katherine shoved her arms into the sleeves of her coat and jammed on her beret.

"Kiss me good-bye," Manya said.

Katherine went over and kissed Manya softly on the cheek. "Good-bye."

Manya held her tightly for a moment, then pushed the stiff little body away. "It's a good thing I know you love me, my clam," she said. Katherine stood awkwardly in the doorway for a moment, then turned and ran downstairs.

Julie was waiting for her, wrapped in a shabby old fur coat and cap, and a long, blue scarf. She was wearing gloves, but almost as soon as they went out she plunged her hands deep into her coat pockets, pulling one of Katherine's hands in with hers. "Your mittens don't look very warm," she said.

Katherine trotted along by her, panting a little.

"You still limp," Julie said.

"Not much. Hardly any, any more."

"And you shouldn't be so out of breath. Do you get enough exercise?"

"I did while I was at school. Gym. I hated it."

"Why?"

"I wasn't any good. And the gym teacher kept asking silly questions about my hip and taking me off to a special room afterward to see if anything could be done about it. And she didn't like me, because I didn't want her to look at me and poke me. I don't want to have exercise, Mother."

"I know what you'd like." Julie squeezed her hand inside the coat pocket. "You'd like fencing. I think it might be good for your hip, too. I want you to get rid of that limp as quickly as possible. Jack Bradley said you ought to outgrow it. We'll go to Georgio Goldoni, on University Place. He's a great fencing master and you'll love him madly anyhow."

"Well, if you want me to fence, I will."

Julie took her hands out of her pockets and turned Katherine around so that she could look at her again. "Three years is a very long time. You were a baby, and now you're grown up and going to take care of me. Aren't you?"

"Oh, yes, Mother."

"What's happened in those three years that was important to you, my darling? I know the facts, what you've been doing. Manya and Nanny and your father have been good about writing when I've been away. But I want to know what's happened that was important just to you. Who are your friends?"

"Pete Burns."

"He's in the play, isn't he?"

"Yes. He's my friend."

"What about friends your own age?"

"I haven't any."

"Other children at school?"

"I didn't like them. And I haven't been at school since the play began. Aunt Manya said she was going to have to send me to the Professional Children's School soon. There was somebody once I would have liked to know."

"Who was that, my baby?"

"It was the day after you were hurt. My birthday. In the afternoon Nanny took me to the park because I didn't have my birthday then. I had it in July with Dr. Bradley. Did he tell you?"

"Yes, darling."

"There were some children in the park I used to play with sometimes and they asked me to play hide-and-seek. And then someone caught me and I was 'it.' And I couldn't catch anyone. Because of my hip, you know. I ran and ran and I couldn't catch anyone and they all laughed at me and almost let me catch them and then ran away and laughed and I kept trying harder and harder to run fast and then I fell down and I cried and they all laughed. I cried because I was mad." At the memory of that afternoon Katherine's cheeks burned with shame. "When I got up they all started yelling and then ran away. So I went in the opposite direction until I came to an underpass."

Telling her story to Julie, Katherine thought it was strange that she should remember it so clearly. But it was one of those things that was indelibly printed in her memory.

27

She had gone into the underpass and stood under the shadowed arch looking at the names and meaningless words and sentences scratched on the walls. A horse passed overhead and the clop of his hoofs vibrated through her body. She leaned against the cold damp wall, staring ahead at the dark stones opposite her, then at the bright sunlight that surged up at the arch from either side but could never get all the way under, and she hated the sunlight. After she had stood there for a little while, breathing hard, a little girl approached from the direction in which the other children had gone. She was about Katherine's age and size, with short, light-brown hair and the largest blue eyes Katherine had ever seen. She was dressed in a gray pleated skirt, a little too short for her, a gray silk blouse, and a black beret. She walked solemnly by herself toward the underpass as though she were far away from everybody in the world. She got halfway into the underpass before she saw Katherine. Then she stopped and stared at her. Katherine stared back. After a while the little girl said, "Do you want to play with me?"

Katherine looked at her for another moment before she answered, "All right."

"What's your name?"

"Katherine Forrester. What's yours?"

"Sarah Courtmont. How old are you?"

"Seven. It's my birthday."

"My birthday's in April. I'm lots nearer eight than you. Do you want to stay under here?"

"I don't care."

"I like it under here. Were you crying?"

"No."

"You almost were. You stay under here. They're going to feed you to the lions in the morning and I'll come save you."

"All right." Katherine leaned against the wall and watched

28

Sarah as she ran out into the bright sunlight, ran easily and well. After she had gone a few yards she turned around, threw back her shoulders, and walked slowly toward Katherine, looking suspiciously to right and left. When she got to the underpass she dashed over to Katherine.

"Come quickly, dark-haired princess. I will save you!" she whispered.

"I can't—my chains—" Katherine strained against invisible bands.

"My sword will slash them," Sarah hissed, brandishing an invisible weapon. "Come now. You are free. Follow me." And she ran out. Katherine followed her, unable to keep up. After a moment Sarah looked around at her. When Katherine ran up panting, she said with interest, "You limp."

"Yes."

"Why?"

"I hurt my hip."

"Just now?"

"No. When I was two."

"What did they do to you?"

"Lots of things."

"What things?"

"Oh—lots of things."

"Did you have a wheelchair?"

"No."

"Crutches?"

"No."

"What then? You must have had things if you still limp."

"A plaster cast."

"Anything else?"

"A brace."

"What kind of a brace?"

"A lot of leather and iron."

"How big was the cast?"

"All my leg and around my middle here."

Sarah stared at Katherine with interest and then said regretfully, "I've never been hurt. Or even very sick. Do you mind limping?"

"Yes!"

"Why?"

"Because."

"Was that why you were almost crying?"

"No."

"Why were you?"

"Because."

"What are you going to be when you grow up?"

"A pianist, like Mother. What are you going to be?"

"An actress. A great and famous actress with my name in lights on all the marquees . . . Will you play with me again?"

"Yes."

"Often?"

"Yes."

"I don't usually come this far. Next time I'll take you to where I play with my gang."

Katherine asked wistfully, "Do you have a gang?"

"Oh, yes. I'm leader. You can play with us, too."

"I—can't run very fast."

"That's all right. We can rescue you from things."

"It—it doesn't matter to you because I limp?"

"I think it's interesting. Besides, you don't limp much anyhow. Does it matter to you?"

"No. Only sometimes in the park."

"Why were you almost crying?"

"Because."

30

"I won't let you play with my gang if you don't tell me why."

"Because—because my mother's been hurt and in a hospital and they won't let me see her."

"How did she hurt herself?"

"I don't know. No one tells me. It was in her car."

"Why don't you just go to the hospital to see her?"

"I don't know where it is."

"Can't you find out?"

"I guess so. But they wouldn't let me go."

"Just sneak out and go. After you go to bed, maybe."

"Oh . . ."

"My father's a lawyer. That's how I know about things. What's yours?"

"A composer. Thomas Forrester. My mother's a pianist. Julia Forrester."

"Is she hurt bad?"

"I don't know."

"I'd go find out if I were you."

"I guess I will."

"Will you come out to the park tomorrow?"

"I guess so."

"Well, if you do, you come under here and me and my gang will rescue you. You're an early Christian and they're going to throw you to the lions. What we started to do today. And you're all tied up so you can't run."

"All right."

Through the underpass came the echo of Nanny's voice calling. "Katherine! Katherine!"

"I've got to go," Katherine said. "Good-bye."

"Good-bye." Sarah held out her hand. "Do not despair, comrade. Tomorrow I and my men will save thee before it is

31

too late. Hark! I hear footsteps. I must go before I am seen. Farewell! Courage! Farewell!" And she was gone.

While she had been talking Katherine had looked out over the horizon. Now she turned back to Julie. "She wasn't there when I went back to the park the next day, and I looked for her for a long time but I never saw her again. I don't know why I remember it so well except maybe because of its being my birthday and it was so awful and you weren't there. I did sneak out and go to the hospital, but they wouldn't let me see you and they phoned Aunt Manya to come take me home."

"My poor sweet," Julie said.

"Mother—"

"Yes, my baby?"

"Where are we going to live? Are we going home?"

"No, darling, we aren't going home."

"Well, why? Doesn't Father want us to come home?"

Julie was silent, and after a while Katherine asked again, "Doesn't he, Mother?"

"Katherine," Julie said, "I told you that I was a very dreadful person for a while after the accident, and when your father wanted to love me and help me I pushed him away. You can only push people so far, or they'll really go away. And that's what happened. Because how could he know that the harder I pushed the more I wanted him to come close, the more I told him to go away and leave me alone the more I needed him with me . . . I've always been a definite person and when I told him to go away enough times, he went . . . Did he ever talk to you about me?"

"No. I only see him for Sunday dinner, you know, and we don't talk much. I play for him, sometimes, or we just sit together. He's been writing lots and lots of music. Most of it's

32

awfully sad and funny. You feel it in your stomach. When we hear it on the radio Aunt Manya cries. She—" Katherine stopped suddenly, remembering Manya reading from the book of poetry and weeping.

"She what, Katherine?"

"She cries a lot, doesn't she? I mean, it doesn't hurt to come out. It's right there and I guess it stops the pain in your chest if it's like that. I don't cry easily. It gets all stopped up and I can't. If we're not going back to Father, where will we live? Will I still have Sunday dinner with him?"

Tears didn't come easily, but Katherine knew that words were coming out much too easily now. Her words came out too easily because Julie's words hadn't really gone into her yet. She walked along the stony path with bits of rust-colored grass sticking up through the snow and ice, and stared at the black charcoaled lines of stone walls drawn across the snow-covered fields and the black charcoaled branches of trees and the gray sky, old lemon-yellow at the horizon. Julie's words were clear and black against the snow, like the trees and the fences and just as far away.

"Where will we go, Mother?" Katherine asked again.

"I've sublet a small apartment on West Tenth Street," Julie said. "We'll stay there till your play closes at any rate. You're a very fine little actress, my baby."

"Have you seen me? Mother, have you seen me?"

"Of course I have. Several times. I couldn't keep away. You don't know how proud of you I was on opening night. And reading the reviews the next morning. And seeing you helped me to decide that I was strong enough to be with you and that you were old enough and strong enough to help me. So tomorrow afternoon we'll go to Tenth Street. You'll go on having Sunday dinner with your father. Are you cold? You're shivering."

"I guess I am cold, a little."

"Shall we go back?"

"All right."

They turned around and started back to the house. It was far up the path ahead of them, but they could see it high up on the hill between the bare branches of the trees. They walked in silence until Julie asked suddenly, her voice hard and tight, "Have you ever seen your father with your Aunt Manya? Do you see them together often?"

"No," Katherine said, and the wind blew through her coat and into her bones and she pressed closer to her mother, trying to shove her mittened hand even deeper into her mother's coat pocket. "Why?" she whispered, and although Julie couldn't possibly have heard the whisper, she answered the question.

"Katherine, I know you're not going to understand this. Your mind is a clear and clean one. Don't try to understand what I'm going to say with your mind. It's something you'll understand with your heart someday." She paused, and they continued up the hill until they had almost reached the house. Then Julie stopped and took her hands in their cream-colored pigskin gloves out of her pockets and put them on Katherine's shoulders and looked into Katherine's eyes. "Your Aunt Manya and your father love each other," she said. "They've loved each other for quite a long time now. And it's good; for them, it's right. You must know that."

Julie turned away and started to walk quickly down the path. Katherine made a movement to follow her, but stood still after she had taken a few steps, and waited. She stood in the middle of the path, kicking against the snow with one toe, looking down at the path for a long time. Then she walked slowly over to the stone wall at the edge of the path, stepped ankle-deep into the cold snow, and clambered up onto the stones and sat there. The yellow at the horizon was gone now; the entire sky was the color of the inside of an oyster shell and seemed to press against the naked earth, to be clamped over it like a shell, so that it became more and more difficult to breathe. Katherine sat on the wall motionless and thoughtless. Her mind seemed completely empty. Her mind felt the way your chest feels when you are running hard and fall flat and knock all the wind out of you. And thought coming back into her mind hurt just as much as breath coming back into your body.

Slowly she pulled off one of her mittens and drew her finger across her cheek and down onto her neck several times. Then she put her hand back into the mitten, back into her pocket. "I love your mother more than I would my own sister, and the last thing I want in the world is to hurt her," Manya had said, and again Katherine remembered Manya reading from *The Oxford Book of English Verse* and weeping. She tried to remember her father from Sunday to Sunday as she had seen him for the past three years, but he seemed always the same, shabby, vague, preoccupied, listening intently while she played the piano but the rest of the time not paying much attention to her. —I should have been told—she thought.—I should have been told about Mother nearly dying and about everything. I should have been told.—

She sat there on the stone wall saying over and over, I should have been told, until her mind went empty again, and she felt the icy cold of the stones through her coat and the wet cold of the snow that had slid into her shoes. Her hands, curled tight in the mittens and pressed into her pockets, were numb. She climbed off the wall, looking down the road. Her mother was nowhere to be seen, so she turned around and walked back toward the house.

The door to the library was open, and Manya was standing there waiting. She stood very straight in the center of the doorway, watching Katherine come toward her. She stood there in the center of the doorway like a criminal awaiting sentence. And looking at Manya, Katherine knew that what she did or said would matter tremendously to her aunt, that all Manya's passionate intensity was concentrated on waiting for Katherine to speak. Katherine stopped still for a moment in the hall, looking at Manya Sergeievna in her black wool dress with the heavy Russian silver cross, and knew that she couldn't speak. So she pulled off her mittens and her beret, hugged herself, and said, "I'm cold."

Manya stood in the doorway, quivering, for a moment longer; then she looked at Katherine's body instead of at Katherine's mind, and came toward her. "Katyusha, you're frozen."

Katherine slipped past her through the doorway and crossed the library to the fireplace. She crouched down on the hearth bench, shivering. Manya followed her into the library.

"Katya," she began, and bent down and put her hand on Katherine's head. Katherine did not move, but her whole body stiffened; the deep shivers that were shaking her stopped. Manya took her hand away.

"You shall have some hot wine," she said, and went out.

Katherine sat there staring into the fire, and the touch of Manya's hand on her hair burned into her head. She sat there until Manya came in with a glass of hot red wine and sugar with a cinnamon stick in it and gave it to her. She held the glass in a white linen napkin and drank slowly, while the comforting warmth from the sweet, spiced wine began to fill her body. Manya stood by her, watching her dumbly. The heavy silence hung unbroken until Charlot came in, and announced, "Masha says lunch is ready, Aunt Manya. Where's Mrs. Forrester?"

Manya turned to Katherine, "Where *is* Julie, baby?"

"She's still out walking. She wasn't ready to come in. I was cold."

"I'll go and find her." Manya went out.

"No, please—" Katherine stammered.

Charlot squatted down beside her on the hearth bench. "It's too bad you don't look like your mother," he said.

"Yes."

"My mother knew your mother."

"She did?"

"My mother was American, too. She was a dancer. My father was French. He was a poet. My mother and your mother and Aunt Manya all knew each other in Paris. My mother and father were both killed in an automobile accident last year in Aix-les-Bains. So Aunt Manya sent for me, because I didn't have anybody and there wasn't any money. But I work for her. I'm not just living on charity. I work hard. I milk the cow and take care of the chickens and I help in the garden. I'll do a lot more in the garden when spring comes. I earn my living here."

"That's sort of ungrateful, isn't it?" Katherine asked.

"What do you mean?"—indignantly.

"When people like Aunt Manya do things for you, they don't want to be paid back for them. And when you do things for people like Aunt Manya, you don't do it because you owe it to them. You do it just because you want to."

"My mother said you shouldn't take things from people. And she said you should watch out about doing things for them. She told me an old Russian proverb that says, 'Now I've done you a favor, when are you going to kick me in the behind?' "

37

"I know what your mother was talking about," Katherine said, "but you don't."

"You think you're awfully clever, don't you?" Charlot glared into the fire.

"No—no, I don't."

"Aren't you going to finish your wine?"

"I guess so."

"Because if you don't want it, I'll drink it for you."

"No. I want it."

"Well, drink it, then."

"I am." Katherine took a big gulp and stared at Charlot. Charlot had thick dark hair and large, dark eyes, with the longest lashes she had ever seen. He had thin tight lines at either side of his mouth that made him look grown up, not at all like a child, but the lines disappeared when he smiled, especially when he smiled at Julie, and made him look almost as young as Katherine. She stared at Charlot and he stared at her, at her dark-blue eyes that looked accusingly into people, that were difficult to read.

"You don't look like your father, either," he said.

Again Katherine stiffened. "How do you know? You don't know my father," she said.

"Oh, yes I do." Charlot stuck his feet out in front of him, almost into the fire. "He's very tall, and he has lots of hair that's sort of no color, more brown than anything, I guess, and he looks at you and doesn't see you and talks to you and doesn't remember what he says, and he sits and fiddles at the piano for hours, and then he suddenly starts writing things down, and he yells like anything if anybody interrupts him."

"How do you know?" Katherine demanded. "How do you know?"

"He's out here lots." Charlot pulled his feet out of the fire-place.

"All by himself?"

"No. With Aunt Manya."

"That's crazy."

"No. He's out here lots."

"It's crazy. I live with Aunt Manya. She's in town all week. She just goes out to the country Saturday nights. And Father couldn't be with her then, because I have Sunday dinner with him. Every Sunday."

"He comes out with your Aunt Manya Saturday night and takes the eleven o'clock train into New York on Sunday. Sometimes I drive him to the station. Then he comes back on the four o'clock train. He's a very nice man."

"Yes . . ."

"They're all three of them very nice people. Your mother and Aunt Manya and your father."

"Yes . . ."

"Aunt Manya and your father talk about your mother lots. At the table, I mean. That's when I hear what they talk about. They've told me lots about her. They love her a very great deal. But I guess your father would, anyhow, wouldn't he? It's too bad he didn't come out this week end."

"Yes . . ."

"What's the matter?"

"Nothing. I—I'm just cold."

Charlot sprang up, his face suddenly twisted with unhappiness, the lines on either side of his mouth standing out white. "I've said something wrong."

"No. I'm just cold."

"Please. What did I say?"

"Nothing."

39

"I always say the wrong thing. I always make people hate me. Please don't look at me like that."

"Like what?"

"Hating me."

"I don't hate you."

"I didn't mean to sound ungrateful to Aunt Manya. I love her very much. Would your mother think I sounded ungrateful?"

"I don't know."

"But would she?"

"Sort of, I guess."

"It's really because I *don't* want to be ungrateful, you see, only I make it sound wrong."

"I know."

"You're not hating me?"

"No."

"I wish you wouldn't look at me like that."

"I can't help it."

Charlot knelt down in front of her and stared at her solemnly. "If anything's wrong, your mother can make it all right."

Katherine bent her head and looked at her feet, at her wet brown shoes and the little dark wet stains on the rug where the snow had melted off them. Charlot put his hand gently on the back of her neck, and stroked it. Katherine sprang up and crossed the room quickly.

"Don't be nice to me—please don't be nice to me. I mustn't cry. It would be awful if I cried."

The front door banged and she went back to the fireplace and sat down. Charlot sat down beside her, putting his arm around her. "It'll be all right," he said. "Everything'll be all right."

"Don't be nice to me." Katherine whispered fiercely, turn

ing around as she heard footsteps. Julie and Manya came in.

"Have you and Charlot made friends?" Julie asked. She had her arm around Manya as though she were giving her strength.

Charlot stood up and smiled at Julie, and the lines on either side of his mouth disappeared.

"Come along," Julie said. "I'm ravenous. Charlot, take Katherine in to lunch."

ANYA and Julie and Katherine drove into town just in time to go to the theater. As soon as she had her make-up and costume on, Katherine went to Pete's dressing room.

"Are you busy, Pete?"

"No, kitten. Come in."

"Pete," she said, before she got in the door. "I saw Mother. Aunt Manya took me to her and I'm going to live with her."

"Are you happy, baby?"

"Yes."

"But something's wrong?"

"Sort of. Things are always funny. They're never the way you think they're going to be."

"I know. Is your mother different? Is that it?"

"Oh, no! No! That isn't it at all! If it were just Mother it would be wonderful, except for her not playing. That isn't it at all. I told you because I thought maybe you'd like to meet Mother."

"I'd love to, kitten." He didn't ask her any questions, and she had a feeling that he knew, that he'd known she was back with her mother, that he'd known about Manya and her father all along.

After the play she introduced him to Julie, and then Julie took her downtown to Tenth Street, to a small delightful apartment looking out on a garden with a little naked statue in the center. She gave Katherine her bath and some milk

42

toast, and Katherine felt lulled and happy again. The next day she played for her mother, while Julie stood by her, nodding approvingly, then sat down next to her, and worked with her for several hours. Every day they worked together, and other lessons were forgotten.

"You read too much, and you're way ahead of yourself anyhow," Julie said, "but if you want to be a pianist, you're way behind."

They went for long walks together, and Julie made Katherine take fencing lessons. She wasn't very good at the footwork because of her hip, but her handwork was highly praised, and the atmosphere of the Salle was so warm and friendly, there was so much sincere appreciation for true artists and for anyone who was struggling to be one, that Katherine looked forward to her lessons three times a week.

For a month they were peaceful and happy together. Even the first Sunday, when they both went to have lunch with Tom and all three of them were strained and miserable, seemed just one bad isolated day, and didn't color the days that came before or after it.

In the evening, after the theater, Julie called for Katherine and took her home. Sometimes they stopped at a drugstore and Katherine had a milk shake, but usually they went straight home and Julie made Katherine soup or hot chocolate or milk toast. Once on a Saturday evening Dr. Jack Bradley came back to the dressing room to get Katherine. He sometimes came to the apartment to have tea, and once had re-examined Katherine's hip thoroughly in his office, promising Julie that the limp would be quite gone by the time Katherine was grown.

He knocked on the dressing-room door that Saturday night, and called, "Katy!"

Katherine called back, "Come in." She was pulling a gray-blue sweater over her head, and her face emerged still shiny with traces of cold cream. "Where's Mother?" she asked.

"Talking to your Aunt Manya."

"Did you see the play tonight?"

"Um-hum."

"Did you like it?"

"I did indeed, kitten."

"Aunt Manya's wonderful, isn't she?"

"Yes."

"Mother says she could watch Aunt Manya every night and never get tired of her. Mother says she has infinite life and variation in her work. Mother says she's great because she works both with her brains and her guts and not just one or the other."

"Mother says hurry up," Dr. Bradley said.

"I'm all ready. I just have to put my towel over my tray. Isn't it pretty? It's blue. It's handwoven. It's a nice color blue, isn't it?"

"Very nice. Ready now?"

"Yes."

"Come along, then."

Katherine locked the dressing-room door carefully, and they went down the iron stairs to Manya's dressing room, which was just off the stage. Manya was at her dressing table, most of her make-up still on, her long, dark hair loose over a crimson dressing gown. Julie was curled up on Manya's chaise longue, looking small and pale in her blue tweed suit, the scar on her face and neck showing strongly in the bright light.

Manya reached out and pulled Katherine close to her. "You gave an extra-good performance tonight, baby," she said.

"Oh."

44

"Come along." Dr. Bradley loomed big and impatient in the doorway.

Julie got up from the couch and stretched. Then she kissed the top of Manya's head and tweaked her nose. "See you Monday," she said, and they left.

They went to a small bar on Forty-fourth Street, and sat down at a table in an alcove with faded murals on the walls reminiscent of Watteau. There was a lamp on the table with a warm pink shade, and the orchestra wasn't too loud and was playing nostalgic tunes from the Noel Coward plays. "A lovely setting, isn't it?" Julie murmured.

Dr. Bradley grinned at Katherine. "Well, kitten, do you think I'm corrupting you, bringing you to a place like this?"

"Oh, no."

"What'll you have? Scotch and soda, like your mother?"

"I don't like Scotch. Could I have a lemonade?"

"I think it might be arranged."

Dr. Bradley gave the order, but it had scarcely been brought when the headwaiter tapped his shoulder and called him to the telephone.

"Do you like Jack Bradley?" Julie asked.

"Yes. He gave me half his birthday once."

"Have you seen him much these past three years?"

"No. Aunt Manya had Dr. Koteliansky whenever I was sick."

"She and Jack never got along very well. That's true. He's helped me a lot."

"Has he?"

"Helped me to get back a lot of my self-respect." Julie laughed a little. "He still thinks I'm beautiful."

"You are."

"You love me, darling."

"Charlot thinks you're beautiful. Pete does, too."

"Let's not go into it. Lemonade good?"

"Um-hum."

Dr. Bradley came back to the table looking very glum. "It's the Petersen boy," he said. "I'm quite sure he's all right, but that mother of his is having fits, so I'll have to go. I don't suppose you'll wait for me, Julie?"

"I have to take Katherine home."

"Well, maybe I could come down to the apartment later on."

"Not tonight, Jack. I'm tired. And Katherine and I have to get up early tomorrow to fence."

"Well, good night, then." He leaned across the table and kissed Julie gently, then kissed Katherine on top of the head. They watched him weave his way through the tables and out.

"He wants me to marry him," Julie said.

"Oh."

Julie stared intently at Katherine, but the deep-blue eyes staring back into hers were unreadable. "I'm not going to," she said.

"Oh."

"Do you think I should?"

"I don't know."

"Would you like me to?"

"No."

"He's very sweet and gentle. Understanding, too. But it's useless to try to turn to somebody you're just fond of, when what you really need is something more. Besides, I have you and we're very happy together, aren't we, baby?"

"Oh, yes!"

"Poor Jack didn't have time for his whisky. Mustn't let it go to waste. I'll drink it. Do you want another lemonade, kitten?"

"Yes, please."

Julie beckoned to the waiter. "A double Scotch and soda and a lemonade, please . . . Katherine."

"Yes, Mother."

"Are you really happy with me?"

"Oh, yes, Mother!"

"I'm not working you too hard at your music?"

"No."

"It would be wicked of me to drive you into doing what I wanted just because I can't do it myself any more."

"I like it. I like being with you all day. I didn't like school. I didn't like anybody and nobody liked me. This lemonade's awful sour."

"We'll ask for some more sugar."

"No. I like it sour."

Julie finished Jack Bradley's whisky and began on her own. She drank it quickly, and suddenly her eyes filled with tears. "Let's get out of here. Oh, Christ, let's get out of here," she said. Katherine followed her out. They stood on the corner and waited for a taxi. Julie waved violently at each one that came along, but they were all taken. It was fifteen minutes before an empty one came along and pulled up at the curb, and then, before Julie could get to it, a tall man in a top hat and tails had opened the door and was climbing in. Julie ran up to the cab, held the door, and put her head in.

"I've been waiting here fifteen minutes with my little girl. This is my cab. Get out."

The man didn't move. He leaned back in the cab and smiled weakly at Julie. "Well, really, I—"

Julie glared at him. "Get the hell out," she said.

"Well, I—" the man began again, then looked into Julie's face and climbed out, waving his arms vaguely. "That child shouldn't be out so late anyhow," he muttered. "I've a good mind to report you."

"To whom?" Julie asked. She leaned against the street lamp, and her scar showed livid.

Katherine pulled her mother's arm. "Come on, Mother," she begged, "please come on." She climbed into the taxi, pulling Julie after her, and slammed the door. "Thirty-five West Tenth Street, please," she told the taxi driver, who grinned insolently and started.

Julie leaned back in the corner of the taxi. "Bastard," she muttered, then clamped her mouth tight shut. She didn't say anything until they were in the apartment and she had turned on Katherine's bath. Then all she said was "Hurry up," and went into the kitchen. Katherine turned off the bath and followed her. Julie was taking a bottle of milk out of the icebox and she turned savagely as Katherine came in.

"Will you go take your bath?" she said, between her teeth.

Katherine stood terrified in the doorway watching her mother with the half-empty bottle of milk in her hand. Julie's teeth were clenched together to keep her mouth from trembling, and she glared at Katherine until the child turned and left. Katherine turned the water on in her tub again and undressed. But when she turned the water off and climbed in, she could hear Julie banging about in the kitchen. Sometimes she could hear her mother's voice, but she couldn't get the words.

She washed and dried herself automatically, all her energy concentrated on listening. As she pulled on her flannel pajamas, she heard her mother go into the living room, bumping into a chair and swearing, and then she heard the piano. She stood very still, one arm stuck half in the sleeve of her bathrobe, and listened. Her mother was playing the *Gigue* from Bach's Fifth French Suite. Katherine remembered it very well, and it was the happiest music she knew. She stood there and listened to the music coming clear and brilliant from the piano, and she could only sense dimly, not understand, the difference between the way her mother was playing now and the way she had played before the accident, could only feel that something had been there and was lost, that the effortless, childlike grace of her mother's playing was gone, and that the rich, mature passion that had come with such magnificent contrast was held back by the broken bones of the shoulder. Katherine stood there, half in and half out of her bathrobe, until her mother suddenly banged down on the piano keys with a discordant crash, and she heard her go back to the kitchen. Katherine went into the living room, tying her bathrobe belt; went over to the piano; stroked the dark wood gently. A half-empty glass of whisky was standing by the music rack. Katherine stopped stroking the piano and looked at it for a moment, then went into the kitchen.

Julie was pouring hot milk from a saucepan over a charred piece of toast in a blue bowl; her hand was shaking so that half of the milk was spilling on the table. She pushed the bowl at Katherine and said, "Eat this." Then she put the saucepan in the sink and turned the cold-water tap on full force so that it spurted into the saucepan and splashed out back at her. She turned it off and stood there for a moment. When she spoke, her voice was low and controlled. "I'd always heard of the body being a prison. It never seemed one to me. It seemed like an instrument, and some people were good instruments, and some were not. I was a very fine one, and what I cared about most in the world was perfecting and improving my instrument so that if any higher power should want to speak through me I'd be ready. But, Jesus God, Katherine." She wheeled around suddenly and faced

49

her daughter. "I know now what they meant when they said the body is a prison. There is so much in me that wants to come out! And it's all locked in—it's locked in, and it's battering against me every second!" She held her hands out and looked at them for a moment; then she dropped them to her sides as though they were very heavy and she couldn't bear the weight of them any longer. "Everything that I am," she cried, "everything I've worked for, everything I've learned from my living, all the hundreds of things I want to say— they're all locked in, and then they stop being good—they turn into devils—it's as though I were filled with a thousand devils!"

She paused for a moment, very still, almost as though she had stopped breathing, stopped existing, then she turned abruptly and came over to the table and banged her fist down on it. She stood there for a long time and stared at Katherine, who stared back, motionless. Finally Julie leaned over the table, very close to Katherine, breathing heavily into her face, and said, "Why aren't you eating?"

"I'm not hungry. I think I want to go to bed. I think I'm sleepy," Katherine said.

"All right. Go to bed, then." Julie stalked out of the kitchen, and Katherine followed her. She climbed into bed silently and lay down, still in her bathrobe, and pulled the covers over her. Julie opened the window wide, came over to the bed, and looked down at Katherine for several minutes. Then she turned out the light and slammed the door.

Katherine lay motionless and tense for a short time. Then, suddenly, unaccountably, her whole body relaxed, and she fell into an exhausted sleep.

When she awoke it was morning. She lay in bed and waited, because Julie always came in to wake her up when breakfast was ready. It was desperately hard to lie there doing nothing, not even thinking, but she knew that she had to. When she realized that she still had her bathrobe on, she sat up in bed and pulled it off, flinging it over the foot, then lay down again and wrapped the covers over her shoulders. When Julie came in, still in her pajamas and bathrobe, Katherine closed her eyes and pretended to be asleep. Julie sat down on the bed beside her and kissed the tip of her nose and pulled it gently.

"Wake up, kitten," she said. "Wake up. Breakfast is ready, and we have a fencing lesson."

Katherine looked at her mother for a moment. Then she jumped out of bed, and suddenly she felt as light as air. "I'll be ready in a second, Mother," she said.

Katherine's play ran until well into the spring. A week before it closed, Julie took Katherine out to dinner and ordered a bottle of Château Neuve du Pape.

"How would you like to go to college, kitten?" she asked.

"College! But I don't even go to school."

Julie laughed. "Well, you see, baby, I've been offered a position in the music department at Smith College and I'm going to take it. In the first place, we haven't any more money left. Your grandmother, your father's mother, left me quite a lot. She left it to me, not to your father, because she loved me and wanted me to have it, so I've felt all right about using it. But my hospital bills, et cetera, et cetera, took up most of it, as well as everything I'd made, and now there isn't anything left. In the second place, I want to do something. Working with you is wonderful, my darling, but I have a tendency to drive you harder than you ought to be driven, and in the long run that would do you more harm than good. You grasp things so quickly that it's a temptation to push you on and on, far beyond your years. But that would be a transitory kind of progress. You need time to absorb, in between leaps."

"Oh," Katherine said, and sipped her wine.

"They have a very good music department there, you know, and they've offered me a wonderful salary. They wanted me to go to Curtis, but I want to have some practice at teaching before I tackle a lot of people who are really serious about their music—or think they are. I'm really a creator rather than a critic, so I don't know how good a teacher I shall be. Maybe I'll be rotten, and this is one way to find out."

"You're a wonderful teacher."

"No, my kitten. You're a wonderful student. It's rather amazing that I can work so well with you. Usually mothers and daughters squabble like hell. Maybe it's because we were away from each other just at the time when you were becoming yourself and realizing that other people are individuals, too. We aren't stale. We're still discovering each other . . . I must be drinking too much. I'm talking a blue streak. You're not very talkative, are you, my chicken? You talked a lot more when you were a baby."

"Well, where is Smith College?" Katherine asked.

"It's in Northampton, Massachusetts. I'm going to send you to Aunt Manya's for this last week of the play, while I go up and find a house for us. They have a summer school of music there, and I start teaching in just a little over a month. And we're going to have a nice place to live in. I've got a good salary, and we're going to have a white house with a garden."

"I'd rather not go to Aunt Manya's, if you don't mind." Katherine concentrated very hard on cutting her meat into tiny pieces.

"She wants very much to have you. And Nanny'll be there. You'll like being with Nanny, won't you? Nanny's going back to England, you know, and you may not have a chance to see her again."

Life without Nanny to bully her when necessary seemed inconceivable, but Katherine couldn't realize it might ever happen; right now she couldn't even think about it. "Well, Father'll be there, too, lots and lots," she said. "And I don't like it. It makes me feel funny." Katherine didn't look at Julie. She kept staring down at her plate and at the little bits of roast beef she had cut up. She started arranging them in a neat circle around her peas.

Julie poured herself another glass of wine. "Baby. You love your father. And you love Aunt Manya. And once we leave New York, you won't see either of them for a long time. Let them have you this one week."

Still Katherine didn't look at Julie. "If you want me to. All right," she said. And they ate in silence until their dessert was brought in. Then Julie began to pour herself another glass of wine, and Katherine reached over and caught her wrist. "You told me to stop you," she said.

"Oh, let me have just one more glass."

"You told me to stop you when I thought you'd had enough."

"I hate like hell to go to Smith College. Come on. Let me have another glass."

"No."

"Please?"

"No."

Julie put the bottle down and they ate their dessert.

53

HEY lived in a small white house with a garden for four years. Four happy years. Even the periods when Julie was morose and bitter and Katherine couldn't stop her from drinking too much faded out as she looked back on them. She remembered only sitting at the piano and playing, while her mother stood over her, and strength poured into her; remembered sitting curled up in the big, blue wing chair in the corner, looking at the room through a haze of smoke and listening, until she fell asleep, to the discussions that lasted until far into the night; remembered the garden and her mother out in it every moment she could spare, digging and planting and growing things; remembered her first concert in Sage Hall and Julie kissing her very solemnly afterward and crying a little and not saying a word.

In the spring of their fourth year there, when Katherine was fourteen, Julie caught a cold. For the past few months she had consistently been smoking and drinking more than she should—just enough more so that only Katherine knew that it was too much—and when she got the cold, she wouldn't stop going, she wouldn't have a doctor, and she wouldn't go to bed.

"I'm much better if I don't give in to things," she said. "It's only when you give in to things that they get you. Remember that."

"I'll remember." Katherine looked at her mother's too-bright eyes and frowned. "But I wish you'd stay in today,

54

Mother. It's cold and windy again. And your cough's much worse, anyhow."

"The wind on my face is just what I want," Julie said. "I feel hot and smothered. If I get out, maybe I can breathe." She pulled on her old fur coat and opened the door.

"Wear your hat," Katherine said.

"Nonsense. I never wear a hat. It's spring now, anyhow."

"Please wear it."

"Oh, all right, little bully." Julie jammed her fur cap on her head and stalked out.

Katherine didn't go to any classes that day, but waited for her mother to come back. She sat at the piano, practicing. When she heard Julie at the door, she jumped up and ran into the hall. Julie came in and shut the door and leaned against it as though she could hardly stand.

"I think I'll go and lie down just for a little while," she said, and dragged herself slowly upstairs. Katherine followed her and helped her undress. "Wake me in a couple of hours," Julie said, "I promised the Brissarts I'd go over there for tea."

Katherine went into her own room and read for two hours. Then she went back to her mother's room. Julie's cheeks were flushed with fever, and she was breathing with great effort. She looked at Katherine and tried to grin.

"I think the Brissarts will have to do without me today. Phone them, will you?" She spoke with difficulty and coughed heavily. The coughing shook her whole body, and tears came into her eyes with the effort to catch her breath. Little cold drops of sweat stood out on her face, and the scar across her cheek was crimson. Katherine wanted to put her arms around her and hold her to stop this horrible coughing, but she stood still by the foot of the bed and waited. When Julie lay down again, her face was very pale, around the

55

mouth almost blue. "Go and phone the Brissarts," she whispered.

Katherine went downstairs and phoned the Brissarts. Then she phoned the doctor her mother had called in when Katherine had had flu the winter before. It was nine o'clock that evening before he came. Katherine sat by Julie's bed, watching the struggle to breathe become harder and harder. Once Julie looked at her and whispered, "I can't breathe," and again, "Katherine, go away."

But Katherine didn't move. She sat quietly in the straight chair by Julie's bed. When it began to grow dark, she asked her mother if she wanted a light, but Julie shook her head; and as it grew completely dark and Katherine became only a small shadow by the bed, her mother stopped being conscious that she was there. She no longer tried to suppress her battle for air; and in listening to her mother fighting against a power stronger than she was, Katherine suddenly knew that Julie was going to die. She had read somewhere that an ancient Greek philosopher had said that the thing that was Life lay in the pupil of a person's eye, because with death, the eye loses its power to hold a reflection. She wanted desperately to put on the light, to lean over her mother and see if she could still see her reflection in her mother's eye, but she sat very still and didn't move even when Julie coughed and she was afraid the coughing would kill her outright. She said over and over again in her mind—God, please make Mother be all right, dear God, please make my mother be all right—until the words stopped making sense and got all jumbled, and she found herself saying—Mother, please make my God be all right.—

When the doctor finally came, he ordered Julie to the hospital, and went downstairs to call the ambulance. Julie was in the hospital for two days before she died. Then

Katherine called her father and Aunt Manya. It was evening before she reached them. Manya answered the phone. Her voice was warm and delighted.

"Katyusha! Katyusha, my baby!" she said, and Katherine heard her call away from the phone, "Tom, it's Katherine!"

"Mother is dead," Katherine said into the telephone. "Mother is dead. She died this morning. I thought you and Father ought to know."

"We'll come. We'll leave at once," Manya answered.

"I can manage by myself," Katherine said. "I'd rather."

"We'll come. Do you want to speak to your father now?"

"No."

"We'll come," Manya said, and hung up.

Katherine went upstairs and bathed, and brushed her hair and braided it again. Then she went into her mother's room. She had had to lie to be alone this evening, promising each group of well-meaning faculty members that she was going to be at someone else's house until her father and Aunt Manya arrived. She went into her mother's room and stood in the doorway for a minute. She hadn't been in the room since Julie had been taken to the hospital, and the bedclothes were still all tumbled as she had left them. Katherine flung herself down on the bed and lay there for a long time. Then she got up and made the bed carefully, and straightened up the room. She went to her mother's jewel box, and put on her mother's wrist watch, a handsome one with a silver strap. Then she took out a heavy, old, gold locket that had belonged to her father's mother, which Julie had loved very much. In one side of the locket was a picture of her grandmother as a young girl. The other side was empty. Katherine stared at the picture of her grandmother, and might almost have been staring at herself—the same heavy, dark hair, the same small, pale face with the large eyes, the pupils very full, the iris

57

so dark a purply-blue that it was difficult to see where the pupil left off and the iris began. Katherine said to the picture, "I wish I'd known you. You loved my mother. If you hadn't died, maybe nothing would have happened." She put the locket down, ran into her room, and took out of her desk a snapshot, taken the summer before by one of the students, of Julie at her piano at Sage Hall. She went back to her mother's room, cut out the picture carefully, and fitted it into the other side of the locket; then she put the locket around her neck, under her sweater, so that it felt cold and yet somehow comforting against her flesh. If she put her hand up, she could feel it, and no one would know she was reaching out for strength.

She went downstairs and opened the piano. "I'll play for you now," she said, and then again, "I'll play for you."

It was long after midnight when her father and Aunt Manya arrived. She lifted her hands from the piano keys and rubbed the back of her neck Then she closed the piano and went to the door.

Manya had been crying, and when she saw Katherine she began to cry again. She put her arms around her and held her close, and her furs were soft to lean against, and had the faint exotic fragrance that Manya's clothes always had. Her father held her close, too, clumsily. But she didn't want to be held by anyone, to feel anyone's body against hers, to get comfort from any human being.

"She's at the undertaker's," she said. "We can go there now if you like. I think it would be easier if we went in the car. Everything's been taken care of. Everyone's been very kind."

"Why are you alone?" Manya demanded.

"I didn't want anybody. I lied to them. Everybody thinks I'm with someone else."

58

At the undertaker's Katherine stayed outside, while her father and Manya went in to Julie. When they came out, she said, "Wait a minute," and went in. She couldn't help going in, although she was afraid to look at her mother too often, afraid that she might remember her mother dead instead of alive. Julie with the life gone from her, Julie just a pale mask, was very unlike Julie alive, although Katherine was not quite sure why. It was like the difference between her playing before and after her shoulder and arm had been crushed. Katherine stood looking down at her mother, and her hand reached up and caught hold of the locket lying close against her breast beneath her sweater. She had come to look again at her mother, hoping that somehow she might get help from her, that in the short while she still had to look at her mother's body she might find something of her and be strengthened. But Julie's body was an instrument, even now, with her fingers folded together and the scar across the cheek showing much more strongly in death than in life; even now Julie's body was an instrument; not a prison that remains the same even when the prisoner is gone, but an instrument, a piano with the sounding board broken and the strings all snapped; nothing, when its music is taken away. Katherine rubbed her fingers against the heavy gold locket, turned away from her mother, and went out to Manya and Tom.

FTER the funeral Manya took Katherine back to the country with her. Tom stayed there, too, but Manya went back into town, where her play was in its last three weeks. Katherine had the same tiny blue-paneled room she had had before. They arrived quite early in the afternoon. Katherine left Tom downstairs and went up to her room and locked the door. She unpacked slowly, very carefully. She would probably be in this room for quite a while. On her chest of drawers she put the picture of her mother, taken just before her last concert in Carnegie Hall, and on the small bed table she put a picture of Julie and herself, taken when she was five. The only picture she had of her mother since the accident was the snapshot in the locket, because Julie had refused to have any pictures taken. She finished unpacking and was sitting on the bed, staring out the window, when there was a knock on the door.

"Who is it?" she asked.

"Charlot," a voice answered.

"Oh." She got up, unlocked the door, and let him in. Charlot was eighteen now, and he looked older; but he still moved with the same leonine grace, and his lashes were as long and black as ever. His hands were very brown and long and strong, with a black line of dirt under the nails and earth ground deep into them. He held them out.

"I ought to wash my hands, but I've been working and I wanted to see you. You still don't look like your mother."

60

"No," Katherine said.

"I run the place now." Charlot sat down on the bed beside her. "We have all our own vegetables and we have pigs and three cows and a heifer. I've built new chicken coops, too. And the garden is much more beautiful than it used to be. Do you have a picture of your mother I could have?"

"No," Katherine said. "But maybe Aunt Manya has."

"I'd rather not ask her. Will you ask her for me?"

"Why?"

"She's always teased me and said I was in love with your mother."

"Were you?"

"You don't have to be in love with a person to love her."

"I'll see if Aunt Manya has a picture," Katherine said.

"Thank you."

"These are the only ones I have."

Charlot studied the two pictures very carefully. Katherine watched his face closely. She saw that there were tears in his eyes, even though he clenched his teeth to keep them back. "If I show you something, do you promise never to tell?" she asked.

"Whom would I tell?"

"You wouldn't tell Aunt Manya or Father?"

"Of course not."

Katherine pulled out the locket and opened it. Charlot moved closer to her, with his arm around her so that he could see better, and looked long and steadily at the picture of Julie. Then he turned to the picture opposite it. "Who's that?"

"My grandmother."

"She looks like you."

"I know."

"Your mother's mother?"

"No. Father's."

"Oh."

"Mother loved her very much. And she adored Mother. She died when I was two, so I don't remember her very well. She was a singer."

"Oh."

"She sang at all the courts of Europe."

"She doesn't look like that sort of person."

"She wasn't. That's why Mother said she was wonderful. She gave this locket to Mother."

"You haven't cried, have you?" Charlot asked.

"No. How did you know?"

"I could tell by your eyes."

"They thought it was dreadful of me not to cry. I think Aunt Manya and Father understand, but none of the people at Smith do. They think I don't care."

"I understand," Charlot said.

"Yes. I know."

"Wouldn't you like to cry?"

"I don't know."

"You wouldn't hurt inside here so much if you cried. After my mother and father were killed, I felt much better when I cried. When I got to America, I started re-reading some of Father's poems, the ones to Mother. And then I cried—you won't tell anyone?"

"No."

"Maybe you might be like your mother, even if you don't look like her."

"I wish I could someday. I wish it more than anything. But I don't think I could ever be strong and wonderful, like Mother." She shut the locket and slipped it inside her sweater again. "I think I'll . . ." she began, then stopped and shook her head.

"You think you'll what?"

"I don't know. I don't know what I'll do."

"Did you know we're going to England in August?"

"To England!"

"Yes. Aunt Manya is going to do a play in London."

"Is Father going, too?"

"He's her husband." The lines on either side of Charlot's mouth showed white. "I didn't use to think that anything that hurt anybody could have any good in it, but I guess it can."

"Yes. Mother said that."

"Will you talk to me a lot about your mother?"

"Yes. Will I go to England, too?"

"Of course. I'm going to Paris. To study. Aunt Manya is going to lend me the money, but I'll pay her back. I'm going to study medicine. I'm going to be a doctor, and I'm going to be a veterinarian, too. Do you like animals?"

"I love them. Mother and I had a dog, the most beautiful Norwegian elkhound you've ever seen. He was called Boërre. You pronounce it like 'butter' in French, but it isn't. He was run over last Christmas by a bunch of Amherst boys. I was really afraid Mother was going to kill them all. He was such a wonderful dog. We felt so empty without him. Maybe if you'd been a veterinarian, you could have saved him. Mother thought he should have been saved, but the man was so stupid, and he didn't care. He said that if nature wouldn't save him he couldn't do anything. Mother said he was all wrong and Boërre could have lived if someone had really known what to do."

"It's a funny thing about nature," Charlot said. "How she's called Mother Nature, and it's true; when you're unhappy and it's all through you so your whole body aches with the unhappiness, if you go out alone and press yourself close

63

against the earth, you get comfort. But I think that's because it's only when you're dead that nature is a mother, and when you go and lie tight against the earth, you're sort of trying to get as close to it as you do when you're dead. When you're alive nature doesn't care. She doesn't give a damn. But when you're dead she becomes your mother and takes you back to herself again. When you die you stop being yourself and become part of nature; you go back to being earth and air and water and fire."

Katherine stood up. "Charlot—"

"What's the matter?"

"You don't believe that Mother *is* now?"

"I didn't say that."

"But do you? Do you believe that Mother *is* now—herself, somewhere, actively living, *herself*?"

"Well, what you believe about things like that is just your own personal opinion, isn't it?"

"You don't think she is. You think she's just nothing, don't you?"

"Well, that needn't stop you from thinking she's still herself somewhere, need it?"

Katherine backed away from the bed and stood against the chest of drawers. "But, Charlot, I saw her when she was dead! I saw Mother, and it just wasn't Mother. It's like looking at a photograph; it looks like the person, but the person isn't there. *Mother* wasn't there! Not what's really her! And if she wasn't there, she's got to be somewhere!"

"Yes," said Charlot slowly, "but what is a soul without a body, without senses? Can you imagine existing, being yourself, if you couldn't see? Or hear? Or feel? And, after all, we think with our brains. How could you be yourself if you couldn't even think?"

Katherine began to cry, tears of fury. "I don't care! It's all

64

crazy!" she cried. "If you die and then you're just nothing, there isn't any point! There isn't any point to anything! Why do we live at all if we die and stop being! Mother wasn't ready to be stopped! Nobody's ready to be stopped. We don't have *time* to be ready to be stopped! It's all crazy!"

"I shouldn't have talked. I'm sorry. Katherine, I'm terribly sorry. It was stupid of me."

"It's crazy! It's just crazy!" Katherine shouted at him again. "You, going to be a doctor! You ought to know better! If you can't see well, you get glasses and then you can see, but it's not the glasses that are doing the seeing—it's you! It's not the eyes that are doing the seeing, either—it's you! I don't think Mother's eyes are seeing now, but *she* is! She's *got* to be! I think we're given rotten bodies on earth. I bet Mother's got a much better one now. You're just crazy! You go away!" The tears were streaming down her cheeks, and she stamped as she shouted at him.

Charlot jumped up and caught her to him and held her. "Katherine, stop. Stop, Katherine, stop," he said over and over. She fought him, hitting him and trying to bite, but he was much the stronger and finally held her so that she stood pressed against him, panting. "Katherine, forgive me, forgive me," he said, and kissed her very softly on the cheek. She clenched her teeth together tightly, snarling like a little animal, and almost wrenched herself free. "Listen, please listen," Charlot said, the lines on either side of his mouth standing out very white. "I haven't had anybody to talk to. I haven't had anybody to talk to since I came to this country. Aunt Manya's beautiful and I love her. I love to be with her and watch her; and she's brilliant, too, she isn't just beautiful, but I can't talk to her. And I can't talk to your father. He's always off in a cloud, and only Aunt Manya can get through to him. I've needed someone to talk to. I'm a person

65

who needs someone. And that week your mother was staying here, before you came, she let me talk to her, and it was so wonderful. It's the most wonderful week I can remember. It wasn't that I meant anything to her. It's just that she was wonderful. And you're her daughter, and so I thought maybe I could talk to you. I forgot for a minute that you weren't somehow your mother, and how you must feel. Please, please don't hate me."

As he was talking, Katherine's body relaxed slowly, and Charlot let her go. She sat down on the bed again, her shoulders drooping. "I don't hate you. Only don't talk like that. I don't want to be frightened—I'm not strong enough—I haven't anybody to help me any more—I'm not strong enough . . . Have you a handkerchief?"

"Here. It's really clean."

"I cried."

"Yes, I know."

"I wish I hadn't. Now I just want to lie down and cry."

"Why don't you?"

"I mustn't. Mother said I mustn't give in to things."

"She never gave in to things, did she?"

"No."

"Are you going to be a pianist like your mother?"

"Yes."

"Will you play for me?"

"If you like."

"Do you play well?"

"Yes."

"Will you play for me now?"

"Where's Father?"

"He's probably in the lodge. That's where he works. Aunt Manya had it fixed up for him. She had one of the pianos put there for him. Will you play now?"

66

"All right."

They went downstairs. Katherine sat down at the piano and began to play. She didn't hear Tom when he came in and sat down by the piano just out of sight. She played for over two hours. Then she turned to Charlot, saying, "I didn't mean to play so long. I'm sorry."

Tom got up and lumbered around to her from behind the tail of the piano, where he had been sitting, and put a sheet of music manuscript in front of her. "Try this."

Katherine played, recognizing her father's music—a simple little melody in B minor, almost like a folk song, but with great passion and strength underlying its simplicity. When she had finished, Tom said nothing about his composition. He took it back and stood looking down at her. "You play Bach very well indeed, my dear," he said at last.

Katherine looked down at the keyboard. "Mother said when you were unhappy or confused, Bach was the person to play. With almost everybody else you can think, but with Bach there's nothing but the music. It's true, you know."

"Yes, I know," Tom said. He stood leaning on the piano. Twice he seemed about to speak; then he waved his arms a little, helplessly, and wandered out.

The summer dragged by, hot and sluggish. Long hours spent at the piano. Walks in the evening with Charlot. Walks in silence up the narrow path to the mountaintop, Charlot leading, pausing every once in a while to pick a delicate green fern, to look up at the evening sky through the green-and-gold light that filtered through the trees. Occasionally rabbits with small jaunty tails scurried across the path, so close that their warm fur brushed against Katherine's feet. The birds sang more freely in the dim green light on the

evening mountainside than anywhere else, sang with a peculiar piercing sadness,

> *Annihilating all that's made*
> *To a green thought in a green shade.*

When she had practiced until she ached with fatigue,
when dinner with Manya and Tom had seemed almost un-
endurable—so difficult did she find it to fight against the
warm blanket of love and tenderness and pity they were constantly throwing over her, in this heat, when all she wanted
was coldness—then the path up the mountain seemed the
only bearable thing in the world; and even it stretched out,
with its roots reaching up to trip her, its stones pressing into
her shoes to bruise her feet; and Charlot stalked on ahead,
indifferent, selfish, lost in his own thoughts, whistling *Ma
Mie* over and over again, up and down the scale, up and
down the scale. On these evenings it always came as a slap
of surprise when the trees cleared, and they came out onto
the flat top of the mountain. It was strange how bare the
mountaintop was; red-and-green clumps of sumac were the
tallest growth. Mostly it was bare patches of flat rock, with
sharp green grasses growing around, grasses on which Charlot used to blow with a raucous knifing whistle. A low
crooked stone wall ran along the edge of the flatness; on its
other side was a ledge of rock that seemed to lean out over
space. Beneath it was a deep drop to a small useless field filled
with stones, which ended in woods again; from the ledge,
too, they could see a great sweep of mountains curling in
purple shadows around the horizon.

If the horror of dinner had been prolonged or if she were
too tired to climb as quickly as usual, by the time they reached
the clearing the sun would have just dropped behind the
mountains. On such nights Katherine wanted to wail at the

lost sun, "Why couldn't you wait! Why couldn't you wait!" and she would glare at Charlot's back silhouetted ahead of her against the streaks of red and yellow splashed above the mountains.

One evening she turned and ran from the stiff silhouette of his back, as her anger at the sun's having already set brought tears to her eyes; dashed through the long grass into the dimness of the woods, not stopping or turning as Charlot called after her, "Katherine!" but plunging, down, down, blinded by tears. There was no path and she had to leap wildly over fallen trees, slide down bare rocks already slippery with dew. Once she ran through a long bramble vine and felt the sharp thorns tearing at her ankles, but she was going with such momentum now that she couldn't stop herself, until at last she felt herself falling and she saw the ground coming up at her. It didn't hurt, because she fell onto a bed of soft springy moss, and suddenly she realized that she'd fallen headlong into a ring made up of the smallest and most delicate toadstools she had ever seen. Beyond the ring was a pool, almost as round as the ring, almost the same size, lying delicately in the evening light like a bubble of quicksilver, surrounded by moss and ferns. Around the ring of toadstools and the ring of the pool was a larger ring of white birches that spread up and down the mountainside and mingled with the pines and firs. Katherine drew in her breath at the beauty of the spot; she was still sprawled on the moss where she had fallen, tears wet on her cheeks, her braids swinging a little as the wind shook them. She crawled on her hands and knees to the pool's edge and lay down by it, listening to the deep throatings of frogs as the last color drained from the sky and the stars came out.

The birches around her were silvery and mysterious, holding in themselves the moonlight and starlight of years gone by. The pool had caught it, too, and when she put her hand in and started little ripples moving in clear perfect circles to the edge of the pool, she could see the hidden silver for a moment until the water was quiet again. She lay there, listening to the whispering in the trees, the low chunking of the frogs, the sweet lapping of the water. For the first time since Julie's death she felt a kind of peace that was not the nervous hypnotism of work at the piano, but that seemed to reach all the way inside her and suddenly made her exhaustion a simple thing, almost beautiful, because now she could close her eyes and sleep.

*L*ATE in August they sailed, two weeks after Charlot, who had to get to Paris early. Katherine wrote to Pete Burns, hoping she might see him, but he was away with a summer stock company, and she spent the day in New York shopping with Manya. They went on board a little after eleven. Tom had arranged for Katherine and Manya to share a cabin, while he had an adjoining one, but after the boat had slipped out of the harbor and the last lights of the shore had vanished in the haze of a summer night, Katherine turned to Manya, who was leaning back against her pillows, smoking, and said, "Aunt Manya."

"What, Katyusha?"

"I think it's awfully foolish for you and Father not to be in the same cabin when you know you'd much rather. And I'd rather be by myself anyhow."

Manya looked for a long moment at her stepdaughter, sitting with her knees hunched up, her fourteen-year-old body very childish in her white cotton underclothes, looked with her warm dark eyes into Katherine's deep blue ones. Then she said, "All right, darling. If you think you'd be happier."

"I would."

Manya got up and went into Tom's cabin. Katherine could hear them arguing for quite a long time before Manya came back and said, "All right, Katya. I'll help you move a few of your things in for tonight. The steward can change the bags in the morning."

71

It was a small, slow boat. Manya loved the voyage and knew that Tom hated the publicity that invariably would come with their passage on one of the large fast liners. They spent the days lying in their deck chairs, reading or gazing at the ocean; often Manya would disappear into one of the salons to write innumerable long letters; sometimes she would drag Tom and Katherine up to the sports deck for a game of shuffleboard or deck tennis, or take them for long walks around and around the promenade deck, while the wind blew her dark hair back tight against her temples and whipped bright color into her smooth beautiful cheeks, so that the occupants of the deck chairs could not help looking up from their books and admiring her. Once, playing a game of deck tennis, Katherine felt her bad hip giving way and fell, breaking her fall with her left arm in order to protect her hip, and giving her wrist a slight sprain. Before Manya or Tom had a chance to say anything or to follow her, she announced that she was going to the ship's doctor to have it strapped, wheeled about and left them. She could feel the pulses in her wrist pounding in time to the engines. She held it in her right hand, not tightly, because that hurt, but just enough to give it support. The ship lurched, and she grimaced a little. The nurse, writing busily in a red-and-black ledger, looked up at her and smiled. "It is very rough today, no?" she said in slow English.

"Quite rough, but I don't mind." Katherine smiled back at her, because the nurse, in every other way undistinguished, had hair that reminded her of Julie's.

"Oh. But do you know," the nurse leaned forward confidentially, "I do, sometimes. I feel so strange—here—" She put her hands over her stomach and looked at Katherine plaintively. Then she turned back to her ledger with a brisk nod. "The Herr Doktor will be out in a moment."

The door opened, and a young man with a blue-striped dressing gown and a sea-green face came out, followed by the doctor, looming tall and resplendent in the doorway. He looked at her over the young man's head, caught her eye, and shaped the words *"mal de mer"* carefully with his lips. The young man staggered out, clutching a little box of pills; and the doctor sat down in a creaking chair opposite Katherine, held his sides firmly, and shook back and forth with silent laughter, throwing his head far back so that the innumerable scars slashed across his face caught the light.

"Herr Doktor," the nurse said, "the young lady has been waiting." Katherine was pleased because the nurse had called her a young lady and not a little girl, as so many people still did because she was so small and her dark braids so long.

"Aha!" said the doctor, sitting up very straight and fixing his round blue eyes on Katherine. "Not seasick?"

"No," said Katherine, very thankful that she wasn't. "I fell playing deck tennis and I think I sprained my wrist."

"Aha!" said the doctor again, pinning her against the wall with his pale-blue stare. Then he sprang out of his chair, helped her up, and holding her elbow with so firm a grip that she could feel each finger pressing separately into her arm, he led her into his little office. "So!" he said, seating her in the chair by his desk. "I am Doctor Barna. Doctor Otto Barna. Your name, please?" He sat down and leaned far back in his chair, so that again the light fell on his face.

"Katherine Forrester." Katherine's glance wandered from his scars to the portrait in a silver frame on his desk.

The doctor followed her gaze. "Ah, you look at my wife, Miss Katherine?"

"She's very beautiful," Katherine said, studying the pale face of the girl, the shadowed eyes, the firm, sad mouth.

"Yes. She is very beautiful," Doctor Barna said abruptly,

73

clipping his consonants with sharp precision. "Let me see your wrist, please."

Katherine held her wrist out to him, trying not to wince as he felt it. She watched his eyes suddenly lose all trace of feeling, watched them become cold and sharp and clear as a microscope. After a moment he put her hand carefully in her lap, and his eyes once more became intimate, personal. "You are still in school?" he asked, reaching for a large roll of adhesive tape.

"Yes," said Katherine. "At least, I ought to be." The doctor's blue eyes darted over the top of the desk until he found a pair of bright scissors that seemed to Katherine inexpressibly cold and cruel-looking. "Are you going to strap my wrist?" she asked.

"Yes," he said. "You will please come to the office again tomorrow morning during office hours."

"All right." She held out her wrist again and he began to strap it, talking briskly.

"You are perhaps going to school in Germany, Miss Katherine?"

"No. We're getting off at Southampton."

"Aha! But you should come to Germany. I'm sorry—I hurt?"

"A little."

"I will try to be careful." Then he looked at her quizzically for a moment. "You will be dancing tonight?"

"Oh—I—I don't know."

"But yes. It will be quite gala. The first dance of the voyage." He cut off the adhesive tape and slid his fingers up her arm. "May I have the honor of a dance with you?"

"Oh! Yes—" Katherine stood up a little hastily.

"Until tonight, then, Miss Katherine?" He smiled at her warmly, intimately, and pressed his fingers against her arm.

74

"Yes—" She half smiled back; he loosened his fingers slowly and led her to the door.

Manya was waiting outside. Katherine smiled at herself in a kind of grim satisfaction because Manya had not presumed to follow her into the doctor's office. "Darling Katya," she said, "Are you all right? You took so long that I came down. Nothing more than a sprain, is it?"

"No. I had to wait a while, Aunt Manya, that was all."

Katherine moved to lead the way out, and the doctor stood in the doorway tc his office, smiling a little.

"Until tonight," he called as she left.

"What was that?" Manya asked.

"He asked if he could dance with me tonight," answered Katherine, staring with guarded eyes at Manya's quickly pleased, open ones.

Manya burst into a peal of delighted laughter. "Darling, how lovely! You really are growing up, aren't you? And your father and I still thinking of you as a baby."

"Don't be silly, Aunt Manya." Katherine reddened and looked down at the black-and-white-checked linoleum floor of the passage.

"But wait till I tell Tom you've hooked the ship's doctor!" Manya clutched the child's arm as the ship lurched and Katherine fell against the wall.

"Ouch, my wrist," she said, jerking away.

"Oh, I'm sorry, darling!" Manya's teasing smile quickly became kind, although the shape of her lips hardly changed. "Don't you want to lie down until lunch? Come along to your cabin."

"No, I'm all right. Let's go up on deck." Katherine walked forward impatiently, and Manya followed with the puzzled, affectionate stare that came so often to her face when she was with her stepchild.

That night she helped Katherine dress in the blue taffeta evening dress she had bought for her in New York. She sat on Katherine's bed, smoking, wearing a crimson silk embroidered blouse she had brought from Russia and a long, black evening skirt. "He's really most gorgeous and divine!" she said, smiling at Katherine's reflection in the mirror.

"Who?" Katherine asked, bending down and fastening the strap of her gold evening slipper.

"Your doctor, my sweet. All those wonderful scars he got at Heidelberg. It must have been Heidelberg. I knew a student once from Heidelberg—" She checked herself as she looked again at Katherine. "Would you like to wear my moonstone clip in your hair, darling?"

"If you're not afraid of my losing it." Katherine fastened her other slipper, fumbling with the clasp.

"Come here. Let me do your hair. We'll put it up in honor of the occasion, even if Tom does have a fit." She held out her hand for the comb, looking keenly at Katherine's cheeks, which were red from stooping. "Darling . . ."

"Yes." Katherine knelt down and bent her head as Manya began to comb and brush the thick, dark hair.

"Don't be—" Manya hesitated a moment. "Don't be too excited about his asking you to dance tonight."

"I'm not quite a baby," Katherine said quickly.

"Of course not, Katya. I know you're a little old woman, but—" Manya shrugged her shoulders. She held the shimmering moonstone clip against the dark hair first in one position, then in another, until she was satisfied. "There! You look really lovely, Katya. Wait a minute and I'll be ready. It's late. Your father will have a tantrum if we keep him waiting."

"All right . . . Thank you, Aunt Manya." Katherine sat

76

on the edge of the bed where she could see herself in the mirror, and waited.

As usual, she was silent all through dinner. Every once in a while Manya looked at her and smiled, and then she began to eat savagely. Once, as she was looking about the room, she caught sight of the doctor sitting at the captain's table. A large woman in a dress covered with bronze-colored sequins was sitting on one side of him, a thin woman in stringy black lace on the other. He was talking intimately to the woman in sequins, leaning toward her and smiling up into her face, but all of a sudden he turned and saw Katherine, and his blue gimlet eyes lit up with recognition. He smiled and nodded at her, and when she half-smiled back, a little shy, he lifted his arm and waved violently. Katherine looked away from her father and Manya as she waved back; but her hand was undecided, her cheeks crimson.

Her father looked at her, his eyes losing their usual vagueness as he saw her waving at someone across the dining room. "Well, Katherine. What is this?"

Katherine's cheeks became redder and she took a sip of water, pressing her teeth against the firm edge of the glass. Manya squeezed her knee under the table and answered Tom laughingly, "He's the doctor who strapped her wrist after you knocked her over playing deck tennis, darlingest. And so he's asked her to dance tonight and I think it will be lovely. We can all admire his divine Heidelberg scars—so romantic!"

"How is your wrist, kitten?" her father asked. "Feel any better?"

"It's all right. May I have crêpes Suzettes for dessert?"

They went into the grand salon for coffee. The floor was bare, the orchestra tuning up. The conductor was a little man with a sly, black mustache; the first violinist had mustaches that drooped like those of a wet walrus. As the conductor stepped up on the platform, Katherine saw the doctor come in and head for their table. She caught her breath and looked at Manya out of the corner of her eye, but Manya had just seen the lady in bronze sequins sitting under the balcony beside a long man with an ascetic, cadaverous face, and was laughing as she pointed them out to Tom.

The doctor smiled and bowed stiffly as he came up to them. "Good evening, Miss Katherine. May I sit down?"

"Yes, of course. Aunt Manya, Father—this is Dr. Barna. My father, Mr. Forrester, and my—my—aunt, Madame Sergeievna."

The doctor bowed. "I did not realize I was in such distinguished company. I am not intruding?"

"Not at all," Manya said. "Do sit down, Dr. Barna."

The doctor kissed Manya's hand, bowed deeply to Tom. For a moment before he sat down, his pale-blue eyes wandered over a blonde English girl at the next table, looked her up and down, then returned to Katherine. She flinched a little under his stare, felt naked, looked down at the ash tray on the table and watched the smoke curl up from Manya's cigarette.

The orchestra struck up a Strauss waltz. The English girl turned from her table and waved at the doctor. "Hello, Dr. Barna."

He rose and bowed to her.

"They tell me the floor's wonderful," the English girl said.

"It is."

"Do let's dance, shall we?" The English girl smiled at him possessively, provocatively. Her dress was very low cut, completely bare over the shoulders. A pale-green orchid perched

78

high on top of her over-elaborate curls. Her nails were long and their polish almost black. "Or am I interrupting?" She spoke with an insolent pseudo-well-bred drawl.

"Not at all," the doctor said. "Excuse me just a moment—" and bowed to Tom, Manya and Katherine as the English girl seemed to drift into his arms. Katherine watched her grace and confidence and wished she were reading, sprawled on the bed in her cabin.

"He's a beautiful dancer," Manya said. "He'll do you good, Katyusha."

"Yes." Katherine had not been in a ballroom since the days of dancing school long ago in New York. Desperately needing proof that she was out of swaddling clothes, she asked, "Please, could I have a cigarette, Father?"

"Being very grown up, tonight, eh? Like to dance?"

"No. I'd rather watch. You go ahead with Aunt Manya."

"Are you sure you don't mind, darling?" Manya asked.

"I'd rather watch."

Tom lit one of his Egyptian cigarettes and handed it to her. She tried to watch them as they danced, Tom stiff, but a good dancer nevertheless, Manya moving with her usual graceful certainty. While Julie had had the gift of being able to lose herself in a crowd, Manya could not help standing out. Then Katherine's eyes sought out the doctor; she saw him whisper something to the English girl, then smile at the lady in bronze sequins, while Katherine squirmed in embarrassment at the coy glance he got in return. But his eyes were vacant and his smile just as facile, as a South American girl in a brilliant cotton print waltzed by. Katherine felt suddenly forlorn, and pressed her fingers (clutching the locket) against her lips to keep them from trembling. Then she held the cigarette to her lips, and for a moment she felt quite

79

poised and self-sufficient as she drew in the smoke, held it in her mouth, and finally blew it out, trying to hold the cigarette in her curled fingers in the same way Julie had.

The music stopped, and she choked a little as the doctor and the English girl came back. The English girl was smiling; her eyes were shiny, and she did not glance over at Katherine's table.

"That was wonderful," she said, sinking into her chair and fitting a cigarette into a long ivory holder. The doctor struck a match and leaned very close to her as he lit the cigarette. The music began again as Manya and Tom came back to the table. The doctor kissed the English girl's hand, then bowed deeply to Manya. "Madame Sergeievna, may I have the honor?"

"Of course, I should be delighted!" Manya smiled her famous gracious smile, and Katherine noticed her father watching them with an expression half of pride, half of jealousy. Because with the doctor Manya was able to dance as she never could with Tom, almost everyone still sitting at the little tables watched them, holding cigarettes and cups of coffee poised in mid-air. Several of the couples on the floor went to the side and watched them, too. When he was dancing with Manya the doctor was so busy executing graceful and intricate steps that he had no time for glances and smiles at other women on the floor. When the music stopped and they came back to the table, Manya was flushed and radiant.

"Will my wife give me the honor of another dance?" Tom asked, emphasizing the 'wife.'

Manya gave no reaction as she sat down and began to fan herself. "Tomoushka, I'm exhausted. Let me sit this one out."

The doctor raised his eyebrows very slightly as Tom pointed the word 'wife', but Katherine knew that she need never be worried about his asking any questions. He turned to her, "Miss Katherine, may I have the pleasure?"

Katherine was suddenly completely panic-stricken. Manya kicked her gently under the table, so she said, "Oh, yes, I'd love to," then added falteringly, "but I'm not a—not a very—"

The doctor took her elbow, and once more she felt each one of his fingers press separately into her arm. He bent his head so that she could feel his breath warm against her ear and whispered, "Now I have done my duty. What were you going to say, Miss Katherine?"

"Only—only that I'm not a very good dancer."

"Aha!" he said, and she looked away from the round, blue eyes to the couples rapidly filling the floor. He poised her quite still in front of him, then held her very tightly and started slowly, in precise time to the music. Katherine closed her eyes and felt herself stiffen. "You must not be so stiff," he said, pressing her closely to him. "It is too bad you do not go to Germany, Miss Katherine."

"Yes . . . I've always wanted to go to Germany." She opened her eyes, because he was holding her so closely that it would have been almost impossible not to follow him.

"My wife lives in Munich," he said.

"Oh, I've heard about Munich. My—my—lots of beautiful museums and things." She had been about to say, "My mother studied for a while in Munich," but she could not bring herself to speak of her mother to him.

"So? Relax, Miss Katherine. You must not think."

"I'm sorry."

"Your—Madame Sergeievna is very beautiful."

"Yes."

"And a very great actress. I have seen her on several occasions when I have been in New York. Once I even sent her flowers. Red and purple anemones. You must try not to look at your feet."

Katherine looked up and across his shoulder. The lady in black lace was leaning over the balcony, trying to catch his eye, but she could see him nodding and smiling at someone behind her. The music stopped, and his eyes came back to her face, paused at her eyes, and wandered down to her lips. He leaned toward her. "Mmmm, mmm, mmm," he said, making kissing sounds with his mouth. Katherine drew back, sickening, afraid that in a minute he really would kiss her. But he released her hand and began clapping enthusiastically. "Aha!" he said. "Wonderful! You dance very well, Miss Katherine."

"Thank you very much," Katherine said breathlessly. They turned back to the table. "How does the wrist feel?" he asked, suddenly sounding almost paternal.

"All right, thank you."

"Good. Don't forget to come to my office tomorrow morning."

But she couldn't forget it. He reminded her of it every morning and evening for four days. Once Katherine overheard Tom and Manya talking about him in their cabin, when they thought she was on deck.

"It's absurd," Tom was saying. "Really, Manya, I don't see why you let the child see so much of that man. You should at least go down to the office with her. There's nothing the matter with her wrist any longer."

"It still pains her."

"Well, anyhow."

"She's your daughter, Tom. If you want to forbid her to see Dr. Barna, it's your privilege to do so." Manya was rolling her "r's" even more than usual.

"You know I don't want to do that. But Katherine is still

very much a child, and I don't like the idea of that lecherous old roué . . ."

"Tomoushka doushka!" Manya burst into a peal of laughter. "He's very charming and it's high time Katherine learned how to cope with men, especially if she's going to be isolated in a boarding school for the next few years—"

It was the first time Katherine had heard of her being sent to boarding school, and she left her cabin in a fury and went down to Dr. Barna's office.

The little nurse with hair like Julie's was sitting in her usual place, writing in the big ledger. "Good morning," she said as Katherine came in. "I think Dr. Barna is waiting for you. You're later than usual this morning." Her face was deliberately blank, her eyes almost angry.

"I'm sorry," Katherine said. The nurse pressed a little bell, and at the signal the doctor opened the door. He loomed up larger than ever, and his scars stood out white on his face.

"Come in, Miss Katherine," he said. He took her arm, but she felt a difference in the grasp. She sat down in the chair by his desk and noticed that the portrait of his wife was lying flat in front of him. He removed the adhesive tape from her wrist, his fingers as firm and gentle as usual, but his eyes were preoccupied. Somehow she could not look at him; she focused her eyes on the picture. He followed her gaze.

"I do not think we need strap the wrist again," he said, and she stood up to go. "Miss Katherine—"

"Yes . . ."

"I had a cable from Munich this morning. My wife is very ill."

"Oh—I'm so sorry . . ." She caught her breath and looked away from the blue eyes and the scars that stood out so prominently.

"So—so I shall not be dancing tonight. You understand?"

He had her hand in his and was twisting her fingers back and forth so that they hurt. But she knew that this time he was unconscious of them as fingers, that they were only something to hold on to. "You understand?" he asked again.

"Yes . . . of course . . ."

He dropped her hand and she walked out of the room, inadequate, confused. She wanted to speak, but she knew there were no words. She was unusually cross with Tom and Manya all day.

They sat at their usual table for coffee that night. Katherine sipped her demitasse carefully and asked for a cigarette. "Here's Romeo, Katyusha," said Manya as Katherine lit the cigarette from her father's match. She looked up quickly, saw him come through the doorway and walk toward them as the music started up, acknowledging the various women darting glances and smiles at him.

"May I have the pleasure, Miss Katherine?"

"Of course." She stood up; he led her to the dance floor and waltzed her silently across the room to the door. "I would like to go outside for a moment," he said.

"All right." Katherine watched the pale-blue eyes wavering about, the quick smiles and nods.

He led her out on the deck and stood beside her looking down at the sea. He reached out and caught hold of her hand. It seemed as though he were trying to get strength from it. Then he turned as though to take her into his arms, but instead walked abruptly back to the music and light of the salon. "This is quite absurd of me," he murmured. The music stopped for a moment and he took her back to the table, bowed absently, and wandered off.

Manya and Tom were dancing. Katherine looked down at her unsmoked cigarette still burning by Manya's crushed-out ones in the ash tray. When she looked up, she could see the doctor dancing with the lady in bronze sequins. He was making kissing motions with his lips at the air in front of her mouth.

When Tom and Manya came back, Katherine rose. "I'm tired. I think I'll go to bed," she murmured, and went down to her cabin, feeling quite sick.

She didn't see the doctor again except to nod "good day" until the night of the ship's concert. The day of the concert dawned gray and wet. When she woke up Katherine could see the rain slanting against her porthole. The decks were almost empty; people had congregated in the lounges and salons. Katherine put on her coat and went out on deck. For a long time she stood against the wet railing, watching the rain hiss on the wrinkled gray skin of the sea. Occasionally a gull swooped near her, telling her that the trip was almost over, that they were near land. There was one gull with only one leg that seemed to go by her part of the railing more frequently than the others. Sometimes it flew with its one leg dangling instead of tucked under it like the others, seeming to flaunt its affliction in a most un-gull-like way; and Katherine disliked it for this.

When she felt a cool hand put over her eyes and heard Manya's deep voice suddenly become a shrill cockney one for her benefit—"Guess 'oo?"—she was unreasonably angry, and jerked away, not answering. Manya stood beside her, dropping an arm lightly about Katherine's shoulder, but not attempting to draw her close. She, too, stared out at the water, at the sky that was so nearly the same color as the water that the horizon was almost indefinable; stared, too, at the sweeping gulls. When she spoke, it was almost as though she had forgotten Katherine's presence.

"I keep watching these sea gulls and thinking of Julie.

85

Not that strange one with the dangling left leg, but the free, proud ones."

At the mention of her mother's name something seemed to tighten up inside Katherine. She clutched at the railing, looking fixedly at the water, as Manya went on talking.

"She told me that the reason she knew she could never marry Jack Bradley was because of a ferry ride they took together. They stood at the back of the boat all the way over to Staten Island—it was always New York Julie wanted to see. She loved to watch it through the snow, disappearing and getting softer and more like a dream—Julie and I used to ride on the ferry often when we were first in New York together and were poor and hungry and frightened because people had thought we were good in Paris and in New York no one seemed to know we were alive . . . but it did become kind to us . . . And the sea gulls. You know how the sea gulls fly across with the ferry—how beautiful they are, gliding with the wind and being part of it . . . Julie said that the day she rode across with Jack Bradley it was windy and snowy, and there was a pigeon trying to fly with the gulls. And while the gulls were lifting their wings so lazily and almost seeming to drift forward, the pigeon's poor wings were flapping desperately, and the wind beat against its breast, and sometimes it would be driven backward in spite of the breathless flapping of its wings. But whenever there'd be the least pause in the wind, it would beat forward again, and somehow it managed to keep up with the ferry and with the gulls that circled round it. And then, just as they almost reached Staten Island, it got driven way back—and Julie couldn't see it—and when the boat stopped she wanted to wait. She wanted to see if the pigeon got safely to land. But Jack was in a hurry. He was cold and he wanted coffee; so he wouldn't wait."

Tom had come up in time to hear the last part of the story. He was in a bad mood; people had kept coming into the small dining room, where he was trying to practice for the evening's concert on a bad upright piano; his sulky face was very like Katherine's. "There are far more pigeons than gulls," he said. "Sometimes I don't believe there are any gulls. And I know there isn't any land. I wonder if pigeons can swim? If they can, it isn't so bad."

"Julie was a gull," Manya said softly.

"I still don't see why you don't play at the concert tonight, Katherine," Tom said. "It would be good practice for you."

"Oh, leave the child alone, Tomoushka." Manya was laughing at him softly, turning up the corners of his mouth with her long fingers. "If she feels she isn't ready to play in public, she undoubtedly knows best."

Looking unwillingly into Manya's eyes, Tom suddenly stopped frowning and smiled with his rare childlike charm, in the face of which Katherine could never be cross for long. "All right, kitten. I'm just a cross, officious, old parent. I hate the thought of this damn concert so myself that I can't bear anyone else's getting out of it. Manya—"

"All I did was say I wouldn't perform unless you did, too," Manya said hastily. "I don't know what on earth to do for the poor fools. They expect something classical, I suppose, something that will raise the roof off the salon. I don't know what I shall do for them. It's all going to be a frightful bore. Do you want me to put your hair up for you, Katya?"

"No," Katherine said. "I'll wear it down. Thank you." She did not know quite why she had refused so violently and rudely to play at the ship's concert. It probably would have been good practice. Perhaps it was only because Manya had asked her, or perhaps because she had mentioned Julie when she asked. Katherine didn't know. She only felt miserable and confused.

The concert opened with a selection by the ship's orchestra; then the first violinist squeaked and screeched through some Paganini. When Tom played some of his own compositions, illustrating them with a short and witty lecture that set everybody laughing and applauding, Katherine could not help feeling proud of him, and, looking at his face, which was still like a little boy's, and at his shaggy no-colored hair, at his long clumsy body that nevertheless looked comfortable in tails, she felt a strong desire to protect him, followed by a lethargy in which a voice inside her clamored that she was the one who needed protection, that she had no time to protect others.

The English girl sang *Orpheus with his Lute* in a high not-unpleasant voice, and was greeted with enthusiastic applause. Then came the eternal magician, with his fumbling card tricks.

A wind that rolled the ship about had joined the rain; the lights in the salon seemed brighter because of the storm outside. The rain and the wind and the turbulent ocean seemed to draw people together, to make them more friendly, to make them fond of one another simply because they were all human beings in a ship that was not very big when compared with the vastness of the rain-veiled ocean that surrounded it. So they laughed at the silly jokes of the amateur comedian, applauded the *Londonderry Air* squeezed out of a fat little boy's flute, listened attentively to a young man with a wavering Adam's apple give an arm-waving rendition of one of the soliloquies from *Hamlet*. When Manya's turn came, a hushed and expectant silence fell over them all. Katherine had not seen Manya act since she had played with her in the Rostand play when she was ten, and she

88

was suddenly filled with a desire that all these people gathered about in their best evening clothes should think her wonderful.

Instead of going straight to the platform, Manya went over to the group of folding chairs where the members of the orchestra were now sitting, still holding their instruments, and borrowed the guitar that the second violinist occasionally used when they played gypsy airs. Then she beckoned to Tom and whispered to him; he smiled and sat down at the piano.

"I was going to do a long and tragic speech from *Phèdre*," Manya said, smiling at her audience, "but I've had my eye on this guitar all evening, and if you don't mind, I'd like to sing you a few Russian and French songs instead."

With an easy little jump she was up on the piano with the guitar, and Tom began to play softly. As Manya broke into her song, something happened inside Katherine. It was as though something that had been stretched to its utmost limit inside her now snapped, and something warm spread all through her; it wasn't until Manya had sung several songs that she realized that this warm feeling was love.

She remembered that Julie had talked sometimes about how wonderfully Manya sang with the guitar; she remembered that Julie had never stopped being Manya's friend; she knew as she listened to Manya sing that she loved and adored her—not in the way she had adored Julie, but warmly, securely, like a child again. Perhaps this singing of Manya's meant more to Katherine than her acting ever would or could, since it was always music that moved her most deeply. All she knew was that she was happy again, and it was good.

Manya had one of those haunting voices that can sometimes be light and childlike, sometimes deep and full of tears, and with her singing the formal part of the concert came to an end. The audience crowded around the small stage, demanding more songs; the orchestra joined in with Manya's guitar and Tom's piano; the lady in bronze sequins fumed because she was not going to have a chance to sing *Caro Nome*. When Manya sang the sweetly sentimental *Ma Mie* that Charlot had whistled up and down the scale, up and down the scale, as he climbed the mountain, Katherine felt the tears rush into her eyes. Then she felt a hand on her shoulder, and looking up, saw the doctor.

"There is a very great artist," he said.

Katherine nodded.

"Only a great artist can take those simple, beautiful songs and sing them into the hearts of everyone present. What a liquid voice! And when she is on the stage! I bow down to her, I kiss her feet. Ah, Miss Katherine, I am very happy. Today I received a cable that my wife is out of danger, and now Madame Sergeievna sings so beautifully, and the concert turns out not to be a bore after all!"

He put his arm around her, and it was the arm of a father. She leaned against him and watched Manya and Tom, and her love for them overflowed within her like a fountain. Perhaps if she hadn't tried so desperately and successfully all summer to avoid seeing them together except at meals, this would have happened sooner. Now the relief of being able to love them again was greater than she could bear, and she had to leave the salon, to run down to her cabin and cry. She cried very hard and then stopped, feeling happy and sleepy. She took a hot bath, a wonderful bath of hot salt water that stung her face and eyes as she rubbed off her tears with a washcloth filled with the special salt-water soap that even so didn't lather. When Manya came down she was in bed, half asleep. Manya stood in the doorway, framed in the yellow light from the other cabin, and looked over at Katherine's bed, but did not attempt to come in, so Katherine called, "Aunt Manya."

Manya sat down on the edge of the bed, looking very beautiful in her dark full skirt and peasant blouse, her face flushed and her eyes shining from the triumphant ovation her songs had received; but her eyes softened as she watched Katherine, the pale face looking very childish with the dark braids lying coiled beside it on the pillow, one hand clutching the heavy gold locket.

"Aunt Manya—" Katherine whispered.

"What is it, darling? Are you all right? Why did you run out on my singing?"

Katherine squirmed around until she was kneeling in the bed, and flung herself at Manya. "Please kiss me good night," she said.

As she felt Manya's tender arms go quickly around her, felt Manya's lips brush softly against her cheek, she was a child again, completely protected and happy.

Uт they sent her to boarding school, her father and Aunt Manya, to an English boarding school in Switzerland. She went with a kind of fighting resentment that slowly turned into a bewildered misery. The years were rolled off her, and she was turned into a little girl again, but it was no help. She stood in the middle-school common room with her nose pressed against the windowpane and wept. When she unscrewed her eyes enough to look out for a moment, all she saw was gray fog and the branches of the plane trees, thick and furry, through it. The lake and the mountains across the lake were as invisible as though they weren't there at all. Her stomach jerked as she thought how strange it would be if the fog lifted suddenly and there were nothing but a great gaping hole with space showing through, all empty and black. The idea was so startling that she stopped crying and tried to imagine what it would be like without the lake and the mountains. The older girls listening to *Good Night, Sweetheart* on the tinny gramophone would scream with terror, but Katherine would just stand there quietly by the window and watch. Maybe no one would notice her, and they would all run out of the room and she would be there, all by herself. She would be really alone, and she could break the silly record and just sit there quietly, with no one to bother her. They would all run out and fall into space, and she would stand by the window and watch them disappear and smile.

"Katherine."

Katherine pressed her nose harder against the window-pane.

"What?"

"Come away for a minute. I've got something to tell you. Oh, you ass, you've been crying again."

"No, I haven't, Sheila."

"Hunh," the other girl said. "Come along."

"What do you want?" Katherine stared out of the window.

"I said I wanted to tell you something. Something awfully interesting. If you don't come along I won't tell you. I thought you'd like to know."

"All right," Katherine said. Sheila took her arm and led her out of the common room and up the back stairs. "Where are you going?" Katherine asked.

"To the room. It's the only place we can be alone."

"But we aren't allowed—" Katherine began.

"To hell with the rules." Sheila shook her head violently, and her dull-brown hair with the frizzy permanent flew about her face. She pushed it away and took Katherine firmly by the hand so that she couldn't escape. "Aren't you shocked because I swore?" she asked.

Katherine smiled faintly. "No. What do you want to tell me?"

"Wait till we get to the room." Sheila led her along the corridor and into one of the dormitories.

"Well?" Katherine sat on one of the beds and held the tip of a dark braid firmly in each hand.

"Good Lord, you'd think you were doing me a favor in listening," Sheila said. "Not many people would tell you things, Katherine Forrester. Nobody likes you."

Katherine flushed and kicked her feet against the edge of the bed. "Do many people tell you things?"

"I wouldn't listen." Sheila tossed her head again. "I'm getting out. That's what I wanted to tell you."

"What do you mean?" Katherine looked up quickly, and Sheila walked self-consciously over to one of the white bureaus between the beds and sat down by it.

"Just what I said." She opened the bottom drawer and began rummaging around in it. "I'm leaving next Saturday. Just one week."

"But how can you?" Katherine watched, amused, while Sheila pulled a compact out of the drawer and powdered her nose, then smeared a little lipstick on her lips.

"I'll get into a frightful row if they find me with this. But I'm hanged if I care." Sheila rouged her cheeks gingerly. "I've only another week of this dungeon. Ever used make-up?"

"Yes."

Sheila looked skeptical. "Well, maybe it's because you're an American. They say Americans go in for this stuff frightfully young." Sheila's mother was American, and she considered herself a great connoisseur of American language and manners, although the largest body of water she had ever crossed was the English Channel. She added, "You've got to promise not to tell about my leaving."

"All right."

"I just wrote Mummy and she said she'd come and get me." Sheila rolled her make-up in a uniform blouse and put it back in the drawer. Then she pulled out a pink lace brassière and held it up. "Do you have any of these?"

"No."

"I say! Well, don't you think you ought to?"

"Why?"

"Well, don't you just think you ought to?"

"Why should I? I'm perfectly flat."

94

"Well, I don't think it's really decent not to."

"That's silly."

Sheila changed the subject. "I'll tell you why I told you about my getting out."

"Why?" Katherine asked, wishing she would hurry.

"I think you ought to leave, too."

"But this is just the beginning of the term."

"You're awfully silly," Sheila said. "You don't like it here, do you?"

"Yes."

"Don't lie. You know you hate it. You're always crying. Don't think Pen and I don't hear you at night, even if you do put your pillow over your head. It's not going to get any better. Why don't you write your mother?"

"She's dead."

"Your father, then," said Sheila, looking away, a little embarrassed.

"I don't want to bother him."

"Gosh, you *are* queer," Sheila said. "I should think your being unhappy would bother him."

"He doesn't know I'm unhappy."

"But haven't you told him?"

"No." Katherine wandered over to the window. It had never occurred to her that it might be possible to leave the school.

"Wouldn't you like to leave school?" Sheila persisted.

"Of course."

"Then I think you're an ass if you don't write your father. Where is he?"

"London."

"What does he do?"

"He's a composer."

"Gosh, I should think you'd like to be with him."

"I do." Katherine turned away from the window and walked between the beds to Sheila. "Is your mother really going to take you away?"

"Of course. I don't tell lies even if you do."

Katherine didn't get angry. It wasn't worth while to get angry with Sheila. "You mean all you did was write her and she said she'd come and get you?"

"That's all. Are you going to write your father?"

"I don't know. You'd better wash that stuff off your face, Sheila. If anyone sees you, you'll get into an awful row."

"I'll take it off with cold cream," Sheila said, unrolling a jar from her gym bloomers. "It's awfully bad for your face to use soap and water." She began to smear the cream on her face, unconscious of the door opening and the stern stare of their form mistress. Katherine saw her first and backed toward the window.

"Well, Sheila!" the form mistress said, ignoring Katherine. Sheila clutched the cold-cream jar to her and glared at the mistress. Katherine stood with her back to the window and looked apprehensively at the gold pince-nez perched on the mistress's nose, then dropped her eyes along the blue serge dress to the floor.

"Go wash that stuff off your face immediately, Sheila," the mistress said, then turned to Katherine. When she spoke her voice was softer. "What are you doing here, Katherine?"

"I was—I was just with Sheila, Miss Halsey," Katherine said, tears rising quickly to her eyes at the note of kindness in the mistress's voice.

"Well, run along to the infirmary sitting room and wait for me there. I want to have a talk with you."

Katherine left obediently and walked slowly down the corridor, stepping carefully in the centers of the diamond patterns on the carpet. She turned the handle of the door to the infirmary nervously, but Miss Anderson, the nurse, was not at the desk, and she slipped into the tiny sitting room unseen. The fire was lighted, but she went over to one of the windows and peered out into the fog. It was beginning to lift a little, and she could see the plane trees more clearly. Their bare branches looked ugly to her, and she stared beyond them, trying to see down the mountainside. But the lake and the mountains beyond it were still invisible. She wondered again if they were really still there. Was it possible for them just to disappear? People died and were never seen again . . . She did not hear the door open, and she jumped when she heard Miss Halsey's voice.

"What are you thinking of, Katherine?"

"Nothing."

"Oh, but you must have been thinking of something."

"Just that it looks cold and you can't see the lake."

"Come over and sit down," Miss Halsey said.

Katherine walked over to the couch and sat stiffly on the edge.

"Is Sheila a very good friend of yours?" Miss Halsey asked.

"No."

"You seem to see rather a lot of her."

Katherine shrugged her shoulders. She couldn't tell Miss Halsey she didn't talk to Sheila from choice. "She's all right."

"I don't think she's very good for you," Miss Halsey said. "Why don't you go around more with the other girls in your form?"

—They're incredibly childish and they don't like me— Katherine thought, but she merely said, "I don't know," and looked down at her feet. Miss Halsey put an arm around her tenderly.

97

"Why are you so stiff and unrelaxed, Katherine?" Miss Halsey asked. "People would like you, if you'd only let them."

Katherine pressed her lips together. Miss Halsey's arm felt heavy about her, and she wanted to jerk away. The mistress held her arm around the stiff little body for a moment, then stood up wearily. "All right, Katherine. Run along back to the common room."

Katherine left without speaking and went downstairs. In the common room there was still a group around the gramophone, and some of them were singing the words . . . "Good night, Sweetheart" . . . Sheila wasn't there, and Katherine was glad. She went over to her locker, ignoring and ignored by the groups of girls she passed, and pulled out her writing paper. She sat cross-legged on a table near one of the windows and began writing a letter to her father.

She didn't have a chance to speak to Sheila again until after dinner. Then she drew her aside and whispered, "I wrote my father this afternoon."

"Gosh, that's ripping," Sheila said. "Do you want me to tell you a joke?"

"No." Katherine turned away in disgust.

In the common room a group of girls were playing cards on the floor. Penelope Deerenforth, her other roommate, who was captain of the form, was dealing out the cards swiftly, her tongue sticking out of one corner of her mouth.

"That fool of a Halsey is going to put the bureau in front of the window again tonight."

"Been going on one of your sleepwalking toots, Lady Macbeth?" Ginny Merritt asked.

"So it seems," Pen said, and looked up and saw Katherine. "Hello, Katherine. What are you doing?"

"Nothing." Katherine moved away, but Ginny stopped her.

"There's something we think Pen ought to say to you."

"Oh?" Katherine said. "What?"

Pen reddened. "Well—I don't mean to sound pompous or anything because of being captain of the form or anything, but we sort of think it would be nicer if you undressed under your bathrobe the way the rest of us do."

"Oh."

"I mean, it really isn't done, not to, you know."

"Isn't it?"

"No."

"Well, I can't see what difference it makes as long as you're not deformed or rolling in fat, but if it upsets you to see me undress out in the open, I'll take cover." She looked at them with all the scorn she could muster and walked away, but as she left, Ginny leaned out and tripped her up, and she fell. Loud laughter. She scrambled up and ran from the room. It would be four days before she could hear from her father or Aunt Manya.

On Wednesday there was no letter for her. But there would be one the next day. Surely there would be one the next day. On Thursday morning she stood by the mail table fifteen minutes before the earliest possible moment when she could expect the students' mail to be brought out. When she saw Miss Halsey she wanted to leave, but she saw that the form mistress was coming straight to her, so she slid down from the table and waited.

"Miss Valentine wants to see you in her office, Katherine." Miss Halsey looked at her strangely.

The headmistress was sitting at her desk with a letter in her hand. Katherine's heart jumped as she recognized her father's handwriting.

"Good morning, Katherine," Miss Valentine said. "Sit down."

Katherine sat rigidly in a straight chair by the desk, her eyes glued to the letter.

"I have a letter from your father here. He says you are unhappy. What's the matter?" Miss Valentine looked at Katherine's thin face and watched her jaw set stubbornly. "He says that you don't like the girls. Are they unkind to you?"

Katherine said nothing and stared at Miss Valentine, but the headmistress felt that the gaze did not stop at her eyes or meet them but went on and on into space.

"There must be some reason for your being unhappy," she persisted. Katherine's jaw set more firmly and her eyes became more distant. "Sheila Hughes-Gibbs is a good friend of yours, isn't she?" Miss Valentine asked.

"No." Katherine bit the word off and clasped her fingers tightly around the polished arms of the chair the way she did at the dentist's when she was afraid he was going to hurt.

"Who is your friend, then? Isn't there someone you like especially?"

"No." Her mouth began to tremble, no matter how tightly she pressed her lips together. This wasn't fair. It had never occurred to her that her father might write to Miss Valentine. Manya should never have let him.

Miss Valentine watched Katherine's eyes fill and wanted to take her in her arms—she looked so small for her fourteen years in spite of the old little face—but she remembered what Miss Halsey had told her, and was afraid. "Who is unkind to you, Katherine?" she asked.

Katherine shook her head. But the headmistress persisted with questions until her brain felt heavy and dizzy.

"But surely there must be some who tease you more than

the others. Your letter made your father and your aunt very unhappy. They want you to stay here and have fun with other girls your own age, fun you've missed for several years now. And how can I help you if you don't help me a little? Who is the one who teases you most?"

Katherine looked down at the floor and felt worn out. "Nobody."

"How about Virginia?" Katherine said nothing. "Does she tease you?"

"Nobody teases me."

"But your father said in his letter that the girls teased you."

"Nobody teases me," Katherine said. "Please let's stop talking about this. If I have to stay, I will."

"Does Penelope tease you?"

"No."

"Penelope and Virginia are the ringleaders in your form. If you don't tell me it was someone else, I shall have to blame it on them."

"But I tell you it wasn't anyone! No one teases me!" Katherine said loudly.

Miss Valentine then asked very gently, switching her entire manner, "Do you really want to leave, Katherine? It would make your father very unhappy."

Katherine shook her head. She wished she'd never written the letter, that she'd done what she wanted to do on Saturday afternoon, and stayed in the common room instead of going with Sheila.

Miss Valentine watched her, and again wanted to gather the thin little figure up, and again remembered Miss Halsey. "You'll try to stay and be happy, won't you, dear?"

"Yes."

"Run along, then, or you'll be late to your class."

Katherine turned and left the office, then ran to the mail table. She read the letter from her father quickly and turned and ran into the bathroom, choking with sobs. She hated her father, she hated Sheila, most of all she hated herself. She tried to cry quietly, but every once in a while a great sob would come out. She was desperately afraid that someone would come in. The first class had already begun, and she stayed in the bathroom the full half hour, washing her face with cold water. The thought of going into class late with her face all streaked with tears was not to be borne. She went up as the bell rang and slipped into her seat.

After supper she went into the common room and tried to read, but she had turned only a few pages before Sheila came up to her and tugged one of her long braids. "Come on up to the room. I want to tell you something."

"No."

"Why not?"

"I don't want to, that's all."

"Don't you want to hear?" Sheila stared at Katherine with astonishment in her little pop eyes.

"I don't care."

"Well, all right. It doesn't make any difference to me. I don't particularly want to tell you. I just thought you'd like to know."

"I want to read," Katherine said.

Sheila put her hand over the page. "Well, wait a minute. Can't you talk like a decent human being for a while? I say, what do you suppose Ginny and Pen were doing in Valentine's room all afternoon?"

Katherine's stomach turned over.—Oh, dear God, why did I write that letter?—she thought. "I don't know. Were they there?"

102

"All afternoon," Sheila said. "I expect they're going to be expelled."

"Oh, no!"

"Um-hum. They were crying awfully hard, and they aren't here now. Oh, I say, did I tell you I decided not to leave, after all?"

"No."

"So I wrote Mummy and told her never to mind about coming for me. My aunt! Here they come now! I bet Val gave it to them. They still look blobby."

Katherine stared at Ginny and Pen with terrified eyes, as they stood in the doorway, looking about the room, then turned and came straight toward her. She dropped her eyes to her book, jerked away from Sheila, and tried to read. Her heart was pounding violently.

"Well, Katherine Forrester?" Ginny said. Katherine looked into their hostile faces. Sheila's mouth was open, and her little eyes were filled with curiosity. Katherine sat silent as a stone. She looked from Ginny to Pen and felt cold all over.

"So you're a tattletale, too," Ginny said.

"No, I'm not."

"Yes, you are." Pen's prim little mouth was hard. "You got us into one beastly mess with your sniveling to old Valentine."

"Are you—are you going to be expelled?" Katherine whispered.

"Oh, so you thought you could expel me, did you?" Ginny laughed. "Well, you were mistaken there, Miss Sneak. I'm still here, and I can make things pretty unpleasant for you from now on, if I choose, I can tell you."

"We don't want tattletales around," Pen said.

Sheila couldn't restrain herself any longer. "What'd she do?"

"Just wrote her father and said I wasn't being nice to her, and then told Miss Valentine what a beast I was," Ginny said angrily.

"Well, I call that dirty." Sheila looked Katherine up and down coolly.

"Dirty's no word for it," Ginny said. "Come along, Pen. I can't stand talking with such filth any longer tonight." They turned and walked over to the gramophone. Katherine could hear them talking loudly.

"Gosh, they're going to make life fun for you," Sheila said. "I bet you'll be glad when you get out."

Katherine closed her book with a bang. Her voice rose shrilly. "Leave me alone for a minute, can't you!" She walked over to the window and looked down the mountainside. It was a clear night, and she could see the lake and the deep shadows of the mountains across the way. She wished that they would disappear, that in their place would be space, a great empty hole, all black. And she would run out of doors and leap into the space that had been mountains and lake, and be all alone forever.

Then she was conscious of someone at her side. It was Pen, pulling at the sleeve of her blouse rather timidly. "I say, Katherine—" she began.

But Katherine pulled away fiercely. "Leave me alone!" she shouted. Out of the common room she ran, out of the school building, down the path lined by plane trees waving angry branches at her, panting, running, until she bumped headlong into someone.

"Watch out, little one," said a pleasant voice, and she looked up through the darkness into Charlot's face. The

104

accent, too, had been Charlot's.—Now I'm going out of my mind—she thought.—Charlot, here!—

Charlot, if it was Charlot, put an arm about her waist and led her down the path to the Music and Art building. In the light shining out from the building she saw that it was not Charlot, but someone a good deal older. Still, someone who had the same tense mouth with the tight lines drawn on either side, the same long dark eyelashes, the same grace of movement.

"I'm awfully sorry," she said. "And I thought you were someone else."

"Did you?" He looked down at her. "And I thought you were a lot younger than you are. What's the matter?"

"I was running."

"Out of delight?"

"No."

"To get away from the school for a few moments?"

"Yes."

"You're not crying?"

"No, I don't think so."

"Not sure?"

"Yes. I'm sure."

"Are you all right?"

"Yes. Thank you."

"I'll leave you here, then." He smiled at her, and went into the Music and Art building.

As Katherine started down the path, she saw a light go on at the far side of the building, and she turned and went toward it. Music poured out toward her as she walked slowly, quietly, up to the window. Crouching against the wall, she listened. He was playing (for she knew without looking that it was the stranger she had run into), playing a Bach

105

Toccata and Fugue that had been one of Julie's favorites. Her cheek pressed against the rough gray stone of the building, she listened until she heard the bell that meant she would have to run back to school if she was not to be late —and to be late on top of everything that had happened would be sheer stupidity. She ran. And in her mind ran the grievance that had been there since her first day in the place. Manya had chosen this school because Miss Valentine drew her piano teachers from the Montreux Conservatory, but not one music lesson had Katherine had, because the teacher to whom she was assigned was off on a tour and would be late getting back to town. And half an hour a day was all she was allowed to practice. She made up her mind she would speak to Miss Valentine about it the next day. She must have a music teacher, any music teacher, if she was to stay sane in this place. Because her misery was making her neglect her music. During her practice period she sat looking blankly at the keys, aching all over with loneliness for her mother, longing for Julie to lash her into work, to scold her, to swear at her. She would think—I must practice, I must. Mother'd be so furious with me.—But she couldn't work.

But the next morning Miss Halsey called Katherine up to her desk, told her that her music master was back in Montreux, that his name was Monsieur Justin Michel Vigneras, that her first lesson was to be at five that afternoon—adding crossly that Monsieur Vigneras was the most expensive of the music masters and that she hoped Katherine would apply herself to her piano lessons better than she had to her schoolwork.

At five Katherine knocked on his door in the Music and Art building, her heart beating violently, because she was almost sure that it was the door to the studio from which the

106

music had poured so wonderfully the night before. The same pleasant French voice said, "Come in," and she pushed the door open and stood in the doorway.

Monsieur Justin Michel Vigneras did not turn around. He stood leaning against the piano, looking bored and sulky, and this expression seemed even more like Charlot than the composed adult one of the night before. Sheila was at the piano, struggling with a Mozart *Sonatina*. She looked up in relief as Katherine arrived, jumped up quickly, and ran her fingers through the permanent wave that had become frizzy from the indignant washings of Miss Anderson, the school nurse.

Monsieur Vigneras' mouth set. "Finish," he said.

Sheila pouted, sat down, and began the *Sonatina* again.

"Not the whole thing." Justin Michel Vigneras raised his eyebrows. "Just from where you left off, please!"

"I don't remember where I left off." Sheila stuck her hands out in front of her. The girls were not allowed to have long or lacquered fingernails, but Sheila had managed to keep the little finger of her left hand free from inspection, and the nail curved out from it, long and pointed, in contrast to the short clipped nails on her other fingers.

Justin Michel Vigneras pointed to the music. "Here. Begin here."

Sheila began to play and labored through to the end. "May I go now?"

"You certainly may. And if this term you would kindly practice at least half an hour between lessons, it would be less painful to us both."

"I practice half an hour every day except Friday, Saturday, and Sunday—that's the week end," Sheila said righteously.

"And play at least one scale a week."

"All right," Sheila said, her pout gone and her best smile

107

on, the heavy bands on her teeth in childish contrast to her permanent wave. "Good-bye, monsieur."

"Good-bye. And cut that absurd fingernail." He took a white silk handkerchief with a blue border out of his pocket and blew his nose. Then he turned to Katherine, looking at her for the first time as Sheila went by her and shut the door.

He smiled at her, and she thought—It must have been an omen, his playing last night, and my hearing him. I'm glad I felt so awful and had to run and run. Otherwise, none of it would have happened.—

"Aren't you my little friend of last night?" he asked.

"Yes. I am."

"Your name, please?"

"Katherine Forrester."

"What age have you?"

"Fifteen."

"You have studied the piano before?"

"Yes."

"Very well. Play something for me. Something not too long. I will probably stop you before you get very far, anyhow."

Katherine sat down at the piano; her hands felt cold and clammy; she was trembling. She reached up and felt for her mother's locket with unsteady fingers.—I'm behaving like an idiot, a damned idiot—she said to herself. —If I let myself get all panicky like this I'll play badly. Mother'd be disgusted with me.—She clenched her hands tightly together for a moment to steady them, then began a Scarlatti *Sonata*. Once she had begun to play, the fear left her. Her sureness of the music gave her courage, and she played well. When she had finished, Monsieur Vigneras was no longer leaning against the piano.

But the first thing he said was, "Do you speak French?"

"Yes, a little," Katherine answered, surprised and rather disappointed, because his English was very good and she knew she had played well. "I understand it all right."

He spoke in French. When he spoke his own language, his voice deepened and a new warmth came. "Play something else."

Katherine turned back to the piano and played the Bach *Prelude and Fugue in F major*.

"Now some Beethoven." When she had finished he asked, "With whom have you studied?"

"With my mother."

"Who is your mother?"

"Julie Forrester."

"Is she a musician?"

"Yes, she—she—" Katherine's face grew crimson because he didn't know her mother was dead. "She was a very well known pianist in America."

"I will look her up. Where is she?" So he hadn't noticed the past tense.

"She—she's dead."

"Oh. I'm sorry. When?"

"Last April. The seventeenth."

"She was training you to be a pianist?"

"Yes."

"Then why in God's name are you here?"

"Father wanted me to have some conventional education. I haven't been to school since I was ten. And I don't imagine he and Aunt Manya much wanted me around."

"Who is Aunt Manya?"

"My father's wife . . . They love me a lot, both of them, and I love them, I adore them both, but after all, what would they do with me? I'd just be in the way, and Aunt Manya's opening in London, so . . ."

109

"Opening what?"

"Opening in a play."

"Oh. Well, we'll see what I can do for you. Have you done much Chopin?"

"The *Etudes* and the *F major Ballade*. Just because I wanted to, though. I wasn't really ready for it."

"Well, we'll see what I can do for you. You shouldn't be here. Half an hour's practice every day."

"I'll do more. I'll sneak it in somehow."

She was suddenly terribly happy, with that sudden winging up of something inside her breast that seemed like the flight of a bird. She sang as she left the Music and Art building and went back to school, sang as she walked down the corridor, until Miss Halsey stopped her sharply. —I don't care—she thought angrily, trying to keep the wonderful feeling from going. —I can learn here, the way Mother would have wanted me to. I'll study and make her proud of me. Nothing else matters.—

She slipped out of the preparation hall and upstairs to one of the empty practice rooms. It wasn't used because the piano was so bad, but it was better than nothing. She went in and shut the door, standing by the window in the dark. The mountain sloped in terraces down to the lights of Montreux and the lake; and across the lake the mountains of France stood, shadowy in spite of the clear outline the snow gave them against the sky. Two lake steamers were moving slowly on the water in opposite directions, two small bands of gold lights approaching each other and crossing. In a straight line down the mountain ran the funicular, and, winding around, ran the small train. They were the only lights on the mountainside, and they seemed like something magic. Leaning there with her nose pressed against the windowpane, Katherine suddenly felt a sense of peace and strength. "I will lift up mine eyes unto the hills, from whence cometh my help," she whispered, then withdrew from the window, turned on the unprotected ceiling light that glared down at her, sat down at the dreadful piano with the squeaking pedals and practiced until time for dinner. She went into dinner with a consciousness of her strength, of great indifference to the things that had been making her so miserable—a consciousness that was too conscious to be real. But she sat through dinner thinking of her music lesson, thinking of Justin Michel Vigneras, thinking of Julie.

Throughout the dining room the liquid clinking of spoons against glass dishes made a clear sound like myriads of little bells. She listened to them ringing softly, trying to shut out all distinct words, so that the sound of conversation was like a chorus of voices echoing a pagan prayer in a faraway temple. Sucking her cherries slowly, she arranged the eight pips in a pattern around her saucer. It would be beautiful in a temple with bells and everybody praying. She remembered going to church with her Nanny, remembered the sound of the huge organ, the light filtering in golden dusty shafts across the nave, the jangling of bells, intonings of prayers, clear, high voices of choir boys that seemed to shine like the light from the candles burning everywhere, the intense clicking of rosaries—and excitement slid up her spine like a crack up a pane of glass.

Exultantly she thought—I'm alone, I'm alone, and I don't care, because everything's so terribly thrilling and beautiful.—

"What are you thinking of, Katherine?" Miss Halsey leaned toward her from the head of the table.

"I was thinking," she said slowly, feeling that now they

could not get at her, that now she would not give them power, "of how in counterpoint—"

But before she could go any further Ginny broke in scornfully. "Oh, Katherine's showing off again."

"Virginia!" Miss Halsey said sharply, looking at Katherine, and Katherine felt the hot blood surging to her face.

"I was not!" she burst out hotly.

"Never mind, Katherine," said Miss Halsey, and Katherine knew that they had triumphed again. She stared fixedly at the school shield above the side door to keep the tears from her eyes, and it dilated and contracted, blurred and sharpened, dilated and contracted, blurred and sharpened. She heard the roar of chairs being pushed back and stood up hastily, hearing Miss Valentine's grace only as a cruel murmur against her ears. She stood still as the staff and the upper tables marched out, then followed Penelope Deerenforth, forgetting to put her napkin in the rack, followed Pen through the passage, down the stairs and into the Anglican chapel.

When she told Monsieur Vigneras that she had to use the bad piano on the fourth floor he gave her special permission to use the piano in his studio in the evenings, and the world changed for her. For his studio had nothing to do with the school, with rules and regulations. It was part of her mother's world, the world to which someday she would belong. Every day led up to the moment after dinner when she could walk down the path to the Music and Art building and walk into Justin's studio. Justin's studio. Her home, her heart, her life.

And then she found another home that was really part of the studio. One afternoon after her lesson she climbed up into an old elm tree that was near the building. Half its branches hung over the gray stone wall that marked the school boundaries. The first Saturday afternoon she climbed up in it to read, she discovered that from its branches she could see through the trees to the gray slate roof of a deserted old château. Although she was afraid of hurting her hip, she swung herself out onto the lowest branch, which hung over the stone wall, and dropped down onto a soft deep pile of leaves. The grass and weeds had grown up so that she could not see where there had been paths, and she pushed her way through. Every once in a while she would come upon a little marble statue half hidden by the long grasses, a small Pan blowing on his pipes, a sad-faced Grecian lady with no arms, a little naked boy with pigeons on his shoulders. At the château the grass had grown high through the cracks in the terrace. One of the heavy, dark shutters was open and swung back and forth crookedly on a single rusty hinge. The glass of the long window was gone, so she could walk right in to what had once been a huge and magnificent salon. There was still quite a lot of furniture covered with sheets, and in one corner, by the fireplace, the biggest fireplace she had ever seen, she discovered an old organ with a good many stops. She pulled the sheet back and sat down, pumped air into it, and began to play. At first the organ wheezed and choked and gasped, but then the tone came clear and sweet, and she played the Bach *C minor Toccata*, and then everything she knew by Bach. When she had finished, it was long past time for tea, almost time for dinner, and she knew she must get back to school. If she were found out, she would never have a chance to go there again, even if she weren't expelled. She covered the organ carefully and slipped out. When she got back to the stone wall, she saw that she was going to have a difficult time getting over it from this side, for there was no tree to help her; but she managed to clamber up with the aid of some niches

113

where stones had fallen out, and lay panting on the top, her hip aching. She climbed down as soon as she had caught her breath and went back to school. But the château was there for her to go back to every Saturday afternoon.

In her mind she always went there with Justin, as she called Monsieur Vigneras to herself. Not Justin, the way Sheila or the others called him, but in a special way all her own; and the château she went to with Justin was the château of a hundred years ago, with the portraits and tapestries on the walls, and all the furniture intact; and the spinet she had found in one of the small upstairs sitting rooms restrung; and beautiful copper pots and pans shining in the kitchen.

Katherine spent the Christmas holidays with her father and Aunt Manya in London. Charlot stayed in Paris, so she didn't see him, and Nanny was in Scotland, so she couldn't see her; and her father and Aunt Manya were loving and gay and busy all the time. But when she got back to school, something wonderful and astounding happened.

She was assigned to the same room, with Pen, and this time Ginny Merritt, and she was given the bed by the window, so she could lie in bed at night and look down the mountainside at the lake and across to the mountains of France. There was a new girl in the form. Katherine saw her when she got into line for dinner. She had on the navy-blue school uniform and she was standing casually in line, perfectly at ease, talking in an animated voice to Ginny Merritt. There was something familiar about her, but Katherine was not sure what it was. It was more the way she was standing than her crisp English speech. Her voice was deep, rich, a little monotonous. When they sat down at the table Katherine could see her face better. She must

114

have been about Katherine's age, but she looked older, and she had the biggest blue eyes Katherine had ever seen.

"I say," Ginny said. "This is Sarah Courtmont, everybody. She's going to be in our form. Please introduce yourselves."

In a flash Katherine remembered. Of course she remembered. Sarah Courtmont. The little girl in the gray pleated skirt and silk blouse she had played with in Central Park, who had been going to save her from the lions. It might be impossible, but it couldn't be anyone else.

She said nothing. She sat quietly at the table, not talking, listening to the muffled clink of spoons against soup plates, and the roar of talk that came and went like waves. When she pressed her fingers rapidly against her ears, the sound of voices really did sound like waves, like the ocean sound you hear when you listen to a sea shell.

After dinner was over she wanted to speak to Sarah, but if Sarah didn't recognize her, she wouldn't say anything. She went into the common room, climbed up onto one of the lockers and lay there with *Dombey and Son*. Sarah came in with the others and joined the group at the gramophone. She seemed perfectly at home; she knew what to say to other people; she had been the leader of her gang in Central Park.

But this night Katherine couldn't concentrate the way she usually could. *Good Night, Sweetheart* kept intruding into *Dombey and Son,* so she climbed down from the locker and went off toward one of the practice rooms, although she would have to answer roll call in just a few minutes. As she went upstairs she almost bumped into Miss Halsey.

"Where are you off to, Katherine?" Miss Halsey asked, as Katherine stood aside to let her pass.

"I thought I'd practice for a little while, Miss Halsey."

"It's almost time for call-over."

115

"I won't be late, Miss Halsey."

"I'd like to speak to you for just a minute, Katherine." Miss Halsey led the way into one of the deserted form rooms and turned on the light. As the light went on, everything outside except the street lamps on the terrace disappeared. The plane trees disappeared, the gym building, the conservatory, the Music and Art building; everything was suddenly gone, and instead the windows mirrored, distorted, the empty desks and chairs of the form room.

Miss Halsey sat down at her desk, and Katherine stood impatiently in front of it. "Did you have a pleasant holiday?" Miss Halsey asked.

"Yes, thank you. Did you?"

"Splendid, thanks. Now, Katherine, aside from your exuberance—your work in English is not bad, and I hear from Miss Wheeler that your History is excellent, but the other mistresses without exception tell me that your work is not acceptable."

"Oh."

"Why is this? I don't think you're stupid."

"No. I'm not."

"Then why is it?"

"I don't know."

"Don't you find the classes interesting?"

"No."

"You don't find the other girls interesting either, do you?"

"Not particularly."

"Don't you think that's rather unhealthy?"

"Well, I'm afraid they don't find me particularly interesting, either."

"Perhaps if you put your mind to turning over a new leaf this term, you might be happier."

"I'm not unhappy."

"Do you think it's good for you to spend so much time alone?"

"Yes."

"I know you have ambitions with your music, but surely if you were with the other girls during your free time instead of practicing or going off by yourself, it would be better. Don't you want your form to accept you and like you?"

"Naturally."

Miss Halsey got up from her desk, came over to Katherine and again put an arm around her. "I'm sure you'd do well if you'd only try harder," she said, drawing Katherine to her. "You're really a sweet little thing, Katherine. Why are you always so cold and distant?"

Again Katherine stood rigid in Miss Halsey's embrace, not speaking, until the mistress dropped her arm. "You may go now, Katherine; but I warn you, you'd better pay more attention to your studies," she said coldly, and, turning, walked stiffly out of the form room.

Katherine turned out the light and watched the plane trees and the buildings and the night outside become visible again. She went over to the window and stood looking out for a moment; then she turned abruptly and went off to her practice room.

The next Saturday afternoon she was climbing up in the elm tree by the wall on her way to the old château, when Sarah hailed her. "Hello, Katherine. What are you doing?"

"I like to sit up here. What are you doing?"

"Just wandering about. I got bored with the mess in the common room and that eternal record of *Good Night, Sweetheart*. I say, haven't I seen you somewhere before?"

"Have you?"

"Well, there's something familiar about you. I can't quite

117

place it. Maybe it's just that you remind me strongly of somebody. But I can't think who. May I climb up, too?"

"If you like."

Sarah pulled herself lightly into the tree and perched on a branch near Katherine. "If you don't want me, for heaven's sake say so and I'll find me another tree."

"No, don't go."

"Sure you don't mind?"

"No. Why? Do I look as though I minded?"

"Yes. A bit. You're rather antisocial anyhow, aren't you?"

"No. I don't think so. Not really."

"I hear you play the piano well."

"Yes."

"Will you play for me?"

"If you really want me to."

"Well, I wouldn't have asked you if I didn't. I say, where *have* I met you before? I'm quite sure I have. I always remember people. I'm sure I've met you."

"Do you remember—" Katherine blurted, and then stopped.

"Do I remember what?"

"Do you remember once in Central Park in New York I was in one of the underpasses and you came along and you were going to save me from the lions. I remember because it was my birthday and except for that it was such a horrible day."

Sarah looked puzzled. "I don't really remember, but I guess that must have been it. Why didn't you tell me before if you remembered?"

"I don't know exactly—"

"We came to England when I was eight, and I haven't been back since. I remember Central Park and New York very well, though. We lived on West Seventy-seventh Street. I say, this is funny, isn't it?"

"Yes," Katherine answered. She looked at Sarah sitting on the next branch swinging her legs, looked at Sarah with the huge, blue eyes and short, light-brown hair, and suddenly she felt very happy.

After Sarah came, things were different. Suddenly she was no longer on the outside. She didn't quite know how it happened, but it did, and that was the important thing. Sarah knew how to walk out of the common room on Saturday afternoon because she was tired of the crowd, and nobody minded or thought it was strange. Usually on Saturday afternoons they went up to the best practice room, which was on the fourth floor. Katherine was signed up for it from four to six, and persuaded Sheila to sign from two to four, knowing that she would never come.

It was a narrow rectangle of a room with a good upright piano for Katherine and a window seat for Sarah to read in or to study parts in her battered volume of Shakespeare. Those were lovely Saturday afternoons.

"Katherine," said Sarah.

"What?"

"Listen." Sarah read aloud in her low, rich voice:

> *"This ae night, this ae night,*
> *Every night and alle,*
> *Fire and sleet and candle-lighte*
> *And Christe receive thy soule."*

"Doesn't that make shivers go up and down your spine in a nice sort of way?"

"Yes. You remind me of Aunt Manya when you read aloud."

Sarah beamed. "You couldn't say anything nicer, ducks."

"Well, it's true."

"It's begun to snow." Sarah twisted around and pressed her nose against the windowpane.

"Has it?"

"It's so nice and warm and comfortable in here. I love Saturday afternoons."

"Um."

"Let's slip over to the château tomorrow afternoon, shall we?"

"Yes, let's!"

"I wish you'd put some music to that thing I just read."

"I will if you'll copy it out for me. Maybe a sort of theme and variations, or maybe a fugue."

"Will you show it to Justin?"

"If it's good enough."

"Miss Halsey would probably think it stinks." Sarah grinned.

"Miss Halsey stinks. You know what she says?"

"What now?"

Katherine wriggled her shoulders and twisted around, trying to rub the back of her neck. "Gosh! I've been playing almost four hours. Would you believe we'd been here that long?"

"No," Sarah said.

"Rub my shoulders, Sarah."

Sarah stretched and came over to Katherine, beginning to knead the muscles of her shoulders and neck. "What were you going to say about Halsey?"

"Halsey says *Don Quixote* is a riotous comedy."

"Isn't it?" Sarah asked.

"*Don Quixote* is one of the greatest tragedies ever written."

Sarah laughed. "Did you tell Halsey that?"

"Yes. And I'll get a rotten mark for my pains. And Father and Aunt Manya'll think I haven't an ounce of brains. I told Justin what I thought and he said I was right . . . Oh, that feels so lovely. Tickle behind my ears . . . Now, look, what I said to Halsey is that Don Quixote is a great man beaten by life; the world has brought him down. His tragedy is not his death. That was a kindness on Cervantes' part. It would have been too cruel to let him live. His tragedy is his realization that he's a fool—" She stopped abruptly and glared at Sarah.

"What are you laughing at?"

"I'm not laughing really," Sarah said. "You just sound so sweet and pompous when you get that professorial air."

"I'm not pompous."

"Of course you are."

" 'You will read fifty more pages for tomorrow and we will have a factual quiz the next day ' . . . I'm so stupid, I've never passed one of Halsey's factual quizzes yet. She probably thinks it's because I'm reading the original instead of the condensed version. Oh, Lord, you know what?"

"What?" Sarah asked obligingly.

"She thinks we're reading the original because we're afraid the condensed version cuts out the dirty parts. She can't possibly imagine our doing it simply because we want to read it the way it was written. Golly, what's the point of coming to school? The only person I've learned anything from is Justin, and music's supposed to be extra-curricular. Mother said that as long as she was alive I'd never have to submit to the idiocies of a conventional education. You know, I don't think Smith was much better, either. Only there you *could* learn if you wanted to; only not many

121

people wanted to, and lots of the ones who did were sort of dreeps. It's crazy. It's all crazy. You know why I get so—het up—about *Don Quixote* being a tragedy, not a comedy?"

"Why? You get het up so easily, Kat."

"Because," Katherine said. "Because—sometimes—I get afraid maybe I'm sort of like Don Quixote. Maybe some day I'll wake up and find out the world I've made up for myself isn't anything like the real one. I mean, here at school we don't get a chance to do anything but make it up. And maybe when I get out in the world I'll wake up in it and see: Katherine, a little fool . . . You know, when you rub my head like that I can just talk and talk and talk and most of the time I haven't any idea what I'm saying."

"Most of the time I haven't, either," Sarah said.

"It's because I haven't had anybody to talk to since Mother died, I guess. Mother was so wonderful to talk to, I got sort of spoiled. I've always wanted to talk to Justin—I've talked and talked to him in my own mind—but when I'm with him I get all tongue-tied and I can't say anything except silly unimportant things, and I want to kick myself for being a fool—and I'm sure he'll think I'm a moron and not worth teaching—"

"You know he'd never think that." But Sarah had learned it was best not to argue.

"It would be better if I didn't say anything. But I just go on and on, talking nonsense. Now where am I? I was talking about us."

"I love the way you wander," Sarah said.

"I don't. Where was I? Oh, yes. Me being confused since I've known you. We've talked so much, Sarah, about everything under the sun. And when you put something into words, it leads to so many other thoughts. And I don't believe in God the way I did—"

122

"Oh, Kat, you shouldn't let what that boy said make so much difference."

"It isn't Charlot's fault. The way I believed before, just sort of blindly, wasn't really good. It was bound to change. It's just that not having it all definite and comfortable is sort of frightening. Stop rubbing me. You're tired."

"No I'm not."

"Yes, you are. So stop." Sarah rubbed a moment longer, then sat down on the floor and leaned against the piano. Katherine put her elbows down on the piano keys, cupped her chin in her hands, and went on talking. "I do wish I believed in God still. It's not that I don't believe in Him, Sarah. It's just that I don't know. Remember what you said to me last week? Nothing is certain, except that nothing is certain. I keep thinking about that . . ." She paused. After a while she asked, "Isn't Pen Deerenforth mad because we've been seeing so much of each other? You were *her* friend when you first came."

"No. She likes you, too. Everybody does, now. They just didn't know you before. I've talked a lot to Penny about you."

"I think Penny must be a lot nicer than I am," Katherine said slowly. "If I were Penny, I wouldn't like me."

"Why not?"

"I don't know. I just wouldn't."

There was a knock at the door and Sarah said, "Come in."

Penelope Deerenforth opened the door a crack, stuck her head in, and peered near sightedly through her glasses, then came in all the way and shut the door. "I thought I'd find you two here. Hello."

"Talk of the devil," Sarah grinned.

"Were you?" Pen asked.

"Um-hum."

"What were you saying?" Pen's face lit up with immediate interest.

"He has cloven hoofs," Katherine said, "and a long tail, and a face just like yours."

"Thanks."

"You're quite welcome," Sarah said.

"What I really wanted to ask you," Pen plunked herself on the window seat, "is, does either of you want to go to the cinema tonight?"

"To the cinema!" Katherine and Sarah spoke at once.

"Yes. There's some sort of educational thing in Montreux, and Val's arranged for any of the upper school who want to, to go. I'm supposed to get names."

"Oh, gorgeous. Let's go. Educational or not, it's the nearest thing to professional theater we'll get here, even if it's illegitimate. O.K., Kat?" Sarah asked.

"I ought to practice."

Pen pushed up her steel-rimmed glasses, which always slipped down her nose. "Forget your career for once. Come along and have some fun. Besides, it'll be good for Sarah, and we won't have another chance to go to Montreux till half-term."

"Well—" Katherine rubbed her finger against the music rack. "All right."

Pen suddenly began to laugh. "Oh, did you hear Sheila's latest?"

"What?"

"She thinks the street-walking scene from *Macbeth* is wonderful."

Both Katherine and Sarah groaned.

"Speaking of street-walking," Pen said, "I was wandering around in my sleep again last night, and woke up in the middle of Miss Halsey's room! Isn't that a riot! Thank heaven

124

I didn't wake her. She was snoring like a log. Wouldn't you know Halsey'd snore! So I just got back to my own bed as quickly as possible. I was sure I'd wake you or Ginny, Kat, but you were sleeping like logs, too. You weren't snoring, at any rate, thank goodness. One night I found myself crouching out on the balcony like an animal in a cage. Oh, and another thing I came up to ask—I don't suppose one of you wants to come down to the common room and make a fourth at bridge?"

"Not me, thanks." Katherine was definite.

"Sarah?"

"No . . ." Sarah said. "I guess not."

"Oh, come along."

"Unh-unh. I'm too comfy here."

"Well, I guess Sheila's in luck, then. Oh, Elkes is taking us tonight, thank heaven, not Halsey or Anderson. Kat, what *have* you done to make Halsey hate you so?"

"I argue too much."

"Yes, you certainly do. My Aunt, Sarah, you missed something, having to go to the dentist Friday. You should have heard Kat pitch into Halsey about *Don Quixote*. I bet she flunks you for that, Kat."

"I bet she does, too," Katherine said.

"You should be more careful. Honestly you should." Pen took off her glasses, spat on them, wiped them on her blue serge uniform, put them back on, took them off again, and wiped them on her slip.

"Here." Katherine handed her a handkerchief. "I haven't much respect for anyone who's as poor a teacher as she is."

"No one's ever failed a certificate exam from one of her classes," Pen said, putting on her glasses and giving the handkerchief back to Katherine.

"Maybe that doesn't mean so much."

From far down the passage Sheila's shrill voice could be heard calling. "Pen! Penny Deerenforth!"

"For heaven's sake go downstairs, Penny, before she comes in here." Sarah pushed Pen toward the door.

"O.K. See you later. You missed a good tea this afternoon. Chocolate blob cake. 'Bye." And Pen went out.

"Sarah," Katherine said.

"What?"

"Look. Tonight after supper I won't go to Montreux. I'd really better go over to Justin's studio and practice. I mean, if he's really been wonderful enough to let me use his studio at night I ought to take advantage of it. And I haven't practiced nearly enough this week."

"You practiced four hours this afternoon."

"I wasn't practicing. I was just fooling around."

"When's your next lesson?"

"Monday."

"Well, O.K., if you really think you should."

"I do."

"Did you give the handkerchief back to him last time?"

"Yes. I hated to. It would have been something of his really to keep. It was such a lovely one, too. The one he used the very first time I saw him. The white silk one with the blue border."

"Why didn't you keep it? He probably wouldn't have remembered."

Katherine looked down at the keyboard. "I couldn't."

"Why?"

"I don't know." Katherine began to do a finger exercise on three notes. "I just couldn't."

"You never told me why you had it," Sarah said.

"I got something in my eye on the way over to the studio. Remember how windy it was last Monday? And he took it

126

out for me and he was so sweet and he put his arm around me and . . . You know, Sarah . . . it's funny . . . but when I gave him the handkerchief right after my lesson on Thursday . . . and left the studio and started to walk back to school . . . I felt . . . I felt the same way I felt when . . . when I stood in the cemetery and watched Mother being lowered into her grave . . . just as lost . . ."

"Katherine!"

"I know it sounds awful. But that's the way I felt, Sarah. I'd been so stupid during the lesson. Not about the music, just me. And I felt, Oh, God, it'll just go on forever, me being such an idiot and Justin never knowing, and it had been so lovely to have the handkerchief to hold. It gave me strength and courage. I'm such a coward, Sarah."

"No, you're not."

"Yes, I am. You'll realize it someday, if you don't now . . . Remember last Sunday, when I talked to you a little bit about Mother and you cried?"

"Yes."

"It's the first time I've been able to talk about Mother, and I'm so glad I did, because now it's easier for me to think about her. I can think now and it doesn't hurt quite so much. You know, Sarah, after I'd given Justin back the handkerchief, I remembered so clearly that afternoon at the cemetery—the sun shining so hard that it hurt—and those awful hypocritical men in black who were bossing everything and looking as if they felt so important—and that awful oblong hole in the ground with the loose dirt piled on one side—and Sarah, it smelled just the way our garden at Smith smelled in the spring when Mother was out in it, planting—Mother had green fingers—and it was so awful to have the most—the most final—thing about Mother's death—smell like anything so alive as the garden in spring, with Mother planting the

127

sweet peas—and all those awful people who didn't give a damn about Mother and me, and they kept trying to make me cry—but I wouldn't—and Sarah, there was a sort of canopy thing over the grave—I don't know why—it certainly didn't look like rain—and the canopy was striped—and gay—"

"Oh, Katherine, it couldn't have been striped."

"But it was. I'm sure it was. I remember it so horribly clearly—Sarah—you don't mind my talking to you?"

"Oh, darling." Sarah's mouth was trembling. "How could I mind?"

"If I talk about it—if I put it into words—maybe it will stop eating my insides out—remembering it—you're sure you don't mind?"

"Katherine."

"Oh, Sarah, you don't know what it was like, watching her —she couldn't breathe and she was struggling so—she wouldn't give in—anybody else would have given in long before Mother did—and I couldn't help her—there wasn't anything I could do to help—there wasn't anything at all— and I need her so—Oh, God, I need her so—" Suddenly she was choked with the sobs she had held back for so long, and she flung herself at Sarah and began to cry.

Sarah was crying, too. She put her arms around Katherine and they sat there on the floor, rocking back and forth, and Sarah murmured over and over, "Oh, Katherine, Katherine darling—"

Katherine's sobs were tearing out of her, and they were so choking, so desperate, that she frightened Sarah. But after a moment she controlled herself. "I'm sorry—I'm sorry—" she whispered. "I didn't mean to cry--it's the first time I've cried—about Mother—I mean, really about Mother—since she died—I'm sorry—"

"Don't, please don't," Sarah said.

"I shouldn't have talked about it—I've never cried before —honestly—last Sunday afternoon in the château I didn't cry—you did—remember—oh, please, please—I need help—I need help—"

"Katherine, darling Katherine, don't, don't. Oh, Kat, don't—"

"I've stopped. I've stopped."

"Don't stop if you don't feel like it."

"I've stopped." Katherine lay quietly with her head on Sarah's lap. Sarah stroked her head and kissed her gently like a baby.

"Kat, it'll be all right, everything'll be all right. Darling Kat, don't hurt so."

There was a sharp knock on the door, and before they could answer, Miss Halsey entered briskly. Katherine jumped up and went to the window, turning her back on Miss Halsey and wiping her eyes with her hand.

"Who is this?" Miss Halsey asked. "Sarah Courtmont and Katherine Forrester?"

"Yes, Miss Halsey," Sarah said.

"What were you doing in here?"

"Katherine was practicing."

"Really? It's strange that I didn't hear the sound of a piano and that you should both be sitting on the floor."

"I'd finished practicing," Katherine said without turning.

"Yes. I imagine you had." Miss Halsey looked with irritation at Katherine's back. "What were you doing?"

"We were talking," Sarah said.

"What about?"

Sarah paused a moment before she answered. "About Katherine's mother."

"What about Katherine's mother?" asked Miss Halsey, misinterpreting the pause.

129

"Nothing," Sarah said.

"I'm sure it was nothing."

"I was telling Sarah how my mother died." Katherine turned from the window and faced Miss Halsey. "Would you like me to repeat it to you?"

"When did your mother die?" Miss Halsey asked, not ungently, her small cat-face turned slightly away.

"Last April. The seventeenth."

"And that's what you were telling Sarah about?" Again Miss Halsey's voice was not ungentle.

But Katherine's voice was hard as she answered. "Yes. Did you want anything in my practice room, Miss Halsey?"

"Your practice room?"

"I'm signed for it from four to six on Saturday afternoon. I believe it's not quite six now."

Miss Halsey shut her mouth very tightly and stood looking at them for a moment. Then she said sharply, "You will please go to your rooms, both of you, and wait."

"Certainly, Miss Halsey," Katherine said. "Come along, Sarah."

"And you're not to talk," Miss Halsey added as they opened the door.

Katherine turned. "You can't treat us as if we were children forever, Miss Halsey."

"Hush, Kat. Come along." Sarah took Katherine's hand and drew her out.

They walked down the corridor and down the stairs in silence. When they reached the room Sarah shared with Sheila, Katherine put her hand on the doorknob. Sarah said, "You'd better not come in with me."

"I'm coming." Katherine set her lips.

"You'd better go on down to your room."

"No," Katherine said and went over to the window.

130

"You shouldn't have talked to Halsey like that. Now we'll really get the devil."

"I know. But she makes me so mad, always snooping around."

"Kat, you let people upset you too much. Look at the way Sheila gets in your hair."

"I can't bear that song she sings. I can't bear it. About the worms crawling in and out of you when you're dead."

"I'll tell her not to."

"No, don't. That would be worse. Her not singing it because of me. She'd be so noble about it. I'm sorry I yelled at Halsey, but she couldn't have picked a worse moment to bounce in. I can't bear people to see I've been crying."

"I don't think she realized you had."

"I don't see why she sent you to your room, too." Katherine was rapping her fingers nervously against the window. "After all, I was the one who was rude to her."

"Oh, well, there's no love lost between Halsey and me, either."

"Maybe, if I eat humble pie and apologize beautifully, she won't do anything to us."

"It'd be worth trying for once, and for heaven's sake, stop drumming on the window."

"I've had four deportment marks already this term. I don't want another of those little sessions with Val."

"Do apologize, Kat. But I mean *really*. Not the way you usually do."

"I'll be marvelous. You won't know me."

"Hunh," Sarah said.

Katherine turned around and leaned against the window. "You know, I took Val at her word once and went to her study to try and talk things over."

"I made that mistake, too."

"She doesn't listen to a word you say. She just gives you a lecture on 'how to get on with people,' shakes your hand, says she knows you'll be happy and a credit to the school, and kicks you out of the study . . . I used to be able to talk to Mother about anything."

"I can't talk to Mamma," Sarah said. "If she thinks I'm unhappy, she gets so miserable herself I can't bear it. She starts to cry and it's awful. I just have to pretend everything's wonderful. And Daddy's always so legal and learned, I can't talk to him."

"Father's so vague," Katherine said. "He's always lost in whatever he's composing, or writing lectures, and I don't like to bother him. And I adore Aunt Manya, but it would be sort of unfair to Father if I went to her instead."

"I wish Halsey'd hurry up and give us our bawling out and our deportment marks and get it over with," Sarah said.

Katherine flung herself down on Sheila's bed. "I'm tired. I'm going to wait in comfort."

Sarah got up and wandered in turn over to the window. "Every time I talk about wanting to be an actress, Mamma cries and has fits. I wish I could get out of school and get off on my own. I hate to have it hanging over my head. I want to go back to America, because I don't think Mamma'd leave Daddy in London and come after me, and I think there's more future in the American theater. Let's have an apartment together in New York."

"Let's!" Katherine said, and Miss Halsey was completely forgotten, and she was happy and excited. "Oh, Sarah, let's!"

"But I want to meet your Aunt Manya first," Sarah said.

"Of course. The minute the Easter holidays begin. We'll have the most marvelous time."

"What time is it now?" Sarah asked.

Katherine looked at her mother's watch. "Five of six."

132

"Sheila'll be up to change for supper any minute now. She's late."

"Doesn't she get on your nerves, Sarah?"

"Heavens, yes. She would if I let her. If Halsey doesn't come before supper, I suppose we should wait."

"We didn't have tea, and I have no intention of missing my supper."

"Katherine, you promised to be good."

"All right. All right. I forgot. I'll be good."

The door burst open and Sheila shouted, "Hello, angels."

"Hello," said Sarah.

"If we'd been playing for money," Sheila pulled her tunic over her head, talking through it in a muffled voice, "I'd have won ten shillings from Ginny and Pen Deerenforth."

"You're quite the card shark, aren't you," Sarah said.

"Halsey's on the rampage about something. She stormed through the common room on her way to Val's study like a typhoon."

Katherine and Sarah exchanged glances.

"She's always on the rampage about something or other," Sarah said.

"You're going to the cinema tonight, aren't you?" Sheila combed her hair. She picked up Sarah's hairbrush. "I never brush my hair. "It's very bad for a permanent to brush it. I need a new perm."

"If you have another permanent, your hair's going up in smoke," Sarah said.

Sheila combed away, unperturbed. "Are you going to the cinema?"

Sarah took her brush and put it back on her bureau. "I am. Kat's going over to Justin's studio to practice."

"Oh, Kat, don't be a dreep. Come along."

"Unh-unh."

"Has Justin said anything to you about his going away?"

Katherine jumped up. "No! What? He's going away? Who told you?"

"I don't know. I think it was Ginny, maybe. I thought maybe he might have said something to you, seeing you're such a pet of his."

"What did Ginny say?"

"Oh, I don't know, Kat. Something about he mightn't come back after the Easter hols. My Cow! Don't get so excited."

"Sarah, I've got to find out."

"Wait just a few minutes, Kat," Sarah said. "You promised you'd behave."

"I can't. I've just got to find out about Justin. If Halsey comes, tell her I'm in the john and I'll be right back." She ran out and downstairs to the common room. Ginny was at the gramophone, listening to the eternal *Good Night, Sweetheart.* Katherine grabbed her by the arm. "Ginny, Sheila said you said something about Monsieur Vigneras' leaving." Even in her excitement she was careful never to call him Justin, except to herself or when she was talking to Sarah.

"Well, I don't know, Kat. I thought I heard Val saying something about his going to Paris after the hols, but I'm not sure."

"If there's anything to it," Pen Deerenforth turned toward them, "he'll probably tell you himself, anyhow, so don't get all upset. Don't you have a lesson Monday? Ask him yourself, then."

"Thanks," Katherine gasped, and turned and ran back to Sarah's room.

As she came up to the door she heard Sarah saying, "It was because Katherine was—dreadfully upset about her mother—she'd never talked about it before, and it sort of made her remember everything. She—she wouldn't have been so rude if she hadn't been upset."

And then Miss Halsey's voice. "I'm sure she was rude, and I'm sure she was upset, but I don't think it was her mother she was upset about."

"But of course it was, Miss Halsey."

"Why did she jump up so quickly when I came in?"

"She didn't want you to see she'd been crying."

And then Miss Valentine's voice, cool and impersonal as always. "You'd better go and find Katherine and bring her here, Sarah."

Katherine opened the door and went straight to Miss Halsey. She tried to sound as much like a polite and penitent young English girl as she could. "Miss Halsey, I want to apologize for having been so rude to you in the music room. I was—upset—and it embarrasses me to have people see me cry and I wasn't very good at controlling myself. I'm terribly sorry. I know my rudeness was entirely unforgivable. It was all my fault, completely. Sarah didn't have anything to do with it."

"To do with what?"

"The rudeness. It was only me." She turned to the headmistress. "Miss Valentine, excuse me for changing the subject, but it's not true that Monsieur Vigneras is leaving after Easter, is it?"

"I don't think this is the time to talk about that, Katherine," Miss Valentine said.

"Please. I've got to know."

Her voice was so intense that the headmistress answered her. "No. He's not leaving. He's going to Paris to give a concert, but he'll be back." Katherine felt the wonderful soaring feeling of relief inside her. No stupid punishment Val chose to impose on her would matter now. She smiled

135

radiantly at Sarah, who took her hand. Miss Halsey turned to Miss Valentine and said "Please," in an impatient voice.

Miss Valentine looked at Katherine. "Were you in the bathroom, Katherine?"

Katherine answered, a little startled, "No."

Miss Valentine turned to Sarah, "Why did you say she was in the bathroom?"

"I don't know," Sarah said.

"Where were you?" Miss Valentine asked Katherine.

"I went down to the common room to see if I could find out if it was true about Monsieur Vigneras' leaving."

"I told you to go to your rooms and stay there." Miss Halsey had a rubber band in her fingers and kept twisting it until Katherine wanted to reach out and snatch it from her.

But all she said was, "I had to find out about Monsieur Vigneras."

"When you are told to do something by one of the mistresses," Miss Valentine said, "you are expected to obey."

"I'm sorry."

Miss Valentine turned back to Sarah. "Why did you lie?"

And again Sarah said helplessly, "I don't know."

"You'd better be careful, Sarah," Miss Halsey said. "You don't want to be kept out of the next form play."

"Oh!" Katherine said suddenly. "That was my fault. I told her to say I was in the bathroom. I thought it would cause less upset. I just remembered. I'm sorry. It was my fault, not Sarah's. The whole thing was."

"What were you doing in the music room?" Miss Valentine asked Sarah.

"We were talking."

"How long had you been in the music room?"

"Ever since lunch."

"Talking the whole time?"

136

"No. Most of the time Katherine was practicing and I was reading."

Miss Halsey cut in. "What were you reading?"

"*The Oxford Book of English Verse*. It belongs to Katherine's aunt, Manya Sergeievna—the actress."

"Do you often sit with Katherine when she practices?" Miss Valentine asked.

"Yes."

"Do you ever go over to Monsieur Vigneras' studio with her at night?"

"No."

"Are you sure?"

"Yes."

"Well," Miss Halsey said, "I saw you and Katherine coming back from the studio one night last week."

"I often go and get Katherine after preparation hours. She can't hear the bell over there."

"Don't you have a watch?" Miss Valentine asked Katherine.

"Yes. But when I'm practicing I forget about the time, and ever since I was awfully late one night, someone's always come to get me. If Sarah doesn't, Sheila or Ginny or Pen Deerenforth do."

"Do you usually spend Saturday afternoon in the common room?"

"No," Katherine said.

"Why not?"

"I'm surrounded by enough people during the week."

"Where do you usually go Saturday afternoon?"

"To the fourth-floor practice room."

"Does Sarah go with you?"

"Often."

"And she reads?"

137

"Yes."

"What do you do Saturday evening?"

"I practice in Monsieur Vigneras' studio."

"Even though there's no preparation?"

"Yes."

"And Sunday afternoons?"

"I practice, usually."

"And when you don't practice?"

"I go to the fourth-floor practice room anyhow."

"Why?"

"Because I like it there."

"Because it's private?"

"Yes."

"Do you go there alone?"

"Often."

"And when you're not alone?"

"Somebody's with me."

"Who?"

"Sarah, usually."

"You see a good deal of Sarah?"

"Yes."

"Why?"

"Because I like her."

"Why?"

"Because I can talk to her."

"You weren't doing anything besides talking and practicing this afternoon in the music room?"

"No."

"Did anyone else come into the music room?"

"Pen Deerenforth."

"What did she want?"

"To ask us about the cinema tonight."

"Are you going?"

"Sarah is. I'm not."

"What are you going to do?"

"Practice."

Miss Valentine turned and focused her cold, brown eyes on Sarah. "Penelope Deerenforth and you were very friendly when you first came to the school, weren't you?"

"Yes," Sarah answered.

"Is she as good a friend now as ever?"

"Yes."

"Are you sure?"

"Of course."

"Whom do you prefer, Penelope or Katherine?"

"Katherine."

"Why?"

"Because I can really talk to Katherine."

Miss Valentine turned to Miss Halsey, who was still twisting the rubber band about on her fingers. "I think you'd better ask Penelope to come here, please."

Miss Halsey snapped the elastic onto her wrist. "Certainly, Miss Valentine." She went out, shutting the door sharply behind her.

"Why are you asking us all these questions?" Katherine said.

Miss Valentine's brown eyes were expressionless as she answered, "Because I want to help you."

"Help us about what?"

"Certain things I think you don't understand."

"Ever since I've been here your only method of helping us has been to confuse us," Katherine said. She knew she shouldn't talk, but it was the only way not to cry.

Sarah laid a restraining hand on her arm. "Kat—"

But Katherine paid no attention, and Miss Valentine stared at her impassively, letting her talk.

139

"I wasn't confused about everything before I came here. People didn't try to read meanings and motives into the simplest things. Miss Halsey doesn't know why I want to read all of *Don Quixote* instead of the condensed version. Miss Anderson doesn't understand why I spend my week ends practicing instead of playing bridge and chattering. But, golly, it's all wrong the way we have to live here. Human beings *have* to be alone once in a while. The only doors that have locks on them are the bathroom doors. In our bedrooms or the practice rooms, or anywhere, you can never be sure you're not going to be interrupted."

"You shouldn't be afraid of being interrupted, if you have nothing to hide," Miss Valentine said.

"It's not a question of having anything to hide. It isn't right for us not to have *some* privacy, to be always surrounded by hordes of gibbering girls. Sometimes I think if I hear another giggle I'll scream. And if you're ever unhappy about anything and want to cry, the only place you can go is the bathroom. Golly, sometimes I think I'm more at home in the bathroom than any other place in school."

"That will do, Katherine," Miss Valentine said.

Katherine spoke quietly. "I'm sorry I was rude to Miss Halsey this afternoon. I think rudeness is unforgivable, and I deserve to be punished for that. But I don't know what all these questions are about."

There was a light knock on the door, and Miss Halsey came in with Pen.

"Thank you, Miss Halsey," Miss Valentine said. "You may go now if you like."

Katherine could see that Miss Halsey did not like, but she bowed stiffly to Miss Valentine and left. Pen looked questioningly at Katherine and Sarah.

"There are one or two questions I'd like to ask you, Penelope," Miss Valentine said.

"Yes, Miss Valentine?" Pen pushed her glasses up on her nose.

"Did you go up to the practice room on the fourth floor this afternoon?"

"Yes, Miss Valentine."

"Who was there?"

"Sarah and Katherine."

"What were they doing?"

"I don't know. Talking, I guess."

"Where were they sitting?"

"I don't remember."

"Think."

"I guess Sarah was on the window seat, and Katherine at the piano."

"Why did you go up there?"

"To ask them about the cinema tonight."

"What did they say?"

"They said they would."

"Both of them?"

"Yes. Katherine thought she ought to practice, but we told her to come to the cinema."

"You changed your mind about that afterward, Katherine?" Miss Valentine asked.

"Yes," Katherine answered.

"Why?"

"Because I knew I ought to practice."

"Did you talk to them about anything else?" Miss Valentine asked Pen.

"I asked them if either of them wanted to come down to the common room and play bridge."

"And?"

"They didn't want to."

"Why?"

"Katherine was practicing, I think, and Sarah said she was too comfortable where she was." Pen kept pushing nervously at her glasses and trying to look at Sarah and Katherine without being seen by Miss Valentine.

"Have you noticed any change in Sarah recently?" Miss Valentine asked Pen.

"No."

"Are you sure?"

"Yes, Miss Valentine."

"Very well, Penelope. You may go now. Will you send Sheila Hughes-Gibbs to me, please?"

"Yes, Miss Valentine." Pen left, managing to give Katherine a comforting poke on her way out.

"Please, Miss Valentine," Katherine said, "I don't know what you're trying to get at, but I think you're on the wrong track."

"Let me be the judge of that."

"Do you really have to drag Sheila into it?"

"Yes. I do."

Katherine ignored Sarah's warning nudge, and her voice galloped on again unsteadily. "St. Christopher's supposed to be the patron saint of travelers, isn't he? It seems to me we're sort of travelers. But I don't think when we get out of here we'll find we've been helped across the river. We're much more apt to find we've been dumped right in the middle of it."

Miss Valentine deliberately ignored her outburst.

"Why didn't you and Sarah tell me that Penelope had asked you to go downstairs and play bridge?"

"I didn't think of it," Katherine said. "Did you, Sarah?"

"No."

142

"I don't know how to play bridge, anyhow," Katherine added, as a knock sounded on the door.

Miss Valentine called "Come in," and Sheila entered.

"Did you send for me, Miss Valentine?" she asked.

"Yes, Sheila. You're Sarah Courtmont's roommate, aren't you?"

"Yes, Miss Valentine."

"Has Katherine Forrester ever been in your room at night?"

"No, Miss Valentine. Why, Miss Valentine?"

"Have you noticed any change in either of them recently?"

"No, Miss Valentine. Why, Miss Valentine?"

"Please simply answer my questions, Sheila."

"Yes, Miss Valentine."

"Have they been off alone more than usual lately?"

"Katherine's always gone off alone."

"Don't the other girls resent that?"

"At first, I guess. We're used to it now."

"And Sarah?"

"Oh, we've all liked Sarah right from the start. She's wonderful at hockey. She's on the team already. And she's always lots of fun."

"Then you've noticed no difference in either Katherine or Sarah?"

"No, Miss Valentine."

"Think."

"No. Katherine's always been a queer bird and Sarah's just the same as ever."

"How has Katherine been queer?"

"Sort of unfriendly. Always off practicing. She's all right when you get used to her ways, though."

"All right, Sheila. That will be all. Thank you. I trust you to say nothing about this."

143

"No, Miss Valentine. Of course not, Miss Valentine," and Sheila left.

"Miss Valentine, *please*," Katherine asked, "what is all this about?"

"Sarah," Miss Valentine said, "will you wait outside for just a minute, please?"

"Yes, Miss Valentine." Sarah gave Katherine's hand a squeeze and went out.

"Your mother is dead, Katherine?" Miss Valentine asked.

Katherine reached up and clutched the locket under her uniform. "Yes."

"You spend the holidays with your father and your stepmother?"

"Yes."

"Do you go out with boys your own age during the holidays?"

"No."

"Why not?"

"I don't know any."

"What do you do?"

"Father and I play a lot on two pianos. And I read. And I often go to the theater with Aunt Manya and sit in her dressing room. And she takes me out to teas and things with her friends."

"Don't you think you may be taking your music a little too seriously?"

"My mother was training me to be a pianist. I've got to let school interrupt as little as possible."

"You might be a better musician, if you learned to live a more normal life."

"I don't consider the life we're given here at school normal."

Miss Valentine changed her tack. Her voice was deceptively gentle as she asked, "Don't you think that perhaps you and Sarah are getting too dependent on each other?"

"No."

"Have you ever kissed Sarah?"

"No."

"Are you telling me the truth?"

"Of course."

"Miss Halsey said that you and Sarah were kissing each other in the music room."

"Miss Halsey's cracked. I was crying, and Sarah was being nice to me. I don't know—maybe she did kiss me. What difference does it make, anyhow?"

"You're very fond of Sarah, aren't you?"

"Of course."

"Sometimes people who are as over-intense about things as you are about your music get over-intense about human beings. I think it would be better if you didn't see Sarah quite so much."

"But that's crazy. I've only been really happy at school since I've known Sarah."

"I'm not going to argue with you, Katherine. I won't forbid you to have anything to do with Sarah, but I want you to promise me not to be alone with her so much."

"That's crazy. I don't get all this."

"Someday you'll understand and be grateful to me," Miss Valentine said. "Will you ask Sarah to come in to me now?"

Katherine stalked out. Sarah was waiting in the passage. "Grateful, hell," Katherine muttered, "Grateful, hell, hell, hell. She wants you now," she said to Sarah.

"Did she do anything to you?" Sarah whispered.

"She's just cracked," Katherine said. "She's completely cracked. Don't listen to her."

Sarah went back into the room. Katherine waited outside.

The first bell for dinner rang, and the girls trooped downstairs. Katherine went into the bathroom and waited until they had all gone by; then she went back and stood in the passage again, in one of the doorways, so that she could not be seen, but could see Miss Valentine when she came out of Sarah's room. It was a long time before Miss Valentine came out. Katherine kept looking at her mother's watch; it was a full half hour before the door opened and Miss Valentine went downstairs. Katherine went back into the room. Sarah was standing miserably by the window, wiping her eyes.

"What did she say?" Katherine asked.

"She—she said I wasn't to tell you," Sarah said, blowing her nose.

"Please—can't you?"

"I don't think I'd better."

Katherine went over to Sarah and put her arm around her. "She's made you unhappy."

"Please don't, Katherine," Sarah said, pulling away. "I'm going down to supper now."

"Are you going to the cinema tonight?" Katherine asked.

"Of course."

"I'd sort of like to talk to you."

"No—" Sarah said.

Katherine held her hand out to Sarah timidly. "Sarah—"

"What?"

"Is something the matter?"

"No."

"Did I do something I shouldn't?"

"No."

"You're not mad at me?"

"No . . . I'm going down to supper now."

"Sarah—"

"What?"

"What was that thing you wanted me to put music to?"

"What thing?"

"That thing you read me this afternoon."

"Oh."

"Do you remember it?"

"Yes."

"Would you say it?"

Sarah recited unhappily:

> "This ae night, this ae night,
> Every night and alle,
> Fire and sleet and candle-lighte,
> And Christe receive thy soule."

"I'll do it tonight," Katherine said.

"All right . . . Oh, Miss Valentine wants to see you in her study at eight."

"Oh."

"I'm going down to supper now . . . Are you coming?"

"In a minute. You go on."

"All right—" Sarah said, turning to go.

"Sarah— What did she say to make you like this? What's happened?"

"Nothing's happened," Sarah said.

"You're different. Everything's different. What has she done?"

"Nothing. I'm going now," Sarah said, and left.

Katherine stared after her. Then she sat down on the edge of Sarah's bed. She reached up and pressed her locket close to her. "Jesus," she whispered, "Jesus, dear Jesus, Jesus—"

When Katherine went to her music lesson on Monday, Justin was sitting at the piano, playing. She stood quietly, leaning against the door until he had finished. When he saw her, he turned around, held out both hands, and smiled at her so sweetly that the tears rushed to her eyes. She went up to him and put her hands into his, looking down at him, trying to keep back the tears.

"What is it?" he asked.

For a moment she could not answer. She just stood still, shaking her head. Then she said, "I don't know."

"Has someone hurt you?"

Wildly she thought—He mustn't be kind to me like this! I don't want him to see me cry—But his eyes looked into hers with interest and concern, and she felt trapped; she wanted to run, to run far, far away; to run where? To run into his arms.

"Has someone hurt you?" he asked again.

At last she nodded.

He held her hands very tightly. "You should get away from here, little one. This is no place for you."

She pulled away from him and turned around because she couldn't stop crying.

He came up to her and put both his hands on her shoulders. "What is it, dear? Do you want to talk to me about it?"

She wanted to talk to him about it. She wanted to talk to him about it more than anything in the world. But she couldn't. She stamped her foot and said fiercely, "It's just that I'm such an utter fool."

"You're not a fool, little one," he said. "You'll be all right. Just get out of this place as soon as you can."

Suddenly she asked, "You're not going away, are you? You're not going away after Easter? You're coming back?"

"Yes. I'm coming back. But I'm going to get away, too, as soon as I can. You're not going to be in Paris for the holidays? You won't be able to hear my concert?"

"No. I'd give anything in the world if I could."

148

He saw that she had stopped crying. "We must get to work," he said.

She went down the path to the château, down the path filled with the wavering yet sharp shadows of plane trees with their ice-black branches; past Justin's studio; up the old oak tree and over the stone wall; paused for a moment by the little boy with the chipped stone pigeon eternally lighting on his shoulder; then pushed through the grasses that pricked through the snow, always choosing a slightly different trail so that no telltale path would be formed; lifted the broken shutter with the old, green, blistered paint; into the salon; into the other world, Julie's world.

Sarah and Pen were there. This she had not counted on. This was not fair. If Sarah had given the château to Pen, Katherine could never go there again.

At the sight of Katherine framed in the window, Sarah's face became suffused with red; her eyes seemed larger and more ice-blue than ever.

"Hello, Kat," she said. "I thought you had a piano lesson this afternoon."

"No. That was just extra last week." Katherine still stood leaning against the dusty woodwork of the long French window. If this was to be the last time she could come to the château (because if it became other people's it became part of their world and was no longer part of Julie's and Justin's and the world she and Sarah had made up), if she could never come here again, they ought to have the decency to go away and leave her alone.

"Well," Pen said, smiling to cover her embarrassment. "This is certainly a gorgeous place, Kat. You and Sarah were beasts to keep it to yourselves."

"If too many people start running over here, Val will find

out." Katherine turned from Pen and looked at Sarah. "I won't come again."

"Good gracious, Kat, why not?" Sarah widened the blue eyes.

"I've too much work to do to waste time over here with a wheezy organ."

"Oh!" Pen said with relief, as the organ was mentioned. "Do play for us, Kat."

Quietly Katherine stripped the organ of its dusty coverings. Instead of playing Bach, as she usually did here, she played the *Brahms-Paganini Variations,* the most noisy, wild, and confused music she knew.

"Phew!" Pen said as she finished. "That wore me out, just listening to it. You're certainly a wizard, Kat. It won't be long before we'll all be saying, 'I knew her when—' Well, we'd better get on back to school, Sarah. It must be nearly time for prep. You coming, Kat?"

"It's one of my practice periods," Katherine said. "If you won't report me, I'll stay here till I have to sign in with Elkes."

"Of course I won't report you." Pen looked indignant and uncomfortable at the same time, and as usual when she didn't know what to do, took off her glasses and wiped them.

"Well, I mean your being head of form and everything—"

"Oh, this is sort of different," Pen said awkwardly, putting her glasses back on. "Coming, Sarah?"

"Yes," Sarah answered, and they opened the window and pushed aside the broken shutter. Katherine was left standing alone by the organ, the light lying in stripes across her uniform as it filtered through broken slats in the shutters. Suddenly she heard the shutter being pushed away again, and Sarah came back into the room.

"I say, Kat—" Sarah said, standing just inside the window.

"Yes."

"I'm sorry."

"What about?" Katherine almost whispered the words.

"Oh, all this mess and sort of everything. You do understand, don't you?"

"No."

"I mean, Val and everything—"

"If you want to start paying attention to what Val says, that's up to you."

"I don't like you to be unhappy."

"I'm not unhappy."

"Sure?"

"Naturally."

"Well—see you later, then—"

"All right."

"In the common room."

"Good-bye." Katherine turned back toward the organ.

"Good-bye." Another push of the shutter, and Sarah was gone again.

Bᴜᴛ there is something about Time. The sun rises and sets. The stars swing slowly across the sky and fade. Clouds fill with rain and snow, empty themselves, and fill again. The moon is born, and dies, and is reborn. Around millions of clocks swing hour hands, and minute hands, and second hands. Around goes the continual circle of the notes of the scale. Around goes the circle of night and day, the circle of weeks forever revolving, and of months, and of years.

By the time Katherine was sixteen, peace had come back. The peace of work at the piano, and an ever-increasing adoration of Justin. The peace of reading every book in the school library, and every book she could beg Manya to send her. She was given the job of playing the organ in chapel, to the eternal resentment of Miss Elkes, who had been proud of her own ability to pound out hymns and psalms. She learned to develop an aloofness that kept her free from the barbs of her formmates, and the change from savagery to at least a kind of civilization is most marked between fourteen and sixteen, so that they began to give her a kind of respect. They were proud of her when she played in a recital at the Montreux Conservatory, winning honors and getting her name in the papers.

Active happiness is not a common state. Active unhappiness is better than dull days. Katherine was seldom in an intermediate stage. If Justin was pleased with her, she sang as she left his studio. If he was moody and preoccupied, she was sure it was because he was angry with her, and she was depressed until her next lesson. She learned to accept seeing Sarah constantly just as a member of her form, but sometimes a casual word would make her remember the peaceful and happy hours in the fourth-floor music room, or the daydreams together in the château on Sunday afternoons, or the hour between tea and prep, and she would feel a panic of loneliness that made her rush in terror to a piano to keep misery from filling her heart. Yet if there were more stars than usual, or if the trees in front of the street lamp made special patterns on the path, a feeling of the great glory of life would come over her. If she woke up in the night, got out of bed and stood by the window, looking down the mountainside, she would think as her heart began to pound with sudden unreasonable excitement, my God, my God, the night keeps being shattered by so many things; that thin steeple jutting into the purple sky pushes it away with cool, sharp blackness; in the raucous clang of somber bells I can feel it shatter and break; from the chalet up the mountain the colored notes of a concertina make it warm with their warmth; the high thin cry of a distant siren splinters it into frightened fragments; the night keeps being shattered by so many things . . .

Then in the spring of her sixteenth year there was the music lesson at the end of which Justin said, "I'm going away."

When something like that is said, there is a hollowness inside you, but no real feeling. "Away? When?"

"This summer. After school closes and I finish up in Montreux. I have a position at the Conservatory in Paris for next year . . . You must be glad with me about that."

"I'm glad for you. I'm awfully glad for you," Katherine said, still empty and unfeeling inside.

"You have one more year of this place after this?"

153

"Yes."

"And then what?"

"May I come to Paris and go on studying with you?"

"You should come to Paris, yes. But whether or not you should study with me is another matter. We're worked together for almost three years now. Maybe you should have a change."

"There'll be all next year," she said, and felt tears tremble in her eyes. She looked down so that he wouldn't see.

But of course he saw. Justin always saw everything. And said nothing.

At last Katherine said, "I could learn from Mother. Whenever she told me anything, it was like turning on a light. It's the same way with you. It would be stupid to change."

"Well," he struck a chord lightly on the piano. "We'll see when the time comes. Meanwhile, I have news for you."

"For me?"

"Yes . . . That Miss Valentine doesn't like you much, does she?"

"No. She can't bear me."

"She doesn't understand you. That's why. She's afraid of people she doesn't understand. And she resents your talent. Although she hopes that someday she'll be able to say, 'Oh, yes, Katherine Forrester was one of my girls. We gave her her first encouragement here at the school. Such a nice little girl. One of my favorite pupils.' Whited sepulchre. I have no patience with disappointed old maids who try to pretend they are Moses the Lawgiver to make up for being thwarted. I had the devil of a time wangling special permission for you."

"Special permission for what?"

"To spend the night in Territet next week."

"The night in Territet!"

"Yes. Julien Quimper will be in town Monday night.

154

He knew your mother and he wants you to play for him."

"Oh—" Katherine gasped.

"I had to be most charming and gallant to your Miss Valentine before she would give you permission. She ended up by being so coy with me that I nearly spoiled it all by being rude. Anyhow, you're to come down to Montreux with me after your lesson on Monday, and you will spend the night with me and my sister in Territet. In the evening we'll go to Quimper's concert, and then you'll play for him. I told your Miss Valentine that you couldn't possibly make the last train back to the school, and that it would be of the utmost importance to your career. It isn't, so don't be nervous about it. I know Quimper will like you. You're his type. And he may be able to help you. And I also thought you might like to meet him because he knew your mother. He admired her very much, and said that if it hadn't been for her accident, she would have been one of the greatest pianists of our time, if not the greatest . . . You're happier now, aren't you?"

"Oh, yes!" Katherine said. "Oh, yes! Thank you ever and ever so much, Monsieur Vigneras."

"Let's get to work," he said. "Let's hear the *Italian Concerto* again. I think that will be a good thing for you to do for Quimper."

The Sunday before Quimper's concert Sarah knocked on the door of the fourth-floor practice room where Katherine was working. "Hello," she said. "Am I bothering you?"

"No." Katherine stopped playing and looked at Sarah, who seated herself on the window seat.

"This is sort of like old times, isn't it?" Sarah asked. Katherine said nothing. "I heard you, so I thought I'd come in for a sec if you didn't mind."

"No. I don't mind!"

155

"Isn't the chemistry assignment foul? I've got to get on downstairs and get Pen to help me with mine. Have you done it yet?"

"No."

"It's frightful—a lot of old algebraic formulas we've all forgotten years ago stuck in the middle of electrons and negatrons . . . I hear you're going to Montreux with Justin tomorrow."

"Yes."

"Ginny told me."

"Oh."

"I s'pose you're awfully excited about that."

"Yes. I am."

"Well, good-bye and good luck."

"Thanks."

Sarah left, and Katherine started practicing again. But for several minutes her fingers trembled, and she could not concentrate. She wished that Sarah had not come.

On Monday at her lesson she played the program Justin had arranged for her to play to Julien Quimper. Then he looked at her and said, "What have you done to yourself?"

"I put my hair up."

"Oh. I see."

Her hair had not gone up since the night when Manya had fixed it on shipboard. Now she no longer felt as though she were playing at being grown up. It seemed incredibly stupid that at the school they were not allowed to wear their hair up until they were in the sixth form. She had had to go into the bathroom of the music and art studio to follow her impulse of putting her dark braids up before this lesson.

"Don't you like it?" she asked.

He looked at her again. "Yes. I like it very much. But all of a sudden you aren't a little girl any more.

156

You're a woman. And quite beautiful. How old are you?"

"Sixteen. Pretty nearly seventeen. I'm not a child."

"In many ways I know you're far beyond your years, little one, but you surprise me nevertheless."

"Do you want me to be a child? Would you like me to be a child?"

Justin laughed. "You're funny."

"No, I'm not!"

"Yes. You are. Funny and sweet . . . Well! We won't have a lesson today. Let's take the next train and get away from this place. Have you everything you need in that little suitcase?"

"Yes."

"Come on, then." He took her coat down and helped her into it, took her beret and dropped it onto the top of her head.

Katherine didn't talk much on the train. She sat next to Justin and listened to him. He talked about himself, his childhood, his music, Julien Quimper, his sister Anne. The white lines on either side of his mouth that made him so much like Charlot relaxed, and his gray-blue eyes were shining and happy. When they got to Montreux, they had to take a streetcar to Territet, then the funicular, and then it was a ten-minute walk up the mountain to the tiny villa where Justin lived with his sister. Anne met them at the door. She was wearing a warm-gray tweed suit, and her hair was very short and curled softly over her head, and her smile as she took Katherine's suitcase was as warm as Justin's.

"I feel as though I know you already," she said, "Justin has talked so much about his prize pupil. But I thought you were a little girl, and I find a young lady. You're to sleep in my room, dear, on this cot by the window. I hope you don't mind, but we haven't an extra room."

"Oh, this is lovely!" Katherine said. "I love being by the

157

window, and they're such beautiful blue blankets, Mlle. Vigneras."

"You must call me Anne, because I'm going to call you Katherine," Justin's sister said.

Katherine spent the rest of the afternoon with Anne, since Justin had a lesson to give in town. Anne showed her an album of pictures of Justin, and in going through an old box of pictures and programs and clippings from all the concerts Anne and Justin had been to when they were children, they came across a picture of Julie when she was very young in Paris.

"Oh!" Katherine gasped. "Oh! It's Mother! Look! It's my mother!"

It was a newspaper picture of Julie in an old black coat and beret, leaning against the curve of a piano, one beautiful hand holding a cigarette, the other stuck deep in her pocket.

Anne watched Katherine for a moment; then she went quickly into her bedroom and came out with a small, blue-leather frame. "This ought to just about fit. Let's see." She took the picture and slipped it into the frame. "It's perfect. Isn't that lucky? There you are, dear."

"For me?"

Anne laughed. "Yes. For you."

"Oh, thank you! Thank you ever and ever so much!"

They had dinner in Montreux at the Montreux Palace. Anne said that it was a great treat for them, a celebration because of Justin's appointment to the Conservatory. They were very gay and very happy. Katherine looked at Justin's face with the tight lines gone, and something seemed to rise up inside her like a bird taking wing.

Julien Quimper's concert was magnificent. Katherine sat between Anne and Justin, and when the lights came on, the tears were streaming down her face. Justin laughed and pulled his handkerchief out of his pocket, the white one with the blue border, and gave it to her. "I love Katherine," he said to Anne. "She always cries whenever music moves or excites her, and she doesn't even know it till you tell her about it."

—He doesn't mean it—Katherine thought—but he said he loved me—

Julien Quimper came back to Territet with them. It was after midnight when they got back, and they talked for over an hour before Katherine began to play. Anne brought out a bottle of wine, and when it was finished Justin brought out another. They were well into the second bottle when Julien Quimper put his hand on Katherine's shoulder and said, "Justin has had more than enough attention for tonight. I want to hear you play. If you have half the talent your mother had—" and then he stopped short. "Go on. Play."

Katherine had refused the wine, because she wanted desperately to play well for her mother's sake and she was afraid it would make her brain and fingers less accurate, but she felt drunk as she rose and went to the piano. Justin came and stood beside her, and she whispered up at him, "I'm afraid."

He bent down and kissed her on the forehead and whispered back to her, "Don't be afraid, my darling, you'll be all right."

She started to play. She was so nervous and excited that she knew she was running away with herself sometimes, but the excitement gave her a new lack of inhibition in her playing, too. When she had finished the short program Justin had prepared, Julian Quimper said, "Do you know the *Gigue* from the Fifth French Suite? Your mother used to play that so you couldn't help being happy and wanting to dance for joy."

159

"I've worked on it some," Katherine answered.

"Play it, then. I'd like to hear you do something in that vein. You tend to stress the melancholy and emotional in your playing. I suppose it's your youth."

"She's generally too reserved and controlled," Justin said. "She's reversing her usual procedure tonight."

Katherine played the *Gigue*. When she had finished, Julien Quimper got up and sat down on the piano bench beside her and put his arm around her. "You've got a lot to learn," he said. "You've got a tremendous lot to learn. How old are you?"

"Almost seventeen."

"Well, I think you're your mother's daughter, my dear. She'd be proud of you if she could have heard you tonight. She was proud of you, wasn't she?"

"I don't know."

"Of course she was. Don't be afraid to say so."

Anne rose. "I think I'd better take Katherine off to bed."

"Are you sleepy?" Julien Quimper asked Katherine.

"No."

"Don't make her go to bed, Anne. She likes being up late." Julien Quimper refilled his glass of wine.

"You go on to bed, Anne," Justin said. "I'll take care of Katherine."

Anne sat down again. "I'll wait."

"It's all right, curlyhead. Go on. You know you have to be up early tomorrow. And you said you had a headache."

Anne pushed her fingers through her cropped hair. "Well, I do."

"Then go on to bed, dear. But let Katherine have a little fun for once. She hates that dreadful school of hers, don't you, little one?"

"Yes."

160

Anne couldn't help yawning. "Would you like to stay up a while longer, Katherine?"

"Oh, yes."

"And she doesn't have to be back at school till noon. I wangled her permission till that late. As long as she catches the eleven-thirty train she'll be all right."

"Well, all right," Anne said, yawning again. "It's all that wine. It always makes me sleepy when I drink too much, and I have had an awful headache. It's been a lovely evening, anyhow. So good night, everyone. Shall I see you again while you're in Montreux, Monsieur Quimper?"

"I'm afraid not, Anne. I'm on to Lausanne tomorrow and then Zurich. So good-bye."

"Good-bye, and thank you," Anne said.

"Good-bye, and thank *you*." Julien Quimper bowed deeply. Anne kissed Katherine good night, pulled her brother's ear, and went off to her room. Julien Quimper filled a wineglass and took it to Katherine. "Now you can drink, little one," he said. "You've played beautifully and it'll do you good. As I remember, your mother liked to drink."

"Yes, she did."

"When she was just a slip of a thing in Paris she could drink many good men under the table. Small, like you, but made of iron. I believed in her right from the first night I met her, in May, in a small café under the chestnut trees. Beautiful and romantic. Only she never fell in love with me. I was desperately in love with her. It's a strange thing, how you can love somebody, how you can be all eaten up inside with needing them—and they simply don't need you. That's all there is to it, and neither of you can do anything about it. And they'll be the same way with someone else, and someone else will be the same way about you and it goes on and on—this desperate need—and only once in a rare million do

161

the same two people need each other." He paused and laughed. "Those are cheerful words, aren't they, child? But I'm afraid they're only too true."

"Yes. I know," Katherine said.

"I doubt very much if you know now," Julien Quimper said, "but unless you're phenomenally lucky, you will know someday."

"Maybe she'll be lucky. I think she'll be lucky." Justin smiled at her.

"No," Katherine shook her head. But inside her she was saying, she was contradicting herself—He kissed me before I began to play, he kissed me to give me courage—

She sat curled up on a corner of the sofa, sipping her wine. Every time she emptied her glass Justin or Julien Quimper filled it again. She sat with her legs tucked under her on the sofa, and the smoke from Justin's cigarettes and Julien Quimper's pipe curled around her head, and their words curled around like the smoke, and Justin's arm was heavy across her shoulders, and she put her head down on it.—My braids are up and I look quite nice—she thought—and my eyes are blue, almost black, like my grandmother's, and Justin looks like Charlot, only he's much more like Mother. I cried, too, when Aunt Manya read out of *The Oxford Book of English Verse* and cried when Sarah read out of *The Oxford Book of English Verse*, I wish she hadn't; it's always something that makes people unhappy, only I won't be unhappy, because Julien Quimper said I was my mother's daughter, and she'd be proud of me, and she wouldn't be proud of me if I was unhappy because of *The Oxford Book of English Verse*, because of what Aunt Manya read, and because of what Sarah read, why should I be unhappy, Justin kissed me before I began to play.—

162

Julien Quimper got up and stretched and kissed Katherine good-bye. She stayed curled up on the sofa while Justin saw Julien Quimper to the door. She closed her eyes, and her thoughts stopped coming in sentences, even stopped coming in words, but she knew when Justin came back and was standing over her.

"You'd better go to bed, little one," he said.

"Yes. I know." She stood up and looked at Justin standing in front of her, and suddenly the white lines on either side of his mouth came out, very strong, and he put his arms around her.

"I'm tired," he said. "Oh, God, I'm tired."

Katherine was in a daze. She stood there with Justin's arms around her, with Justin leaning against her, and suddenly her mind stopped being fuzzy and warm and felt very clear and cold and empty. Then she said, "I guess I drank too much wine. I feel sort of funny."

"I can feel your heart pounding," Justin said. "It's going terribly fast."

"It's the wine," Katherine said.

"No. I don't think it's the wine." He bent down and kissed her very gently, and then again, gently. "You're very exciting, Katherine. Do you know how exciting you are?"

"It's the wine," Katherine said. "I drank too much. I feel funny. I feel funny. I think I'm going to whoops."

"What?" He pushed her away, angry, unbelieving.

"It's the wine," Katherine said. "It's made me feel funny."

Justin put his hands on her shoulders. "You want to be put to bed, is that it? You want to be treated like a baby and put to bed?"

Katherine nodded. Justin went into the bathroom and turned on the bath. He walked unsteadily. Then he stalked into his bedroom without a word. Katherine went into

Anne's room and undressed quietly in the dark without waking her. She slipped into her blue flannel bathrobe, put her pajamas over her arm, and went into the bathroom. When she came out, Justin was standing in the living room in his night clothes.

"All ready?" he asked. She nodded. "Come here," he said. She went up to him and he put his arms around her again. "You're very comforting, little one," he said. "You're very comforting."

"Oh—"

"You've got such a strong, firm little body. I like the feel of it against mine."

Katherine let him lean against her for a long time. Then she said, "My feet are cold."

Justin looked down at Katherine's feet, still red from the hot bath. "My poor baby, of course they are. You should be wearing slippers. Come and sit on the sofa and tuck your feet under you." He led her over to the sofa and she sat down, and he sat down beside her.

"I think I'd better go to bed," she said. "I still feel funny. It's the wine."

"I don't want you to go. I don't want you to go yet. I don't want to be left alone. Don't go just yet."

"All right."

He kissed her again, still very gently. "Let me sleep with you. Come on, let me lie near you."

Katherine looked at him, at the tight lines of his face, the tenseness of his mouth, his gray-blue eyes, suddenly unguarded and unhappy.

"Come on. Let me lie with you. Just for fun," he said.

"I think I'd better go to bed," Katherine repeated. "I still feel funny. It's the wine." She rose and turned toward Anne's room, and Justin let her go. He stood watching her.

"We won't frighten Katherine any more. We'll go to bed, and we won't frighten Katherine any more," he said.

She went into Anne's room and climbed into the small cot by the window and waited. She was afraid he would come in. Of course he wouldn't, with Anne asleep in the room. But she was afraid he would come. She lay on her back, every muscle tense, and waited. She wanted desperately to have him come. —He's got to come. Please let him come and speak to me. Don't let everything be ruined. It wasn't me. He didn't know it was me. It wasn't me he kissed. I was just someone. I was just the person who was there. It would have been whoever was there. It wasn't because it was me. Please make him come in. Please make him come. Don't let it be spoiled. I'll die if he should hate me. Please make him come.—

She heard him go into his room and slam his door. And still she waited. She slipped out of bed, went into the living room again, and crouched down by the fire. She waited there for a long time, until she started drowsing off and waking up again when a log fell, thinking that Justin was coming and everything would be all right. Finally she got up and went back to bed and curled up into a tight little ball for warmth, because inside her she felt very cold; and at last she fell asleep.

She didn't sleep long. She woke up early and lay quietly in bed. After a while Anne got up and dressed in the living room in order not to wake her, and left.

Katherine sat up in bed and put on her bathrobe. She felt the same way she had felt one morning waiting for Julie to come in. But Justin didn't come. After a while she got up and dressed. The clock on the mantel said nine-thirty. She found a piece of paper and a pencil and wrote on it, "I can make the ten o'clock train, so I think I'd better go back to school. I have my carfare and my ticket, so don't worry. Thank you ever so much and please thank Anne for me too. Katherine."

She looked around for a place where Justin would be sure to see the note, and finally left it on the piano.

She went into school through the back gate, and in through the cloakroom. She was just in time for Latin class, and she slipped into her seat without attracting attention.

The rest of Tuesday, and all of Wednesday, and Thursday until time for her piano lesson had a completely nightmare quality. As the time drew near for her lesson, she was so nervous that her hands were cold and clammy, and she had to clasp them tightly together to keep them from trembling. She stood outside the studio for several minutes before she could gather courage to knock. Penelope Deerenforth was at the piano, playing a Handel *Minuet,* competently, but without the least imagination. Katherine stood leaning against the window until she had finished, watching Justin. His face was expressionless. Pen said good-bye to Justin, smiled a little self-consciously, and left.

"Hello—" Katherine said.

"Hello, Katherine." He smiled at her, a purely impersonal smile. "The summer holidays are nearly here, and I shall be leaving, and I'd like to get you started on some new things before I go. Here are some Shostakovitch *Waltzes,* more Chopin *Etudes,* Beethoven's *Fifth Concerto,* and I think you might as well do this Bach *Toccata and Fugue.* Bach is certainly your strong point, and there's no reason to slight him. I thought you also might like to work on this *Kermesse Suite* of your father's. That's a lot of stuff, and I'll only be able to start you on it all, but I thought you would probably like to crowd as much as you can into these last few weeks."

166

"Yes, I would," Katherine said, and they settled down to work. She knew now that he would never mention the night in Territet. And neither would she.

It happened that Justin's last lesson before the summer holidays and his departure for Paris was with Katherine. She came to his studio as usual in her regulation blue tunic and white blouse; her long, heavy braids were not pinned up as they had been the day she went to Territet, but somehow she did not look like a child.

Justin looked at her. "You've grown older."

"Have I?" she asked, and she was angry because she was breathless. She always seemed to be breathless when Justin spoke to her, and she was sure it made her sound wishy-washy and indeterminate.

"Yes. You've grown older. What's happened?"

"Oh, I don't know."

"Who's hurt you?"

"Oh, no one."

"You're not telling the truth, are you?"

"No one's hurt me."

He didn't say anything more until the end of the lesson. Then he said, "Well, this is good-bye, Katherine."

"Yes." She couldn't take her eyes off him; she had to stare at him, to look until the last possible moment.

He saw the misery in her eyes. "What is it?"

"Nothing."

"I'll miss my lessons with you."

"I'll miss them, too."

"You keep on working hard and get out of this place as soon as you can."

"I will."

"Are you going to London for your holidays?"

167

"No."

"Where are you going?"

"Aunt Manya's finished her play, and she isn't going to do another one till autumn, and she's taken a villa in France, above Thônon, because she says it will be a good place for Father to compose."

"And you'll go there?"

"Yes."

"Well, you drop me a line every now and then to let me know how you're getting on, will you?"

"Oh, yes!" —He's given me permission to write him—she thought—he's given me permission to write!—

"We'd better say good-bye now, dear."

"Yes—"

He leaned down and kissed her on both cheeks. "Good-bye, little Katherine."

"Good-bye—"

He pushed her gently, and she turned and stumbled out of the studio. She ran to the elm tree and climbed up into its branches and sat there, her arms clasped tightly around the trunk, sobbing. But through her tears she thought—He hasn't forgotten me. He does know I exist. He told me to write, and he called me little Katherine and dear, and he kissed me good-bye.—

And then came the thought that she might never see him again, and she pressed even more closely to the tree, and the sobs came crowding out so quickly that she had to stop thinking of him and concentrate on getting her breath. She sat there for a long time, clutching the trunk of the tree, pressing her cheek against it until it was patterned from the bark, sat there until she saw Justin leave the studio, carrying the music he hadn't already packed, walking happily, his head held high and proud, out of her life.

ECAUSE she was not going to London, she left an hour before the English train, which took almost all the rest of the school. She carried a big shabby suitcase that had belonged to Julie, and she sat in the train, peering out of the window, thinking of the unaffectionate good-byes she had said to everyone and of her last glimpse of Justin disappearing down the path between the rows of plane trees. There had been no good-bye to Sarah. She hadn't seen Sarah to say good-bye to.

If she thought about it, it seemed impossible that she could once have known Sarah so well, could have been so familiar with the workings of her mind; and could now feel, looking at the same large blue eyes and brown hair, listening to the same decided, self-assured voice, that here was a stranger, someone she had never known and could never know.

The constant repetition of the noise of the wheels turning on the tracks, the shake of the carriages, rhythmic and dissonant at the same time, made words run almost meaninglessly through her head, words turning like the wheels of the train, words jarring against her consciousness like the shaking of the carriages.

Manya met her in Thônon. It was after midnight when she arrived, and she was numb with chill and fatigue. The night was icy although it was almost summer. Manya's face was flushed and shining with cold, not white and pinched

169

like Katherine's. She looked very alive and beautiful in her dark coat and cap. She kissed Katherine warmly.

"My poor baby, you're shivering. Was it a frightful trip? Of course it was. And that heavy suitcase. I'm perfectly sure you carried it the whole way yourself and never gave it to a porter because it was Julie's. Changing trains twice. The café's closed, so I can't get you any coffee. There's a little bistro down the street that may be open. No, I know what's better. I think there's a flask in the car. Come along, darling. Well, can't you kiss me any better than that? Charlot's here. He wanted to come meet you tonight, but I wouldn't let him. He just got in, and he hasn't had any sleep in weeks, so I made him go to bed. Katya, you look so grown up! You're not my baby any more. What have you done to yourself?"

"I've got my hair up." Katherine's teeth were chattering.

Manya took her arm and led her to the car. "Yes. Your hair. It does make a difference, doesn't it? Here, tuck this robe around you. But I don't think it's just the hair, my little Katya. It's in your face, too. Well, after all, you're almost seventeen. I was married at seventeen, and had a child. A little boy. He died when he was two. Tie this scarf over your head. It's much warmer than that stupid hat, and your ears are about to fall off. You grew old very early in the four years you lived with Julie, and I thought going to a school with a lot of girls your own age would really make you a child again, and instead you've the face of a little old woman. Here's the flask. Take a long swig, darling. It'll warm you. Come on, Katyusha, take more than that. That's better. I know you hate the school, baby, and I wanted so to take you away when you wrote us that dreadful letter your first year there, but your father was so determined to have you stay there, to have you live a normal healthy conventional exis- tence. And you know what your father is. But I blame myself . . . I really don't know what Julie would have done, whether she'd have made you stay or not. Anyhow, there's only one more year of it, and then you shall do whatever you like . . . I've been so busy these past years, I've neglected you dreadfully. It's not because I don't love you, darling . . . The reason I never wanted another child after my baby died was that I knew I'd neglect it for my work. I was away on tour when my baby died. I had to be. There wasn't any money and I had to take the first job I could get. I wouldn't ask Leonid—that was his father—but don't blame me for that, Katya; after all, I was very young. Why am I talking like this? So stupid, so thoughtless, when you're so tired. We must get to know each other again this summer. You don't hate the school quite so much now, do you?"

"It's all right."

"Some of your letters—and Katya, you certainly write the least informative letter I've ever read—about a girl called Sarah seemed very happy. But you haven't mentioned her lately. Did she leave?"

"No, she's still there."

"What's the matter? Did you quarrel? All right, darling, don't glower so, I won't press you if you don't want to talk. Only you haven't mentioned her since your first year there, so I thought she must have left. I know how one can get enthusiasms about people, and then find out they're really very dull and not worth bothering with. I read in the paper the other day that your music teacher, Justin Michel What's-his-name's going to Paris to the Conservatory."

"Yes."

"You'll miss him, won't you, Katyusha?"

"Yes."

"Well, darling, don't look as though you were going to bite my head off. You'd better have another swallow."

171

"No."

"I know I'm talking like a foolish old woman, but really, Katya, when you look at me like a little Sphinx I—well, I feel as though I'd gone up in my lines and didn't have the faintest idea what the rest of the play was about, much less what my next lines were, and I have to ad-lib all over the place. You'll have to read the play I'm going to do in the autumn. It's beautiful—a really great play, I think. Your father's going to do music for it. I shall be horribly disappointed if it doesn't go well. Darling, it's lovely to see you again and to have time to really be with you—even if you don't seem a bit pleased at the prospect of a summer with your father and me."

The drive up the mountain took about three-quarters of an hour. Katherine huddled into the robe and tried to make her face completely expressionless as she listened to Manya, because she could see her aunt looking at her worriedly out of the corner of her eye from time to time. She closed her eyes and leaned back, trying not to think, because now that the robe and the whisky had taken away some of her physical numbness, it had taken away her mental numbness, too, and the sudden prospect of a three months' holiday with unlimited time in which to think, and nothing but a year of school without Justin ahead of her, made the tears very close.

"Katya, what is it? Are you ill? Don't you feel well?" Manya asked once, and as usual when she was sincerely worried, her accent vanished.

"I'm just tired," Katherine said.

The villa Manya had taken was large and beautifully furnished. Tom was at the piano in the great hall when they came in. He kissed Katherine absent-mindedly, and went out to the kitchen and made her a delicious omelette. She ate it in silence, while he talked excitedly to Manya about his new

172

violin concerto. Immediately after supper she said, "I'd like to go to bed now, please."

Manya took her up the wide marble stairs. She led Katherine into a bedroom and a dressing room that made her feel as though she had fallen into the middle of a set in a Hollywood studio.

"While I'm making a lot, I'm going to live like a star," Manya said. "You know I've never been able to save anything. Will you be all right here, baby-no-longer-a-baby?"

"Yes. I'll be fine."

"Sleep as long as you like tomorrow morning, and when you want breakfast, ring, and Josef will bring it to you. Your father and I are going to Évian for the day to see some friends, and we won't be back till after dinner. You can come, if you feel like it, but I thought you'd probably rather rest on your first day."

"Yes, I would."

"Charlot is dying to see you, anyhow, and he refused point blank to go to Évian. You know how he is. Good night, Katya darling."

"Good night, Aunt Manya."

"I hope you'll have a happy holiday."

"I will. Good night."

Manya left, and Katherine undressed and got into bed. The hot-water bottle under the covers was still warm, and the warmth of the bed and the whisky soothed her, and she fell asleep instantly.

Early the next evening she went upstairs. Her room had a small balcony that hung over the large terrace downstairs. She put on her coat and went out on the balcony and looked down the mountain to the lake and then across to the mountains. This time she was looking across at the mountains of

173

Switzerland, instead of France, but the same small lake steamers were gold bands of light on the water. Below her, to the left and the right, were the lights of Thônon and Evian and the small scattered groups of lights from the villages on the way up the mountainside. At the edge of the lake she could see the gaily colored lights of a fair, and if she strained her ears, she thought she could hear the music of a carrousel. There were no lights on the mountainside from funicular or train. The only way up was on foot by the *sentier,* or in a car, or with a horse. Immediately below her on the terrace were two cypress trees in huge stone jars, menacing black shadows. She looked at the cypress trees and then at the mountains of Switzerland across the way, impassive, immovable, frighteningly permanent.

"Oh God!" she cried. "I can't!"

From the shadow of one of the cypress trees another shadow emerged, and a voice said, "Katherine."

She stood very still on the balcony, and her heart began to pound violently.—He couldn't be here, Justin couldn't be here.—The voice said again, "Katherine, it's Charlot."

"Hello," she said.

"Hello." He came all the way out of the shadow and stood where the light from the French windows shone on him, and she gasped to see how much more like Justin he was even than she had remembered.

"I slept all day," he said. "I'm sorry."

"Oh, that's all right. I practiced."

"Let's get out of this mausoleum," he said. "There's a *kermesse* down by the water front. Shall we go?"

"Yes, let's," and suddenly her whole body stopped sagging and came to life.—That's the thing to do—she thought—I'll go to the fair with him and I'll be gay and happy.—

"Hurry up," he said. "I'll wait for you downstairs."

174

She ran into her room and turned on all the lights. She opened her closet and pulled out her black velveteen dress with the lace collar and cuffs.—It's schoolgirlish but it's the best I've got—she thought. She went into her dressing room, but she had no make-up, and she stared discontentedly into the mirrors with their bright lights at her small thin face. "Oh, damn," she said, "damn!" and ran down the corridor, opening one door after another, until she found Manya's room and her dressing table. She made up painstakingly and well. She remembered everything Manya had taught her, blending her rouge and eye-shadow skillfully and putting her lipstick on with Manya's best brush. She dabbed perfume behind her ears and put her braids up very carefully. She looked through Manya's jewel box until she found a pair of earrings that had belonged to her mother, and she put them on. In one of Manya's drawers she came across a magnificent old Russian shawl, which she put over her head. She scrawled a note:

"Dear Aunt Manya,
I'm going to a fair with Charlot. I borrowed a scarf and lots of your make-up and Mother's sapphire earrings. I'm sorry. But it was necessary. Katherine."

She left the note on the dressing table, took a last look at herself in the mirror, and hurried down the wide marble staircase.

"Well, you certainly took long enough," Charlot began, as he heard her coming. Then he caught his breath. "Well! Well, Katherine!"

She smiled at him and held out her hand. "Hello, Charlot."

They stood there at the foot of the stairs, holding hands, staring at each other. Charlot looked a great deal older. He

175

looked as old as Justin, although Katherine knew he was only four years older than she was. The lines on either side of his mouth were stronger, his large dark eyes seemed more deeply set, his tense face even less able to relax than it had been before.

"I still don't look like Mother," she said at last.

"No." Charlot kept on looking at her. "But you're yourself now. You weren't before."

She laughed. "That's funny. I feel less myself now than I've ever felt in my life."

"Come on," he said. "Let's go."

They went out to the garage. "Aunt Manya left the Mercedes for us," he said. "She thought we might like to go to the *kermesse* tonight. I didn't mean to sleep all day. I woke up and heard you at the piano, and it put me back to sleep again. That's not very complimentary to your playing, is it?"

"You look tired. I guess you needed sleep."

"Will you play for me when we get back tonight?"

"If you like."

He opened the door to the car. "I'll have to slide through. Sorry. It's parked too close. Here we are. Climb in. Do you want the robe over you?"

"No. I'm warm enough. This shawl's wonderfully warm."

"You look very beautiful." He backed the car out of the garage.

"Do I?"

"Yes. Don't you know that? You, with your great stage experience."

"Don't tease me," she said, soberly. "I'm not a very good actress."

"Don't lie. You know you're good. Don't you?"

"Yes."

"Why did you say it, then?"

176

"I don't know."

"Come along. Tell me."

"Oh, I don't know, Charlot. Anyhow, when our form did a play at school I didn't even get a part, much less in any of the big school plays."

"Did you tell them you'd ever been in a play?"

"Only Sarah. And she promised not to tell."

"Didn't you want them to know?"

"No."

"Why?"

"They wouldn't have liked it."

"Why?"

"I don't know. They just wouldn't."

"Who's Sarah?"

"She's a girl I used to like. She's going to be an actress."

"Don't you like her any more?"

"Oh, yes."

"Then why did you say 'used to like'?"

"Did I say that?"

"You know you did."

"Oh. Well, I don't know why I said it."

"Do you like that school of yours?"

"No. Do you like yours? Studying medicine and things, I mean?"

"Yes."

"Are you good at it, Charlot?"

"Yes."

"I mean really good?"

"Yes." He was driving rapidly, too rapidly for the narrow, winding road. Katherine braced her feet and pushed back against the seat. He looked over at her, and his mouth twisted into a grin. "Nervous?"

"No."

"Yes, you are. But you needn't be. I'm a good driver. We won't go hurtling down the mountainside and into the lake." He drove silently for a while, then asked softly, "Well, Katherine?"

"Well, Charlot?"

"You all right?"

"Yes . . . It's good to see you again, Charlot. Even when I haven't seen you for ages, it's always easy to talk to you."

"And to you," he said.

"It's almost as though you were my brother."

"Listen, darling. I don't want to be a brother to you. So cut that out."

"I'm sorry. I didn't mean to make you cross. I'm sorry."

"Forget it," he said, and scowled through the windshield down the mountainside.

She watched his hands on the steering wheel, the long fingers suddenly tense, the knuckles white so that the soft, dark hairs on his fingers showed more strongly. In the rear-view mirror she saw his face and the lines on either side of his mouth were very tight. But if she blurred her eyes, she could almost pretend he was Justin.

Suddenly he reached over with one hand and pulled the shawl down from her head, touching one of the earrings gently with his finger. "Those belonged to your mother."

"Yes."

"They look well on you."

"I'm glad."

He pulled the shawl back over her head and put his arm around her. "Don't worry. I can drive very well with one hand."

"Oh."

"Do you mind my arm?"

"No."

178

"The first time I saw you," he said, "when you were just a child, was the first time you'd seen your mother since her accident. And then the next time was just after she'd died, and four years had passed, but you were still a child. And now it's three years and you're grown up. Why?"

"I don't know. I guess it was just time for me to grow up."

"I think I want always to be around when important things happen to you. Would you mind?"

"No. I'd like it."

"Has something happened to you now?"

"No."

"But you're not a child any longer."

"Well?"

"You're grown up now. Something must have happened.

"I don't see why. People have to grow up sometime, even if nothing ever happens to them."

"No. That's not so. Some people stay children all their lives. Some people stay children even if things happen to them. Like Aunt Manya. She hasn't had an empty life. As lives go, I'd say she's had a pretty full one, and she's been able to absorb enough of it to be a good actress. And I think she'll go on being a popular and successful actress even when that animal magnetism, or whatever it is she's got, goes. Because her acting has more to it than that. But, anyhow, she's never really grown up. She's still a child and she always will be one. Look at that villa. My God! Your father's a child, too, but in a different way. He's more like a baby who hasn't learned to focus yet. No, that's not right, either. Well, you probably know what I mean. Your mother was an adult. And I think you'll be one. Maybe. You'll either be an adult or you'll go to hell. You'll go to hell anyhow, but you may come out of it instead of staying there. I'm talking incomprehensible rubbish, aren't I?"

179

"No. I don't think so." She reached up and took hold of his hand on her shoulder and held onto it tightly.

He took her to a small café that was already crowded, although it was still early. "Mind if I order for you?"

"No. Go ahead."

"Want some wine?"

"Please."

The music from the merry-go-round was very loud and gay. "Have we got much money to spend, Charlot?"

"Enough to do everything your little heart desires this evening, darling. Shall we ride on the carrousel?"

"Yes, let's!"

Charlot took her hand, and they ran over to the merry-go-round, and she climbed onto a milk-white horse, and Charlot onto an ebony-black one, and they rode around, laughing and shouting at each other, and she got the gold ring twice. They were panting and laughing when they got off, and they walked away, arms entwined, swaying a little.

"What now?" Charlot asked.

"More wine please, Jus—Charlot."

"More wine?"

"Yes, please."

"You are a little dipsomaniac, aren't you? All right, come along."

They went into a little bistro. As Charlot opened the door, the hot air, filled with the heavy odor of wine and beer and smoke, rushed out at them. Katherine felt a little dizzy and clutched Charlot's arm. He led her to a small unoccupied table in the corner at the back and ordered wine.

"Like to drink?" he asked.

"Sometimes."

"Know how much you can take?"

"Yes."

"Won't make yourself sick?"

"No."

"Don't have to worry about you?"

"No."

"You got that one down quickly enough, didn't you?"

"I was thirsty."

"What now? Ferris wheel?"

"All right."

They waited at the foot of the ferris wheel while it wheezed to a stop. The man who ran it was swarthy, and he looked unclean. Katherine pressed close to Charlot and away from the man. He had on a pair of brown trousers covered with grease stains from the machinery of the ferris wheel, and his toes showed through the holes in his canvas shoes. He wore a green silk shirt open very low at the neck, so that the hair curling on his chest showed. On the back of his head he had a green cloth cap and behind his ear stuck a half-smoked stub of a cigarette with lipstick stains on it. With both hands he reached out to pull the lever that stopped the wheel and leered up at Katherine and winked. She felt Charlot's fingers tighten on her arm. The man's hands were gray with dirt, his fingernails too long, and very black. The middle finger of his right hand was gone at the first joint, and the stump was dirty, too.

Katherine and Charlot climbed up onto the chair that was still swinging a little as the ferris wheel stopped. As he strapped them into the chair, the man leaned very close to Katherine, and it seemed to her as his face neared hers that it was going to come closer and closer, getting bigger and bigger until it exploded. But it stopped a few inches away from hers.

"The wine is good here," he said, and laughed. Katherine drew back in her seat.

"Leave the young lady alone," Charlot said sharply.

The man laughed again. "No harm, no harm intended," he said. "Wine is a wonderful thing on a late June evening. A late June evening is a wonderful thing, too, when one is young. I will give you an extra-long ride, because the young lady has a pretty little face, and she still gets frightened easily, and her eyes are the color of the night." He slapped the footboard of their chair sharply, so that it lurched, and then pulled the lever that started the wheel moving. They swung back and up, at first slowly, then gaining speed, until they reached the top of the wheel. At the top they seemed to hang suspended for a moment, then they were out and over and plunging downward. Around again and up to the top, up and just over the edge, and the ferris wheel stopped. Katherine gasped and clutched Charlot.

"He did that on purpose," Charlot said. "Son of a—sorry, dear. I don't like him. I don't like the way he looked at you. Afraid?"

"No."

They looked out over the lake from the top of the ferris wheel. If they jumped they would land in the lake. A small steamer was going by, as gay with lights as the fair. Blown and distorted by the wind they could hear the strains of a Strauss waltz almost drowned out by the blaring of the merry-go-round music.

"Do you still believe in God?" Charlot asked.

"I don't know. Why?"

"I just wondered."

"Oh."

"God didn't make man in his image," Charlot said. "Man made God in *his* image. And not a very good image, either."

182

"Oh, I don't know." Katherine looked at Charlot, at his thin tired face, so strained about the mouth, at the deep circles under his eyes. "I don't know," she said again. "Human beings can be pretty wonderful sometimes. And I guess if we didn't think we had the possibility of being pretty wonderful ourselves, in spite of its being a hell of a world, or maybe it's because of it, there wouldn't be much point in living, would there?"

"Your mother's the only wonderful person I've ever known."

"Well, there you are. That's one at any rate, isn't it? And you think you can be something yourself someday, don't you?"

"No. I think I'm rotten. Rotten as hell."

She reached up and pulled his nose and the gesture felt familiar, and she realized it was Julie's, and suddenly she felt very happy and her eyes began to shine. "Don't talk like that," she said. "You're not rotten. You're one of the few people."

He touched her earrings again with one finger, then felt through her dress the hard comfort of the locket where it lay between her small round breasts, and his arm tightened about her, as the ferris wheel went into motion again. As they reached the bottom, the man pulled the lever so that the wheel moved very slowly.

He leered at Katherine again, and then turned to Charlot. "I hope you appreciate her eyes. She has very beautiful eyes, dark like the night. The most beautiful eyeballs I've ever seen. I'd like to hold them in my hand." He laughed loudly, slapping his thigh, and started the wheel going quickly again, and again as they got just over the top, the wheel lurched to a stop.

183

Katherine peered down through the iron skeleton of the wheel, and the man was laughing at two girls who were over-dressed and over-made-up. One of them had very light blonde hair that curled over her head, and long dangly jet earrings, and she held the stubs of the tickets between her teeth. The other had straight, dark hair, shiny with brilliantine. It was pulled into a tight knot at the nape of her neck, with a soiled artificial rose behind one ear, and tight against her cheeks were two spit curls. She had a cigarette in a long black holder. The man stood with his arm around them both, and they were laughing up at him as though they found him attractive. He strapped them into their chair, slapped their footboard, and started the wheel again. As they reached the bottom, the man pushed the footboard and set their chair swinging violently. "You watch out," he shouted to Charlot. "That's a girl who needs a man who knows women. I know women. It was a woman bit my finger off."

"You watch out, yourself," Charlot shouted back angrily. "You can't insult her. She's not French, she's American. You watch out!"

"Charlot!" Katherine said. "Don't! He doesn't matter."

"I won't have you insulted," he said.

"It doesn't matter. Really it doesn't." She pulled the shawl, which had slipped down on her shoulders, up over her head again. He reached into his pocket and drew out a package of cigarettes, and lit one.

"Could I have it?" she asked.

He put it into her mouth and lit himself another. "You're such a funny little thing," he said.

"I'm not funny."

"Well, you're little, anyway."

"Mother was little, but you never thought of her as being little. You thought of her as being tall. Could we ride on

184

one of the lake steamers sometime? I've always wanted to."

"We'll go tomorrow," he promised.

"Oh, lovely!" She leaned close against Charlot, with his arm tight around her, and put her head down on his shoulder. Everything seemed to be going around, not only the ferris wheel, but the lake, and the mountains, and the lake steamer, and all the people, and all the thoughts in her head. Everything went around and around, until the ferris wheel stopped and the man unstrapped them from their chair.

"Lovely eyeballs," he said. "Love to hold them in my hand. Pretty little teeth, too. Just like little tombstones." And he roared with laughter as Katherine and Charlot left.

"What now?" Charlot asked.

"More wine, please."

"Again?"

"Yes, please."

"Are you sure you should?"

"Of course I'm sure. Unless you think *you've* had enough."

"Don't be silly," he said. "Come along."

In the café they went to this time there was dancing on an improvised dance floor. Charlot ordered the wine and then stood up. "Come along. Let's dance."

"I don't think I know how." She had not danced since the nights on shipboard with Dr. Barna when she was fourteen, when she was a child.

"It's all right," he said. "You've got enough wine in you to be relaxed, and that's all you need."

She stood up, keeping the shawl about her head.

"Leave the shawl," Charlot said. "It'll get in your way."

She stood up in front of him, in the black velveteen dress with the lace collar and cuffs, looking suddenly like a child again, nervous and forlorn.

Charlot put his arm around her. "Come along, baby. Don't

be afraid. It'll be all right. Just look at my nose and don't think of anything else. That's a good girl."

He held her very close to him, as Dr. Barna had, so that his legs pressed against hers; but as the music began, she looked desperately into his face and said, "Oh, Charlot, this is awful."

"Don't be a little idiot," he said, and kissed her neck softly, several times. And suddenly her head seemed to be on fire, and she heard the pounding of the train the day before, saying over and over again, Justin please Justin please Justin please, and she heard Aunt Manya's voice reading the melancholy verses, and the sound of the sobs she had never actually heard.

"You're doing wonderfully," Charlot's voice came in her ear. "You're a beautiful dancer."

And suddenly the spell was broken, and her feet refused to move. "You shouldn't have said that, you shouldn't have said I was good. Now I can't do it any more. Let's sit down, please."

He led her back to the table, and she sat down and began to draw Manya's shawl over her head again.

"No, don't," he said, and leaned forward and pulled at her braids, so that the hairpins scattered about on the table and her braids came down, and she was a schoolgirl again. "Maybe you'd better be a child," he said.

Under the table she stamped in fury. "Charlot! How dare you! How *dare* you!"

He laughed and filled her glass with wine. "Here, adult."

She took the wine and drank it down angrily. "Now you've spoiled everything," she said.

"How have I spoiled it?"

"I didn't want anything to remind me of school. Not anything at all."

186

"And your braids remind you of school?"

"Yes."

"That's easily fixed." He slipped the rubber bands off the ends of her braids and loosened her hair so that it fell about her face and over her shoulders in a heavy dark cloud. "There," he said. "Now put your Russian shawl on, and you'll look as glamorous as Aunt Manya." She pulled the shawl over her head, glowering at him, as he filled her glass again, and his own.

"I've been reading Shakespeare," he said at last.

"Oh. Have you?"

"Yes. I've quite a lot of theories."

"Have you?"

"I think *Lear* is a bad play, but a magnificent poem."

"Oh."

"I'd like to see you play Juliet."

Her eyes softened. "Would you?"

"Have you read all of Shakespeare?"

"Everything except *Timon of Athens*."

"Shall we talk about it sometime?"

"All right."

"Had enough wine for the moment?"

"Um-hum."

"Come along, then."

They went out and walked under the chestnut trees, whose leaves were shaking the soft early summer night, walked until the waltz music faded and only the blaring of the merry-go-round could be heard. Suddenly a loud voice rang out:

"Come and see the animals, the wonderful exhibit of animals, come and bring the children, an education for fifty centimes, fifty centimes only, to pay for the upkeep of the animals, fifty centimes only, come and see the smallest horse

187

in the world, the most poisonous snakes, Medusa the vulture, come and see the great panther and the spotted leopard."

"Shall we?" Charlot asked.

"All right," Katherine answered. Tonight she would say all right to everything.

They went in. The smallest horse in the world was a mangy little pony that stretched his legs out in his tiny cage and looked defiantly at the crowds pushing to see him. "Oh, no!" Katherine cried. She looked at Charlot, and the lines on either side of his mouth stood out like cords, and his nostrils were pinched in with fury.

"Let's go," she said. "I don't want to see any more, Charlot."

"No. Come along." He grabbed her arm and dragged her away. A group of rabbits was huddled up in a corner of a cage, and snakes lay coiled menacingly in insecure-looking glass boxes. In a small wire cage a great panther paced back and forth, his head bowed. Somehow, he reminded her of Charlot.

Suddenly Katherine found the tears streaming down her cheeks. "Take me out, please take me out," she begged. "I can't bear it. All of them shut up in cages, pacing back and forth, shut up in cages, and we can't get out. Let's go, please let's go."

They pushed toward the exit. When they got out, he took her down to a chestnut tree that grew almost in the water of the lake and pulled out his handkerchief and held it out to her. It was a white silk one with a blue border. She flung herself into his arms and clung to him, sobbing, "I can't bear it. Oh, God, I can't bear it!" over and over.

"What can't you bear, darling?" he asked, when she had quieted down.

188

"Nothing. I'm all right. I'm sorry."

He pushed her hair, which had become shaggy like the pony's mane, back from her face and wiped her eyes tenderly. "We'll get some roasted chestnuts," he said. They walked away from the tree and down the path crowded with merry-makers, many of them drunk by now, or amorous, or both, toward the warmth and color of a brazier. Charlot bought a bag of hot chestnuts. "Open your mouth," he said, and she opened obediently. He laughed, "Not as though I were a dentist about to pull a tooth. As though you were going to get something enjoyable. There. Taste good?"

"Um-hum."

"What would you like to do now?"

"More wine, please."

"All right, little toper," he said. "You seem to be able to take it."

They went back to the little bistro, back to the same small table in the corner. Charlot held her hand across the table. "You have very strong hands for so small a creature," he said.

"I want to be strong. That's what I want more than anything."

When they had finished their wine, she said, "Let's go home now, please, Charlot," and they went to the car. He tucked the robe around her, and she leaned against him wearily. "It was a lovely evening," she said. "Is it very late?"

"Two o'clock in the morning. Did you really have a good time?"

"Yes. I had a lovely time." She leaned forward, so that her hair fell about her face from under Manya's Russian shawl, and rubbed her eyes.

"Tired?" he asked.

"A little. It's all that train business yesterday. Traveling can be lovely and it can be awful, too. I rather like the way

189

you drive a car. It was very good wine and it made me feel lovely. The chestnuts were lovely, too. And the white horse I rode on and the black horse you rode on. You do like me, don't you, Charlot?"

"Of course, baby."

"I wish you'd stop calling me baby."

"All right, Katherine."

"Are you tight, Charlot?"

"A little."

"You drank more than I did."

"I know."

"Don't you think I hold it well? I mean, for me?"

"Very well."

"I mean, under the circumstances I ought to have been under the table long ago, oughtn't I?"

"Yes."

"And I'm not a bit, am I?"

"Not a bit."

"I've inherited a strong head from Mother. Shall I play for you when we get back?"

"Don't you want to go to bed?"

"No. Do you? Are you tired? Do you want to go to bed?"

"No."

"Shall I play for you, then?"

"All right, darling."

"Shall we talk about Shakespeare?"

"All right."

"Why are you unhappy, Charlot?"

"What do you mean?"

"Why are you so unhappy?"

"I'm not unhappy."

"Yes, you are. Every time I've seen you you've been unhappy. The first time when I went to Aunt Manya's place

190

in the country you were unhappy and it made you try to be horrid, only you didn't want to be inside you, so you weren't. And then that time after Mother died, you were unhappy and you said such dreadful things; because you were so unhappy about them, you had to say them to someone, and maybe you were right, I don't know. I don't know anything any more except that I've got to believe in something, and I do, I don't know exactly what it is. Because I don't think many of us are enough in ourselves to say anything great in our work; I know I'm not, but I do think if I work hard enough and make myself ready, things can be said through me that are much bigger than I am, and I do believe there's something great somewhere to say them, if I should be ready enough to be chosen. But that wouldn't be enough, you know, if we stop being ourselves, ever, it's not fair, none of it's fair; we're only given a chance to begin and there's no point in beginning if we're not allowed to finish. We're only given enough brain to ask questions, that's the whole trouble, we're only given enough brain to ask questions, not enough to answer them. I'm sorry—I was talking about you. I didn't mean to get off on all this. And you're unhappy now, too. I can see your eyes in the rear-view mirror, and I could see them all the way down the mountain when you didn't know I could, and it was really worse then, because it's somehow a different kind of unhappiness now than it was then. It was so tight and despairing I couldn't bear it, it was the kind I had to try and help you from my soul with, away from you; I sort of had to try and will help into you, but I couldn't touch you. This kind, I could put my arms around you and try to comfort you. I don't like you to be unhappy. Partly unselfishly, because I love you very much, Charlot, and partly selfishly, because when you're unhappy yourself, you don't want anyone else to be unhappy, because that takes away

191

from the importance of your own unhappiness. But it's mostly because I love you that I don't want you to be unhappy. Why are you unhappy? It isn't because of your work, is it? Aunt Manya wrote me that you're considered one of the most brilliant students they've ever had, and that you've earned all kinds of scholarships and things. It isn't because of your work, is it?"

"No, I love my work."

"Have you had an unhappy love affair?"

"No, darling."

"Have you had a love affair?"

"Sort of ones."

"My hair smells nice. Aunt Manya's perfume. I smelled them all and chose the one that smelled most like me, and it still smells. You just sort of don't like people, do you?"

"No. I hate them."

"I hate them, too. But all the world isn't people. That's the point. Do people like you?"

"No."

"Not anyone?"

"No one. There isn't anybody in the world I can talk to."

"You can talk to me. That is, if you want to. I know it isn't any good just to have someone you can talk to. If it isn't someone you want to talk to it's really worse than nothing. But if you ever want me, I'm here, Charlot. Everything's going around and around. It's a lovely feeling. Sort of like when you just begin to go under the laughing gas at the dentist's. I know you need someone to talk to, Charlot, and someone to talk to you."

Charlot drove in silence for several minutes. Then he burst out, "There's so much love in me, and nowhere for it to go!" He laughed, a little bitterly, and went on, quietly, "I thought at first I wanted to be a veterinarian because I love

192

animals so, and I hate people, and animals need good doctors almost more than people do. They can't tell you where they hurt or how. You just have to know. But then I found that love and hate are so close it's sometimes hard to tell which is which, and my love for animals doesn't satisfy me, isn't enough; it isn't enough to have them trust me and to know I can help them. I think I really want people to trust me in the same way, and by my helping them, turn them from things I scorn and despise and hate into things I can love. And sometimes I meet people I want to turn to; I want to give them all the love I have in me, and always I've been pushed away. I talked once to a priest about it, when I was terribly in love with someone and terribly unwanted. I said that I'd never had an unhappy love affair, because I've never been allowed to come close enough to the people I've loved to call it that, and the people I might say I've had affairs with I've never really cared about, nor they for me, thank God. Your mother was the only person I ever really loved who never pushed me away or hurt me, and with her it was more worship than love, and I only saw her that one week she stayed at Aunt Manya's. But I'll never forget her. She's an awfully important part of my life. I think she's an important part of lots of people's lives. More people than we know."

"Yes, I think so, too," Katherine answered.

"The best way I have of knowing what is right and what is wrong is whether or not I think she'd approve. I've done a lot of things she wouldn't approve of. I've been cheap often, because I was lonely and unhappy and frightened because of always being pushed away. When I talked to the priest about it, he said it was because I'd never really been in love with anyone, that my pride and my love of Charlot were always stronger than my love for another human being. I don't know whether he was right or wrong. I don't know why I'm telling you all this. It's because I'm drunk. I'll regret it tomorrow."

"Oh," Katherine said. "Will you?"

"Undoubtedly."

"That's not fair. Unless it made me angry or I took it in the wrong way and let it make things different, you haven't any right to take it out on me. Mother never did."

"All right," Charlot said. "I won't, then. Here we are. Back again. It's raining. Did you know?"

"No. Is it?"

"Yes, a little. Stagger out, baby. Here, I'll take the rug. All right. Come along."

They walked back into the house. In the great hall the fire was blazing, and it was warm and light. Josef told them that Manya and Tom had gone to bed and left them a tray of sandwiches and milk.

"I don't want anything to eat," Katherine said.

"Neither do I." Charlot sat down in front of the fire. "Are you going to play for me now?"

"Of course. What do you want?"

"Do you ever improvise?"

"Um-humh."

"Play about tonight, then, will you?"

"I'll try." Katherine sat down at the piano and began to play softly, meditatively, then slowly gaining speed and gaiety, bringing in the jangling rhythm of the merry-go-round music and the Strauss waltzes. She felt as free and as light as the spring rain that was beginning to fall. She knew she wouldn't be able to remember a note of what she played the next morning, and she wasn't sure she would still like it if she could. But tonight it sounded wonderful, the insistent music of the merry-go-round appearing again and again, and against it the Strauss waltz, sometimes clear and

194

loud, as they had heard it in the restaurant, sometimes soft
and blurred and discordant, as it had sounded from the lake
steamer, as it had sounded heard from the top of the ferris
wheel.

Charlot lay back in his chair, his eyes closed, and she
thought he might be asleep. But as the music died away, he
opened his eyes, got up and came over to her, and sat down
on the piano bench beside her.

"Did you like it?" she asked.

"Every second of it." He put his arm around her and
drew her close to him, and she put her head down on his
shoulder. They sat there that way with the firelight flickering
over them, and Katherine's mind felt strange and detached
from her, and nothing really mattered, because her mind,
which was really thinking quite clearly, was just waiting for
her body to come back to it, only it didn't matter how long it
took. Charlot pressed her close to him, so that her face was
buried in his neck and it was difficult to breathe, and he
kissed her softly on the tip of her ear several times, and his
breath came quick and hard. Then he pulled her head around
with a sudden movement and kissed her on the mouth,
lightly, and then, as she lay quietly in his arms, long and
passionately. When he released her and rose abruptly and
walked over to the fireplace and stared down at the fire with
his back to her, she watched him, and still her mind, which
was thinking clearly, was detached from her body; and now
her body was something she had never had before, something new, and she did not know when it would become part
of her mind, or if it ever would, and it really didn't matter.

After a while she called softly, "Charlot—"

He turned around and faced her. "Well?"

"Hello—"

195

"Hello," he said, and sat down in front of the fireplace. "Let's talk about Shakespeare, shall we?"

"Oh. All right." She sat down on the floor beside him. "All right. You talk."

"I'll talk about Falstaff. Shall I talk about Falstaff?"

"Go ahead."

"You know *Henry IV* well?"

"Naturally."

"Well, I think Falstaff was a hell of a lot more complex than Hal thought he was. I think he was a great actor, but like Aunt Manya, he wasn't always conscious that he was acting. He fluctuated from part to part, and occasionally fooled himself into thinking he was sincere. But mostly he was the cynical and disillusioned courtier—the man of the world who has seen life and knows everything and therefore doesn't bother to reason it out—doesn't bother to be introspective—for after all, what's the use? Life is a pretty grim affair, honor is an empty shell, so why not be merry?"

"Oh," Katherine said. Charlot leaned toward her, then he drew back and went on, and his voice had the strange sound it always had when he was forcing himself to talk, as though his voice had to go around a hard cylinder.

"Why not play with words, with personalities," he said, "and enjoy the laughter and adulation of friends and the mob? Falstaff, if you could see him in tails, is almost Noel Cowardish in his attitude. But in spite of his cynicism, Shakespeare has made him extremely sensitive, with the deep, hidden kind of sensitiveness, the hidden ability to be hurt, that it seems to me all Elizabethans had to a large degree. Falstaff had terrific pride. He adored making quips and jests, but he wanted them to be appreciated. He didn't mind if his friends didn't believe his stories, as long as they listened to them. He adored acting. He thought himself great

196

at it, but he was never as good in the scenes where he and Hal were deliberately assuming parts as when he let the parts assume him. He couldn't bear to let anybody think he was hurt or discomfited. When Hal disclaims him in Part II, he quickly turns to Shallow and the others to assure them that he is not hurt. Hal has to be like that in public, and he, Falstaff, would think it very strange if he weren't."

"Oh," Katherine said again. "Yes, you're right, Charlot."

Charlot smiled at her with his mouth, but his eyes probed deeply into hers as he went on. "Falstaff made no bones about being a coward. He isn't one, and he knows it, but he sees no point in giving up his life before it is time. And he knows that the others don't really think him a coward—and yet he is so concerned with his histrionics that he doesn't realize that that is all the others see—that they don't see Falstaff himself. I think that Shakespeare realized, and it is extremely difficult to realize things about your own age, that it was the very awareness the Elizabethans had for the individual that kept them apart. Each one was so conscious of himself, so passionately introspective, so amazed and overjoyed at being himself, that he didn't have a great deal of time left over for the rest of the world."

"You think you're a little like Falstaff, the Falstaff you see, don't you?" Katherine asked.

"I'm like Falstaff without friends and without an audience," Charlot said. And he put his arms around her again, and kissed her, opening her mouth. She lay back on the floor after his kiss and rolled over and looked into the fire, her hands pressed against her burning cheeks, her tangled hair falling about her face.

"You talk about Shakespeare," Charlot said. "You talk about Shakespeare quickly."

"I don't want to talk about Shakespeare," Katherine whis-

197

pered, and she looked at Charlot and he came to her, and she was pressed close against him.

When she awoke the next morning, the sun was streaming into her room. Manya's bright Russian shawl was flung over the chair where she had left it, and she realized that her hair was down and a mass of snarls. She lay in bed and focused her eyes on the coat and the shawl, and her mind, which had suddenly come back to her body and claimed it again, tried to collect itself. Her head ached, and she rubbed her fingers against it.

—Now I know—she thought—now I know what being with a person is like, but I'm really not any different, I'm not any older, I haven't learned anything except that just the act of being with someone isn't very important, doesn't really change you, unless you let it make you cheap, I guess. It's got to be someone who has part of your soul, someone you want to have part of your soul, someone you want to give the inside of you to, or it doesn't count. So I still don't know about it, the thing that generates power. I got more from Mother and Sarah and Justin, as far as being given power is concerned, than I have from Charlot. It's still something that's got to happen to me, something I've got to learn if I'm really ever to know about things.—

She looked at her mother's watch, and it was after twelve. She dressed, untangled and braided her hair, and went downstairs. Manya and Tom were breakfasting in front of the fire. She kissed them both. "Where's Charlot?" she asked.

"He's still asleep," Manya said.

"Oh."

"Want some breakfast?"

"I guess so."

"Go wake Charlot first, will you, baby? He promised to go to Thônon with me today and get some new shirts."

"Oh. All right." She went upstairs and into Charlot's room. The blinds were drawn, and the room was dim; only the top of Charlot's dark head showed above the bedclothes. She sat down on the bed beside him, uncovered his head, and tweaked his nose gently.

He pulled her down to him and kissed her, and then buried his face in her neck. "You're not angry with me?" he murmured.

"Why should I be angry?"

"Katherine," he said. "Katherine, I do love you so desperately."

"No. You don't. You can't," Katherine said, and her heart began to beat very fast.

"I do. It's always been you I've loved and wanted, only I never realized it until last night."

"But you can't love me, Charlot."

"Why can't I? Of course I can."

"It's just because of what happened last night." Katherine clutched his hand desperately. "You needn't say you love me because of what happened last night. It wasn't your fault."

"I'm not saying it because of last night. Last night, all of it, from the minute you came downstairs with that shawl over your head, looking so beautiful, was what made me realize that I love you, but it isn't because of what happened that I'm saying it, it's because it's true. I love you and I want to marry you."

"No—oh, no, you don't, Charlot."

Charlot sat up quickly and caught hold of her wrists so tightly that it hurt. "You don't want me to love you?"

"Not like that."

"What do you mean?"

"I want you to love me but not like that."

"Then why did you let last night happen? You didn't have to let it happen."

"I don't know why."

"Was it because you were drunk? I didn't think you were that drunk. I didn't think I was that drunk. But if you feel like this now, we must have been."

"No. It wasn't because of the drinking. I wasn't drunk from the drinking."

"What were you drunk from, then?"

"Unhappiness, maybe."

"So you came to me because you were unhappy? Just a cheap second best?"

"No. It wasn't that. I don't know. It was like being hypnotized."

"I didn't try to hypnotize you."

"I don't mean by you. I don't quite know what it was."

"Then you didn't know what you were doing?"

"No, it wasn't that."

"Then what, then?"

"I don't know. But—but I didn't think you cared anything about me, Charlot. I didn't think I mattered to you. That way. I knew you loved me and I loved you, only with me it isn't that way, and I didn't think it was with you."

"If it isn't that way with you, how is it? What other ways are there?"

"Just loving. The way I loved Mother and Sarah. Just loving."

"Oh, I see."

"I just wanted to help you."

"You don't know what you're talking about, do you?"

"I don't know."

"What will you do if you have a baby?"

200

Katherine sat very still for a long time. Then she whispered, "A baby?"

"Yes," Charlot said. "A baby. Hadn't you thought of that?"

"No."

"What will you do if you find out you're going to have my child?"

Katherine took a deep breath. It was as though she were drawing her whole body in tighter. She raised her head and looked at Charlot. "I shall have it."

"Will you marry me if you find out you're going to have it?"

"Of course not."

"What will you do with it?"

"I shall teach it to play the piano and take it to the theater."

"It takes nine months to have a child, Katherine," he said.

"I know that."

There was a long silence. Then Katherine said, "Charlot?"

"Well?"

"How do you know if you're going to have a child? How long does it take before you know?"

"If we were in Paris and I could take you to the right man, we could find out almost immediately. As it is, I guess you'll just have to wait and let nature take its course."

"Well, how will I know? Just if I miss my period?"

"Are you regular?"

"Not particularly."

"When are you due?"

"Oh, I don't know. About three weeks, I think."

"Well, if you just miss one month, it won't be anything to get frantic about. If you miss two, it'll be pretty definite. You may have a bit of morning sickness and dizziness, but that's not infallible. It could be caused by nervousness and fear of having a child. So if that should happen, don't let it worry you too much."

"I'm not afraid."

"Do you want a child?"

"No. It would mess everything all up. I don't think it's good to try to be creative in too many ways at once. Not when you're my age, at any rate. I'd hate like fury to have a child right now."

"Katherine, will you promise me one thing?"

"What?"

"If you do find out you're going to have it, promise me you won't do anything rash like—like having an abortion."

"I told you if it happens I'll have it."

"What will they do at your school if they find out?"

"Oh, there'll be a frightful row, and I'll be expelled. It would be rather fun."

"I wish your mother were alive."

Katherine flung herself across the foot of the bed. "Oh, God! So do I! So do I!"

After a while Charlot asked her, "Katherine, is there anybody else?"

"What?"

"Are you in love with somebody else?"

"I don't quite know."

"Then you are."

"No. No, I don't think I am. It's a different sort of thing. Not like anything else. Anyhow, I know there isn't ever any hope. I'll probably never see him again. And even if I did, it wouldn't be possible. He'd never love me that way. If he ever wanted me, me, Katherine—well, he can always have whatever he wants, as far as I'm concerned. But he'd never want that. Besides, it's different, anyhow. He's so above me. It isn't just that he's older. He's a great artist already, and I'm just a promise that may or may not be fulfilled. I believe it will be fulfilled, and I think he does, too, nevertheless, I'm still just a promise, and that's not enough. I haven't any right ever to bother him or ask to see him, and I'll probably never get the chance again, anyhow."

Charlot's mouth tightened. "Why did you come to wake me if you feel the way you do about me?"

"Aunt Manya asked me to. She said you'd promised to go to Thônon with her to buy some new shirts."

"Well, I'm not going."

"You said you'd take me on one of the lake steamers today."

"Do you want to go?"

"Yes. I do."

"All right. We'll go. I can't talk to you here. Have you had breakfast?"

"No."

"Well, go and eat. I'll be down in a minute. You can tell Aunt Manya I'm not going to Thônon."

Manya insisted on Charlot's going to Thônon for the shirts, so it was just beginning to get dark when Katherine followed him up the gangplank to the small lake steamer.

"First, second, or third class?" he asked her.

"Third, of course. You can't get down to the bow with first or second. Besides, who wants to go first or second, anyhow?"

They went up to the very front of the boat and stood leaning on the railing, looking out, farther apart than they ever had been in their lives. Katherine stood looking down at the water churning up yellow and green on either side of the boat, and suddenly she realized that the color of the churning water was the color of the horizon of the winter sky on

203

the day she had gone for a walk with Julie on Manya's farm, on the day she had first met Charlot, the day that was so indelibly printed in her memory.

She pulled Charlot's sleeve gently. "Charlot—"

"Well?"

"You think I did a very awful thing?"

"I don't know."

"But it wasn't the first time with you, was it?"

"No."

"And when you did it before, feeling the same way I did, you didn't think it was awful?"

"I guess not."

"Then why should it be with me?"

"I don't know."

Again Katherine tugged at his sleeve. "Charlot—"

"Well?"

"Charlot, please be really honest. You're not involved in me, all of you, really and truly, you know you're not. You're not less yourself when you're away from me. Last night you were just attracted to me, and I was to you, and we'd both had a little too much to drink, and we were both—well, you know what I mean. And you want so much to be in love with someone, and have the security of having someone, and you keep hoping you'll find something of Mother in me, and you love me a little extra anyhow just because I'm Mother's daughter and so I'm somehow a little part of her, or at any rate something that was hers, like a handkerchief or a dress, and you just let everything fool you into pretending that it would be good for you to be in love with me. But you're not. Isn't that so?"

"You don't know what you're talking about."

"Yes, I do . . . You said last night that you knew what was right and wrong by thinking how Mother would feel about it. Mother hated dishonesty more than anything in the world. Please—"

"All right," he said after a long while. "I guess it's all true, everything you say."

"Well, then, it's all right, isn't it? There isn't any reason for everything to be spoiled. We had a lovely evening last night, both of us. It'll never be repeated, because it just couldn't be, with us being us. But it was lovely, and there's no need to spoil it by trying to make it ugly when it wasn't, and there's no need for us to spoil our love for each other because of it."

"What about the baby?"

"I may not have one."

"If you do, then I've done a dreadful thing."

"Oh, I see!" she cried. "Now I really understand! If I have a baby, one of us will have to be blamed, and you'd much rather have it be me. It's not so much what other people think that bothers you. I know you're not that kind of a coward. It's that you don't want to have to blame yourself! Well, you're crazy. It isn't your fault any more than mine. You didn't force yourself on me. It was something that was perfectly natural, as natural as breathing, and I don't think anything as natural as that can be sinful. It may be inconvenient, but it's not sinful. Maybe people will make it out as sinful, but it isn't, really, and as long as we know that, it's all right. If it became cheap or too easy, it would be bad—but just last night, all alone, all by itself, you can't make me think it's a sin, and that's that."

He stood there stiffly, staring out over the prow of the boat, the lines on either side of his mouth very white. Gradually she felt his body relax, and he put his arm around her and said, "I wish more than anything in the world that we were in love with each other."

205

"So do I. It would be lovely, wouldn't it? But we're not, and it seems to me that it would just mess up our lives more to pretend we were than to face the truth right now. I think that's what Mother would feel, at any rate. But I do love you very much, Charlot, just plain loving."

The wind was in their faces, and her bangs were blown back and her braids flopped against her shoulders. Leaning against the prow of the boat, with Charlot's arm protectively around her, she suddenly felt at peace, and the words of the old psalm came back to her mind:

> *I will lift up mine eyes unto the hills*
> *From whence cometh my help.*
> *My help cometh from the Lord,*
> *Which made heaven and earth.*
> *He will not suffer thy foot to be moved;*
> *He that keepeth thee will not slumber.*
> *Behold, he that keepeth Israel*
> *Shall neither slumber nor sleep.*
> *The Lord is thy keeper;*
> *The Lord is thy shade upon thy right hand.*
> *The sun shall not smite thee by day,*
> *Nor the moon by night.*
> *The Lord shall preserve thee from all evil;*
> *He shall preserve thy soul.*
> *The Lord shall preserve thy going out and thy coming in*
> *From this time forth, and even for evermore.*

—I do believe in God—she thought. —I do believe in God. The mountains and the lake and the possibility of people like Mother and Justin being born, that's really enough. Even if I have a baby—she thought—it can't make life much more uncertain or strange than it is already. And I don't care what other people think, just people in general, as long as I know I'm all right, and the few people I really care about know it. Right now it's just Justin and I don't know when I'll see him again, but I will see him again, because I will it so intensely.—

"I envy faith," Charlot said suddenly. Silence again between them and the sound of the wind and the waves in their ears.

Katherine said at last, because she knew Charlot wanted her to talk, "Sarah and I divided the world into four classes."

"Did you, darling? What are they?"

"There are People. That's almost everybody. Just people. The kind of people who are hidebound by convention, who have no understanding, no compassion, who are unhappy and don't even know it, and because of their own unhappiness subconsciously enjoy condemning other people in an effort to make them even more unhappy. Then there are real people. They're a very small class, and very wonderful. They're not creators, they're not artists, but they can understand and appreciate consciously, not just animalistically. They don't feel, with People, and with that man in the Old Testament, that anybody who tries to create is automatically condemned. You know the kind of person I mean. Then there's the other kind. The phony artists. The trouble with them is that a lot of times they convince you that they're first-class, and then it's awful when you find out; and they can do a tremendous amount of harm. Then there's the last class of all. Sarah and I called it our kind, but that was presumptuous of us. It's what we want to be, what we must always try to be, or there's no point in living. It's what Mother was, and what Justin is. Don't laugh at me. I know all this sounds awfully pompous and childish. We thought it was very impressive. I see now that it isn't."

"I'm not laughing," Charlot said. And again they were

silent. At last he said, "Someday I'd like to have a ship, an old-fashioned sailing vessel. And I'd like to have you for the figurehead. I'd strap you to the prow of the boat and let your hair stream out in a dark shadow behind you and leave you there for the sea gulls to peck out your eyes."

Katherine said solemnly. "I think I am blind. I don't see things clearly the way I used to. I've become confused, and it's frightening. Mother was so clear. Always. That's why some people thought she was awful, because people who have vision are always condemned. I'm so confused that it's become a kind of physical tiredness. I ache all over with the confusion, and I want to be held in somebody's arms. But it can't be just anybody. I don't mean to sound like a tragic queen. I know I'm just a silly little girl. But it's all right for me to talk to you, isn't it, Charlot?"

"Of course, my darling," he said, and they stood close to one another looking out across the lake, and night fell, softly, hushing them.

After a week Charlot had to go back to Paris. Katherine missed him, but she felt relieved at his departure, too. She took long walks by herself, spent long hours at the piano, read in front of the huge fire at night. Several times Manya tried to talk to her, but she felt so nervous, was so afraid of the sword of Damocles dangling over her head, that she couldn't have talked even if she had wanted to.

In the end, however, she talked. She had gone to bed early with a book. She was still reading when she heard Manya and Tom come upstairs, was still reading half an hour later, when there was a knock on her door.

"Who is it?" she called.

"It's Manya."

"Oh, come in, Aunt Manya."

Manya wore one of her many crimson dressing gowns. Her hair was down, her feet bare. "Katya, is there a Bible here?" she asked, going over to the bookshelves.

"I think there's a French one."

Manya ran her finger across a row of books. "Yes. Here it is." She gave the small black volume to Katherine. "Find me the third verse of the fifth chapter of Romans, will you?" she asked.

Katherine found the place and handed the Bible back to Manya, who read aloud.

"Et non seulement cela, mais nous nous glorifions même dans nos afflictions, sachant que l'affliction produit la patience, et la patience l'épreuve, et l'épreuve l'espérance . . . And not only so, but we glory in tribulations also: knowing that tribulation worketh patience; and patience, experience; and experience, hope."

She put the book back in its place.

"There! I knew I was right. Tom swore it was in The Acts of the Apostles." She looked at Katherine for a moment, then came and sat on the edge of her bed.

"What are you reading, Katya? . . . Proust? He's always struck me as being very boring and depressing, but of course that may be because I read him in Russian, and I don't think Russian's very good for Proust. Even if I don't care for him, I find him very true; don't think he's ever false except that he does see everything through unhealthy eyes. And I do wish he didn't find it necessary to say everything quite so many times. Which one have you? Hmm. *Albertine Disparue*. Well, if you want to read it, it's up to you, darling, but don't flaunt it in front of your father."

"I won't."

"Katya."

"What?"

"I don't mean to pry, dear. I do respect your privacy, you know that. But I hate to see you unhappy."

"I'm all right."

"You're all wrong enough to make me very uneasy about you. Couldn't we have a talk? Are you angry with me because I've been such a neglectful, irresponsible stepparent?"

"Don't be silly. You know I adore you. And I know the beastly school's father's fault."

"Well, then, Katyusha, what is it? You look as though you were waiting for something horrible to happen."

After a moment Katherine looked up at her and said, "I'm afraid I may be going to have a baby."

If Manya was shocked she gave no sign of it.

"Whose?" she asked.

"Charlot's."

"I see."

"You won't tell Father?"

"Of course not . . . We'll go to Évian tomorrow. Dr. Varron is staying there—supposed to be on a holiday, but I know him quite well, and I think he'll see you for my sake."

Katherine felt a great relief as Manya took things out of her hands. "If I have to have one, you'll help me?" she asked.

Manya ignored this question. "When did this happen between you and Charlot?"

"The second night I was here. The night we went to the *kermesse.*"

"Then you haven't really had time to notice any symptoms."

"No. I guess not."

"Well, we won't cross any bridges until we come to them, my child . . . Was it Charlot's fault?"

"No."

"You knew what you were doing?"

"I guess so."

"Had you been drinking?"

"Yes. But I can't blame it on that . . . Are you angry with me?"

"Angry?"

"Do you think I did something dreadful?"

"Are you in love with Charlot?"

"No."

"I feel that I am the last person to have the right to condemn anyone," said Manya, after a pause. "And then I think of words—I think they seem more revealing when you think of words not in your own language. I think of the word passion. And then of compassion." She stood up and pulled her crimson dressing gown about her. "We must try to get some sleep. I'll have Josef call you early and we'll set out for Évian before Tom wakes up. Good night, Katya."

"Good night, Aunt Manya."

There was to be no baby. When they were assured of this, Katherine and Manya wired Charlot in Paris and then both behaved with a kind of childish gaiety that made Tom ask if they had been drinking.

"No," said Manya, "but it's a very good idea. We'll have champagne at dinner to celebrate."

"To celebrate what?" Tom asked.

"Oh, just our all being together and so fond of one another," Manya said.

Only once again during the holidays did she mention the matter. "Kisienka, just because there weren't any disastrous results this time—" she began.

But Katherine cut her short. "Don't worry, Aunt Manya. It won't happen again. Don't feel you're obliged to give me a moral talk. I'll behave with Victorian propriety. Besides,

I'm going back to school soon. I'm safe enough there. You needn't worry."

Manya put her arms around her stepchild. "Oh, darling, I hate to send you back again."

"Never mind," Katherine said. "I understand. Father. I understand why he feels that way about me, too. You've always been wonderful to me, even when I've been horrid and ungrateful. I don't forget that. And then I can remember that thing from Paul you read the other night. I sort of like it. 'Et non seulement cela, mais nous nous glorifions même dans nos afflictions, sachant que l'affliction produit la patience, et la patience l'épreuve, et l'épreuve l'ésperance.'"

ATHERINE'S music teacher during her last year at school was a Monsieur Devault. She hated him at once, hated his little waxed mustaches, his ogling manner, his lack of artistry or perception. He, in turn, thought her arrogant and gave her bad marks because she refused to change from Justin's methods, which had been so like Julie's, to his. She tried to drop the lessons, but had to keep them up, or she would have had to give up the practicing. She knew the poor marks distressed Manya and Tom, but she stuck stubbornly to what she thought was right.

Only one thing happened at the school that year that broke through her shell of work and study and touched her. She was getting ready for bed one night, when the gym teacher, Miss Elkes, whose place at the chapel organ she had taken, knocked on the door and asked her to come to the infirmary for a moment. A little bewildered, Katherine put on her bathrobe and slippers and followed her. The nurse and her form mistress were talking busily in the office. Miss Halsey was spreading a sheet over the long wooden table, while the nurse stood by, holding a tape measure.

"Penelope Deerenforth's been walking in her sleep again," the form mistress said. "I've had to move her chest of drawers in front of the window."

"Probably studying too hard," the nurse said, and turned and saw Katherine. "Hello, Katherine," she said, and smiled at her pleasantly, and, Katherine felt, a little too eagerly.

213

"Katherine," Miss Halsey said. "We've all noticed that you sometimes limp a little."

"Hardly at all any more, Miss Halsey," Katherine said. "Only when I'm terribly tired, and then if I realize it, I can usually cover it."

"Miss Elkes has noticed that you often limp toward the end of gym class."

"Well, gym has hardly been my strong point, Miss Halsey. Besides, I've felt rather tired this year."

"Why?" the nurse asked.

"Oh, I don't know, Miss Anderson." —I'm certainly not going to tell you it's because I read under the bedcovers with a flashlight every night and get up before six to go up to the fourth-floor practice room in the morning, where I know I won't be heard—she thought.

"How old were you when you injured your hip?"

"Two."

"You've never been told to cut out gym?"

"No. A moderate amount of exercise is good for me. I'm not half bad at fencing."

"When was your hip last thoroughly examined by a physician?"

"Oh, I don't know. When I was around ten, I guess."

"Not since?"

"No. There wasn't any need. It's been perfectly all right. It hasn't given me a bit of bother. I'll just never be national sports champion, that's all."

"Wouldn't you like to get rid of that limp?"

"But I am rid of it."

"Miss Elkes says she notices it often."

"Well, I don't intend to be violently athletic when I leave school, Miss Anderson, so I doubt if anyone else will notice

214

it. Besides, even this remnant of a limp will probably disappear eventually, anyhow."

"It doesn't bother you? Make you self-conscious?"

"No. Why should it? There isn't anything there to be self-conscious about."

"Were you ever examined to see if one of your legs is shorter than the other?"

"Oh, I don't know. I suppose so. Dr. Bradley did absolutely everything that had to be done. The last time he examined me, he told me just to forget about it."

"I think possibly the fact that your good leg might be longer than the other may account for your limp, rather than the injury to your hip itself."

"Oh. Well, it really doesn't make much difference, does it?" She was suddenly afraid of the three eager women. "Please—may I go now?"

"No, Katherine, you may not," Miss Halsey said. "Please don't be so impertinent. We're only trying to help you."

"Thank you very much, but there's nothing that needs to be done."

Miss Halsey turned to Miss Anderson, speaking as though Katherine were not there. "Crippled children are often maladjusted."

"I'm not crippled, I'm not a child, and I'm not maladjusted."

"But you were a cripple, weren't you?"

"Only when I was too young to really remember it or be bothered by it. And it was never called by that word."

"You're not particularly intimate with the girls here at school, are you?" Miss Elkes asked.

"No."

"Have you ever had many friends of your own age?"

"No."

215

"Hasn't that made you unhappy?"

"Occasionally."

"Isn't that perhaps what made you—well, too emotional about Sarah Courtmont that time?"

"Need we bring that up?"

"Katherine," Miss Halsey said sharply. "Please try to be less antagonistic. How can we help you?"

"But I've told you I don't want to be helped. Please!"

Miss Elkes went on. "Do you have any friends of your own age out of school?"

"Of course. Certainly. Lots of them."

"Who are they?"

"Well—there's—there's Charlot. Charles Bejart. He's studying medicine. He's a very good friend of mine."

"How did you meet him?"

"He's my Aunt Manya's adopted son."

"Who else?"

"Oh, I don't know. Lots of people. Besides, I don't see what my private life has to do with my hip or my limp. It's my own business, not anybody else's."

Miss Elkes and Miss Halsey nodded to Miss Anderson, who turned to Katherine. "Will you get up on the table, please, Katherine? We'd like to measure your legs. What have you got on under your bathrobe?"

"My underclothes."

"Will you take them off, please?"

Deliberately Katherine took off her bathrobe and undressed.

"Put your robe on again," Miss Anderson said icily.

Katherine smiled at them, put on her bathrobe, and climbed onto the table.

"Is it because of your accident that you are so small?" Miss Elkes asked.

"No. My mother was very small, too. Small and strong. The difference between us is that people know I'm small, and nobody knew she was. It was always a surprise."

"Lie down now, please," Miss Anderson said, and Katherine lay down on the long table draped with the white sheet. Miss Anderson gave one end of the tape measure to Miss Halsey and showed her just where on Katherine's hip to hold it. Miss Elkes stood with a pad and pencil ready. Miss Anderson measured first the right leg, then the left leg, calling the figures out to Miss Elkes. Then she measured both legs again triumphantly.

"Ah," she said, "we were right. The left leg is a little shorter than the right." Miss Elkes and Miss Banks beamed. Miss Anderson turned back to Katherine. "Stand up now, please." Katherine slid down from the table and stood facing them.

"Yes," said Miss Halsey. "It's really quite obvious. Her right hip is higher than her left."

"I like it that way," Katherine said. "May I go now?" She was so angry that it was difficult not to cry.

Miss Anderson nodded, and she left.

The next morning during English class Miss Elkes came into the classroom and went up to Miss Halsey's desk. They whispered together for a moment, then Miss Halsey said, "Katherine Forrester, you're wanted in the infirmary."

Katherine followed Miss Elkes upstairs to the infirmary. The school doctor, whom she mistrusted and disliked, was there. He measured her legs as Miss Anderson had done the night before, and dismissed her without a word. Nothing more was said until two weeks later just after lunch, when Miss Anderson went into the common room and called Katherine.

"I have a present for you, Katherine," she said, as she led

217

the way upstairs. Katherine looked at Miss Anderson suspiciously, as the nurse took a box off the table in the infirmary office. "Here you are," she said, much too cheerfully.

Katherine untied the string and took off the wrapping paper. Then she opened the box. In it was a pair of shoes. The shoe for the right foot was a perfectly ordinary, ugly, black shoe with laces. The shoe for the left foot was a cripple's shoe, built up to raise the left foot higher than the right foot from the ground.

"What's this?" Katherine asked.

"It will make your legs equal in length and you won't limp any more."

"Oh, no."

"What do you mean?"

"I won't wear this thing."

"Katherine, that shoe was very expensive. You don't want your father to pay several pounds for something you don't use, do you?"

"Did you ask Father's permission before you got this—this thing?"

"Your father wrote that we were to do anything in regard to your hip that the doctor thought best."

"But you didn't tell him it would be wearing a thing like this?"

"Don't argue, Katherine. Put the shoes on."

"No. You're crazy. It'll make me limp." She knew she sounded hysterical, but she couldn't help it.

"It may at first, but then it will cure you completely of limping. Come along. Put the shoes on."

"No."

"Do as I say."

"No. I'll never wear it."

"Katherine," Miss Anderson said. "We've tried to be

218

pleasant about this, but you've refused to cooperate. Ever since your first day here you've done your best to make it impossible for people to like you. All the teachers, with rare exceptions, find you exceptionally antagonistic. History is the only course in which you get good marks. Your music, which you seemed to be so proud of and to think so important, has gone down badly, according to Monsieur Devault, who finds you an impossible pupil. You are obviously not very popular with the girls. I am hoping that all this comes from a physical defect. I am trying to correct that defect."

"Do you call making someone who is a perfectly normal healthy person into a cripple correcting a defect?"

"Your left leg is shorter than your right."

"But it doesn't matter! I'm perfectly adjusted to it! I don't limp. I'm perfectly normal, there's nothing to make all this vile, obtuse, unnecessary fuss about. My own doctor, Dr. Bradley, undoubtedly knows that my left leg is shorter than my right. If he'd thought something should be done about it, he'd have done it. You ask him!"

"Where is he?"

"In New York."

"Aren't you being a little bit ridiculous, Katherine?"

Katherine found she could make no effort to control herself. "Well, do you think it's going to make the girls like me any better to see me wearing this thing? I don't want pity, by God! And I won't get pity, anyhow. I'll get laughter and jibes."

"Will you please stop swearing this instant," Miss Anderson said.

"If you thought my limp would make me self-conscious, what do you think this thing will do? Dr. Bradley'd shoot you for being a fool, if he ever saw it."

219

"Put that shoe on, Katherine."

"Never."

Miss Anderson was a large woman, and strong. She went over to Katherine and took both her wrists. "Do you want me to force you?"

Katherine bared her teeth. "Oh, we're going to fight, are we? All right, I'm game."

Miss Anderson dropped Katherine's wrists. "Wait here," she said, and went out of the room.

Katherine walked up and down, stamping angrily, saying over and over under her breath, "I won't, I won't, I won't."

In a very short time Miss Anderson returned with Miss Valentine. Katherine bent down, her lips pressed tightly together, her nostrils curled scornfully, and put on the shoes. Then she walked out of the infirmary, limping, as she had known she would. She went into one of the practice rooms and played angrily until the bell rang for the exercise period, which was a walk that afternoon because of a thin cold drizzle that kept them off the playing fields. Miss Halsey was taking the walk. Katherine went out to the stone path, where the girls from the upper school were assembling, and waited for her name to be called. She tried to cover up the limp the shoes gave her, but the more she tried to hide it, the more exaggerated it seemed to become. Around her the girls were choosing partners for the walk. As yet no one had noticed or remarked upon the terrible shoe.

As Miss Halsey called "Forrester," she looked at Katherine, standing slightly apart, and Katherine saw her eyes, curious and eager, on the shoe. She walked in angry silence.

When her practice period came, during preparation hours, Katherine went down to the cloakroom and took off the shoes and put on her black canvas gym shoes. Miss Anderson had confiscated her regular school shoes when Katherine had taken them off that afternoon.

She put the heavy shoes she had wrenched off her feet under one arm and went to the small side door near the cloakroom. The rain had turned to snow, but underfoot it was wet and slushy, and she knew her feet would be soaked. She went back to the cloakroom, put on her rubber boots, then set out again, and started up the mountain. The path was almost obscured by snow, but she didn't care whether she followed it or not. She pushed her way up. Once she reached the shelter of the trees, the wet snow lashed against her face less cruelly, and it was easier to climb because the wind no longer pushed her breath back down her throat; she could pull herself up by the trees. Her hip hurt, sending the pain all the way down her leg, but she was sure it was just the result of the power of suggestion and the misery and embarrassment the shoes had caused her. If none of this sound and fury had happened, she would be no more conscious of her bad hip now than she had been for the past years. —Mother would knock that woman down for being such a fool—she thought. —Mother would just lay out and whack her for trying to make me into a cripple. I won't have it. They can do anything they want to me, but I won't have it.—

When she thought she had climbed far enough, she stopped, put the shoes down, and looked around for a sharp flat stone. Then she began to dig, under the layer of snow and the layer of fallen leaves, into the rich ground that was frozen hard. She dug until her fingers were numb and bleeding and she had made a good-sized hole. Into this she put the shoes, covering them up again with the earth, pounding it down hard, then putting back the layer of dead leaves and spreading snow on top, until it looked like a very small grave. She looked at it and laughed, broke off a twig and drew a cross on top of the grave and the date. Then she placed a small, round stone at the head and said,

> "Blessed be he that spares these stones,
> But cursed be he that moves my bones."

and started back down the mountain.

When she got back to school, she heard voices in the cloakroom. She stopped, and stood waiting, her heart pounding. Then, —Oh, hell—she thought—they'll have to find out sooner or later—and she pushed open the door of the cloakroom.

Sarah and Penelope Deerenforth were sitting on one of the big boot boxes reading a letter, their heads close together, and they jumped guiltily as Katherine came in.

"Hello," Sarah said, and grinned a little sheepishly.

"Hello," Katherine said, and sat down and pulled off her boots and put on her gym shoes.

"Why the gym shoes?" Pen took off her glasses and put them back on.

"What *were* those weird-looking things you had on this afternoon that made you limp?" Sarah asked.

"They were an idea of Miss Anderson's," Katherine said, tying a double knot in her gym shoes viciously, "to keep me from being self-conscious about my bad hip and to cure the limp I don't have."

"Oh, I say, what a rotten shame." Pen pushed her glasses up her nose and looked at Katherine with sympathy.

"So I've just buried them," Katherine said. "If you want to report me for being out of bounds, et cetera, et cetera, et cetera, I suppose I shall be expelled, but I really don't give a damn." She turned her back to them as her words began

222

to gallop out, clenching her teeth together to keep the tears back.

Pen got up and stood behind her, patting her clumsily on the shoulder. "Don't get so excited, Kat. We wouldn't dream of reporting you. I'd have done exactly the same thing in your place."

"Besides, we haven't any business being down here ourselves during prep," Sarah added. "Let's tell Kat, shall we, Pen?"

Pen blushed and lowered her head. "All right."

"Pen got herself engaged last summer during the hols, and she just got a letter from his mother asking her to stay in London with them for Christmas. She didn't think his mother liked her, and it's a wonderful letter, so everything is all right."

"I'm awfully glad, Pen," Katherine said solemnly.

"He's so wonderful," Pen said. "He's assistant French master at St. Martin's School in Yorkshire. Don't you think I'll make a wonderful assistant master's wife in a boys' school? He was brought up in Paris, so of course he really speaks French, and he's going back to the Sorbonne to study this summer. Mother says I'm much too young to think of marrying yet, but I'm eighteen, and that's old enough to know my own mind. I didn't want to come back this year, but she said if I did she'd let me get married next year, if Edmond and I still wanted to. His name's Edmond Murray-Lyon, by the way. His mother's the most dignified white-haired old lady you've ever seen. She was quite old when Edmond was born, so in a way she's more like a grandmother than a mother. The only thing she likes about me is my brains."

Sarah laughed. "Have you ever heard Pen talk so much, Kat?"

223

"Never," Katherine said, and laughed, too.

"You must promise never to tell anyone," Pen said. "I haven't told anyone except Sarah."

"I promise." Their sharing the secret with her made Katherine very happy, though she knew it was because they had been sorry for her on account of the dreadful shoe.

Pen took off her glasses and looked at them dreamily. "He doesn't mind my glasses," she said. "He says I'm beautiful, and when he wants to kiss me he takes them off and puts them in his pocket." She looked at them and wiped them on the sleeve of her uniform and put them on again. "The first time I saw him was at one of my grandmother's strawberry teas, so of course I didn't have them on, but then he took me to the cinema, and I knew I'd have to wear them or I wouldn't see a thing, so I took them out and I said, 'I have to wear these or I can't see two feet in front of my nose, do you mind awfully?' and he said he didn't mind a bit and I was just as beautiful with them on as I was with them off. I know I'm not a bit beautiful, but it's lovely to have someone say so."

"You have a beautiful body," Katherine said.

"Oh, Katherine!"

"It's true."

"And she has beautiful hair," Sarah said. "Naturally curly, and that beautiful taffy color. I'm so furious I won't be able to be at the wedding. We're going back to the States this Christmas, Kat, so I won't be back next term. I can't say I'm sorry."

"Oh," Katherine said.

"We'll be back in New York, and Daddy promised I could go to Dramatic School. I'm really looking forward to it awfully."

Pen looked at her watch. "It's nearly time for the end of

224

prep," she said, folding her letter. "We'd better go upstairs. I say, Sarah, don't you think we can persuade Halsey to move the chest of drawers away from the window tonight? It spoils the view, and nothing's going to keep me from walking in my sleep when I'm so happy."

Miss Anderson did not notice Katherine in her gym shoes until the next morning after breakfast, when Katherine was going back to her room to make her bed. Then she stopped her in the passage.

"What have you got on your feet?"

"My gym shoes."

"Where are the shoes I gave you yesterday?"

"I don't know."

"What do you mean?"

"I've lost them."

"How could you have lost them?"

"I just have."

"You'd better come with me to Miss Valentine's office."

"All right."

But even two hours in Miss Valentine's office could not make Katherine tell what had happened to the shoes.

"If you will let me wire my Aunt Manya in London to-night, she will wire you or phone back that I am never to wear any such shoes," she said finally, "and as she, as well as Father, is my legal guardian, that ought to satisfy you."

And Manya's furious telephone call settled matters. The shoes were never mentioned again, and everybody but Katherine forgot the matter quickly. Somehow she couldn't seem to throw it right off. Her hip, which she never thought of except when she was doing some sort of exercise that was too difficult for her, began to bother her, and she felt that she was limping all the time. But after a while she forgot

225

about it, and her concentration went back to her music, and reading, and getting the year over with.

When the year had finally gone and there were only a few more days left for ever and ever of this school, which she disliked but knew to be no worse than most other schools, she managed to wangle permission from Manya to go to Paris for a week and stay alone in a small hotel on the Rue Ordener. Charlot happened to have a week off just at that time and would be able to take care of her. Katherine knew that her father heartily disapproved of her doing anything like that alone, but that Manya believed in young people's being on their own as soon as possible, and was her ally. The thought of a week in Paris and a chance to see Justin again was almost unbearably exciting. It was more difficult than ever to sleep, and she read longer and longer each night under the bedclothes. One afternoon, just a few days before the end of term, when she was up in the old elm tree with *Martin Chuzzlewit*, Penelope Deerenforth hailed her.

"I say, Kat, are you up there?"

"Yes," Katherine said shortly, irritated at the interruption.

"Would you mind if I came up for a sec?"

"No, come along."

Pen clambered up, panting, and Katherine reached down and gave her a hand. "I never was the sportsy type," Pen said, settling herself on a branch and straightening her glasses. "Look, Kat, I hear you're going to Paris."

"Yes. I am."

"Well, look, would you mind if I went with you and stayed at the same hotel just for one night?"

"No, of course not. I didn't know you were going to Paris."

"I told you Edmond was going to study at the Sorbonne this summer, didn't I?"

226

"Yes."

"Well, his mother's coming with him, and she's invited me to stay with them for a fortnight, but they won't be in till the next day, and I'd feel rather nervous about staying by myself in a strange hotel, so if you wouldn't mind—"

"Of course, Pen, it's all right. Will you write and ask about a double room for Sunday night or shall I?"

"I'll do it, if you'll give me the address. Thanks very much, Kat, it's very kind of you."

"Don't be silly. It'll be very pleasant."

She left the school without a regret. She resented the fact that Pen was to be with her, because that would keep her from throwing off the school completely, from blotting out its existence. But in the long run it wasn't important.

On her last day there after she had finished packing, she went back to the studio that had been Justin's and still seemed to hold something of his personality; went back to the old château for the first time and played on the organ, which by now was falling apart and wheezing more than ever. Even if she was not able to see Justin during this one week in Paris, she would be in his city, and in the city where Julie had studied; she would write Justin from London; she would study with him in the autumn. Her term in prison had been served.

KATHERINE and Pen talked very little on the trip to Paris. Without the background of school they both became suddenly shy. Innumerable walls rose up between them, larger even than those that had existed at school, where Pen was an integral part of the place and Katherine always an outsider. Charlot took them out to dinner but brought them back to their hotel early, saying that both looked tired and needed a good sleep, and he would be around for Katherine in the morning. He looked, as usual, thin and exhausted, but somehow the strain had gone out of his face; it was no longer the face of someone who was in desperate need of comfort and understanding. When he heard of Pen's engagement, he congratulated her, looked at Katherine a little strangely, and said, "I, too, am engaged." For a moment Katherine felt a terrific pang of jealousy run through her. Charlot was no longer hers, and although she did not want him, it would be difficult to conquer the selfish wish that no one else should have him. "You'll adore her, Katherine," he said. "She's so beautiful, and sincere, and real. She has hair like yours, Miss Deerenforth, but you're obviously English, and she couldn't be anything but French. It's so fantastic that she loves me, Katherine. I can't believe it, I can't imagine myself being so fantastically lucky."

"I told you you weren't in love with me," Katherine said.

He reached across the table and took her hand. "I know, darling. You've always been right about everything. You—you don't regret anything, do you?"

228

"No, Charlot. I don't regret anything."

"You'll see her before you go. She's in Avignon for a friend's wedding now, but she'll be back Sunday morning. You'll love her and she'll love you."

Katherine didn't feel as happy about Charlot's wedding as she felt she should. When they were undressed and in bed, she turned to Pen. "You know I ought to be delirious with joy about Charlot, and I am terribly glad to see him so happy. It's wonderful to see his face so un-tight, but I feel sort of lost, as though something sort of valuable had gone out of my life."

"Was he really in love with you once?" Pen asked. "He sounded as though he had been."

"Just for a very short time."

"Were you in love with him?"

"No. I just—I just somehow wish he'd written me about it."

"What did he mean when he asked if you regretted anything?"

"Oh—nothing."

Pen changed the subject. "I wish I'd known you better at school, Kat."

"I wish you had, too."

"I think we might have been awfully good friends."

"Yes."

"I'm sorry about that mess you had with Sarah."

"I am, too."

"It was all Val's and Halsey's fault, wasn't it?"

"I guess so. Yes. And mine, for not knowing anything about anything. I still don't. Know anything about anything, I mean."

"I'm going to find out soon," Pen said happily. "Shall we turn out the light now, Kat? Are you sleepy?"

"Um-hum. Good night, Pen."

"Good night, Kat."

Katherine woke out of a deep sleep to hear the phone ringing. She reached out drowsily and picked up the receiver. "Hello?"

It was Manya's voice. "Katya, darling, I'm sorry to wake you, but I just got back, and I knew you'd be out cavorting with Charlot and that Justin of yours after tonight, and I wanted to be sure to get you. Now, listen carefully, Katya. We're sailing for New York on Sunday. Oliver Henley phoned me this evening, and he wants me to do the play in New York next winter, and we're closing here on Wednesday, and that will give us just time to get ready to sail on Sunday, and we can spend the summer in Connecticut. The boat sails from Le Havre at midnight, so if Charlot will put you on the boat train, we'll meet you there. Have you got it all straight?"

"Yes. I've got it all straight, but I don't want to go back to America. I want to stay in Paris and study with Justin."

"Oh, my darling, I'm sorry, but I could never persuade your father to let you stay in Paris all by yourself, when you're only seventeen."

"I'll be eighteen in October."

"But you're seventeen now. I know it would be wonderful for you, and I know how much it would mean to you, but he's your father, and he's an angel and a great composer, even if he has a terrible streak of conventionality where you're concerned, and you've got to do what he says till you're eighteen at any rate, and you can study with the best teacher in New York, so please be a good girl for Manya's sake, and take the boat train to Le Havre on Saturday."

"Oh, all right, all right, I'll be there, damn it," Katherine said, and hung up. Then she switched on the bed lamp and looked at her mother's wrist watch. Two o'clock. She glanced at the other bed and noticed that the covers were pushed back and Pen was gone. —She's probably gone to the bathroom—she thought, and turned out the light and lay down again. But with Manya's words still ringing in her ears, she couldn't go back to sleep. —Why in thunder she should have to pick now to go back to New York is beyond me—she thought. —If she could at least have waited until the end of the summer I could have studied with Justin during the summer and that would be better than nothing. I don't know whom to study with in New York. I suppose I'll go to Mother's old teacher and ask him, but I don't even know if he's still alive. He was in his sixties when Mother was still working with him. Why do things always have to be such a hateful mess? Just when I thought everything was going to be all right again . . . Pen's been gone an awfully long time. Oh, Lord, I suppose she's walking in her sleep again, what with all the excitement of meeting her Edmond tomorrow.—

She turned on the light again and got out of bed. Although it was July and the trip on the train the day before had been hot and uncomfortable, the room felt cold, and when she went over to the window and pushed it to, she noticed that it was raining softly. She put on her bathrobe and slippers and opened the door. There was no sign of Pen in the long, dimly lighted passage, and the bathroom, too, was empty. Seized with an overwhelming anxiety, she dressed quickly, and went down to the desk. A sleepy-looking clerk with a too-long mustache was reading a paper, and he eyed her suspiciously.

"I'm sorry to bother you," Katherine said, "but the young

lady I'm with walks in her sleep, and she isn't in the room and I'm worried about her."

"What do you expect me to do about it?" the clerk asked.

"Please help me to find her."

"She's probably in the w.c."

"I looked there. Please. She may have fallen somewhere and hurt herself."

The clerk got up, grunting, and went up in the elevator. Katherine waited at the desk. —I know I'm silly to be frightened—she thought—Mother always teased me for being a worry bug. Pen's always walked in her sleep and nothing's ever happened to her before. I wish tomorrow would come, and everything would be all right. Even though I know tomorrow doesn't always make everything all right. Sometimes it makes what you've been afraid of come true. But I wish tomorrow would come and we were sitting up in bed eating breakfast the way we had planned and waiting for Edmond and Charlot to come. I wish Charlot had written me about his being engaged. He should have written. I wonder what she's like. I bet she isn't worthy of him. I bet she's a bitch. I wish that awful little cockroach of a man would find Pen. Why did he go off and leave me all alone? I don't want to go back to America. I don't want to. It's not fair. I've dreamed so about being in Paris next winter, working with Justin. I should have been allowed to be in Paris next winter.—

The elevator rattled down and the clerk came out. "I can't find her anywhere," he said. "And she couldn't have gone out. I would have seen her. Well, maybe I wouldn't have." He opened the door and looked out, then came back to the desk, rubbing his tobacco-stained mustache with the back of his hand. "If she's out on the streets, there's no use looking for her. You'd better go back on up to bed. She'll probably turn up in the morning." He picked up his news-paper again.

Katherine stared at him helplessly for a moment, then went back upstairs and undressed and climbed into bed, frowning anxiously at the tumbled covers of Pen's empty bed. As she reached out to switch off the light, she remembered that she had closed the window and got up to open it again. And as she put out her hand to open the window, a terrible thought struck her, and she drew back, afraid to touch it. Then she gathered herself together and pulled the long window open and peered down three stories to the courtyard below. It was so dark she could see nothing, but she stayed peering down for a long time, trembling from head to foot. Then she turned suddenly and pulled on her bathrobe and ran downstairs to the desk again.

The night clerk looked up from his paper with irritation. "Now, see here," he said. "I don't want any more of this nonsense tonight."

"Please." Katherine clasped her hands together. "Our window opens onto the court. Please . . . would you . . . go and look . . ."

"You're making a lot of fuss over nothing," the clerk said, pulled a soiled handkerchief out of his pocket, and took some shreds of tobacco out of his mouth. "But if it's the only way to keep you quiet—" He got up and went off, and Katherine was left waiting, leaning against the desk again. This time he wasn't gone long, and Katherine could see that he was very frightened. He went to the telephone and spoke to someone in French so rapid and inarticulate that Katherine could understand only a few words of it.

"What is it?" she asked. "Please, what is it?"

"You'd better go up to your room and wait there," he said. "You'd better go up and wait. What room is it? No, maybe you shouldn't. Oh, I don't know what you'd better do. What's your room number?"

"34a. Did you find her?"

"Yes, I found her."

"Is she—is she all right?"

"I don't know. I don't know anything," he said. "You stay here. No, go up to your room and wait. Yes, that's best. You go up to your room and wait."

The thin, merry-faced porter with the green-baize apron, who had carried their bags up that afternoon, came out from a small door hidden in the shadows.

"Go on up to your room," the night clerk said again. "Go on up. It's best."

Katherine went back to the room and waited, her hands pressed tightly together, her heart pounding so violently that her ears hurt and it was difficult to breathe, trying not to look at the window. She had shut the door, but suddenly she went to it and stood there waiting, until the night clerk and the porter carried Pen in and laid her on the bed.

Her pajamas were soaked with rain and clung to her body. Her fair hair was wet, too, and a strand lay across her face. The rain was wet on her face and mixed with a thin stream of blood that came from her mouth. Her breathing was so shallow that it was barely perceptible.

Katherine ran to her suitcase and got out the slip of paper that had Charlot's number on it. She gave it to the night clerk and said, "Get me this number quickly. It's a doctor. Hurry up." Then she turned to the porter. "Get me some hot-water bottles as quickly as you can. Really hot, and wrap them in towels. Be as quick as you can." Then back to the night clerk. "Get me that number." She pushed them out of the door, then went to the telephone and took off the receiver. After a moment she could hear the clerk ringing

234

Charlot's number. The telephone rang and rang and rang, and she was afraid it would never be answered, but at last a cross voice said, "Well, what is it?"

"I want to speak to Charlot right away, please," she said.

"Doesn't live here," she heard the voice say, and the telephone was hung up.

She jiggled the receiver frantically. "Get that number again," she told the night clerk.

Again the phone rang. This time it wasn't as long before the voice said, "What is it?"

"M. Charles Bejart, please. I want to speak to him at once. It's a matter of life and death."

"Wait a minute," the voice said, and there was another long pause. Katherine looked at Pen lying so motionless on the bed, her wet hair clinging to her face, the thin line of blood oozing out of her mouth. "Oh, God," Katherine whispered, "please, God, please, please, please—"

After a long time she heard Charlot's sleepy voice. "Hello."

"Charlot, this is Katherine," she said. "Pen walks in her sleep, and she walked out of our window on the third floor. She's breathing, but she's not conscious and she's bleeding out of her mouth."

"I'll get hold of du Marsais and come right away," Charlot said.

"Her night clothes are drenched. Should I try to take them off?"

"No. Keep her well covered. Get hot-water bottles, if you can. We'll be over as soon as possible."

"All right." She hung up. Then she took the blankets off her bed and covered Pen with them. She took a towel and wet it gently with warm water and carefully tried to wipe the blood from Pen's face, pushing the wet hair back from her

235

forehead and cheeks. Once Pen opened her eyes, looked at Katherine without recognition, and closed them again. When the porter came in with the hot-water bottles, Katherine packed them around Pen, well wrapped in towels so that they wouldn't be too hot, and covered her with the blankets again.

Out of a pocket in his green-baize apron the porter took Pen's steel glasses-frames and some bits of broken glass and laid them on the blotter on the desk. In her sleep Pen must have automatically reached out and put on her glasses.

Katherine waited until the porter had left. Then she dressed.

It was almost an hour before Charlot came with Dr. du Marsais.

"Is she your sister?" du Marsais asked.

"No. A school friend. She was supposed to meet her fiancé here tomorrow."

"You'd better wait outside."

Katherine went out obediently. This time she didn't have long to wait before Charlot came to her.

"We're taking her to the hospital," he said. "It isn't much use, but she'll be better off there than she would here."

"Is she going to die?"

"I'm afraid so, Katherine."

"Oh."

"This is a dreadful thing for you to have to go through, darling."

"It's a dreadful thing for Pen to have to go through," Katherine said, her voice shaking.

"Dearest," Charlot said, "I'll go with her to the hospital, and I'll stay with her so she won't be alone in case she recovers consciousness." He looked at his watch. "It's five o'clock now. What time is her fiancé supposed to come?"

236

"He said he'd be at the hotel tomorrow at noon."

"You'd better go to bed and get some sleep, then."

"I couldn't sleep. Let me go to the hospital."

"Someone has to be here to meet that young man, and it had better be you. You are to get undressed and get into bed and try to sleep. I'll phone at ten-thirty. Wait here."

Charlot went back into the room again. In a few minutes the door opened and Dr. du Marsais came out. He carried Katherine's pajamas over his arm and held a small twist of paper out to her.

"This contains a very mild sleeping tablet, and I want you to promise to take it." In the dim light his body hardly showed in the dark suit, but his well-groomed hair shone silver, and his voice carried authority.

"All right," Katherine said.

"I've taken another room for you, and you're to go to bed right away and sleep. Charles will telephone and wake you up in plenty of time."

"All right."

The night porter came down the hall with a key in his hand. Katherine and Dr. du Marsais followed him down to the end of the passage, where he opened the door to a small room that looked out on the quiet side street. Dr. du Marsais dismissed him. Then he filled a glass with water and handed it to Katherine.

"Now take the tablet and drink the full glass," he said, and Katherine obeyed mechanically.

Dr. du Marsais turned the bed down, lighted the bed lamp and switched off the ceiling light. "Now get undressed and get into bed," he said. "You're a brave girl." And he left.

Katherine took off her clothes, her blue serge uniform and white shirt, and white regulation underclothes, and got into her pajamas. Nothing was real. She felt nothing at all. She climbed into bed and turned off the light, and waves of drowsiness flooded her whole being. A soft rap on the door roused her.

"Who is it?" she called.

"Charlot."

She let him in, then got back into bed. "What is it?"

"I just wanted to say good night, darling," he said. He sat down beside her, and kissed her gently, and tiptoed out.

The telephone woke her. She answered it, and Charlot's voice came, strong and comforting. "Katherine."

"Hello, Charlot."

"I'm calling from the hospital, darling. Pen is still unconscious, and I'm afraid it can't be more than a few hours now. Perhaps you'd better go back to the room you had together and put her things in her suitcase. When her fiancé and his mother come, if they want to go straight to the hospital, you get a taxi and bring them over. We've tried to get hold of her parents, but couldn't. I wired the address you gave me, and the wire was not received. Perhaps her fiancé will know. We've done everything we can, at any rate. Now, please send downstairs and order some breakfast."

"I'm not hungry."

"Order at least fruit and coffee. Understand?"

"Yes, Charlot."

"I'll see you in a couple of hours, then."

"Yes . . . good-bye."

"Good-bye, little one."

In the room she had shared with Pen both beds were still unmade. On Pen's pillow the blood had dried, and the rumpled bloodstained towel still lay on the washstand. On

238

the green desk blotter lay the steel glasses-frames and the shattered bits of glass. She took Pen's clothes from the back of the chair over which they were neatly folded and put them in the top of her suitcase. Then she took her toothbrush and paste and her comb and brush from the washstand, and packed them, too, and the glasses-frames. When the telephone rang and Mrs. and Mr. Murray-Lyon were announced, she took her coat and hat and went downstairs.

Even if they had not been the only people in the lobby, she would have recognized them at once. Mrs. Murray-Lyon was a tall, white-haired old lady in a dark traveling suit and a Queen Mary hat. Edmond Murray-Lyon was tall, too, with a gentle, good-natured face, thick, brown hair, and a little brush mustache. His face was puckered with anxiety now, and Katherine saw that he already knew that something was wrong.

She went up to them. "I'm Katherine Forrester. I'm a school friend of Pen's who was traveling with her." Suddenly she couldn't go on. She stared helplessly from one to the other.

"What has happened? Please tell me," Edmond said.

"You know Pen walks in her sleep—"

"No. I didn't know."

"Well, she does. At school they called her Lady Macbeth. The window in our room here is a French one, and it's when she's excited or tired that she walks in her sleep, and she was terribly excited about seeing you today, and I guess she was tired from the trip, too, and—and that's what happened."

Edmond's face was very white, and his mother clung to his arm. "You mean she—she walked out of the window in her sleep last night?" he asked.

"Yes. It was the third story, you see, and it was raining. It was just because I had a telephone call around two o'clock last night that I woke up and saw she was gone. I have a friend who is a medical student here in Paris, and I called him at once, and he came right over with a doctor, and they took her to the hospital right away. She's had the best medical care. If you want to go to the hospital, I can take you there at once."

"Of course," Edmond Murray-Lyon said, and they hurried out. As they got into a taxi, he asked, "It's—it's very serious, then?"

"I'm afraid it is."

"Is she conscious?"

"No. She hasn't been."

"Have you seen her?"

"Not since last night, just after it happened. Charlot— my friend— phoned me from the hospital about an hour ago."

"Do they think she'll live?"

Katherine clenched her fists. "No. They don't," she said.

Charlot met them at the hospital and took Edmond and Mrs. Murray-Lyon up to Pen's room. Then he came down to Katherine.

"Her parents are in London at the moment, and the young man will get in touch with them and take care of everything. They'll take her home to England," he said.

"Oh."

"You're coming around the corner to the café with me and have an omelette or something."

"I'm not hungry."

He put his arm around her. "Come along, Katherine."

They sat down at a small round table and Charlot ordered. "Was she a particularly good friend of yours?"

"No. I didn't have any particularly good friends. I never

240

talked to her very much or got to know her at all until yesterday."

"I see."

"I don't understand about people dying, Charlot."

"You mustn't think about it."

"Of course I must think about it! Don't be silly! If you don't think about it and try to figure things out you become —just nothing. If you do think about it, maybe you go crazy. But I'd rather be crazy than nothing. Of course I must think about it!"

"Go on and talk, if it helps you."

"It doesn't help. Nothing helps. When you're alone. You're in love now. It shines out of every atom of you. You're so different because of it, you might almost be another person. And when you're in love, everything you touch has a kind of excitement and glamour. Even death. Besides, you see death so much, don't you, Charlot? that you have to harden yourself to it. But I'm afraid! I'm afraid! Nobody's safe! It's all around, reaching out for you, catching you unawares. Pen wasn't ready to die. She was in love, and she was going to marry Edmond, and she'd have made a good wife and mother; she wasn't one of the bad people we hate. And she was so young! She was only eighteen— just a year older than I am. I don't understand about young people dying. It's bad enough when you're older, and you've lived your life—oh, God, it's bad enough then, but young people, Charlot! Young people oughtn't to die! I'm afraid! I'm afraid!"

"Don't," Charlot said gently.

"I'm sorry. I didn't mean to make a spectacle of myself. But I am afraid. I don't want to die, and death's everywhere. If it could take Pen like that, how do I know it won't take me next? I don't want to die! I've too much to do, and

241

there isn't enough time to do half of it, even if I live to be a very old woman. Death's unfair at any time—but to a young person!"

"Drink your coffee, darling."

"You won't talk, because you know there isn't anything comforting to say. Isn't that true?"

"Drink your coffee."

"It is true."

"Tonight I'll take you to the Moulin Rouge."

"I don't want to go to the Moulin Rouge."

"But you will go."

"I don't know why I want so frightfully to live. A lot of the time I haven't been very happy. And I'm afraid of having to be alone always. I don't want to be alone. But I'm afraid of having to be. I know our bodies are our only means of communication with other people, but isn't it the fact of our having separate bodies that really keeps us apart? Because you see it's awful, but I'm thinking more about myself than about Pen. Is that why?"

"I don't know."

"Now that you're in love, are you still satisfied with the idea of being nothing, of just being finished after you die? Or don't you believe it any more?"

"Don't you want to get in touch with that Justin person of yours while you're in Paris?" Charlot asked her.

"Of course. That's why I came to Paris . . . And he isn't mine."

"Why don't you get in touch with him today?"

"I don't know. I feel sort of funny about it all of a sudden. Maybe I shouldn't bother him."

"Don't be a little fool. Why didn't you write him to tell him you were coming to Paris?"

"I don't know. I just couldn't, somehow."

"Why don't you write a note now and leave it for him?"

"All right. I guess that would be all right."

"Another thing I was thinking of, little one. Wouldn't you rather move to another hotel?"

"You mean because of Pen?"

"Yes."

"No. I don't think so. I don't think I should. I want to. But I don't think I should."

"Why, dear?"

"It's sort of like falling off a horse and not getting back on again. That's not right, but do you know what I mean?"

"Yes, I think so. But I don't think you should torture yourself."

"Well, I—let's not talk about it, Charlot."

"All right, my dear."

"We'd better go back to the hospital now, and see, hadn't we?"

"All right, come along."

As they went into the lobby, they saw Edmond Murray-Lyon and his mother coming out of the elevator.

"It's all over," Edmond said. "She—she never regained consciousness."

Katherine was silent, watching the tight control of his face.

Mrs. Murray-Lyon spoke to her. "Would you do us the kindness of having dinner with my son and me at our hotel tonight? I know there are some things Edmond would like to ask you."

"Yes. I'd be glad to," Katherine answered.

"Will seven o'clock be convenient for you?"

"Yes, of course, any time."

"Edmond will call for you, then."

"Oh, please—he needn't bother. I'll be with Charlot all afternoon and he can drop me off."

"All right. The Meurice, then, at seven o'clock."

"Yes. Thank you very much, Mrs. Murray-Lyon."

"Thank you, my dear."

Katherine took Charlot's arm and watched Mrs. Murray-Lyon lead Edmond out of the hospital. "I want to walk," she said suddenly. "Please let's walk, Charlot."

"All right, darling. Where do you want to go?"

"I don't know. Anywhere."

He took her to the Luxembourg gardens, and there something incredible happened, for coming down a path toward them was Anne Vigneras.

She recognized Katherine at once and hurried toward her. "Katherine! What are you doing in Paris? Why didn't you let Justin know?"

"We—I—I didn't get in till last night. This is Charlot. M. Charles Bejart. Charlot, I'd like you to meet Mademoiselle Vigneras."

Anne shook hands with Charlot. "I'm very glad to meet you. Do you know, you look so much like my brother—has Katherine ever told you?"

"Often," Charlot said. "That's my main attraction for her."

Anne turned back to Katherine. "Come and sit down for a moment, if you have time. Are you busy? I'm intruding, perhaps?"

"No, oh, no, please let's sit down."

Anne led them to an empty bench, sat down, and took Katherine's hand.

"Do you think I—do you think I could see Monsieur Vigneras?" Katherine asked her.

"Of course, darling. How long are you going to be here?"

"Just till Sunday. I have to sail for America on Sunday."

"Oh, what a shame! And Justin isn't here just now. He won't be back till Saturday night."

"Then I shan't see him!" Katherine cried.

"You'll see him Saturday night, of course," Anne said. "But it's a pity you couldn't have had more time with each other. I know he'll be very disappointed. He often talks of you, and wonders how you are getting on with your work. Julien Quimper asks after you, too, whenever he comes to dinner. Justin was quite hurt because you never wrote him after that first letter, Katherine. Why didn't you let him hear from you?"

"I didn't think I ought to bother him unless I had a really good reason."

"Coming to Paris was reason enough, wasn't it? You should have let him know."

"I didn't think I ought to bother him."

"You funny child."

"No. I—"

"Katherine, what is it? What's the matter? Do you want me to go away?"

"No, oh, no, please don't go."

Briefly Charlot told Anne about Pen.

"What a terrible thing," she said, in a quivering voice. "What a terrible, terrible thing. Katherine, won't you come and stay with me this week? It would give me so much pleasure to have you, and then you'd really have a chance to see Justin when he comes home on Saturday night. He's done awfully well, you'll be proud of him, Katherine, he's very highly thought of. Won't you stay with me?"

Charlot said, "It's very kind of you, Mlle Vigneras. I should be much less worried about her if I knew she wasn't alone."

245

"It's all right, then, Katherine? You'll stay with me?"

"You know I'd love it. It just seems like a dreadful imposition."

"On the contrary. It'll be a great pleasure for me. I've been very lonely this past week without Justin. It's all settled, then? Let's move you right now, shall we?"

Justin's apartment was a charming one, four flights up, under the eaves. There was a big room with the piano and a sofa and books and comfortable chairs and a fireplace and warm lamplight, and there were two tiny bedrooms, a bathroom, and a sizable kitchen.

"I'll put you in Justin's room till he comes back," Anne said. "And then on Saturday night, if you don't mind terribly, you can sleep on the divan in the living room. It's really very comfortable. I've slept there often myself. Now I'll light the fire and make some tea, and then you'll play for me, won't you?"

They stayed in front of the fire, drinking quantities of tea, until it was time for Katherine to go to the Meurice to meet the Murray-Lyons. Dinner was a strained, miserable affair. Katherine did her best to answer Edmond's questions, but she found she knew very little about Pen. She knew what she looked like hunched over her desk in the preparation hall, with her glasses sliding down her nose; waving her hand violently in class when the most difficult questions were asked; standing with authority and dignity behind Miss Halsey's desk at form meetings; speaking to the entire school in chapel, punctuating her speech with the characteristic gesture of pushing her glasses up on her nose; leading the "crocodile" to church on Sunday with Sarah (—I ought to write to Sarah about this—Katherine thought); singing happily, off key, at choir practice; and disgracing herself by laughing outright in the middle of the sixth-form play—it

246

was only exterior things like this that Katherine knew about Pen. She knew very little about her inner being.

After dinner Edmond took her back to Justin's apartment, and Charlot was there, and Marcel Desmoulins, a friend of Justin's and Anne's, who, Anne told her, was the finest organist in Paris and played at the Church of Ste Anne. They took her to the Moulin Rouge when Edmond left, and Charlot made her drink a little too much and get very gay, and then they took her home and put her to bed, and she fell asleep at once.

The next morning Anne brought Katherine her breakfast in bed and told her that she had talked to Justin on the telephone and told him everything, and that he was longing to see her, and would be back as early as possible on Saturday night.

As early as possible wasn't until after eleven o'clock. They knew he was coming, because they heard him running up the stairs, two at a time. Anne ran to the door and opened it, and he kissed her and picked her up and swung her around, and then he kissed Katherine, too, and picked her up and held her off at arm's length.

"That's what you get for being such a little thing," he said. "You haven't changed a bit, except now you look ninety instead of seventy-five." He put her down. "And your hair looks as though it was used to being up. Do you ever wear it down any more? Just two long dark braids flapping against your shoulders?"

"Only when I get ready for bed. How are you? Are you all right?"

"Yes, I'm all right, little one. How are you? Can you still play the piano? Sit down and play for me. At once."

Katherine sat down and played. She would never forget that night as long as she lived. They didn't go to bed at all.

Anne curled up on the sofa and slept, and Katherine and Justin sat at the piano and worked. Worked until she was completely sure of herself again, and the doubts she had had about her music vanished.

"I wanted so much to be in Paris next winter and study with you," she said, looking out at the dawn coming over the rooftops.

"You'll be all right," Justin said.

"But look at tonight! Look how much I've learned tonight! You don't ever know enough to be able to work just by yourself."

"There are plenty of people in America who can probably teach you far more than I ever could."

"I don't know. You and Mother are the only people I've ever learned from. You know, I was failed in music at school last year."

"I don't doubt it, with that bastard Devault. Nevertheless, you've made great strides by yourself, little one."

"Have I? Have I really?"

"You know you have. I've just been able to tighten a few things for you tonight, to clarify a few points. Have you any idea whom you'll go to when you get back to America?"

"I don't know. Albert Peytz was Mother's teacher. I thought I'd ask him, if he's still alive."

"He ought to be able to suggest someone. Look at Anne, she's sound asleep, poor darling."

"Oh—it's all my fault. I'm sorry."

"It's my fault, infant. Don't worry. It's not the first time Anne's dozed away all night in this fashion. She'll be all right. But how about you? Are you very tired?"

"I'm not a bit tired. I haven't felt so wonderful in ages."

"Back ache?"

"Not really."

Justin got up and stood behind her at the piano and massaged her neck and shoulders. "Now, you write me from America."

"I will."

"You write me. Not just one short funny little note. Real letters. Promise?"

"I promise."

"Do you know how to make coffee?"

"No."

"Neither do I. And we mustn't wake Anne. I know a good café that's open all night, just around the corner. Want to come with me and get some coffee?"

"Yes. I'd love to."

They went downstairs and out into the street. Day was beginning to come, but the shadows still clung to the buildings. The café around the corner still lay deep in darkness, but you could tell that day was very near because the lamp had lost its brilliance. They sat down and Justin ordered coffee.

"As long as things happen to you, you'll be all right," he said. "You're strong enough to take them, and as long as things happen to you, you'll learn and be all right. Remember that, no matter how dreadful things may seem sometimes."

"I've got an awful lot to learn," Katherine said.

"Yes, you have indeed, little one. But the thing that most gives me faith in you is that what does happen to you penetrates. It doesn't just brush off the surface. It goes into you, and is there for you to make use of when you're ready for it."

"Even useless horrible things, like Pen's dying that way?"

"Even things like that."

"How do I know I'm going to live long enough to be able to make use of the things that have happened to me?"

"You mustn't be afraid of death."

"I am."

"Fear is a terrible thing."

"I know."

"I think fear and covetousness are the most terrible things in the world, the greatest destroyers. They eat the insides out of one and leave only the shell. I don't want you to be afraid."

"But I am."

"I've always been proud of you, because I've thought of you as one of the brave ones."

"I'm not. I'm a coward. And I'm all alone with my fear. I'm all alone and I'm afraid of being alone and I'm afraid of dying and I'm afraid of being afraid. Now do you despise me and want to disown me?"

"No. Because I still think you are one of the brave ones. Basically."

"If you ever stopped believing in me, I shouldn't be afraid of death any more. I should want it."

"You mustn't say that."

"But it's true."

"You shouldn't let one person's opinion be so important."

"But it is."

"I don't think I'll ever stop believing in you. Not as long as you're you. And if you stop being you, my opinion won't matter to you any more, so that's all right. But don't stop being you. I don't think you will."

"As soon as I possibly can I am coming back to Paris and study with you. Would that be all right?"

"Of course."

"It's all Father's fault, my having to go back to America. I love Father, you understand, he's a darling, but he's such a fool, and he knows it, he knows he's absent-minded and crazy, but I do think he puts it on a bit because he knows people think it's charming, but he really is crazy to think he ought to counterbalance it by being frightfully conventional about me and my bringing up, and it's all wrong, I know Mother would say it was wrong. And Aunt Manya will think I'm right about wanting to come back to Paris to study with you, too. Aunt Manya's been on my side all along, and I know she's argued with Father, but Father's so stubborn that once he gets his mind made up about something, even Aunt Manya can't make him change it."

"It's going to be very hard," Justin said, "for people to realize you're grown up, Katherine. You're such a tiny thing. And I think you're a very great mixture of grown-up-ness and complete babyishness, in spite of your ancient little face. You know, the reason I know you're a nice girl is because Anne isn't jealous of you. Anne's a very jealous person, would you believe that? It's her worst fault, and it's only because she's a very strong person that she's been able to conquer it. If ever I should fall in love and want to marry, she'll make a wonderful sister-in-law and friend, but I must say she's been very disagreeable sometimes when I've been attracted to the wrong people. Have you seen Marcel Desmoulins the organist while you've been here?"

"Yes, several times."

"I think Anne's a little bit in love with him, don't you?"

"Yes, I do."

"And I know he's head over heels in love with her. It would be a very good thing for them both . . . I'm a terrible letter writer, but I'll try to drop you a line around Christmas time."

"Oh, would you?"

"I'll try. But don't hate me forever if I don't."

"I won't."

"When do you have to leave, little one?"

"Charlot is coming for me at twelve. I have to have lunch with him and his fiancée and then they're going to put me on the boat train."

"Who is this Charlot?"

"He's a very old friend of mine. Charles Bejart."

"Are you in love with him?"

"Oh, no. He's like a brother."

"Sure?"

"Yes."

"That's good. I don't want you to go around being in love with someone who's engaged to someone else. Let's go, my dear. It seems like a huge amount of stairs up to my garret, doesn't it?"

"I don't mind them."

At the foot of the stairs Justin stopped and turned toward her. For a moment Katherine thought he was going to kiss her, but he just smiled and started up. On the landing he paused. It was very dark. She stood still and waited. Although they were not touching, it seemed that she could feel him.

"There is something," he said, "that I should have apologized to you about a long time ago."

"Never mind," Katherine whispered. "You've never hurt me. I understand."

"You do, don't you?"

The landing seemed full of their presence and of something growing, burning with a clear flame between them that lit up the dark and made it alive. Neither of them spoke. Neither of them moved.

After a long time Justin sighed softly, blowing the flame out, unwillingly, regretfully.

252

Anne was still asleep on the sofa.

"Do you want to try to take a nap until your friend comes?" Justin asked, his voice very casual.

"No. I'm not a bit sleepy. But you do if you want to." Katherine's voice was equally casual.

"I'm not sleepy either, little one. Shall we play some records?"

"Wouldn't we wake Anne?"

"If we wake her, she'll cook us some breakfast. There's method in my madness."

"Oh, that would be mean!"

"Anne doesn't mind. Besides, if she's going to marry Marcel Desmoulins, she'll be cooking breakfast for him instead of me before long. Shall we have the *Brandenburg Concertos*? All six of them?"

"That would be lovely."

Justin put on the first *Brandenburg Concerto*, and Anne rolled over on the sofa and stretched and yawned. "Want your breakfast, do you?" she asked.

"That's right," Justin said, and grinned at Katherine.

Anne got up, ran her fingers through her short curly hair, and smoothed down her skirt. "My clothes look as though I'd slept in them. Strange, isn't it?" she said and went into the kitchen. Justin put more logs on the fire, and they listened to records and sat over breakfast until Charlot came at twelve with his fiancée.

With one look at Pauline Marat, Katherine knew she should feel happy about Charlot. Pauline Marat was a slender young Parisienne, on the tall side, beautifully dressed, with softly waved fair hair under a small black hat. Her eyes were dark-gray and very far apart and had the deep black line under the lashes that looks like heavy mascara but is natural, and that is almost unique with French women. Her nose was delicate and hooked, a little too long, her mouth firm and sweet, the upper lip narrow, the lower lip quite full. She couldn't keep her eyes off Charlot, and it was evident that she adored him. When she shook hands with Katherine, her grip was steady and strong.

"Come along, little one," Charlot said. "I'm going to take you to the most marvelous place for lunch. I couldn't take you before, because it's a place I never go to without Pauline."

Katherine turned to Anne. "I can't thank you for this week—I—it's meant so much to me—I—I do thank you ever and ever so much."

Anne kissed her. "I loved having you, dear. You know that."

Then Katherine turned to Justin. "I guess it's really good-bye this time."

He came up to her and put his hands on her shoulders. "Not at all. You mustn't forget that you've promised to come back to Paris and study with me as soon as you possibly can."

"I won't forget. I won't forget. But America seems such a long way off."

"Not really. It's only as far as you make it in your mind."

"Then it's right here."

He kissed her on both cheeks. "Good-bye, little one."

"Good-bye—and thank you."

She went downstairs with Charlot and Pauline.

HEN she went back to the apartment where she and Julie had lived on Tenth Street (How long ago was it? Nearly eight years), the street, and its ailanthus trees, and the house itself, seemed to have shrunk. Katherine walked up and down before it until she felt that she must look like a suspicious character, trying to pretend that she was ten once more, trying to pretend that Julie was up in the top floor of the apartment—and somehow trying to pretend that Justin was there, too. But Julie wasn't there. Justin wasn't there. Katherine wandered up and down Tenth Street until long after dark, then went back to the apartment Manya had taken overlooking the East River.

Tom had gone out of town to give a series of lectures. She found Manya back from her rehearsal, sitting in front of the fireplace, gazing into the flames. Katherine stood in the doorway of the shadowy room and watched Manya, getting pleasure and satisfaction from the weary grace of her aunt's pose, from the firelight flickering over the beautiful face. After a while she said, "Aunt Manya."

Manya turned around and held her arms out. "Katyusha, I'm so glad you're home. I'm in the depths of gloom."

Katherine sat on the hearth bench and put her head on Manya's knee. "What are you gloomy about?"

Manya sighed. "We had an abominable first reading. Everyone is terrible. After all the trouble Oliver Henley and I had recasting the thing over here, nobody is right. I read

255

badly. Sometimes I can't help thinking: Now I'm successful, now I'm at the top, my name in lights, my picture in the papers; but in a few years, when I shall be a far better actress than I am now, perhaps my beauty will be gone, perhaps I'll be forgotten, unable to get a job. Now I'm at the top, but if the play flops here, maybe that'll start me on the downgrade. I don't mean in the quality of my acting. That I control. But in my name, in my popularity. It's bound to happen sooner or later. It always does. I know I'm a fool to let it matter. I know it doesn't, really. But it seems very bleak. Very dreary." She laughed and held her fingers with all their rings out to the blaze. "Maybe you'll have to take to writing me fake fan letters in my old age, Katya. But if you dare!"

Katherine rubbed her head drowsily against Manya's knee. "I'm gloomy, too," she said.

"Why, baby?"

"I'll be eighteen next month. And what have I to show for it?"

"Well, what?" Manya asked.

"Not much, it doesn't seem to me. I ought to be more in control of my playing than I am. Technically I'm all right, but I haven't any emotional control—no ability to sustain. And after all, any fool can acquire technique. And I haven't done much living. You and Mother'd both done much more living than I have when you were my age."

"Had we?"

"Of course!" Impatiently. "I've gone on letting you and Father take care of me. But when I'm eighteen, I'll be of age."

"You're not of age till you're twenty-one."

"You're of age enough to marry."

"Thinking of marriage?"

"No! But I ought to support myself."

Manya shook her gently. "If you're still not supporting yourself by the time you're twenty-one, I won't hold you back. But until then you owe it to your mother, and to your father and to me, to study, to work like the devil at your piano."

"That's what I wanted. To study with Justin in Paris."

"There are other teachers besides Justin, Katherine."

Katherine. So Manya was beginning to get annoyed. She tried to explain. "But it was so *easy* for me to learn from Justin, Aunt Manya."

"Perhaps it would be better for you if it weren't so easy."

"I had all last year with that horrible creature."

"Are you sure he was as bad as all that?"

"I'm sure."

"Well, my child, perhaps it's just a different point of view. I don't suppose age ever has or ever will understand youth."

"That's rubbish."

"It's all right, darling. I know you're upset and I'm not being any help. You feel older now than you ever will in your life. I know the summer was dull for you. And I know you want an apartment of your own. But just thank your old Manya that your father isn't sending you to college. I finally argued him out of it, but it was quite a job."

"Oh, my golly," said Katherine, "I didn't know he wanted that."

"He did. And even if we'd stayed abroad, I don't think he'd have considered allowing you to stay in Paris alone, and I doubt if Charlot and that very nice Pauline of his would have liked having you on their hands for their honeymoon; so I'm afraid studying with Justin would have been impossible in any case. I've made an appointment for you tomorrow at twelve with your mother's old teacher. He's about ninety now, and impossible to get on with, I hear. Julie was

257

practically his last pupil; but he may be able to give you some advice . . . I think we'd better have a drink. A fine way you picked to cheer me up. Your career! Good Lord! What about mine!"

"I *am* grateful, Aunt Manya," Katherine said softly.

"And don't start that again." Manya kissed her lightly on the forehead, went over to the cupboard and got out a bottle of wine.

Katherine saw her mother's old teacher the next morning. Although it was a warm September day, he sat huddled in rugs next to an open fire, complaining bitterly because the steam heat wasn't turned on. Pulling out a crooked pair of steel-rimmed glasses, he looked at her for a long time, first with them on, then with them off.

"Well?" he said. "What did you say your name was?"

"Katherine Forrester."

"Julie Forrester's daughter?" Incredulously.

"Yes."

"You don't look in the least like your mother," he said, taking off his glasses and putting them away as though the interview were over. Katherine stood in front of him, waiting. "Well?" he asked. "What are you hanging around for?"

—This is a fine mess—she thought. In the corner of the room, half buried under piles of music, she saw a piano.

"You'd better close your eyes," she said to him, and went over to it, not looking at him again before she began to play, fearful of losing her courage. She played for quite a while. Not a sound from the bundle of blankets huddled in front of the fireplace. —I'm just going to play till something happens—she thought. Finally she began on some of the things Julie had studied with the old man, hoping this might bring some sort of response. It did. Suddenly he shouted in a voice

258

that had amazing power: "Harold! Harold! Come here at once!"

—Now I'm going to be thrown out—Katherine thought—taken by the scruff of my presumptuous neck and booted out on the street.—

An elderly valet came hurrying in. "Yes, Mr. Peytz? What is it, Mr. Peytz?"

"Clear off that piano!" the old man shouted from his chair. "Clear it off, you cream-faced loon! I can't hear properly! I want the lid raised!"

Harold hastened to sweep the piles of music onto the floor, Katherine helping him, the old man roaring in the meantime, "Can you stand a decrepit and ancient old man for a teacher? Can you, hey?"

Studying with Albert Peytz was not easy, but it was stimulating, and, since he had been Julie's teacher, it reminded her in ways of her lessons with her mother. He demanded so much work of her that after a month Manya had to go and talk with him, to swear loudly and picturesquely at him (for that was the language Albert Peytz best understood), to tell him that he might be a slave driver but that Katherine was not plying the oars in a Roman galley and that it was not necessary for him to flick the whip so constantly. She forbade Katherine to practice more than five hours a day, at least until she had gained back some of the weight she had lost.

But more potent than Manya's threats in cutting down on the work proved to be Pete Burns. Katherine kept meaning to look him up. She knew that he had a good part in Paul LeStrade's latest play, and that his reviews had been splendid. He had talked to Manya over the phone and sent Katherine his regards. She intended to go backstage one night and see him, but somehow she never did. Her lesson

259

fell on the next day, and Mr. Peytz would be angry with her if she didn't know the whole of the presto movement; or she had had a bad lesson the day before and mustn't repeat it.

When she did meet Pete Burns, it was at a Sunday evening concert at Carnegie. She was sitting in the top balcony, but came down during intermission to smoke and collect a few leaflets about other performers. She recognized him at once, standing there smoking, looking bored and a little sullen. As she walked by him, she said softly, "Pete Burns."

He turned. "Why, hello! How are you! It's been centuries, hasn't it?"

She realized that although he knew he knew her, he had no idea who she was. "Quite a long time," she answered "How are you?"

"Fine! Great! How are you? You're looking wonderful! Lovelier every time I see you. Working now?"

"In a way. I'm looking forward to seeing your show. I've heard wonderful things about you."

"Well—" He was pleased and embarrassed. "It's a wonderful part, and perfect for me. It's my first big break, so it means a lot to me. Look, why don't you come and sit with me this half? My date couldn't come at the last minute, and I've got this empty seat—"

"All right," she said. "I'd like to."

"What was that last show you were in?" he asked. "I remember you perfectly in it, and I was trying to think of the name just the other night."

—Oh, Pete, you rat.—"I haven't been in a play for eight years now."

He looked at her, bewildered for a moment, then laughed, sheepishly, ingratiatingly. "All right. I give up. Who the devil are you? I know that I know you quite well, it's infuriating."

260

"Well, the last and only show I was in, you were in too," she said.

"Oh, Lord. Eight years ago. . . . No! My God, no! It isn't the baby!"

"Which baby do you mean?"

"Kitten! But you're grown up! You're a woman! I sent my love to a little girl with long braids down her back."

"You haven't changed much, Pete."

"If I look at you now and think of you then—I must be hoaryheaded and potbellied. Kitten, it's good to see you! Come, let's sit down!"

Pete had seats in a second-tier box. During the next portion of the concert they kept turning and half-smiling at each other. The pianist was dull; once Katherine turned to Pete and whispered, "I can play better than that!"

And he whispered back, "Prove it!"

The bar he took her to afterward was crowded. He knew his way well, pushing through to a small empty table at the very back, almost in the kitchen, shouting greetings to the barkeeper, and to many of the people at the tables. Smoke curled in soft, choking clouds over their heads; there was a strong odor of beer; Katherine sat drinking Scotch and soda and smiling at Pete. She felt comfortable and happy.

"Now," said Pete, "you've had enough." As he took her glass away, it seemed as though they had never been apart, as though he were still the strong Pete who protected her and scolded her whenever he thought it necessary. "Just because—" he began, then stopped.

"Just because what?"

"Nothing, kitten."

"You were going to say just because Mother—?"

"Perhaps."

"That hasn't anything to do with it."

261

"Hasn't it?"

"No."

"O. K. Don't pay any attention to your Uncle Pete. I really haven't any right to try and boss you now that you've grown up, so go ahead and drink. But it's time for us to go home anyhow. I have to get up early for a radio program tomorrow. You'll come to my show tomorrow night?"

"I'd like to."

"O.K. I'll leave a ticket in your name at the box office. Only one, because I want you to go out with me afterward."

"That'll be lovely."

"My God, you've grown up!" he said again.

"What did you expect?"

"I told you. A little girl. A little girl in pigtails. How's Madame Sergeievna's play coming along?"

"Oh, all right now, I think. It opens in a week."

"Been to any rehearsals?"

"A couple, now that they've got a theater."

"What do you think?"

"If it's not a hit, it's a crime."

"What matinee?"

"Thursday."

"Good. I can see it. Come along, kitten. I'll take you home in a taxi. But never expect such service again. I'm still a subway boy, in spite of my present prosperity."

She got into the habit of calling for Pete after his show. She would spend the evening practicing, then take a crosstown bus over to the West Side and walk to Pete's theater. Then they would go to Pete's favorite café, the Purple Pigeon; or sometimes he would buy a bottle of Scotch and they would go to his hotel on Forty-eighth Street; or occasionally Manya would ask them for a late supper with her.

Katherine was very grateful for Pete. Somehow, music

had not been enough to cure the restlessness that obsessed her body and soul. Pete was solid comfort; he was like warming your hands in front of a fire in winter; he was like coming into a darkened room and turning on the lamps; most of all he seemed to her like a small but very seaworthy boat taking her across a large body of water from one point of land to another. This was comforting, because she loved and adored the land she had left and did not know what the land she was approaching would be like. By making the journey easy he seemed to promise that the shore would be pleasant.

"You're very fond of Pete, aren't you?" Manya asked one evening, not long before her play left for a two weeks' try-out in Boston.

"Of course. I always have been. He takes care of me. He's sort of like a hunk of my childhood, of when Mother was alive."

"Falling in love with him?"

"With Pete! Good heavens no! He's like my older brother!"

Sometimes she wondered why Pete did not let her see more of the other members of his company. They seemed pleasant and exciting people to her, but although he looked upon them with complete camaraderie as far as he was concerned, it was with complete disapproval as far as she was concerned. "You're too young and innocent to get mixed up with a shady theater bunch," he tried to explain.

"Good heavens, Pete, I'm eighteen, and I've been mixed up with the theater all my life. After all, Manya Sergeievna is my stepmother."

"That's different."

"Why?"

"Baby, I'm not going to explain. You do as I tell you."

"All right. But I am not as innocent as you think."

"You're a little floosie, then, but I'm going to reform you."

263

At the Purple Pigeon he couldn't prevent people from joining them. He seemed to have been in shows with almost everyone who came in—as well as chorus girls who twined their arms about his neck, kissing him effusively, looking curiously out of the corners of their eyes at Katherine. Heavily painted older women, most of them disappointed leading ladies or out-grown ingenues, who had to struggle desperately now for character roles, would come over to their table and try to get them to move to one of the large tables in the middle of the room; but Pete always refused, sometimes rudely, always with the manner of a king speaking to bothersome subjects. "It won't do you any good to know them, kitten. Maybe we shouldn't come here so often."

"You know them all so well. If you don't like them, why?"

"I have fun with them."

"Why shouldn't I?"

"In the first place, you're not an actress."

"What's that got to do with it?"

"Lots."

This attitude of his she did not understand, but she rather enjoyed being bossed by him. It left her nothing to cope with but her own practicing, and with Albert Peytz as teacher, that was plenty.

One evening, when she was working on a new Bach Fugue, she forgot the time, and when she looked at Julie's watch (still around her wrist with its silver strap) it was eleven-thirty. Pete's show broke at eleven, and she was always there by eleven-five. She flung on her coat and tore downstairs. A cold November rain was falling; street lamps shone in the puddles; her shoes were thin and would be soaked through before she reached the theater. As she stepped out of the house, she saw her bus and started to run, but just as she neared it, waving pleadingly to the driver, it slithered off into the rainy night. The anger, the misery, the humiliation of it! The bus lumbered down the street, disregarding the small furious figure on the corner that was ready to weep with desperation. She would probably have to wait fifteen minutes before another bus came along. It would be almost quicker to walk, and even so, Pete would be sure to have left, he would think she wasn't coming, he would be angry with her, he would think she was standing him up, and if there was one thing Pete couldn't bear it was being stood up.

Rain beat against her face. She had forgotten her hat, and her hair became a heavy, wet mass coiled icily about her head. The few remaining leaves of the trees struggling to grow in small square patches cut in the cement sidewalk caught the light from the street lamps and shone like small dark mirrors. Katherine saw a taxi and waved to it. Incredibly, it was empty. If, on a rainy night, a taxi came by and was empty, perhaps Pete might have waited for her after all.

The taxi crawled across town like a wet, half-drowned bug. Rain beat against the windows and against the square insert of glass in the roof. The rain was so heavy now and flooded the windows with such a continuous stream that when she peered out, it was like looking at a city under water. The figures passing on the street, collars up, hats down, wavered strangely as they moved. The tall trunks of lampposts were not straight, but crooked as lightning. Shop windows spilled their yellow light, which seemed to mingle with the rain and become part of it. Oil from the cars made the deep puddles in the street shine with the colors of the spectrum as they caught the light.

Katherine reached into her coat pocket and found she had forgotten her money. Panic seized her. It was a quarter to twelve. Pete would never have waited. Thank heaven, there was Bill, the doorman!

The taxi drew up at the stage door. "Wait a minute, please," she told the driver, and ran down the long narrow alley, where the rain dripped in cold streams from the fire escapes. She opened the stage door and rushed in. "Bill, is Pete here?" she gasped.

"No, honey, he left about fifteen minutes ago," Bill told her. "He was waiting for you. Seemed kind of mad because you didn't come. Phoned you a couple of times, but didn't get no answer. Sugar, you're soaked to the skin. Watch out you don't get pneumonia."

"Oh, I'll be all right. I never catch cold. Bill, I've got a taxi outside, and I forgot my money. Can you lend me a couple of dollars? I'll pay you back tomorrow night."

"Sure thing, doll," he said, fishing in his pocket. "I'll go out and pay it for you. Mr. LeStrade's still here, and he'll want a taxi. I'll tell it to wait. If he comes out, you tell him I've gone to hold him a taxi."

Katherine sat down on the air cushion Bill kept on his chair. She could hear Paul LeStrade whistling in his dressing room. She wondered why he was so late; usually he was off with some little blonde ten minutes after the curtain fell. Now he came out of his dressing room alone, looking very splendid and almost as young as he would have liked to look.

As he noticed Katherine, he raised his eyebrows for a moment, then remembered that she was usually around after the performance and probably wasn't looking for his autograph.

"Is it still raining?" he asked her. "You seem very wet." It was the first time he had condescended to speak to her.

"Yes," she said. "It's very wet. Bill said to tell you he was holding a taxi for you, Mr. LeStrade." She had stood up

266

when he spoke to her, partly because she still had the school-girl habit of standing when an older person addressed her, and partly because she respected him as an actor, no matter what Pete might say about his private life and his little blondes.

"If Bill is holding a taxi for me, I'd better drop you off," he said. "You look too wet to go on plowing about in the rain."

"Thank you very much, but I'm not going anywhere in particular. I've got to find someone I was supposed to meet. The only reason I'm here now is that I've got to borrow a nickel from Bill to get home on. I forgot my money."

Mr. LeStrade drew a ten-dollar bill out of his wallet and handed it to her. "You shouldn't go around with only a nickel. Take this."

"Thank you, but a nickel is really all I need. I've just got to have the nickel, in case I don't find the person I'm looking for."

"Whom are you looking for?"

"Peter Burns."

"Oh. The young man who's stealing the show, eh? Stood you up, has he?"

"No! I was going to meet him here, and I was late and just got here a minute ago, so of course he thought I wasn't coming and left."

Bill came back in. He was quite wet just from going through the alley to the taxi and back. "I have a taxi waiting for you, Mr. LeStrade," he said.

"Thank you. That's very considerate of you." Mr. Le-Strade put his wallet away and turned back to Katherine. "Now, where are you going to look for this young man of yours?"

"Oh, just about."

267

"You must have some idea where you're going, child."

"Well, I thought maybe I'd go and look in the Purple Pigeon."

"All right. We'll go to the Purple Pigeon together. You're too wet to go out in the rain by yourself and get wetter. Besides, it's late."

Katherine did not want to go with Mr. LeStrade, but she didn't know how to refuse. She had a feeling that if she found Pete while she was with the older actor, Pete would not like it at all. But she followed Mr. LeStrade out into the alley, and climbed uncomfortably into the taxi as he held the door open for her.

"Now. What is your name?" he asked, leaning back against the slippery leather seat.

"Katherine Forrester."

"Forrester. Any relation to Manya Sergeievna? Isn't she married to that composer, Forrester?"

"Yes. She's my stepmother."

"Oh. So I suppose you go to the American Academy. You're planning to be an actress, of course."

"No."

"No? Oh, so you're going to marry your young man."

"Pete? Good gracious, no. He's just a friend."

"You seem very anxious to find this friend. Is this the right place? Is this where you want to look for him?"

"Yes. Thank you very much for dropping me off."

"I'm not dropping you off. I'm coming in with you." Telling the driver to wait, Mr. LeStrade opened the door for her.

But Pete wasn't at the Purple Pigeon. The barkeeper recognized her as she came in, a little ahead of Mr. LeStrade, and called to her. "Pete was here, looking for you a while ago, but he's gone on."

"Oh. Thanks," she said, and turned back to Mr. LeStrade.

"Well," he said, "now what are you going to do?"

"I guess I'll go to his hotel."

"Where is it?"

"Forty-eighth Street."

"I'll take you there."

"Oh, please don't bother. It's just down the street. I can walk there perfectly easily. I'm so wet it doesn't matter if I get any wetter. Besides, I never catch cold."

"You come along with me," Mr. LeStrade said, and she had to follow him.

She felt trapped. It was really very singular behavior, she thought, for a star, to take a taxi and conduct a strange, drenched young woman about town on a search for a young man who had stolen the notices from him in his latest play.

The taxi pulled up in front of Pete's hotel, and she hurried into the lobby, making for the house phone. "Mr. Burns' room, please, 70," she said.

No answer came from Pete's room, and she had to hang up and go to the desk. "Did Mr. Burns leave any message for me?" she asked the night clerk, but he shook his head.

"Well?" Mr. LeStrade asked her.

"I don't know. There're a couple more night clubs I can try. You've been awfully kind to help me. Thank you ever so much."

But he wasn't going to leave her in the lobby of Pete's hotel. "Perhaps he's gone to your home?" he suggested.

"No. There wouldn't be anyone to let him in. Aunt Manya's in Boston with her play, and Father's off on a lecture tour."

"You're all alone there at night? No servants?"

"Not till noon. And there's no point in Dunyasha's staying late when Aunt Manya's not there to get supper for, because I'd expected to go out with Pete."

"Well, you'd better come to my hotel with me and have a drink to warm you up. You're shivering."

"Oh, no, thank you very much. I'm all right. Truly."

"You need a drink. Come along," he said, taking her by the arm.

The taxi was still waiting for them when they left Pete's hotel. She knew that Mr. LeStrade had rooms in several hotels so that there would be no trouble between any of his five ex-wives, and she wondered where they would go. Fortunately, the hotel he named was quite close, and they didn't have a long taxi ride. The elevator in the hotel was like the lobby, all gilt and mirrors, and they went up and up. The suite he took her to was evidently one of his least personal apartments. There was nothing about it to mark it as belonging to anyone. Not a picture. Not a book. It was like a hotel room before the luggage of the new occupant has been brought in. But both the twin beds in the bedroom were turned down for the night, and a pair of black silk pajamas was laid out on one. Mr. LeStrade called downstairs for a bottle of whisky, explaining that his wife (though he didn't say which one) was in Hollywood, while Katherine went to the window and looked down on the wet lights of the city below, which shone and quivered like reflections in a lake.

All of a sudden she felt his arm about her. "Perhaps you don't realize it, but I've been watching you every evening when you've come back to meet your young man."

She knew this was not true. In the first place, she was not Mr. LeStrade's type. In the second place, he was so busy with his wife-of-the-evening and the autograph hunters who had managed to get backstage or were waiting out in the alley that he had no time for her. So she said nothing.

But he did not seem to expect an answer. "You have a very intelligent, sensitive, lovely little face. I think you must have suffered, in spite of being so young. How old are you? No, don't tell me. You could be anywhere between fifteen and twenty-eight, and I don't want to know where in the procession of years you come. So you don't want to be an actress, and that incredible young actor Peter Burns is only a friend to you. I am glad of that, at any rate; you are far too good for him. So. I look at that little face and those eyes and all that wet dark hair and those eyelashes wet from rain as though from tears, and I think, if this little thing is not an actress, she must be an artist of some kind. Do you paint? Do you sing?"

"I play the piano."

"Do you play it well?"

"Yes," she said, for even to a famous actor like Mr. Le-Strade she could not minimize her ability. She wished he would take his arm away.

"Let me see your hands," he said. She held them out. Turning her away from the dark mirror of the window, he held her hands under a lamp. "Yes," he said. "Those are a pianist's hands. They have the breadth and the strength. Someday you must play for me. I have a very fine Steinway."

A waiter came up with a tray on which were two glasses with ice, soda water, and a bottle of Scotch. Mr. LeStrade fixed her a very stiff drink, which she swallowed quickly because she felt chilled to the marrow, and her marrow, if indeed she had any by this time, was frozen solid. All this in spite of the heat that was coming up through the radiator pipes. But the whisky warmed her quickly, burning its way cleanly down her throat.

Mr. LeStrade held her face to his and tried to kiss her; turning aside, she pressed her mouth against the expensive, dark wool of his coat, so that his kiss landed on her neck. She pulled away and said firmly, although she was very fright-

271

ened, "Thank you very much for the taxi and the whisky. I've got to go home now. I have a lesson tomorrow morning, and if I don't get a good night's sleep and play well, my teacher will be very angry."

To her surprise, Mr. LeStrade made no objection. He simply dropped his hands and said without a trace of irritation, "All right, darling, if that's the way you want it," and poured himself another drink as she opened the door.

Once she was down on the street, she remembered again that she had no money, and it was a long walk home. This time she could not take a taxi and expect someone to pay for it, since Manya's apartment was half of a private house and there was no doorman. Neither could she go back to Mr. LeStrade to ask for help.

The rain had settled into a steady, thin drizzle. She could feel the fresh cold and wet oozing from the pavement through the thin soles of her shoes, and soon she could feel the actual slosh of the water against her stockinged feet. Her hair kept getting heavier and heavier as it got wetter, until all she wanted was to take a pair of scissors and cut off the masses of braids. She was so exhausted that it was impossible to walk quickly. It took her over an hour to get home.

Once in the apartment, she turned on all the lights, lit the fire and drew herself a hot bath. The effect of Mr. LeStrade's Scotch had worn off, and she was shivering and wretched again. She sat in the hot tub until her skin was bright red and she was pouring with sweat. Then she put on her pajamas, wrapped herself in an old dressing gown of her father's and crouched in front of the fire to dry her hair. Now there were too many lights, and her eyes ached; when she got up to turn off the lights, she paused at the liquor cabinet and poured herself a stiff drink of brandy. Then she crouched in front of the fire again, holding long strands of her hair out to the blaze. Although the brandy made her drunk, she was careful not to let her hair get near the flames. —I've no wish to set myself on fire—she thought, and sat there, the grateful warmth pouring into her until the fire crumbled down to a few red coals. Then she stumbled into bed and fell asleep.

She was awakened by the telephone. She took off the receiver, to hear Pete's furious voice.

"Katherine! Where were you last night?"

She thought of her frantic hunt for Pete; the inside of her throat was hot and sore; she was angry with him for being angry. "What do you mean, where was I?" Her voice was a hoarse croak.

This he didn't seem to notice. "I kept calling till after three. A fine way for you to behave, the minute Madame Sergeievna goes out of town and leaves you alone. You were supposed to meet me after the show."

"I did."

"What do you mean, you did? I stayed till almost midnight."

"I was practicing, and I forgot about the time. And then when I got to the theater, Bill said you'd just left."

"Well, why the hell didn't you come home? What did you do then? That was just midnight. I kept calling you till after three. Where were you?"

She could not tell Pete she had been hunting for him.

"I just went out and had a drink."

"Alone?"

"No. I was with someone."

"Who?"

"Do you have to know everyone I see, Pete?"

"Are you going to deign to meet me after the show tonight?"

"Of course. I'm awfully sorry about last night."

"Like hell you are."

"Honestly I am, Pete."

"You were so sorry you couldn't come home and wait for me the way you would have if you'd had any sense, but had to go out drinking with someone else."

"Don't scold me, Pete. I've an awful sore throat."

"Serves you right. And drinking isn't a glamorous thing, my girl. Causes a lot of unnecessary and stupid messes. And you do far too much of it, especially for someone your age."

"I *won't* be scolded!" she cried, and hung up.

It was a bad music lesson. It was a bad day. Her throat hurt so that she could hardly swallow; her head ached; her eyes stung; when the cook, Dunyasha, scolded her for not eating, she wanted to burst into tears or to throw something; instead, she glowered down at the bright polished surface of the table, clenching her teeth until the tears stopped trembling in her eyes. She got to the theater to meet Pete before the curtain went up on the last act.

Mr. LeStrade came out of his dressing room just as Pete came out of his. "Well, my little friend of last night," Mr. LeStrade said, coming up to her and kissing her as though he had known her intimately all his life, "how are you to-night?"

"Fine, thank you."

"Did you get home all right last night?"

"Oh, yes."

"You'd better take care of this little girl, Mr. Burns," Mr. LeStrade said to Pete. "I think she needs to have someone take care of her."

"I'll take care of her, you needn't worry, Mr. LeStrade," Pete said. "Are you ready, Katherine?"

274

When they were out in the alley, the cement still holding puddles from the rain the night before, Pete grabbed her arm with such ferocity that she cried out in pain. "So you were out with him last night."

"Yes, I was. Please let go my arm, Pete. You're hurting."

"Where did you go with him?"

"To his hotel."

"Which of the five?"

"That's my own business."

"You went up to his rooms alone with him?"

"I can take care of myself, Pete."

"Well, it certainly doesn't seem so."

"He just said he'd give me a drink before I went home—after I'd missed you, of course."

"So you stayed with him till after three. I'm ashamed of you, Katherine."

"You haven't anything to be ashamed of."

"Are you sure?"

"Naturally."

"He didn't try any of his funny business?"

"No. He was very nice about it."

"Nice or not, I don't like your seeing him, and I don't want you to go out with him again."

"I run my own life, Pete."

"That's all very fine, but you're not to go out with him again. What would Madame Sergeievna say?"

"Aunt Manya trusts me, whether you do or not."

"Why the hell couldn't you have gone home and waited for me?" Pete said savagely. "I wanted to talk to you last night."

"You can talk to me tonight, can't you?"

"I wanted to talk to you last night. I had it all planned. It was going to be a very special night. Oh, skip it. We'll go to the Purple Pigeon, and you are not to have more than two drinks."

"All right, Pete. I'll do whatever you say."

At the Purple Pigeon she sat supporting her aching head in her hands. Smoke stung her eyes; voices roared in her ears like a mighty, malignant ocean; her back ached so that she could not sit still in her chair but kept squirming miserably, trying unsuccessfully to get into a comfortable position.

"Please, Pete, let's go to your hotel," she wailed.

He looked at her flushed face, at her eyes with the deep circles under them, and asked anxiously, "Throat still sore?"

"Yes. Awfully. The smoke hurts it. Please let's go to your hotel."

"All right, kitten little. Of course. Come on. But maybe I'd better take you home to bed."

"I want to go to your hotel and have another drink."

He realized that she was not fit to be argued with. "All right. Come along."

Once she got up to his room, she flung herself down on his bed. Immediately the room began to go around in slow, gentle circles. "Around and around, like the pavane of the stars," she said.

"What?"

"Nothing. Pour me a drink, please."

He stood by his washbasin and rinsed out a glass. The electric-light bulb that hung from the ceiling swung slightly, and his shadow on the whitewashed wall swung, too, so that he seemed to be dancing a grotesque undulating dance as he rinsed the glass and poured some whisky into it. The dance frightened her, and she closed her eyes. As darkness rushed upon her, she seemed to be sinking; the bed must somehow have disappeared, and she was falling down, down into the bottomless pit. She opened her eyes quickly. Pete was bending over her with the glass of whisky.

"Are you all right, kitten?"

"Sure, I'm fine," she answered hoarsely, raising herself on one elbow to drink the whisky. Like fire it burnt its way down inside her, like strong, cleansing fire. The light bulb still swung from the ceiling, and the shadows of the furniture danced weirdly as the room swam around. She did not know whether it was worse to have her eyes open and to watch this grinning senseless dance (for it seemed to have a personality, to be leering at her diabolically) or to close her eyes and feel herself dropping through darkness, through unmeasured space.

"Look," she heard Pete say. "For an actor, I can be very inarticulate. But there's something I want to say to you." He stood with his back to her, looking out the window, breathing quickly and audibly.

"Look," Pete said, leaving the window to sit down on the edge of the bed beside her, and taking hold of one of her hands and twisting the fingers. "Look, I've wanted to say this for a long time now, and I meant to do it last night. I had it all prepared for last night. I could have done it beautifully then, but now for some reason it's very hard. Look," he said, and lapsed into silence again.

Katherine had barely heard him. Her mind kept swinging around in vague taunting circles, like the room and the dancing shadows, and she remembered suddenly the whirling merry-go-round at the *kermesse* and thought—I didn't learn anything from Charlot, I didn't learn anything at all, because here I am with Pete, and I don't know anything, I don't know anything, I don't know what to do or what to say.—

"Look," Pete said, "I love you and I want to marry you. Will you?"

She couldn't say anything. She didn't know why, but she couldn't open her mouth to say yes, although she knew now that the answer was yes and always had been yes to Pete. She looked down at his big hand, because of the way it was twisting her fingers, and she began to cry and she thought —I'm crazy, I don't know what's the matter with me, I'm so happy, I'm crying, and then there's this awful cloud coming over me, and I can't see, I'm afraid.—

She cried very quietly, and Pete was unaware of it until his fingers became wet with her tears.

"Look," he said again. "I know your music means more to you than I do. It'll always mean more to you than anyone in the world. And that's right. That's good. That's the way I am about the theater. And it won't make any difference to your music if you marry me, because we're both that way about what we care about. If I were a businessman, who wanted to arrange your time to suit mine, it would be different, but it wouldn't be that way, it—" And then he felt his fingers close to her cheek wet with her tears.

"Oh, don't—" he whispered, his face appalled and frightened. He looked at her face drenched and blurred with tears, and she looked into his gray eyes with their thick, short, black lashes, his gray eyes that were trying to find out what was making her cry, and his face was so puckered and puzzled and loving that all of a sudden her tears stopped; the room stood still; the shadows stopped their dance against the whitewashed walls.

"I love you, too, Pete," she said. "I want to marry you." She pressed close to him, rubbing her face against the harsh, dark wool of his coat, until his hand came down under her chin and he raised her face and looked into her eyes for a long time before he kissed her.

When he kissed her, they both seemed to become very weak, almost to melt into each other, and they had to lean close together, gasping for breath. They kissed again with a sort of franticness, as though in a moment some terrible invisible power would tear them apart; they clung together desperately, trying to press so near that no part of their bodies would be really separate. Because they had both wanted to kiss for so long, because they had never really touched each other before, they were afraid to stop, and they strained with their whole bodies pushing against each other for a long time before Katherine moved away suddenly and said, "I keep forgetting, but my throat is very sore, and you don't want to catch cold and have to miss a performance."

"I'm not afraid of you," Pete said, drawing her close to him again.

"Yes, but I am." Katherine pulled away. "I don't want to give you anything. I feel very funny, Pete."

"How, funny, kitten?"

"I ache all over, not just my throat; and my head is very big, like a balloon, and I'm so hot. Could we have the window open, please?"

"It is open. It's quite cold here."

"But I'm hot," Katherine said, getting up and going over to the window, pushing it up as far as it would go. The rain had turned to snow, a soft quiet snow that fell gently, with the lightness of breathing, and that seemed serene and friendly after the hurried beating of the rain of the night before.

"Pete, would you take me home, please?" she asked.

They left the hotel in silence. Out on the street Pete

279

stopped, and Katherine watched the small dry powdery snowflakes drop onto his eyelashes and cling there. He was watching the snow fall onto her, too, dusting her thick masses of dark hair with glistening white.

"You ought to wear a hat. I'm going to take you home in a taxi," he said.

"No. Please let's walk."

"It's too far."

"We've done it plenty of times before."

"You're in no condition to walk tonight."

"Well, just a little way, at any rate. The wind on my face is just what I need. I feel hot and smothered. If we walk some, maybe I can breathe."

She did not know whether she had said these words consciously or subconsciously. She knew they were familiar. Searching back through the devious channels of her mind, she remembered. These were the words, or at least they were very similar to the words, that Julie had spoken before she went out on that terrible day when she was so ill. Katherine remembered almost every word Julie had said that day. They were branded in her memory with a white-hot iron of pain, seared into her forever. —Only—she thought—I do not think I am going to die.—

Nonetheless, she clutched Pete's arm very tightly as they walked along, lifting her hot face to the cool drift of snow. The people they passed suddenly began making hideous faces at her. One man stuck out a long bifurcated tongue like a serpent's and flicked it at her. A woman, heavily made up, but rather beautiful, suddenly spat all her teeth into her outstretched palm, and the teeth lay there, grinning gumlessly at her. When the woman put them back into her mouth, she turned into Miss Halsey.

"Pete," Katherine said, relieved to hear her voice coming

out almost normally. "I think I have DT's. How much whisky did you give me?"

"Not enough for that," Pete said. "Why, baby? What's the matter?"

Katherine decided not to explain. "I'm going to be a tee-totalitarian. That's what they're called, isn't it? And go around to all the bars and cafés with a hatchet and make everybody stop drinking. I'll give speeches on the evils of booze and wear my hatchet over my shoulder, like that woman out West, what was her name? They made a movie about her. I think Marlene Dietrich played her. Anyhow, she wore pants, and got her man in the end, and everybody learned that liquor is a devil."

At this all the houses on either side of the street began to grin at her evilly and leaned toward her, so that it seemed she could feel their heavy breath.

"I think I'd like to get home quicker than on my feet," she said. "Get a taxi, Pete, quick."

But a taxi late on a snowy night is not easy to get quickly. Pete had a shrill taxi-calling whistle, but all the taxis going by were full.

All the taxis going by were strange creatures, animate in themselves, and each one, at the sound of Pete's whistle, jumped or reared up or reacted in some strange and lurid way.

"I'm sure this one's empty," Pete said, and whistled piercingly.

At this noise not only did Katherine's head split open so that the snow could fall into it uninterruptedly, but the top of the taxi burst open too, and out of the gaping rent was blown a man in top hat and tails. He was Mr. LeStrade, and he was blown up and up until he was lost over the roofs of the buildings.

"Is this taxi safe?" Katherine asked anxiously, laying a restraining hand on Pete's arm.

"Sure, kitten, of course," he said reassuringly, leading her toward it.

"We won't get blown out?"

"No, sweetheart." And he opened the door and helped her in. She leaned against him, squeezing her eyes tight shut, so that she should not see the taxi driver, who was not a man at all but a gorilla in a bright-red sweater. But it would never do to tell Pete this.

"Are you all right, kitten?"

She nodded, burying her face against his shoulder.

"I'll make you some hot lemonade," he said, "and you'll feel better once you get into bed."

He spoke quietly, not sounding at all worried. Then he did not know the dreadful things she was seeing, the strange twists and turns her mind was taking. At all costs he must not know, or he might not love her any more.

The gorilla finally pulled the taxi up in front of a house. It was a strange house that Katherine had never seen before, made entirely of shocking-pink marble. She thought for a moment of telling Pete that she did not live here, but as he paid the gorilla, who had fortunately (and it was fortunately, she was sure, although she did not know why) turned into a rosy-red flamingo, she decided that she would go wherever Pete wanted to take her.

When she got out of the taxi and a sharp blast of wind from the river struck like a whip across her face, her mind cleared. They went into the house and up the stairs, and it was quite safely Manya's apartment; if she reached out her hand, the light switch was on the wall on the right by the big white bookcase.

She did not turn on the light. Suddenly she and Pete were pressed together again in the darkness, very close all the way down, his lips on hers, their arms clinging desperately, their torsos and legs pushing together as though in a denial of the body's power to keep people apart. Then her arms seemed to lose their strength to cling, her body to press against his, even to stand, and he was holding her, saving her, and her mouth was open and her whole body was on fire, burning up and becoming air.

After a time she realized that Pete had picked her up and carried her into the bedroom, and that she was lying on her bed. Quite clearly she said, "I'm a phoenix. I burned all up, and out of my ashes I sprang again."

"What, sweetheart?"

"I'm all right now, Pete. I feel much better. Go into the living room and light the fire and I'll get undressed."

"You'd better get right into bed."

"My hair's wet from the snow. I want to dry it in front of the fire. Besides, I'm all right now. Something burst inside my head when you kissed me, and I burned all up like the phoenix and I'm clear again. Clear as crystal. Don't you worry."

She undressed very guardedly, looking around the room from time to time to make sure that nothing in it turned into anything else. But everything remained normal. Her throat was a burning column of liquid fire, iron bands were tightening closer every second around her head, but in spite of the pain, or perhaps because of it, her mind remained clear, her desk remained a desk, the bed a bed. All the furniture obligingly stayed furniture and did not turn into something with an animate and evil life of its own.

She came into the living room and sat down on the hearth bench in front of the fire Pete had built. He was not in the room, but in a moment he came back with a steaming glass of lemonade wrapped in a dish towel.

"Here, kitten little," he said. "I put some spike in it, but not much. I don't think all this whisky's good for your cold."

She held the lemonade in both hands, sipping the hot sweet syrup slowly, while Pete unbraided her hair and held the soft, damp strands out to the blaze.

"A boy I used to loathe," he said, "used to talk about his desire to run barefoot through people's hair. I know now what he meant."

"I have too much of it," Katherine said. "I think I'll cut it."

"If you dare!"

"Mother wore her hair very short, and it was so nice."

"Darling," Pete said slowly. "I adored your mother. She was a great and wonderful woman. But you've got to grow up to be yourself, you know, and not a shadow of someone you could never really resemble."

"I know, Pete. You're quite right. It's just that Mother was always so firm and strong—she always knew everything."

"Perhaps she just never let you know when she didn't."

"I'm glad you haven't got the lamps on, Pete. It's nice just with the fire."

"When will you marry me?" he asked.

"Whenever you say."

"What about Paris and studying with that Justin of yours?"

"You're Paris. You're more than Paris."

"Shall we tell your father and Madame Sergeievna right away?"

"Oh, Pete!" she said. "Aunt Manya'll be your stepmother-in-law!"

"That's why I'm marrying you," he said. "Didn't you know?"

"I've finished my lemonade," she said. "I suppose I'd better go to bed. My hair's about dry."

He took the glass away from her, picked her up, and carried her into her bedroom. She lay quietly in his arms and stayed very still when he put her on the bed and pulled the covers over her. Bending down, he kissed her very softly, as one kisses a very small child, little gentle kisses on her eyes and cheeks; then he tiptoed noiselessly away.

But before he reached the door, the lamp in the corner suddenly began to nod up and down, grinning at her insanely. Her mind, which had been so clear and safe since he kissed her in the hall, was filled with the dirty waves that come after a storm. "Pete!" she almost screamed. "Stay just five minutes!"

He came back into the room and stood looking down at her. "Is your throat worse?"

"No. I'm all right, I'm all right. Just stay with me for five minutes."

He lay down beside her, on the eiderdown, putting his arms around her. Immediately she fell asleep. When she woke up, she no longer felt the firm heaviness of his body through the eiderdown. Opening her eyes, she saw him standing by her, shaking a thermometer.

"I'm going to take your temperature," he said. "I should have thought of it long ago. I found the thermometer in your Aunt Manya's bathroom. If you have any temp, you've got to see a doctor first thing in the morning. Put this under your tongue."

She opened her mouth obediently and lay looking up at Pete. She saw now that his eyes with their short, straight, black lashes sticking out were indeed very worried. Had he realized, then, the strange things her mind had been doing all evening?

285

He looked at his watch carefully, then drew the thermometer out of her mouth and held it under the lamp. "All right," he said, "we won't wait till morning. You've got to see a doctor tonight."

"It's much too late."

"I don't care how late it is. You're going to see a doctor."

"Have I got very much, then?"

"None of your business."

"Who else's business is it?"

"Kitten, my darling, I want you to see a doctor. Now what's your doctor's name, so I can look up his phone number?"

The lamp in the corner was nodding and leering at her again. She sprang out of bed and went running through the cold halls, her eiderdown about her shoulders, a corner of it flapping against her legs. Pete came tearing after her.

"Where do you think you're going!" he shouted.

"If I'm going to die, I want to die in Aunt Manya's room." She looked at him, thinking how stupid he was not to understand. "I like the lamps in Aunt Manya's room better."

He carried her quickly into Manya's room and laid her on the bed, tucking the eiderdown around her. "Now, give me your doctor's name," he said. "Katherine! What is your doctor's name?"

"I don't remember Aunt Manya's doctor. It's a long Russian name. Mother used to have Dr. Jack Bradley, but Aunt Manya doesn't like him."

"B-r-a-d-l-e-y?"

"Yes."

"Is he the one who wanted to marry your mother?"

"Yes. How did you know?"

"It was town gossip. I just wanted to know because it will

be a good way to identify you to him. How long since you've seen him?"

"Not since I was ten."

Pete was talking busily, in a matter-of-fact voice as he leafed through the phone book. "Thank God, the bastard hasn't a private number. Residence," he said, mumbling the number to himself before he dialed it. Katherine could hear the phone ringing and ringing before it was answered.

"Dr. Bradley?" Pete said into the phone. "This is Peter Burns. I'm calling for Katherine Forrester. She is the daughter of Julie Forrester, whom I believe you knew."

Katherine heard what sounded like a snarl at the other end of the wire, but Pete went on. "She has a very high temperature, too high to wait until morning. If you could possibly come . . . That's swell, thank you." And he gave the address, said "That's swell, thank you," again, and hung up.

"He's coming over," he said to Katherine. "Now try to sleep, baby."

"There is a man standing in front of Aunt Manya's bureau," Katherine said distinctly. "Don't let him take Mother's sapphire earrings." This was the first time she had not been able to control to a certain extent the words she was going to say to Pete. "Make him go away! Don't let him take Mother's earrings!" she wailed, burying her face against Pete's shoulder.

"It's all right, dearest darling," he said. "I won't let him take anything. Sleep now. Sleep till the doctor comes."

"You won't go away?"

"I'll stay right here."

"But don't catch my cold, will you?"

"I won't."

She lay down, clutching his hand again, and drifted

quickly into sleep, sleep that was somehow like plunging into the fiery furnace of Shadrach, Meshach and Abednego. But through the wild hot breath that burned her cheeks, that was consuming her, she heard Pete quoting softly the lines from Shakespeare that every actor knows:

> "Sleep dwell in thine eyes, peace in thy breast;—
> Would I were sleep and peace, so sweet to rest!"

"Kitten. Kitten. The doctor's here." She heard Pete's voice, and she opened her eyes, only to close them again quickly, because the beautiful words that seemed to be brushing gently against her mind like butterflies disappeared as she saw two skeletons wearing men's suits leaning over her. She heard words coming out of her mouth, but she did not know what they were. There was a feeling of being forcibly taken away from Manya's bed, a shrill wailing, and the throb of wheels moving under her. There were the white walls of a room closing in on her and crushing her. There were pills which she swallowed, a great upheaval inside her as she vomited into a curved white pan, more pills, and a sleep as black as velvet. The only thing that was clear was sitting up in bed and screaming furiously, "I will not die! I absolutely and positively refuse to die!"

She did not die. Sulfa drugs brought the fever down and left her weak and exhausted, but with her brain gratefully clear.

Dr. Bradley stood by her bed. "Well, hello, Katy."

"Hello."

"You don't think I'm a skeleton this morning?"

"My goodness, did I think that?"

"You did. Feeling better?"

"I'm all right. May I go home?"

"Well, not for a while yet."

"Why not?" Impatiently.

He laughed. "I see you have a little of Julie in you. Let me see. How long has it been since I've seen you? About eight years?"

"About."

"It doesn't seem four years since she died . . . and it seems forty. That was her locket."

"Yes."

"You fought like a little wildcat to keep it on."

"I did?" Then suddenly, without any warning, a thought stabbed into her mind. "I've got to see Pete!" she cried.

"Your young man?"

"Yes. I've got to see him."

"All right, Katy, but I don't want you to have any visitors for a couple of days."

"I've got to see Pete."

"You'll have to wait."

"I can't! It's terribly important!" She sat up wildly.

Dr. Bradley pushed her gently down on her pillows. "Katherine. Do you want to send your temperature up again?"

"No, but please let me see Pete, please let me see him, please!"

"Why is it so important?"

"I've got to tell him about Charlot!"

"What about Charlot?"

"I've got to tell Pete about him, please, I've simply got to, my temperature will go up again if I don't see him, honestly it will. Please, please, Dr. Bradley!"

"If your temperature stays down all day, you can see him tomorrow."

"Please—today!"

"No, Katherine. It's no use arguing. You'll have to wait and see if your temperature stays down."

"Do you think it will stay down?"

"If you have anything like the recuperative power of your mother, it will. Where is your father? Where is that Manya Sergeievna? Why aren't they taking better care of you? Julie wouldn't like this at all."

"Father's on the coast on his lecture tour and Aunt Manya's in Boston with her play. She opens in New York next week. After all, they didn't know I was going to get flu."

"Well, she's run herself up a pretty bill with telephone calls. I never could gather where she was, or what she was doing, or why she couldn't come back to town unless you were dying."

"She was having dress rehearsals and rewritings for New York and all kinds of things. Of course she couldn't come!"

"She left you all alone in that apartment? No one to take care of you?"

"I'm perfectly capable of taking care of myself. I'm not ten years old any longer. And the cook comes in at noon every day. I'm sorry Pete woke you up so late the other night. I told him to wait till morning, but he wouldn't."

"It's a good thing he didn't. Or your precious Manya Sergeievna might have had to come back from Boston. When anything hits you, it hits you hard, doesn't it?"

"Yes. But I didn't die, at any rate."

"No. You didn't die."

Pete came the next afternoon. He bent over the bed, kissing her gently, smoothing back the hair from her forehead with tender clumsy hands.

"You didn't catch anything from me?" she asked anxiously.

"No, kitten. Look at me. Bursting with health."

290

She pulled him down to her. "Do I look like the last act of *Camille?*" she whispered. "Marguerite Gautier on her deathbed?"

"Exactly."

"Only you aren't Armand Duval. You're someone Marguerite never met. You'd never throw money at me and strike me and knock me down, would you?"

"If I thought you were unfaithful to me, there's no telling what I might not do."

"Pete," she said, pushing him away quickly. "There's something I have to tell you."

—Why do I have to tell him about Charlot?—she thought miserably. —After the way he behaved about Mr. LeStrade and everything. I'm so scared. I'm so scared. If he hates me because of it, I can't bear it; but I've got to tell him, and if he hates me and doesn't understand, it will prove we could never understand or know each other, and I will want to die; I will want to die, but I've got to tell him.—

He took both her hands tightly in his. "You've got to marry me. You can't change your mind, even if you were delirious when you accepted me."

"I haven't changed my mind. But, Pete."

"What, kitten little?"

"There was a boy. Charlot. Charles Bejart. Aunt Manya's adopted son. He's in Paris now, and he's going to be married. He loved Mother very much, and once . . . once for a while he thought he was in love with me. And we went to a *kermesse.* Down on the water front. Lake Geneva. Merry-go-rounds and ferris wheels. The man who ran the ferris wheel was horrible and dirty. And I was so unhappy, and Charlot was unhappy, too. And he reminded me of Justin. He looked so much like him. He even talked like him . . . It wasn't that I was ever—ever in love with Justin, you know, it was quite different . . . only that was partly why. And I was terribly drunk. And it didn't seem wrong, Pete. It just seemed something perfectly natural. And sort of inevitable. But maybe that was because . . ."

"Because of what, dear?"

"Oh, I don't know. Maybe because of being drunk . . . Well . . . that's what I had to tell you . . . If you don't love me now . . ."

Pete's hand went on clumsily and tenderly stroking her forehead. "Look, kitten little, I think I'd better do some talking, too. How could what you've just told me make me stop loving you? I love you more, if anything. But I've got to tell you some things, too."

"All right, Pete."

"I've wanted you. I've wanted you since the first evening I saw you at Carnegie and you told me you were the same little girl I'd known eight years ago. And it's only because I knew it was more than just wanting you that I didn't try to get you right away. But there's been so much more than just that in my feeling for you, and I've known for so long that I wanted to marry you, and I knew I could wait and that I should wait. But look, kitten. There've been lots of other girls I've wanted, and that was all, and I've had them. And I've hurt some of them badly. Not for several years now, but I used to do dreadful things to people, and not even care . . . But I think the fact that I've hurt other people and know it will keep me from hurting you . . . But I've been bad, my darling, and I'm not even afraid to tell you, because I know you'll understand. I promise you that I'm clean and healthy. I haven't done anything that could ever hurt you in that way. But I've been very wild in my day, kitten, and you'd better know it right now."

"Oh."

292

His hand dropped from her forehead and lay near her cheek on the pillow. "Have I hurt you badly?"

She leaned her cheek against his hand. "No."

"If I've hurt you, it's the only time I'll hurt you, kitten."

"You haven't hurt me, Pete. It doesn't matter. I love you, and I know you love me, and that's all that matters."

New York, like most of the great cities of the world, can be the most horrible place and the most wonderful. Suddenly for Katherine it flared into the most wonderful. Sometimes, after she was out of the hospital, after Manya's play had opened and settled down to a long run, after Tom had come back from the coast and Pete and Katherine had told them that they were engaged, after Pete had been taken to see Albert Peytz, looked up and down and grudgingly approved, sometimes Katherine would stand in front of the mirror and say, "Look, Katherine. This is happiness. This is what being happy is really like. Don't be unconscious of it for a single minute."

They did so many things together. All the usual things, the drive in a hansom cab in Central Park, so that she could feel like Marguerite Gautier; the riding across and across on the Staten Island ferry; up and down, up and down on the Fifth Avenue bus; the walks in the cold winter whiteness of Washington Square and Central Park; the splurges at the Casino Russe. Then there were things that were special for them, things that belonged to Katherine and Pete. Long talks with the bartender at the Purple Pigeon after the place was closed, chairs were up on tables, and mops and buckets dominated the floor. Pete burning his mouth on anchovy pizza down in the Village in a restaurant that smelled of garlic and strong soap. Long walks all over town, past the red brick walls of the convent on Eighty-second

293

Street, down St. Luke's Place past the fireman's grave and the house that had once been a mayor's with its two slender lampposts in front of it, down Hudson Street where four pale little boys were crouched solemnly in a doorway late at night, singing with intensity:

> "There's something on the end of the hook
>   The end of the hook
>   The end of the hook
> There's something on the end of the hook . . ."

Then there was the jelly lady up on Ninth Avenue, where they bought lemon butter and gooseberry jam; and a special restaurant in Chinatown; and evenings when they would just go home and Pete would stretch out on the floor and listen and doze while Katherine played.

Then there came the night when they went, as they often did, down to the Village to eat pizza and drink cheap white wine. Katherine loved going to the Village. Always they walked past Julie's old apartment on Tenth Street, and she seemed to gather extra strength, though she felt strong and clear as she had never felt before.

They went to their usual table with the heavy white tablecloth, so hastily dried and ironed that it still felt damp and seemed roughdried. Pete ordered the pizza and wine, and they sat looking at each other across the damp rough tablecloth, smiling into each other's eyes.

"Happy?" Pete asked.

She nodded. "And you?"

He nodded, too.

Katherine didn't notice when a couple came into the restaurant and sat at the table behind her, until she heard her name spoken in a voice that was very familiar, a voice

294

that had English inflections even stronger than those the school had left on Katherine.

"Katherine Forrester—"

Katherine felt the hollow feeling in the pit of the stomach, the sudden jerk of heart, constriction of throat. She turned around.

It was Sarah. Sarah and a blond young man. Sarah had a gray squirrel coat flung over her chair. She wore a red embroidered wool dress that would have been perfect for Manya but was not too becoming to Sarah's figure or her pale complexion. Nevertheless, she seemed so secure in her own awareness of her beauty that most people would have complimented her on the becoming dress.

"Hello, Sarah—" Katherine said.

Sarah seemed to have become years older since she had left school, to be not at all taken aback by this meeting that somehow hit Katherine in the pit of her stomach. "I saw your Aunt Manya's play," Sarah said, "so I thought you were probably back in America. How are you? This is Felix Bodeway, by the way—Katherine Forrester and—" She smiled at Pete, widening those huge, cold, blue eyes. "I don't know your name."

"My fiancé," Katherine said. "Peter Burns."

"Oh!" Sarah exclaimed. "That's why I thought I knew you!" She turned back to her companion. "He's in the Paul LeStrade play. You remember, Felix, we saw it when it first opened. He had all the wonderful notices . . . Felix wants me to marry him," she said to Katherine. "Do you think I should?"

"Well, I don't know."

"I say, it *is* good to see you again," Sarah said. "And going to be married, too! When, Kat?"

295

"We promised Aunt Manya and Father we'd wait a year," Katherine said, "so that makes it next November, I guess."

"At the Little Church Around the Corner? Will you let me come to the wedding? A big wedding or a little one? Kat, how exciting! You're the first of my friends to get married! Sheila wrote that she was engaged, but you know Sheila! I don't believe it for a minute." She seemed to have forgotten that there had ever been any doors closed between her and Katherine. "Do let's pull our tables together, shall we?"

Somehow, Katherine didn't want to and looked toward Pete for help, but Sarah and Felix had already pushed their chairs back, so she had to stand while they joined the two small tables with their rough white tablecloths together. Katherine went around beside Pete and sat down, rubbing her fingers over the firm comfort of his knee; Sarah and Felix sat opposite them. Katherine was so busy watching Sarah that she didn't look much at Felix, though she liked his light well-modulated voice.

"Do you know this place?" he asked.

"Yes," Pete said. "We come here every once in a while."

"I've been coming here for ages." Felix opened the fingers of one white well-kept hand, the nails clean and shining. On one finger he wore a ring, a silver ring with a skull. "Mostly Sarah and I go to a little tavern below Washington Square, but I discovered tonight that she'd never had pizza."

"I love pizza on a cold night," Katherine said softly, looking across the table at Sarah in her vivid embroidered dress.

"Well, Kat, what are you doing?" Sarah asked. "Still your piano?"

"Yes."

"You'll like Felix, then. He's a musician, too. A composer. And he plays the violin magnificently."

296

Felix accepted her praise complacently. "I've long been a great admirer of your father's, Miss Forrester," Felix said, twitching his bow tie straight with his white polished hands, which he could not seem to keep still.

"Oh, but you mustn't call Kat 'Miss Forrester,'" Sarah said, and smiling at Pete, she added, "because I'm going to call 'Mr. Burns' Peter, if such a well-known young actor doesn't mind a mere American Academy student being familiar."

"So you're an actress?" Pete asked her.

"Um-hum. I'm quite good, aren't I, Kat?"

"Yes. You're very good."

It had never been difficult for Sarah to talk, either seriously, intensely, or lightly, laughingly, as she was doing now. She ate her pizza, raved over it obligingly, drank her wine, as her conversation seemed to flit across the table like a little bright bird.

"I say," she said, "do come up to my apartment for a bit. We're really just beginning to talk, and Kat and I have so much to catch up on. Do come."

"It must be awfully late," Katherine said, "and I have a lesson tomorrow."

"The same old Kat!" Sarah cried. "How's Justin? Have you heard from him! Oh, do come for just a sec. I shan't beg you to stay, but just come and have one glass of beer. It's only around the corner."

They went to Sarah's apartment, a furnished room just off the Square, with two studio couches and a few pieces of very modernistic furniture painted yellow. A large colored picture of Manya that had been the cover of the Sunday Supplement of the *News* was framed and hung over one studio couch; a photograph of Paul LeStrade, framed with a yellow mat to make it equally large, hung over the other.

"Know LeStrade?" Pete asked.

Sarah blushed a little. "No. Daddy got it for me for Christmas. He does income tax for him. I think he's magnificent. I thought he was wonderful in your show."

"He has quite a technique," Pete said shortly.

"Do sit down." Sarah waved her arm in a gesture that took in the whole room and all the yellow furniture. "The couches are the most comfortable."

"LeStrade thinks Katherine's quite wonderful," Pete said, following his habit of pursuing a subject through thick and thin.

"Oh, Pete, don't be silly!"

"He's always talking about you, kitten. Gets me off into the wings and goes on about what a sweet, sensitive, little thing you are."

The icebox in Sarah's apartment was an old-fashioned wooden one and it, too, was painted yellow. Sarah peered into it, then turned around with a tragic gesture. "The beer's all gone!"

"Oh, well, never mind," Katherine said.

"But I do mind! I mind terribly! I wanted us to sit and have a glass of beer, and we're going to. Pete, would you come to the corner with me while I buy some?"

"We don't really need beer, Sarah," Katherine tried again. "We've got to go in just a minute."

"But not without a glass of beer. Do come with me, won't you, Pete? I want so to ask you about your play and your performance, and that would bore Kat and Felix."

Pete stood up, giving Katherine's shoulder a little squeeze. Bending down, he whispered, "We'll drink one glass quickly and go, sweetheart," and kissed the tip of her ear.

As the yellow-painted door slammed behind them, Felix looked at Katherine. "Well, shall we talk or shall we just sit?"

298

"Whatever you say."

"Shall I tell you about myself?"

"All right."

He sat hunched up on a low, yellow, wooden bench, holding the tip of his nose between two curved fingers in a way that he had. His blond hair was a little too shaggy, and a lock fell across his forehead and over one eye. "I'm a window cleaner," he said.

"A window cleaner and a musician?"

"No 'and'. Music is my window cleaning. If I weren't so sick of it, I'd quote the Bible. You know that bit. Through a glass darkly. That's how people see. It's as though nobody was out in the world. You know what I mean? We're all shut up in rooms. Everybody. And nobody can ever get in to anybody else's room. That's because we've got bodies. And the only way we can have contact with people is through the windows in our rooms. You get what I mean? And some people have more windows than others. And everybody's windows get dirty. So there have to be window cleaners. I'm one. At least maybe I will be one someday. That's what I want to be."

"Oh."

"The trouble is that my own windows need cleaning."

"Do they?"

"Sometimes I read things and I can see out better. Usually it's music (you must play for me). Or a great actress. Or a painting. Usually I just get drunk, so I can forget I'm locked up all by myself in a room and it's foggy outside . . . You know, Miss Forrester—Katherine—I don't talk this way to most people. I can't talk this way to Sarah. It's just easy, somehow, to say things to you. How old are you, Katherine?"

"Eighteen."

"I'm twenty-one. An old man. You haven't been out in

299

the world long, have you? I've been rattling about the Village since I was seventeen. A very fascinating and amusing place. Where do you live? With your father and step mother over on the East River?"

"Yes."

"You see how much I know about you? That's what you get for being a child of famous people. I make it a point to find out the address and phone number of everybody I admire, whether they're in the book or not . . . I'm not in the least in love with Sarah. Nor she with me. But it might be convenient for us to marry. She's got enough money coming to her, and we get on very well. We could live together very comfortably. Does your Pete have money?"

"Just what he makes."

"Do you?"

"Until I'm twenty-one."

"What do you mean? Most people—Sarah, for instance—come into their money when they're twenty-one."

"When I'm twenty-one, I will not take any more money from Father and Aunt Manya."

"Your mother didn't leave you any money?"

"No," she said, and was surprised at not resenting his questions. But they were asked in such an ingenuous fashion that it would be difficult to be angry with him. Watching him again twist his blue-and-white speckled bow tie into position, she was conscious that Felix Bodeway had a great deal of charm; but it was a kind of charm that made her nervous and excited; she was glad when the door opened and Pete and Sarah came back, Pete carrying a brown paper bag with the beer.

Sarah poured the beer and sat cross-legged on the floor in front of her low, yellow table. "I saw two nuns today," she said.

300

Felix raised his eyebrows, took off his huge silver ring and held it between his teeth.

"What?" Pete asked.

"I was walking down the street and I saw two nuns."

"Here we go," Felix said through the ring.

"Don't you know the superstition?" Sarah asked.

Katherine and Pete shook their heads.

"If you see two nuns on the street, it's very bad. It means you have to wait a long time for the things you want most. I've never been a patient woman."

"And you didn't use to be superstitious," Katherine said. "You used to tease me because I always wished on the first star and didn't like to see the new moon first through a window."

"Oh, but I'm superstitious now," Sarah said, waving her arms airily. "All theater people are superstitious. I'll bet your Aunt Manya's superstitious."

"Aunt Manya was born superstitious."

"Well, some are born superstitious, some acquire superstition, and some have superstition thrust upon 'em."

Felix spat out his ring. "I think it's quite wicked to be superstitious about nuns."

"Oh, I'm sorry, Felix," Sarah said. "I keep forgetting how awfully religious you are . . . He keeps going to churches and things." She turned to Katherine and Pete.

Felix flushed. "It wouldn't hurt you to remember some of the things you were brought up on," he said.

Katherine remembered Sarah in her neat navy tunic and tie, her white starched school shirt, kneeling devoutly in the Anglican chapel at school, and looked at her now kneeling in front of her yellow table, in her crimson dress, with the gold loop-earrings swinging through her soft, brown hair.

"Don't let's be cross with each other," Sarah said, "and I'll

301

explain about the nuns. If you see one nun, it's wonderful. Three is worse than two, and four in a row is death to someone you love. I never see one nun. Never. Always two. It seems as though I'd have to be patient always."

"When I finish spending the ten dollars I started with tonight, I won't have a cent in the world," Felix said.

Knowing that it was expected of her, Katherine obligingly asked him what he was going to do, and indeed most people did what Felix Bodeway expected and wanted them to do.

"Go jump in the Hudson."

"But what'll you really do?"

"Go jump off Brooklyn Bridge. There was a man once who did. I forget his name. He said he'd do anything once. I think he was a gangster. A very high-class gangster. And someone said there was one thing he wouldn't do once and that was jump off Brooklyn Bridge. He bet him something like ten thousand dollars. So he did it."

"Did he live?" Pete asked.

"Oh, sure. Some people say he didn't really do it. Some people say a taxi driver threw a dummy off the bridge and this guy was already in the water. I don't know. Personally, I think he did it. They stopped five taxicabs with him in them, trying to get up on the bridge in the first place. If someone offered me another ten dollars I'd do it, much less ten thousand . . ."

"I say, Kat!" Sarah said suddenly. "I've just had the most wonderful idea!"

Katherine was half asleep, but she opened her eyes. "What?"

"The girl I was sharing this dump with left the Academy because she got a part in the Chicago company of that putrid musical—What's its name?—and I'm sick and tired of this yellow artsy-craftsiness. And you remember at school we

302

used to talk about having an apartment in New York together—well, do let's!"

"I'm too sleepy to think about anything sensibly right
now," Katherine said, warming with pleasure because Sarah
had asked her, nevertheless. "And I'd have to talk to Aunt
Manya and Father. But I'll call you tomorrow if you'll give
me your number."

"I haven't a phone. That's another reason I want to move.
But I'll call you if that'll be all right."

Katherine looked at Sarah in the embroidered dress,
listened to the deep, monotonous voice, and felt great relief
at being once again freely fond of her. She wondered how
she herself would look with gold loop-earrings and an ivory
cigarette holder.

Pete took her uptown on the subway, then walked her
to Manya's apartment. It was very late. The streets were
almost empty, the lamps beginning to get dim. They walked
slowly, their arms around each other because there was no
one around, while the stars faded and the sky grew pale at
its edges.

"Tired?" Pete asked softly.

"Just sleepy."

"Go right to bed, kitten."

"I will. And I won't have a good lesson tomorrow."

"Just tell Mr. Albert Peytz that it wasn't my fault this
time, will you?"

"Um-hum. Did you like Sarah?"

"Cute little trick. Plenty to her, too. But don't you ever
dare go around affecting gypsy earrings and a cigarette
holder. She's much too English a type for that costume, but
she's going through her Village period the way kids go
through mumps and measles. If you do share an apartment
with her this winter, don't catch it."

"I won't."

"Promise?"

"I promise . . . Pete, do you think I should?"

"Should what?"

"Share an apartment with Sarah?"

"The idea has its points, kitten. But you talk to Madame Sergeievna about it."

Katherine was surprised at Manya's enthusiasm when she suggested having an apartment with Sarah.

"Katyusha, I think it'll be very good for you. I love and respect Pete, but you're very young to think of marriage, and it will do you good to live among a lot of young people. You can use your mother's old furniture, if you like. It's all in storage. We couldn't bear to throw it away."

"That'll be lovely, about the furniture, Aunt Manya, but it's not going to make me change my mind about Pete," Katherine said, a little stiffly.

"Katya, of course not. That's not what I meant. I just think it will be good for you to see a lot of mixed young people. I have never thought much of boarding school as a preparation for life . . . even though . . . and then of course you'll see your father and me often. Sunday dinners when we don't go to the country, and I'll expect you to come to the theater often . . . Yes, it'll be very good for you, my child. I've heard of your Sarah's father, and he's highly thought of as a lawyer. Does income tax for Paul LeStrade and a lot of the others. I'm thinking of having him do mine. Bring Sarah backstage to meet me after the performance—not this week, darling, because I'm frightfully busy, but soon."

Katherine found the apartment. Tenth Street was unfortunately out of the question. In the middle of January the only apartments still left were far too big and expensive or too small for a piano. But on Eleventh Street, between West Fourth and Bleecker Streets, she found an apartment on the top floor of an old house that seemed to her quite perfect. She loved West Eleventh Street, with its ginko and ailanthus trees, its quietness, its old-world flavor. The apartment consisted of a living room, a very small bedroom, an adequate kitchenette, and a bathroom.

Getting Julie's things out of storage was like finding a bit of her mother all over again. She had not realized that all of Julie's things had been saved. Here was the large writing table, the mahogany music rack, the portrait of Tom's mother that as usual might have been a portrait of Katherine. Here were the red velvet drapes, the blue ginger jar, the books, and the music. Some of the music had belonged to old Mrs. Forrester and was so ancient and yellowed that it crumbled with dust as Katherine put it into the music rack, but she kept even torn brown scraps of pages because it was music that her grandmother had used, music that Julie had used; it had a life of its own; it would be like murder to throw it away.

Sarah came back from the Academy and found Katherine sitting on the floor among barrels of china and boxes of books, excelsior strewn all around. Together they set to work to put order into their home.

There was just room in the bedroom for one bed, Julie's small mahogany bed with the woodwork carved into swan's heads at the foot and head. They decided to take turns sleeping on the huge couch in front of the fireplace, which could be made up into a reasonably comfortable bed, though the bedclothes would have to be folded into the hall closet during the day.

On the first night they spent in the apartment they had a

party with Pete and Felix and a lot of Sarah's friends from the Academy. Katherine made a heaping dish of spaghetti, and Sarah opened innumerable bottles of beer. Smoke and laughter filled the room. Felix played gypsy airs on his violin; Katherine played Chopin waltzes on her mother's piano, which Manya and Tom had had restrung and polished for her; Sarah played *Petrouchka,* and *Gaité Parisienne* and a lot of Jean Sablon and Charles Trenet records on her portable phonograph. Katherine stood in the kitchen, making more spaghetti, and watched the boys and girls sprawled about the living room, sitting on the chairs, on the couch, on the floor. Standing over the stove, she tried to make herself an isolated observer, to watch this scene from a way of life that seemed to her gay and carefree and happy.

But when at last everyone had gone, she flung the windows wide open and let the cold night air rush in. Emptying overflowing ash trays, Sarah shivered. "I say, Kat, must you?"

"Yes," Katherine said definitely. "We've got to clear out all this smell of beer and smoke and other people's air. Golly, parties make a mess."

"They do, but they're fun," Sarah said, turning on the water in the sink full force, while Katherine swept the floor.

When at last the apartment was spotless again and they had had hot baths and were in their pajamas, Sarah came into the living room and perched on the arm of the sofa where Katherine was to sleep.

"I say, Kat—"

"What?"

Sarah spoke very rapidly, as though what she had to say was difficult for her and the only way to do it was to get it over with as quickly as possible. "I want to apologize for the way I behaved at school about that mess we got in with

306

Halsey and Val. I've been kicking myself for being such a silly, scared idiot ever since. I should have known that people like Halsey and Val are always bats about things like that and scared to death of them because they really don't know anything. I really knew they were bats, but I guess it was sort of my sense of self-preservation coming to the fore. You've been wonderful not to say anything about it, but I felt we had to clear it up. When I saw you in the restaurant, I wanted so awfully to be friends again the way we used to be. You don't find many people who feel the same way about things that you do, and when you do find them you ought to hang on to them. Will you forgive me?"

"Of course," said Katherine, smiling a little shyly at Sarah sitting nervously on the arm of the couch. "Of course, Sarah. But there isn't anything to forgive. It wasn't your fault. Let's forget about it, shall we? Let's forget about the whole beastly school. Let's just remember that we met in Central Park and that we could talk to each other."

Sarah slid off the arm of the couch and huddled against Katherine's feet. "Thanks—thanks ever so much, Kat. I'm so awfully happy about all this—it's all so frightfully exciting, having our own apartment the way we'd planned. This is much nicer than that awful artsy-craftsy furnished room I was in, and your mother's things are so nice, just what I'd expect her to have had. I feel as though I knew her, darling."

"I know."

"Mamma wants us for dinner tomorrow night, now that she's back from Florida. Do you mind? She lets me do what I like, but she'd sort of like to look you over, even though Daddy and your Aunt Manya did have lunch together last week, when you were looking for the place. Kat, that picture on the piano is so wonderful of your mother. Is that the one you said Justin's sister gave you? Oh, Kat, I love our apartment! Really, when I think of your getting married to Pete next year and going off and leaving me, I feel quite awful. Maybe I'd better marry Felix, after all. I do like your Pete. And everybody says he's going to be a great actor someday. Well, maybe I can be his leading lady . . . Kat—"

From a daze of sleep Katherine answered, "Hm?"

"Another thing I've wanted to say. I've felt so awful over it I couldn't bring myself to say anything about it before, but I do want to thank you for having written me about Pen."

"You were her best friend."

"I still can't quite believe it."

"I know."

"Pen was so healthy and so normal. Somehow, you only expect sickly or extraordinary people to die young."

"Yes."

Sarah stretched and yawned. "I'm terribly tired. Are you?"

"Um-hum."

"But it's a lovely feeling. I've got to set the alarm clock for tomorrow, or I won't get to class on time. Do you mind? I'll try not to wake you."

"No, please do. I want to get up early and practice."

"All right, fine. Good night, Kat."

"Good night, Sarah."

The next night Katherine took Sarah backstage to meet Manya. Irina, Manya's old theater maid, who was still with her, was sitting just outside the dressing room, reading a newspaper.

"Irina, will you find out if Aunt Manya'll see me for a minute, please?" Katherine asked her.

Irina smiled at Katherine, got up, and went into the dressing room, coming out a moment later to say, "She's brushing her teeth, but go right in, Miss Katherine."

Manya was all dressed, the crimson dressing gown flung over her chair. Katherine pushed Sarah ahead of her, saying, "Aunt Manya, this is Sarah."

Manya turned to Sarah with her famous smile, put her toothbrush down, and held out her hand. "So this is Sarah," she said, her accent very heavy, her "r" very rolling. "I remember you from Katherine's letters back at that dreadful school, and I had such a charming lunch with your father at the Algonquin the other day. Katya wrote me, I remember, how wonderful you were in all the school plays, and how you almost had to play both Romeo and Juliet. Whom did you end up playing?"

"Mercutio," Sarah said, laughing.

Manya looked her up and down. "I'd like to have seen you do Mercutio. So you're at the Academy now?"

"Yes," Sarah answered. "I wonder—I wonder if I could ask a tremendous favor of you, Madame Sergeievna?"

"You could ask," Manya said.

"We're going to do Tchekov's *The Three Sisters* a week from Tuesday afternoon at the Empire, and we wondered if you might possibly care to come and see our work—and tell us what you think of us. It would mean so very much to us all."

Manya looked at Sarah. "You, I take it, are playing Masha?"

"Yes."

"I'll come," Manya said. "But I'm not at all sure you ought to ask me to tell you what I think of you, because I shall do exactly that."

"But that's what we want, Madame Sergeievna," Sarah said.

Manya reached for her coat. "I shall be especially severe because you are doing Tchekov. Because I am a Russian and have a deep love for Tchekov, and a deep gratitude to him, I am very severe to people who do him injustice and who misread him. And I am afraid you children will not be able to help doing him injustice and misreading him. However, if I see *anything* that is good, I will tell you that, too." She held out her coat to Sarah, who helped her into it. "I'm very glad to have met you at last, Miss Courtmont, and glad you and Katya have an apartment together. I've kept away because I know how much more fun it is to do things for yourselves, but now that you are settled, you must ask me for tea. You've a good face for the stage, Miss Courtmont, and a nice quality. Your voice is a bit thin, in spite of the fact that it's deep, but I think it's because you don't know how to use it yet. Expand your diaphragm."

Sarah took a deep breath and did her best, but Manya laughed.

"Pathetic! That's something you'd better take care of. Look at mine. There! Now feel it. See? Hard as iron. That's the way yours should be. Katya's is better than yours. But you have very good speech, Miss Courtmont, and your voice is well modulated and pleasant. Yes, I shall be interested to see you play Masha a week from Tuesday. What time?"

"Two-thirty."

"Will you be prompt? I don't like to be kept waiting. It puts me in a bad mood, not one conducive to kind criticism."

"We'll be prompt," Sarah said. "We'll try awfully hard to be prompt, at any rate."

"Well, good night, dear," Manya said. "Good night, Kisienka, my baby. Don't stay out too late with Pete." And she smiled at Sarah again and left.

Sarah flung her arms around Katherine. "Oh, Kat!" she said. "Oh, Kat! I can't believe it! I'm too terrified, I shall

310

die, I know I shall! Oh, thank God for you, Kat darling! Oh, I forgot to tell her I'd have tickets for her at the box office. She'll know, won't she? You'll tell her anyhow, won't you, Kat? I can't bear it, I'm so excited. Oh, Lord, they said there wouldn't be any reserved seats. Well, they'll have to reserve seats for her, they'll reserve seats for her, of course. Do you and Pete know Mr. LeStrade well enough to—no, I guess you don't. It doesn't really matter, anyhow. Oh, Kat, she's so wonderful and beautiful! I can't believe it! Wait till I tell the gang at school tomorrow! Just wait!"

"Come along," Katherine said, patting her on the back. "Pete and Felix are waiting outside."

At Sarah's and Felix's request they went, instead of to the Purple Pigeon, to the little tavern below Washington Square that Sarah and Felix were so fond of. Some dirty crooked steps led to the entrance; the bar was by the door, and its heavy stench rushed up to meet them. It smelled, somehow, stronger and more stale than the bar at the Purple Pigeon. They sat down at a small table against the wall. The table was ringed and wet from other people's glasses; half-smoked cigarettes filled the ash tray. Sarah waved until a waiter came over and took their order. With a dirty napkin he wiped off the table, then emptied the ash tray into the napkin.

At the bar sat what Katherine thought at first was a man. After a while Sarah nudged her and said, "That's Sighing Susan. She comes here almost every night."

Startled, Katherine stared at the creature again and realized that it was indeed a woman, or what had perhaps once been a woman. Now it wore a man's suit, shirt, and tie; its hair was cut short; out of a dead-white face glared a pair of despairing eyes. Feeling Katherine's gaze, the creature turned and looked at her, and that look was branded into

Katherine's body; it was as though it left a physical mark. She turned away quickly and looked at Pete, who was lighting a cigarette with fingers that were perfectly steady.

There was a juke box opposite their table. A fat woman in a silk dress with badly dyed hair put a nickel in it, and as the music came blaring forth, she began to dance with a young blonde girl in slacks. As she danced by their table she smiled suggestively at Katherine. Katherine looked wildly around, but saw nothing of comfort. There were two young men sitting close together at the bar, holding hands; an old woman lay sleeping drunkenly, sprawled across her table, red wine dripping through her fingers onto the floor.

Pete looked at Katherine and saw her white face, her dark eyes huge and afraid, so he began to talk very quickly, very gaily, taking her hand and holding it in his. "Once when I was playing stock, I was a butler and I had to pass around a tray during the second act, a tray of raspberry ices, fifteen raspberry ices, though they were never actually used or eaten. And one night the prop man got tired of taking care of fifteen melting raspberry ices and substituted instead fifteen brand-new red tennis balls. And of course he neglected to tell me. So that was the night I had to trip, very slightly, as I came in with the tray, and the fifteen red tennis balls bounced all over the stage."

But Katherine could not laugh with the others. She stood up. "I'm awfully sorry, but I have a headache and I don't feel very well. I think I'd better go home."

Pete stood up, too. "Of course, darling. I'll take you." He helped her into her coat, left some money with Felix, and took her out.

The air in Washington Square was so fresh and clear that it seemed as though she had forgotten what cold clean air could smell like. The stars were crisp and bright, they almost

312

seemed to crackle in the iciness of the night, and they were so thick that, looking up through the bare branches of the trees, it seemed like an unobstructed country sky. Katherine clutched Pete's arm and breathed deeply.

"Let's sit down for a minute," she begged.

"You won't catch cold?"

"No. I—I want to get myself cleaned out of that air. Then I want to go home and take a bath."

"I shouldn't have let you go there."

"Did you know what it was going to be like?"

"I had a pretty good idea. There are a lot of dumps like that in that neighborhood. I used to go to them quite a lot a few years ago."

"*You* did, Pete!"

"Yes, kitten. I went through the same stage Sarah's going through. Thank God, I got out of it. Some people don't. Just see that you don't get into it. I don't think you will. Sarah'll snap out of it. She's a nice kid. Probably talented. Lots of ambition and drive, at any rate, which sometimes gets you further than talent. Beautiful blue eyes. But heaven preserve me from these Academy friends of hers. Just warn me whenever they're going to be around. And I'm not sure what I think of that Felix creature. Seems sort of swish."

"What's swish?"

"Oh . . . never mind, kitten. You've had enough unpleasantness for one night. Did you know your Aunt Manya and I had quite a talk about your sharing this apartment with Sarah?"

"No! She didn't tell me!"

"We both agreed that it would be good for you. Now I'm not so sure."

"But you like Sarah, don't you, Pete?"

"Yes. I like Sarah very much, sweetheart."

313

"I met Sarah first when I was seven. In Central Park. So I can hardly remember a time when I haven't wanted her as a friend. But mostly I haven't had her."

"I'd better take you home now, darling. Your little nose is like ice."

"Then I'm a healthy puppy."

"Come along, sweetheart."

"All right."

When they got back to the apartment on Eleventh Street, Pete kissed her at the door. "I'm not coming up with you."

"Why not?"

"Because I think you ought to take your bath and get right to bed. You look tired."

"Sarah'll probably wake me when she comes in."

"Don't let her."

"But I'm sleeping in the living room, so she can't help it."

"That Sarah knows a good thing when she sees it."

"What, Pete?"

"Nothing."

"But what do you mean, Pete?"

"Sarah's a clever girl, and she'll use any means to obtain her end. I think she'll go far . . . Good night, kitten."

"Good night, Pete."

"Try to forget about that place."

"Is it good to forget about anything there *is*? I mean, even if I forget about it, it'll be there anyhow. That's what's so awful—that things—people—like that—should *be*."

"Try to forget it for tonight anyhow, and sleep. I don't like those circles spreading out like fans under your eyes. If you don't watch out, you'll have gray hair."

"I think gray hair's pretty."

"Go to bed, creature!"

314

"All right . . . kiss me good night, Pete . . . good night, my dearest darlingest . . . good night . . ."

She watched him walk away from her, down the quiet street, past the ginko and ailanthus trees, their bones stripped bare to the winter night. She felt a desperate need to get away from the city and see the country earth lying naked under the star-clustered sky, cadaverous, its bones dark with ice and dark with stones, while water ran wild and clean under the ice in streams and rivers. And suddenly she was homesick for the plane trees lining the walk to Justin's music studio, homesick for the lights of Montreux and the funicular and little train twinkling up the mountainside, the clear black mirror of the lake, and the shadows of the mountains hunched like great shoulders across the way.

But she clumped up to the apartment slowly, panting a little, and lit the fire of cannel coal that one of the Academy students had brought them as a housewarming present. After a long hot bath and an ice-cold glass of milk she felt better, made up her couch, and climbed in between the cold clean sheets. She was just about to reach up to turn off the light, when she heard a key in the lock and Sarah came in, followed by Felix.

"Feeling better, Kat?" Sarah asked.

"I'm all right now, thanks."

"I'm going to bathe. Do you mind if Felix stays and talks to you? Or does your head still ache too much?"

"No. It's all right."

Sarah went into the bedroom and Felix squatted in front of the fireplace.

"Maybe we shouldn't have taken you there," he said.

"Why?"

"You didn't like it, did you?"

"No."

315

"Does it make you think less of me?"

"I don't know."

"Sarah thinks it'll help her acting—to see all kinds of people. And they make very good liverwurst sandwiches there."

"Oh."

"You love Pete very much, don't you?"

"Of course."

"Sarah tried very hard to love me."

"Did she?"

"Yes. And I tried very hard to love her."

"Why?"

"Because I need someone so desperately, I guess."

"But it isn't Sarah you need?"

"No. Is there ever anyone who doesn't need someone?"

"I don't think so."

"Maybe I know why everyone's so rotten."

"Do you?"

"My father used to say that Adam and Eve were a case of primordial incest. And ever since then the human race has been degenerating through intermarriage."

"Oh."

"Are you very happy, Katherine Forrester?"

"Yes."

"But you're unhappy, too, aren't you?"

"What do you mean?"

"I don't think happiness is real unless there's some pain in it."

"Don't you, window cleaner?" Katherine sat up in bed, pulling the eiderdown around her, and stared at the shaggy blond youth crouched in front of the fire.

"For the last week," he said, "while you and Sarah were

316

finding this place and fixing it, I used to walk over to the East River every night and stand in front of your house."

"Why?"

"I felt so lost."

"Lost?"

"I was unhappy, and I wanted to come to you . . . I walked all the way across town and everybody was so ugly and I felt as though I were in some horrible nightmare forest . . . only I was walking on a tiny path, and at the end of that path there'd be a cottage with a light in the window and smoke coming out of the chimney. The way it is in fairy tales. Only for me—when I'd get to the end of the path, the cottage was dark, and the fire had gone out, and the door was bolted."

"What did you do then?"

"I went home and felt terribly sorry for myself. And I got very drunk. That night, and the next night, and the next."

"And then?"

"And then I didn't have any more money."

"So?"

"So I went and borrowed some from someone. And I hated myself worse than ever."

"Oh."

"The awful thing is that when I'm drunk I glory in the filth and misery. No matter what goes wrong, my great cure-all is to make up for myself some other much worse situation, in which I can go through more than human man can endure, and come out somehow pure and whole. Or with at least a chance of getting myself back."

Sarah came out of the bedroom in her pajamas and bathrobe. "What are you two talking about so solemnly? Your tie's crooked again, Felix."

Automatically Felix straightened the little bow tie with his soft white hands. "We were talking about life in general."

"As usual. I'm all ready for bed now, so you'd better get on home. We have to set the alarm again for tomorrow morning, and we've got to get some sleep."

"O.K. Good night, Sal. Good night, Katherine Forrester."

"Good night, Felix Bodeway."

When the door had slammed behind him, Sarah perched again on the arm of the couch. "I wanted to come home and go to bed without waking you, Kat, but Felix insisted he had to talk to you."

"Oh, it didn't matter."

"Headache really better?"

"Um-hum."

"Felix didn't think you liked our place."

"I didn't."

"Why?"

"I thought it was filthy."

"Well, we won't go there again if you don't like it. I'm getting sort of sick of it, anyhow. But it was just around the corner from my old apartment. We'll go to your Purple Pigeon. Although that's not too clean either, Miss Forrester. Golly, I've got to do some more work on Masha before I go to sleep. Kat, isn't it wonderful about your Aunt Manya's coming to see *The Three Sisters*? Please pray for me. It's so desperately important. Will she really come and have tea with us? You know how busy she is. Will she mind my having her picture up? It's all so frightfully thrilling! Good night, Kat darling!"

"Good night, Sarah."

Katherine and Pete went with Manya to see *The Three Sisters*. Katherine had not been allowed to go to any rehearsals, and she had not seen Sarah since the last school play.

Manya was in one of her gloomy silent moods and didn't talk much. She scowled down at her program until the curtain went up; then she stared fixedly at the stage. Katherine slipped one of her hands into Pete's and sat watching *The Three Sisters;* she felt completely protected and safe because Pete's hand was entirely covering hers; her hand was lost in his and no one else could touch her.

Watching Sarah, Katherine felt that she was very good. She knew how to take the stage and hold it. She was born with the authority that it takes many people years of struggle to acquire. And in her make-up and costume she looked arrestingly beautiful, her huge eyes shining like pale blue stars. Katherine felt that Sarah was the only one of the students on the stage of the Empire that afternoon who had a gift of any importance.

Manya went backstage after the performance, taking Pete and Katherine with her, and was immediately surrounded by a horde of babbling, excited students. When the asbestos curtain was lowered, she sat down on a straight chair and analyzed for them the production as a whole, carefully and critically, and then each one of the individual performances. She left Sarah till the last, and Katherine, watching the other girl, could not tell what she was thinking or feeling, could only see the huge light-blue eyes fixed on Manya.

At last Manya turned to her. "And you, Miss Courtmont. There is no question that the only real performance this afternoon was yours. Nevertheless, you were appallingly bad. I didn't think you were going to be quite so bad. And you committed several sins that I find it difficult to forgive. In the first place, you insisted on making Masha consistently charming. In the first act Masha is disagreeable. She is cross and unpleasant. Have you ever read Tchekov's letters?"

"No."

Manya went on firmly. "If you disagree with me about my criticism of your Masha, go to the Public Library and read the letters Tchekov wrote to his wife during the period in which *The Three Sisters* was being produced. His Masha is not a charming-tragic person. She is tragic, yes, but not wistfully, tearfully tragic, as you make her. Tchekov says she is 'given to laughing and being cross.' You only laughed twice during the entire play, I noticed. And you were never cross. Tell me. Was it because you didn't understand the role, or because you were afraid of making Masha unsympathetic?"

"I don't know," Sarah said, looking at her feet in their red-leather espadrilles.

"And that mournful face you went around with! Masha should never be mournful. When I played Masha I laughed so much and was so cross that I nearly drove my director crazy. But I was trying to get as close as I could to what Tchekov wanted. He says, 'Don't make a mournful face in a single act. Angry, yes, but not mournful. People who have borne a grief in their hearts for a long time get used to it and only whistle and often sink into thought.' But you wouldn't know that yet, would you? Only once, Miss Courtmont, did I see you thinking this afternoon, and that was the best moment you had. That was the moment that gives me hope for your future. But your confession scene in the third act, Miss Courtmont! Aren't you ashamed of it? Don't you know how wrong it was? All that storming about. Tchekov says Masha should never leave her couch. You ran about as though someone was chasing you, and you screamed and wailed until I was ready to scream and wail myself. And you seemed ashamed of yourself. The last thing in the world Masha feels is shame. Tchekov says, 'Masha's repentance in Act III isn't repentance at all, but only frank conversation. Take it nervously, but not desperately; don't scream, smile just occasionally, and the great thing is to do it so that the exhaustion of the night may be felt.' You were fresh as a feather, Miss Courtmont. Your third act couldn't have been worse."

"I'm sorry," Sarah said.

"Why are you sorry? There's nothing to be sorry about. I'd rather have you be terrible than mediocre. And in the moments when you were good you were excellent. But you're simply not ready to play a part like Masha. You aren't anything as a human being yet. You're still wishy-washy. Your most definite quality at the moment is your self-centeredness. You have the welfare of Miss Sarah Courtmont, and Miss Sarah Courtmont alone, in mind, and if other people have to be sacrificed, you'll sacrifice them. That's all right in moderation. But watch out for it. It may make for quick success, but it'll be bad for you as an actress in the long run, if you don't check it. You have great potentialities of power and strength, but as yet they are only potentialities that come out in spite of yourself. Guard them. Use them. Don't kill them. Because you can kill them, you know. There are some things that can't die, but there is nothing that can't be murdered . . .

"At any rate, whenever I am casting, or whenever Oliver Henley is doing a play, I'll see that you get a reading. In the meantime, work hard, and go to the Public Library and read Tchekov's letters. I've got to go home now and have some food and rest before I go to the theater. Good-bye, and thank you all very much for a most interesting afternoon."

The students and the directress all thanked Manya effusively. Katherine watched Sarah's face and saw the tears in her eyes. "I hope you know," she said, putting her arm about Sarah's shoulder, "that Aunt Manya thinks you're marvelous."

"Marvelous!"

"Yes. Marvelous. That's just her way of telling you."

"What Sarah needs," Pete said, "is a drink. Come along."

They went over to the Purple Pigeon. Pete ordered Sarah a Scotch and soda, and Dubonnet for himself and Katherine.

"Look, sweetie," he said to Sarah. "You aren't letting what Madame Sergeievna said get you down, are you? Because you're a fool if you do. If she hadn't thought your work was worth while and you were worth bothering about, she'd never have given you a criticism like that, or offered to get you readings. And she meant it when she said she'd rather have you definitely bad than indefinitely middling. Drink down that Scotch, and when you've thought it over a while longer, you'll be happy. As for me, I've never read Mr. Tchekov's letters—though now I'm going to—and I didn't see Madame Sergeievna's production of the play, and you certainly impressed me. I thought you were swell."

Sarah drank the Scotch. "You're an angel, Pete. I do feel less as though I'd been tied to the clapper of a bell striking twelve. I've got to go now. I promised the gang I'd meet them at Walgreen's so I won't be home for dinner, Kat. You're going out with Pete anyhow, aren't you?"

"She's going to cook for me," Pete said. "I've bought a huge bag of groceries. Wine, too. You're going to miss a swell dinner, Sal."

"Oh, well—I'm not very hungry, anyhow. I just want a cup of coffee and a sandwich. Kat, Felix says he wants to come down this evening—later, after Pete's show breaks. You'll be through practicing by then, won't you?"

"I guess so."

"So I thought we could all have some Rhine wine and seltzer together or something. O.K.?"

"Um-hum."

"So good-bye till later."

"Good-bye, Sarah."

When she had gone, Pete turned to Katherine. "I thought she was damn good, didn't you, kitten?"

"Yes. I did. So did Aunt Manya."

"Yup. That talk was good for Miss Courtmont. She needed it. Maybe she'll be a good leading lady for me some-day. We're good foils for each other. Shall we splurge and take a taxi home, kitten?"

After Pete had left for the theater, Katherine settled down to the piano. She had a feeling that Albert Peytz was going to give her one of his famous explosions; for during her last few lessons he had been unnaturally, ominously quiet, listening to her, criticizing her much too gently, giving her very little work. —But she practiced until Felix rang her bell a little before eleven.

"I know I'm early," he shouted up the stairs, as she leaned over the banisters, calling down, "Who is it?"

He came panting up, out of breath, his coat falling off, his blond hair disheveled. "Can we light the fire?" he asked, straightening his tie.

"Go ahead."

"Katherine Forrester, be a darling and make me some tea. I'm congealed to the bone." As Katherine went into the kitchen and put the kettle on, he called after her, "Sarah said Sergeievna gave her a terrific dressing down."

"Aunt Manya thought she was swell," Katherine called back, turning on the hot water too hard and splashing herself as she filled the kettle. Back in the living room, she stretched out on the sofa. "If Aunt Manya hadn't thought Sarah was really good, she would either have practically ignored her or just told her point-blank she didn't belong in the theater."

"Sure? Sal's feeling sort of depressed."

"Of course I'm sure."

"That's O. K. then. Go see if my hot water's ready."

In the kitchen the lid of the kettle was gently lifting and shutting again while a soft hiss of steam came out of the spout. Katherine made the tea and brought it in.

"You're very good to me," Felix said.

"Because I make you tea?"

"Never desert me! Promise me you'll never desert me!" he begged impetuously.

"Why should I?"

"I don't know. I just get scared . . . Why is it so easy for me to talk to you?"

"I don't know."

"Sometimes I wish I never had to talk—to be a human being—to be involved in any human relationships. When I'm composing or working at my violin, I'm good, and the music's good, and there isn't anything else in the world. When I was a little boy, I knew my music was going to be so wonderful for people. I would play and play in the great concert halls and all the people who listened to me would be happier and better people because they had listened. So last year I got a job in one of those Village night clubs and I desecrated my violin by playing low and passionate music on it. And I became low and passionate myself . . . I wish you could help me, Katherine Forrester, but there are some things I can't talk even to you about."

To Katherine, lying sprawled on the big couch, it seemed that there was nothing Felix Bodeway couldn't talk about, nothing he couldn't put into words as facile as they were intense. And maybe that was good, she thought, maybe that was a way of exorcising things that worry you. For when you put something into words, it becomes an affair of the intellect as well as of the emotions, and therefore loses some of its fearsome power.

The light from the cannel-coal fire fell on Felix's fair hair, on his pale face, his undernourished body, and soft delicate fingers with the small golden hairs on them. Then the front door opened and Sarah and Pete came in, flushed and clean from the cold, carrying bottles of Rhine wine and seltzer.

"I called for Pete after his show," Sarah said. "I thought we might as well come down together. Don't move, Kat. I'll fix the drinks."

Pete sat down on the sofa beside Katherine. "Practice hard this evening, kitten?"

"Pretty hard."

"Everything all right?"

"Yes, Pete."

"Do you ever walk along the streets and look at the people and feel you're a race apart?" Felix asked. "I suppose I'm being asinine again . . . But it doesn't matter, black and white and yellow, French, English, American, Polish, Greek. That's not the way the world's divided up. It's not that simple. More complications we've made for ourselves. I walk along the streets and I'm a race apart. I used to think it was just artists. That all artists were a race of their own. But it's even smaller than that. It's the smallest group of all, my race. At least, that's the way it seems to me."

"Pete!" Sarah called from the kitchen. "This beastly ice tray's stuck. Come help me with it, will you?"

"Sure thing, Sal." Pete ambled off.

"Katherine the Forrester," Felix said.

"Yes, Bodeway the window cleaner?"

"You're very fond of Sarah, aren't you?"

"Yes."

"But you're in love with Pete."

"Yes . . . why?"

"Nothing. I just wondered."

"What did you wonder?"

"Nothing in particular. Know Sarah well?"

"No. Not awfully, if I stop to think about it. I guess I know her about as well as anyone does. But Sarah's not easy to know well."

"No. Doesn't give herself. Smart girl. Likes to take. Glad I don't have to marry her. When are you going to marry Pete?"

"I told you. Next November."

"Pray for November to come quickly."

"Why?"

"You'll be happier when you're married."

"I couldn't be happier than I am now."

"You're really happy?"

"Happier than I've ever been in my life."

"I want you to be happy, Katherine Forrester."

"Well, look at me! Look at everything I've got to be happy about! My music. Pete. This beautiful wonderful glorious apartment with Sarah. Everything I've ever dreamed of having."

Pete came back in the living room with the wine. "You know, kitten, something occurred to me tonight."

"What, Pete?"

"You know the part of LeStrade's daughter? That bit in the last act?"

"Um-hum."

"Gert Kendall, the girl who's playing it, is leaving for Hollywood at the end of the month. I was wondering if

Sarah mightn't be able to step into it. She even looks like Gert."

"Oh, Pete, that would be wonderful!"

Sarah sat down in front of the fire next to Felix. "I don't dare think about it. Pete said he'd speak to the stage manager tomorrow before the matinee. Oh, Kat, wouldn't it be wonderful! That would show Madame Sergeievna, wouldn't it? But it's one of those things that don't happen."

The things that don't happen are often the very ones that do. Especially in the theater. One young actress will spend years tramping from office to office and never get a job. Another, of equal talent, through knowing a well-thought-of young actor, will be given a chance before she has even started to look for one. The stage manager was willing to give Sarah a reading. He liked her. Paul LeStrade heard her and liked her. It was a small part, but one that she was singularly right for at this particular stage of her development. And Sarah was only too glad to leave the Academy and join what she considered the "grown-up" world of the theater.

Sarah's being in the play didn't seem at first to change the routine of life much. It meant that Katherine and Pete saw more of Sarah and Felix in the daytime. It meant that often Katherine did not call for Pete at the theater but waited for him to come home with Sarah. It meant that Sarah was often included in their plans for the future, as Pete's leading lady— for of course they would all be famous stars. Felix would compose great piano concertos for Katherine, and double concertos for them to play, while Sarah and Pete were in the most successful plays on Broadway. They would all have a glorious, glamorous and illustrious life.

Katherine saw to it that her father heard Felix play, and showed him some of Felix's compositions. "Well?" she asked him eagerly, when she went up to the apartment for dinner.

327

"He's undeniably very talented," Tom said. "Quite brilliant. Perhaps too brilliant."

"What do you mean, Father?"

"I can't quite explain, baby, but somehow I don't think he'll get very far, your friend Felix Bodeway. There's something too showy, too lightweight. It seems to me he's burning himself out with one quick burst of flame. Of course, I may be quite wrong."

"He's an attractive boy," Manya said. "Charming. But somehow, I agree with your father. He struck me as being lightweight, too. And he has the honest blue eyes of the congenital liar."

"But you think Sarah's good, don't you, Aunt Manya?"

"Yes. I think Sarah's very good. And I think she has the drive that Bodeway lacks . . . I like your friends, Katya, but I think you're a great deal more important than any of them, and I hope you're not neglecting your work because of them."

"I don't think I'm neglecting it."

"I know what fun it is to be your age and part of a congenial group of young people. Especially in a big city like New York, and especially when you all have high ideals—as I think your friends have, from the little I saw of them that one afternoon at tea—and a very good tea you prepared too, my Katyusha. But—"

"But what?"

"Nothing. I guess Pete will take care of you."

"Of course he will."

"You and Pete are just as happy as ever?"

"Yes. Of course. Why?"

"Don't sound like a snapping turtle, Katya! I just thought you looked tired and a little distraught, and I was worried about you."

"Have you noticed anything?"

"What do you mean?"

"Have you noticed anything that would make you ask if Pete and I were as happy as ever?"

"Of course not. What should I notice?" Manya answered, but she didn't look at Katherine, and she held her very tenderly when she kissed her good-bye before leaving for the theater. At the door she turned back.

"Katya, why don't you and Pete drive out to the country with your father and me this week end?"

"Oh! That would be lovely, Aunt Manya!"

"I don't know why I haven't thought of it before—so stupid of me—self-centered, selfish old woman. Meet us at the stage door Saturday night. Your father'll have the car there. It will be lovely to have you, darling. So, until then. Kiss me again. Good-bye, my precious."

"Good-bye, Aunt Manya."

It was a wonderful week end. Katherine and Pete felt alone and allied and close, as they had not felt since the night she came down with flu. On Sunday evening, after dinner, they took a long walk. Katherine wore one of Manya's old fur coats, Pete carried a heavy fur rug. The March evening was clear and cold. They stumbled slowly up the mountain. The path was covered with patches of ice and snow shining white, like marble, like broken statues in the twilight. The air around them was of that peculiar greenish-blue that is only to be seen on an evening that is still wintry, before the trees have spread out their leaves.

Most of the trees were still quite bare and black. But if you looked up at some of them, the sharpness of their outline against the sky was gone; there was the faintest fuzziness in their silhouettes. Where the trees cleared, at the top of the mountain, the snow was almost gone, except for a few

329

patches by the stone wall. The sumac bushes seemed like frowsy old women, with their long dead, brown leaves still clinging tenaciously to them. Katherine and Pete spread Manya's fur rug on the flat rock that seemed to lean out over space and sat down on it to watch the stars come out, to watch the moon rise slowly from behind the mountains. It was a waning moon, and, though just beyond fullness, quite late in rising. When it slipped up over the edge of the mountains, it seemed very fragile, almost of eggshell consistency, or like a skull that has been washed paper-thin by centuries of salt ocean waves, with darker patches where the bone has been almost worn through.

Katherine sat very close to Pete, her head against his shoulder, his arm holding her warm and secure. Every once in a while he would kiss her very gently. When he said, "Kitten, we ought to be alone together more," it was as though he were reading her thoughts.

"Yes," she nodded.

"I wish you didn't have the apartment with Sarah."

"Why, Pete?"

"I thought if you got away from your father and Madame Sergeievna, you'd be more mine. But Felix is always around, and those dreadful kids from the Academy. We're never alone any more."

"I wish we could be."

"We'll make it a point to be. Shall we, kitten?"

"Please let's, Pete."

She leaned against his shoulder, watching the thin shell of moon and the stars dimmed for a wide arc around it, and thought of the times they had been alone, of their walks together, evenings in Pete's room, evenings in Katherine's room at Manya's when the leaves were still falling. As the stars made a pattern across the sky, so her thoughts seemed to make a pattern as they crossed her mind.

Out of the trees below them rose a large night bird with a great flapping of wings, screaming its path across the sky, jolting Katherine out of thought and into speech again.

"It's a funny thing," she said.

"What, kitten?"

"I've been thinking mostly in the past tense."

"Don't you usually?"

"No. I usually think in the future."

"What were you thinking about?"

"Oh—life with a capital L, and—"

"And what?"

"You and me."

"Me and you in the past tense?"

"Sort of as if we were both memories. Does that mean anything bad?"

"It probably means we've sat here too long and you're in a cramped position and it's very cold. The moon's hidden. We'd better go down."

Clouds were racing across the sky. All that could be seen of the moon, now high above them, was a misty glow whenever the clouds were thinnest. Pete helped Katherine up.

"I guess I am pretty stiff. My foot's half asleep. Pete—"

"What, sweetheart?"

"Don't let go my hand."

"I won't."

"Not once all the way down the mountain."

"All right, baby." He picked her up and held her in his arms for a moment. "You're such a funny little thing. I love you so very much."

"I love you, Pete."

"One minute I think you know so much, and the next minute you don't know anything; you're just a child with a face shiny from being scrubbed with soap and water . . . Why can't it be like this always? We get so messy and unsimple."

"I know."

"It's so beautifully simple now. I love you and here we are."

"Yes."

"Ready?"

"Yes."

"Sure you know the way down the path?"

"Yes."

"Let's start, then."

"You won't let go my hand?"

"Afraid?"

"Yes."

They left the top of the mountain and plunged into the shadow of the March night trees. Black across the clouds flapped the cormorant, screaming as it plummeted downward and disappeared into the woods.

Far too soon they were back in New York. Far too soon did Albert Peytz give Katherine the blowing up to which she was entitled. The anger of Albert Peytz was an impressive sight. He stood up, holding his blanket around him with furious fingers; his white eyebrows seemed to stand on end with rage; little blue veins came out in his old cheeks, and his high forehead seemed to have the thin-boned consistency of the waning moon in Connecticut the week end before. When Katherine saw him struggling out of his chair after she had finished playing, her own fingers began to twitch nervously.

"I know it wasn't very good," she said, swinging around on the piano bench.

"Good! Good!" He sputtered so that he could hardly speak. "Who do you think you are! Good!! Good!! God! Do you think I am going to go on teaching a gutless little idiot like you? I'm old, I deserve a rest, I was having a rest, and then you come along and for your mother's sake I give up my comfortable detective story and wear myself out teaching you, deliberately cutting my life span—and I like life, let me tell you! I don't want to die early for an ungrateful, lazy, stupid, thankless, spineless little fool! Harold! Harold! Come here at once!"

Harold came hurrying in, breathless as usual. "Yes, Mr. Peytz, yes, Mr. Peytz, what is it?"

"Go into my room at once and bring me the third album from the left on the fourth shelf. Hurry up, you crawling tortoise. I said at once!"

Katherine stood very still, as if mesmerized by the old man's fury.

"Don't you know it's bad for me to lose my temper and get excited?" Mr. Peytz stormed at her. "I might have a stroke, or a heart attack, and you and your ungrateful idiocy would be responsible. Mark that! Harold! What are you doing in there? Taking a bath? I thought I told you to hurry!"

Harold came panting in with an album of records. "Here I am, Mr. Peytz. I came as quickly as I could."

"Well, I wouldn't admit it if I were you. Twenty years younger than I am! Are you suffering from premature senility? Well, turn on the victrola and give it a chance to warm up. Have you no initiative?"

Fumblingly Harold turned on the victrola.

"All right," Mr. Peytz shouted, "Play the fourth record, and have the kindness to put the first side on first. If you look

333

carefully with those half-sightless eyes of yours, you will see that it is marked 'A.' As for you, Katherine, you will please sit down and listen carefully."

Katherine sat down. She felt ashamed and sullen as the first notes of the record poured forth the Bach *Chromatic Fantasy and Fugue,* on which she had been working. Then, all at once, she sat up very straight. "But—" she began.

"Sh!" Albert Peytz raised his hand imperiously for silence. "Listen!"

She listened. When Harold went to turn the record, she gasped. "But it sounds like Mother!"

"It is your mother," Albert Peytz said. "Be quiet and listen."

She sat very still through to the end of the *Chromatic Fantasy and Fugue.*

"Very well," he said. "You may go now, Harold." Then he turned to Katherine. "Now you will play it."

"No."

"Play it!"

She sat down at the piano. "I can't—" she wailed, dropping her hands in her lap.

"Go on!" Albert Peytz roared. "Play it!"

She played the music with a sort of desperation that left her limp. When she had finished, Albert Peytz sat looking at her for a long time. When he spoke, his voice was quite calm and gentle.

"Perhaps it was not altogether bad for you to dissipate a little. It is not entirely good to be too serious. But you have enjoyed yourself long enough. It is time to stop the fun and settle down to some serious work. You are engaged to the most wonderful young man in the world, and that is very fine. In some ways your music has a quality now that it didn't have before, a quality that is approaching what your mother had at your age. But, my dear child, you *must* give it more uninterrupted concentration—unless you want to give it up altogether. I know you have practiced five hours a day, but those five hours have been whenever you could fit them in, and in order to fit them in, many times you have gone without sleep and food. You are too thin; there are deep purple circles under your eyes; and your fingers are nervous, they never stop moving, playing a bit of this and a bit of that on the chair arm or the table. You are so happy, and your face is so radiant, that most of the time one doesn't see how worn and tired it is; but whenever you relax and look thoughtful, you seem so tired as to be almost ill, and I have noticed that sometimes you limp. It will not do. If you still want to be a musician, you must mend your ways."

"Why didn't you play me Mother's records before? Why didn't you let me know you had them?" Katherine demanded.

Albert Peytz's voice was ominously calm. "Didn't you hear anything I said to you?"

"Yes," Katherine answered quickly. "I heard. I know. You're quite right. I'll do anything you say. I promise you . . . But why didn't you play me Mother's records before? You know—you know what it would have meant to me."

"It would have meant too much to you," Albert Peytz said. "And you have your own personality, your own style. I don't want you to become a second-rate imitation of your mother, when you can be a musician in your own right. But I'll make you a promise, too, child. If you work hard for the next few months, I'll give you the record I played you. The rest you'll have, of course, after I die, which I hope won't be for some time. Go home now, and work. In two weeks we'll make a recording of you doing the *Chromatic Fantasy*. You have that long to prepare it. If you don't dillydally, it will be long enough. I'm tired now. We won't go on with this

335

lesson. Go home. And if you're not going to work, don't ever come back here again."

When she got back to Eleventh Street, where the ailanthus and the ginko trees were beginning to show small shoots of delicate green, she had the same feeling of exhaustion and weakness that she got when she had drunk too much the night before. As she put her latchkey in the lock, she noticed that there was a letter in the mailbox and she drew it out, not glancing at it until she got upstairs. When she looked at the envelope and saw that it was postmarked Paris, she began to tremble violently.

—It's from Charlot or Pauline—she said to herself, slitting the letter open carefully. The signature, "Anne Desmoulins," puzzled her, until she remembered the organist. Inside the two sheets of blue note paper was a single white one. The signature read "Justin."

She read Anne's letter first.

They had meant to write at Christmas, but there had been Anne's marriage. She was very happy. Justin still had the attic apartment. They had bumped into Pauline and Charlot once and gone out and had a cognac together. Everyone had said wonderful things about Katherine. How was she?

With shaking fingers she unfolded Justin's letter. Justin had not been in her mind for a long time. —It's like God— she thought. —When you're happy and have everything you want, you don't need Him, you forget to pray. But when He reminds you of Himself, you fall pale and tremble before His glory.—

"Why haven't you written?" Justin demanded. "I thought I told you to write. How is your music coming? With whom are you studying? Did your mother's old teacher suggest someone satisfactory? I miss you. Katherine, if ever you betray me by becoming mediocre, if ever you dishonor your work, I will come to America and strangle you with my own hands."

There was an excitement about plunging into work again that made her wake up feeling fresh and energetic at six when she had gone to bed at three the night before. She forgot to eat unless Sarah or Pete forcibly dragged her away from the piano. Sarah bought earplugs, and fortunately there were an oboist and a cellist in the house, as well as several people who kept their radios on loudly all day, so there were no complaints when Katherine practiced one finger-exercise for hours at a time. She made her recording of the *Chromatic Fantasy* for Mr. Peytz, who was pleased. She felt renewed life and strength pouring into her fingers and arms. Only in the evening after the show did she see Pete. Sometimes they stayed in the apartment with Sarah and Felix. Sometimes they went for long walks together, in the Square, in St. Luke's Place, in their old haunts of early winter. Katherine walked leaning close against Pete, exhausted but completely happy, not talking much, just knowing the comforting nearness of Pete, watching the slow glow of his cigarette, feeling her own strong hands suddenly lost and small in the strength of his, while the moon waxed and waned, stars blossomed and faded in the sky, and window boxes seemed to unfold outside the Eleventh Street houses like the fan-shaped leaves of the ginko trees.

On Sarah's birthday they gave a party. Katherine suddenly felt so tired that cold sweat broke out on her forehead and upper lip as she stood in the kitchen making blini. As she came in with a trayful, she heard Sarah saying to a dark man whom Felix had brought, ". . . next winter when the show's on the road . . ."

337

Quickly she turned to Pete. "Are you going on the road next winter, Pete?"

"I wanted to talk to you about that," he said. "Come on downstairs for a minute."

They walked slowly down the sleeping street; the stars were already beginning to dim out. "The announcement of the tour just came tonight," he said. "I didn't think there'd be one."

"Do you have to go?"

"They're raising my salary. Twenty-five dollars more a week. That's a good sum. I can save a lot out of that. We have to think of such things, you know, sweetheart."

"Yes, I know . . . But couldn't you get something here in town? You've had quite a lot of publicity out of this show, you're quite important now. And you've been on the road so much. Do you have to go, Pete?"

"I don't know. I think so," he said. "I've never had much respect for people who sign up for a show, play it in New York, and then refuse to go on the road. And then, aside from that, there's the money. If it weren't for you, sure, I might stay in New York. I know I'd get something. But I wouldn't have the salary LeStrade offered me, though why in hell he wants me I don't know, except maybe he thinks I'm less of a menace to him in his own show than going into a lead in something here in town. Then, if I did get something here, it mightn't run. I might be out of work all winter. I'm not the only man in New York, no matter what my notices were. One hit doesn't necessarily mean anything. I've seen people make a tremendous hit and never do anything again. This part is very right for me, and I've still got a lot to learn from it. But the most important thing is you. If I didn't have you to think of, I'd probably chuck the show and take my chances on something else. But there *is* you."

338

"I thought one of the wonderful things about us was that we were never, in any way, going to interfere with each other's careers."

"You're not interfering with my career. It just swings the balance. Anyhow, you'd be interfering in my career if I didn't go on the road because of you."

"That's logic nohow contrariwise," Katherine said, as they turned up the street again.

Pete dropped his cigarette and ground it out with his heel. "The show closes the end of June. We don't leave till the first of September. We'll have all July and August together."

"How long will you be gone?" Dropping her cigarette, she buried her hand in Pete's pocket the way she had done in Julie's.

"All season, I expect."

"Oh. Is Sarah going?"

"Sure. Why?"

"I just wondered . . . I'll be awfully lonely."

"You'll have Felix. Maybe it'll be very good for you, anyhow. You can go to bed at night instead of sitting up with me. And you'll never notice we're gone all day while you're at your piano. Just don't forget to eat once in a while."

At the corner Katherine leaned suddenly very heavily against Pete. "I'm terribly tired. Dear God, I'm so tired."

Pete put his arm around her and half-carried her back up the street. This time he stopped in front of the door. "Sweetheart—"

"What, Pete?"

"So I don't think we should marry until I get back from the road. Because God knows where I'll be in November."

"Oh."

"It's damnable, but it's only sensible."

"That's putting it off almost a whole year."

"Does it matter very much to you?"

"Yes. It does."

"I wasn't sure."

"Sure of what?"

"How much it would matter."

"Oh, Pete!"

"But it really isn't a whole year, precious. Only spring instead of winter."

"It seems like a whole year."

"We'd better go upstairs."

"I know."

Pete kissed her gently, as he would kiss a tired child. She leaned against him, completely limp and exhausted, and he picked her up and carried her up the four flights of stairs.

Sarah was playing Strauss waltzes on the victrola, and Felix was joining in with his violin. Katherine stood in the doorway, and the room went around and around with the dancers. Past her, caught up in the whirlpool, revolved Sarah and Pete, and suddenly she was being whirled about by the dark man Felix had brought. Around and around like the moon and earth and sun and stars, like the hands of the clock, the days of the year, the merry-go-round at Thônon. Everything swirled around until it resolved itself in blackness and she was lying on the bed in the tiny bedroom, with Sarah, Pete, and Felix clutching his violin to his chest, looking down at her with anxious eyes. She sat up quickly, then fell back again as the room began to revolve. "What's going on?" she asked.

"You passed out cold," Sarah said.

Pete went out and came back a moment later with a cup. "Here's some black coffee, darling."

She drank it down quickly, then sat up again, tentatively.

340

"I'm all right now," she said. A Noel Coward record was on the victrola in the other room, sounding quite loud because the voices were subdued.

"I'm going to tell the crowd to go home," Sarah said.

"Don't be silly. I'm all right now."

"You ought to get to bed. I'm going to get them to go."

"It'll spoil your birthday party."

"It's practically morning. They've been here long enough. You stay here and I'll get rid of everybody and clean up and fix your bed. Pete will help me."

"No." Katherine said. "Let Pete stay here. Felix will help you. And don't bother about cleaning up. I'll do it in the morning. You shouldn't have to clean up after your own birthday party."

"We'll do it," Sarah said. "Come on, Felix."

They went out. The light bulb from the bed lamp was bright in her eyes, but she felt too tired to reach out to turn it off. "Turn out the light, please, Pete," she said.

For the first moment after he switched off the lamp the room was completely dark. Then the light resolved itself in a thin square around the closed door, and settled, paler, gray instead of golden, in the rectangle of the window.

Pete began to rub his fingers gently against the nape of her neck. "You've been working too hard."

"Yes. I guess so."

"You'll have to stop."

"I can't very well."

"I'm not going to have you bullied by that slave driver Peytz."

"No," she said. "It isn't his fault. It's not too much work. It's not enough sleep."

"No matter what it is," Pete said, "we've got to put an end to it."

341

"Um," Katherine said vaguely, thinking that would satisfy him.

But it didn't. She was practicing the next morning, when the doorbell rang. She pushed the buzzer and shouted, "Who is it?" crossly down the stairs. Manya came hurrying up. "Oh, hello, Aunt Manya. I didn't mean to snarl. I was working."

Manya kissed her; Katherine sat down on the sofa; Manya stood by the fireplace, frowning at her. "Pete phoned me this morning, Katya."

"Oh, did he? What about?" she asked guardedly.

"What do you mean by fainting?"

"Oh—I don't know."

"We're going to find out. Put on your coat and hat."

"I have to work."

"You are coming to the doctor with me. I've made your appointment with your precious Dr. Bradley instead of Leonid, so just be thankful. Get your coat and hat."

Katherine knew that when Manya used that tone of voice there was no use arguing with her. She got up.

There was nothing wrong with her but exhaustion and undernourishment. With some irritation Dr. Bradley ordered her to spend two weeks at Manya's place in the country. Manya would speak to Mr. Peytz.

Now that they were making her give in, she felt relieved. It would be good to go to the country to the small blue-paneled room, to go to bed early and sleep late in a bed that was a bed and not a sofa that had to be put together and taken apart night and morning (it had seemed the simplest thing for Sarah to remain in the bedroom and Katherine in the living room; Katherine was the smaller of the two and fitted the sofa better); to eat good meals slowly and without

342

nervously feeling that she must rush. It would be a relief to have no conflict for a short time in her mind between her piano and Pete. There was the necessity of doing justice, of doing more than justice, to her music, so that she would not betray Julie or Justin or Albert Peytz—or herself; and there was the necessity of time to be with Pete, partly because of Pete, but mostly because of herself, since Pete had become as much an integral essential part of her life as breathing and music.

It was a quiet and peaceful two weeks. Manya pampered her over the week ends, read to her, rubbed her head, kneaded the tense muscles in her back. She slept and ate and walked in the fresh spring air, transplanted bulbs from the house to the garden, fed Manya's chickens, the Leghorns, the Cochin Chinas, the Orpingtons. At night there were the clear myriads of country stars to look at or Manya's record collection to listen to in front of the wood fire that was so fresh and fragrant and clean-smelling after the cannel coal.

She went back to the city feeling newly alive and on her toes with energy, her battery recharged, her nerves calm, her body fresh and strong. But when Sarah and Pete came hurrying to the door when she got back to the apartment, she knew that something was wrong. Pete's face was drawn, and there was a stubborn set to his mouth. Sarah put her arms around Katherine and kissed her very tenderly, very lovingly, easy tears coming quickly to her eyes.

"What on earth's the matter?" Katherine asked. "Has something awful happened since I was away?" Pete shook his head. "Felix hasn't gone and committed suicide or anything, has he?" Again Pete shook his head. "Well, for heaven's sake, you two! I come back looking as healthy as a young Greek god, and you both look at me as though you'd just learned I'd been stricken with an incurable disease." As she saw the tears spill over in Sarah's eyes, she suddenly felt panic. "I haven't, have I?"

Again Sarah put her arms about her, "Oh, my God, darling, of course not."

Katherine looked hard into Sarah's eyes and felt that they were bright with more than tears. She pulled away and turned automatically toward the piano.

"Mr. Peytz called to see if you were back and how you were," Sarah said.

"Oh."

"You do look well, Kat."

"Yes. I'm fine. But there's something the matter. What is it?"

"Nothing's the matter. Honestly."

"Look," Pete said. "We're all acting stupidly about nothing. We're going to take you out tonight, kitten. Good French food and wine. Come for us after the show."

"O.K." Katherine said. "I think I'll come and see it tonight." Then, looking at them, she changed her mind, she wasn't quite sure why. "No. I guess I'll go and see Aunt Manya's. I haven't seen it in a long time."

Manya's play was a long one and broke almost half an hour later than Paul LeStrade's. Pete and Sarah had their make-up off and were waiting for her when she went around to their stage door. They each took her arm, very affectionately. Katherine thought—I wish Pete and I could have been alone tonight.—

They hadn't been in the restaurant very long when Katherine saw Felix in the doorway, looking over the tables, fingering his bow tie. She waved at him. "There's Felix."

Pete looked annoyed. "I didn't tell Felix where we were going on purpose. I wanted to be alone with you."

—But, my God—Katherine thought—we aren't alone. I

344

love Sarah, I always will, but when it's Pete and me, even Sarah makes someone else.—

Felix's eyes lit up as he saw them, and he hurried over to their table.

"How did you know we were here?" Pete asked, not concealing his irritation.

"Oh, I have my little F.B.I. men," Felix said, and ordered a Scotch and soda.

Sarah looked at him across the table. "Felix, you've been drinking."

"Not so much. But I'm going to have to, to keep my spirits up, aren't I? The unwanted guest, or words to that effect. But if you don't mind, or rather, even though you do, because I know you do, I'm going to stick around. I'm very fond of Katherine Forrester, and I don't like to see her get a dirty deal."

"What are you talking about?" Katherine asked sharply.

"Look," Pete said. "I know you mean well, Felix, but this thing is between the three of us, and if you want to help Katherine, the best thing for you to do is to leave us alone."

Katherine stood up. "Don't go, Felix. Stay and take my place, will you? I'm sort of tired, and I think I'll go home. I got used to going to bed early while I was in the country."

"I'll take you home," Felix said.

"Kitten, please stay," Pete said, in the same breath.

"I'm going home, and I want to go alone." Her voice was quite definite; it sounded flattened out, a tube that had been crushed.

When she was out on the street, she was aware that all three of them were following her. She walked very quickly, trying to ignore them, trying to shake them off as she hurried toward the subway.

She remembered, incongruously, it seemed, the way the

storms had been sometimes over the lake at school. Clouds, gray angry ones, rolled up and filled the valley between the two mountain ranges, the mountains of France and the mountains of Switzerland, rising up behind the school. Then, suddenly, there would be a rift in the clouds, and a shaft of very bright sunlight would sharply, swiftly, thrust itself out and splash down onto the lake. Understanding had come now, with the dazzle and clarity of one of those shafts of sunlight.

Pete caught up with her and took her arm, but she pulled away, saying quietly, "Please."

Walking rapidly through the busy night streets, they passed newspaper stands, the bright glare of movie houses, old women selling corsages of gardenias and violets. As they turned down the subway stairs, Sarah gasped, "But this is like a nightmare!"

Inside the subway station the air was stale. Katherine went to the newsstand and bought a paper, which she opened and held in front of her all the way downtown. Although there was no danger of tears, she felt as though she were stripped, as though she could bear to have no one look at her, especially Pete or Sarah or Felix.

When they reached the apartment house, Pete said, "Look, Felix, please go home."

Sarah added, "Please, Felix. Let us have this out between ourselves."

"There isn't anything to have out, is there?" Katherine said.

Felix turned to her. "Do you want me to go or stay?"

"I suppose you'd better go," she said, turning her back on them and pulling out her latchkey. She climbed the stairs quickly, listening to the sound of Pete's and Sarah's feet behind her.

346

Automatically, Sarah turned on the lights and lit the fire. Katherine went to the hall closet and pulled down her sheets and blankets. "There isn't any need to talk, is there? I understand. I have a music lesson tomorrow and I want to sleep. Go home, Pete, or go out with Sarah, whichever you prefer. Just let me go to bed."

Sarah stood with her back to the room, staring down into the fire, tears spilling through her fingers. "I couldn't help it, Kat, honestly I couldn't."

Katherine tucked in the bottom sheet, pulling it very smooth and tight. "I suppose this has been coming for a long time. Now that I look back I can see it. I understand. You've been working together. The same play. You're both in the theater. I'm a musician. I guess I've neglected Pete for my music. Sarah's much more beautiful than I am, more interesting, you have more things in common. It's quite understandable, I realize that."

Pete handed her the top sheet and helped tuck it in. "It was all my fault, not Sarah's," he said.

Sarah didn't look away from the fire, but continued to stand there, crying. "No. If anyone is to blame, I am."

"It doesn't really matter whose fault it was, does it?" Katherine said. "The blanket, please, Pete."

"We couldn't even run away from it," Pete said, "because of the show, you know."

"I understand," Katherine said again. "It had started even before we went to Connecticut for the week end, hadn't it, Pete?"

"A little."

"Because even then, before Mr. Peytz spoke to me, I was practicing too much, more than was fair to you. And then, after that all I needed was to go away for two weeks. It's quite simple. But I don't know . . ."

347

"What?" Pete asked, taking her pillow off a chair and putting it on the couch.

"I don't know what. My bed's all ready. Would you mind going? I want to go to bed. My lesson tomorrow . . ."

"Your music—it's terribly important to you, isn't it?" Pete asked.

"Of course."

"More important than I am."

"We don't need to go into relativity." Every word she said seemed to her unreal. This was not Katherine Forrester talking, but someone else saying words that had nothing to do with her, using a judgment of which she personally had no understanding. But since this strange person seemed to be saying and doing things that were more or less reasonable under the circumstances, Katherine let her go on controlling matters. "I suppose we'll have to tell Father and Aunt Manya."

"I suppose so," Pete said. "Do you want me to? I will, if you want me to. If you think it would be better."

"No. I'll do it," the strange person in charge of the situation said. "By the way, how did Felix know?"

"I don't know," Pete said. "I guess he just knew."

Katherine went to the closet and brought out her pajamas and bathrobe. "I think we've said everything we need to. Please go, will you?"

"Coming, Sarah?" Pete asked.

"I don't know . . . Do you want me to go, Kat?"

"It doesn't matter to me what you do. I just want to go to bed. I'm sleepy."

"Well, I guess I'll go," Sarah said.

Katherine listened to them go downstairs. She undressed and took a bath. When she was in pajamas and bathrobe and had turned out the lights, she opened the windows wide and

348

stood staring down at the court below, at the single ailanthus tree growing up through the shallow, unfertile ground, at the wooden fence with the paint peeling off, at the hardness of the cement of the courtyard. She went over to the piano and sat down in the darkness, but she didn't play. She thought, but it was still not Katherine Forrester but someone else thinking. Nevertheless, words formed and came out of her mind. —I can't be unhappy, I can't be really unhappy —she thought—because I don't want to die.—

She was awake when Sarah came back. Although she knew Sarah couldn't see her lying there on the couch, with the light from the fire almost dead, she closed her eyes. Sarah got ready for bed quietly, tiptoeing so as not to disturb her, but instead of going into her room, she stopped at the foot of the couch, looking down at Katherine, who had opened her eyes and was staring up at her in the hazy, golden light coming in from the bedroom door.

"Kat, are you awake?"

"Yes."

"Look." (And Katherine noticed that Sarah had picked up Pete's way of saying "Look" before starting anything important.) "Look," Sarah said. "What do you want to do about the apartment?"

"Oh. I'd forgotten about that."

"Do you want to go? or do you want me to go? Or what?"

"I don't know."

"Do you want me to go, then?"

"I guess you'd better."

"I couldn't—just stay—could I?"

"It would be sort of difficult."

"When do you want me to go?"

"Could you go tomorrow?"

"I guess so."

"Where will you go?"

"I'm not sure. I don't want to go home, although, God knows, Mamma'd be glad to have me. Maybe I will, for a few days. Or maybe I'll take a room in Pete's hotel."

"We've paid the rent here through the end of the month," Katherine said. "I'll pay you back your share."

"Don't be silly . . . Kat . . ."

"What?"

"Look, Kat, I just want to say . . ."

"What?"

"Maybe—maybe it doesn't do any good to say things, but there is something I do want to say."

"All right." Katherine knew that Sarah would say her little speech and then feel a great deal better. She lay on the sofa, watching Sarah's profile, dim and beautiful in the light from the bedroom, and waited for the speech. She still felt very calm, very untouched. It was as though the power of feeling had been cut off, as though the nerves had been temporarily anesthetized.

"Look," Sarah said again, "I just want you to know how—how sorry I am—about everything." She spoke slowly. The words came out with difficulty. Katherine was not sure how much of it was real sincerity, painful honesty, and how much was just a very good scene from a second-rate problem play. "About—about everything," Sarah repeated. "I've always brought you nothing but unhappiness. Every time I've had anything to do with you, except that very first time I met you in Central Park. At school. All that mess with Val and Halsey. I was bad about that. And Pete. I don't know. I've been bad about that, too. I guess I could have stopped it, if I'd wanted to. But I didn't want to. I tried to make Pete fall in love with me. I did it deliberately. Whenever you were practicing. Or when we were at the theater. I knew what I was

350

doing. And you made it so easy for me. I love Pete so desperately that hurting you didn't seem—didn't seem big enough to keep me from trying to get him. I've never really thought of anyone but myself. I don't think I ever will. So you mustn't blame Pete. I am the one who is culpable. You see, I've never loved anyone before Pete. It's awfully important to me."

"I know, I understand," Katherine said. "Do go to bed, Sarah."

"But, Kat, I want you to realize I do love you so very tenderly. You've meant more to me than anyone in the world, until Pete came. And Pete loves you too, so very much—"

"All right," Katherine said. "And I love you and Pete, so everybody loves everybody, and you've had too much wine. Go on to bed."

"All right. I'm going . . . You want me to leave tomorrow?"

"Please. I'll stay away all day. Do you think you can have everything out by six?"

"I think so."

"You can leave your keys in the mailbox."

"All right. Good night, Kat." Sarah's shoulders began to shake with sobs.

"Good night," Katherine said.

Sarah slid off the arm of the couch and went into the bedroom, shutting the door. Katherine heard her fling herself down on the bed and sob and sob, easily, loosely, like a child. She knew that Sarah wanted her to come in to her, to comfort her, to tell her that everything was going to be all right. But she didn't move. After a while the crying stopped.

She got up early the next morning, before Sarah was awake, dressed, and made herself some coffee. Then she knocked on the bedroom door. Sarah rolled over sleepily.

351

"You'd better get up and start to clear your things out," Katherine said. "I'm going now. I left some coffee for you."

Once she was downstairs, she went into the drugstore on the corner. She hadn't wanted to call Manya while Sarah was in the apartment, and she remembered that she hadn't called the night before to say she was home from the country. Manya answered the phone by her bed.

"Hello, Aunt Manya. It's Katherine."

"Hello, my darling."

"Did I wake you?"

"No. I was awake. Dunyasha brought me my breakfast half an hour ago. I was reading scripts. So. How are you?"

"Oh, I'm very healthy."

"Something wrong?"

Katherine was silent. She tried to speak and couldn't. Although she was still feeling nothing, the person who had been in control of her anesthetized senses and thoughts the night before was no longer there.

"Katyusha!"

"I'm still here."

"Is something wrong?"

Again Katherine was silent.

"Is Pete all right?"

Now words could come. "Yes. Pete's all right. Will you tell Father, please, that we aren't getting married?"

Now Manya was silent at her end of the wire.

"Tell him, will you?" Katherine asked.

"I'll tell him. Is it Sarah?"

"Did everyone know about it but me!" Katherine exclaimed, with more feeling in her voice than had been there since she got back from the country.

"No, my darling, it isn't that . . . I just sense these things . . . I always have . . . Will you come to us?"

352

"No. Sarah's leaving the apartment. She's leaving today. If you don't mind, I'd rather stay."

"Don't you think you'd better come to us?"

"No. I'd rather stay."

"Are you all right?"

"Of course."

"I want to see you. Will you come and have lunch with me?"

"No. Please."

"What are you going to do?"

"I'm going to the movies."

"All day, until Sarah leaves?"

"Sarah'll be gone at six. And I have a lesson."

"But still—"

"We'll have to stop talking. My nickel's almost up."

"Where are you?"

"The drugstore."

"What's the number? I'll call you back."

"No."

"Are you going home at six?"

"Yes."

"Will you phone me this evening then? Before I leave for the theater?"

"All right. There goes my nickel. Good-bye."

She went to her lesson. She went to the movies. At six she went back to Eleventh Street. Opened the mailbox. The keys were there, so she climbed the stairs, rubbing her eyes, which ached from the strain of so many movies. She did not know whether Sarah had gone home to her family or taken a room in Pete's hotel; perhaps it was best for her not to know.

Since the furniture of their apartment had all been Julie's, Katherine had expected it to look more or less like itself, even with all Sarah's things gone. When she opened the door, the mutilated living room hit her eyes with a shock. The gaps where Sarah's books had been on the shelves were like missing teeth. Even in the short months they had hung there, the pictures of Manya and Paul LeStrade had made marks on the wall. The victrola and the painted stool it stood on were gone; there were no more records. The desk lamp looked decapitated, with Sarah's yellow shade off. Her rag rug was gone, leaving a bare patch in front of the fireplace; the cannel coal was piled neatly on the hearth, because the black coal scuttle had been Sarah's. Her green Finnish bowl was off the table, her yellow and red cushions gone from the couch. The room looked betrayed, desecrated, humiliated.

Somehow, the bedroom was not so bad. Only the furniture remained. The door to Sarah's empty closet stood open; her brush and comb and the pictures of her parents were gone from the bureau; the drawers were empty.

So Katherine took her bed clothes out of the closet in the hall and made the bed. —This was *Mother's* bed—she told herself sternly.

Then she went into the living room and phoned Manya. "Here I am," she said. "I promised I'd phone."

"Thank you, darling. How are you?"

"I'm all right."

"Movies good?"

"Mostly pretty feeble."

"Will you speak to your father?"

"Must I?"

"Of course not, dear, if you don't want to. Sarah gone?"

"Yes."

"What are you doing tomorrow?"

"Practicing."

"Not going out?"

354

"I don't think so. I've got to work. I hardly touched the piano while I was in the country . . . well, good night, Aunt Manya, unless there's anything else you want to say."

"I can't think of anything."

"Good night, then. I hope it's a good performance this evening."

"Thank you. Good night, Katya, my darling."

Katherine straightened up the room, pushing the books on the shelves together, trying as far as she could to make the room look complete. But it was impossible. She boiled an egg and drank a glass of milk for dinner, because it would be foolish to undo the physical good the two weeks in the country had done her. Then she practiced until quite late, when the doorbell rang stridently.

Pushing the piano bench back so violently that it fell over, she tore to the door and pushed the buzzer, calling breathlessly over the banisters, "Who is it?"

"Felix."

She turned without answering, and went slowly back into the room, and righted the piano bench. Of course, it couldn't have been Pete. But her heart was beating heavily.

Felix came in, panting from the climb. "Am I disturbing you?"

"I was practicing."

"Don't you think you ought to stop for a while?"

"No."

"Sarah called me and told me she'd left."

"Oh . . . Did she tell you to come around tonight?"

"No. I wanted to."

"Well, I wish you'd go away, Felix."

"Wouldn't you come out for a drink with me?"

"No. Please go away, Felix, and don't come back." She

355

spoke coldly, sharply, aware that she was being cruel, and ashamed of herself before she spoke. Nevertheless, she spoke.

Felix looked as though she had struck him. He sat down on the sofa, moving jerkily, like a marionette. "What have I done?" he gasped.

Katherine stood leaning against the piano. "You haven't done anything. I'm sorry. I didn't mean to hurt you."

"Then, what is it? Why are you driving me out like this, if I haven't done anything? You're my very favorite person in the world, and I thought you were a little fond of me. Why must I go away?"

"It isn't you," Katherine said. "I'm very fond of you, window cleaner."

"You see, you called me 'window cleaner' again," Felix said excitedly. "You haven't called me that in ages. That's a good sign, that you should call me that, isn't it? And if you're fond of me, why should you send me away?"

"It isn't you," Katherine said again. "It's what you stand for."

"What do you mean?"

"I don't like so many things that you're part of. That awful tavern you and Sarah took me to. Your way of life. The people who came to our parties—your friends. They're part of your world. I think, of Sarah's world. And maybe Pete's. At least, they don't bother him. They bother me. Awfully. I don't want anything more to do with them. And you're so much part of everything I want to forget that I just can't go on seeing you. I've got to cut everything off, clean and sharp. I've *got* to, don't you understand? That's why I don't want to see you, even though I'm fond of you and will miss you very much. But I *can't* see anyone who belongs irremediably to things I want to put behind me forever. That's all."

"I see," Felix said. He looked white and unhappy. Deep,

brown smudges were under his eyes. He twisted at his bow tie with his pale, smooth hands. Then he stood up. "I see."

"I'm awfully sorry, Felix."

"I can't say I understand," he said. "I mean, I understand what you mean, but I don't think you're right. I know—"

"What?"

"I know you won't change your mind. So, you won't mind if—if I go on seeing Sarah and Pete?"

"Of course not."

"If you do mind, I won't, even if you won't let me see you."

"Why should I mind?"

"I mean, Sarah's an old friend, and—"

"Of course, Felix. It would be silly not to see them . . . Good-bye . . ."

"Will you kiss me good-bye?"

"If you like." She kissed him lightly, then pushed him gently toward the door. "Good-bye, Felix, dear."

"Good-bye, Katherine."

She shut the door after him and turned back to the piano.

Sleep did not come easily that night. Through closed eyes Katherine saw an unending procession of ugly, distorted images, and then these images turned in upon herself. Great waves of terror swept over her, and she sat up in bed, putting her hands over her ears as though to shut out the sound of a scream she had never actually heard. Getting out of bed, she went to the window and looked down to the courtyard below. From the window of Sarah's bedroom—no, her own bedroom—it looked very far down. The cement that lay there waiting seemed harder than rock. Standing there, leaning against the window, she felt very dizzy, seemed to feel her body falling, falling, while the cement reached up to hit and crush it.

357

She shuddered violently, shook herself, closed the window tightly, and went back to bed. No, that was silly, that was stupid. She needed the air, and besides, simply closing the window would do no good. So she got out of bed, opened the window wide, came back and sat on the edge of the bed for a moment, then turned on the light.

With restless fingers she rummaged through her things until she found her mother's old Venetian silver dinner bell with the ivory handle. Then she took the cord to her bathrobe and tied one end of it to the bell. The other end she tied firmly to her ankle.

She got into bed, burrowed down under the covers, tucking the bell between the mattress and the sheets so that it would not ring and disturb her when she turned in bed. —That ought to do it—she thought. —If I get out of bed the bell will ring and that certainly ought to wake me.—

She pulled the covers over her head and tried again to sleep, but her mind was wide awake, and image after image continued to come before it, much too sharp and clear, until she was shivering with horror.

The emotion of acute fear awoke her other emotions. She began to ache all over with misery, with a desperate ungovernable unhappiness that made her forget the fear that had roused it.

She tried to reason with herself. This was a shameful way to behave. Her mother could never have behaved like this, have let herself go completely, have allowed fear and desolation to enter her fortifications of unfeeling calm and completely destroy them. —Mother would despise me—she thought, reaching down in the bed to unfasten the bathrobe cord, the symbol of her weakness, from her ankle. But when her fingers touched the twisted wool of the cord, they would not move to untie it. "I can't," she wailed, and flung herself back on the pillow again. Her eyes stung with unwilling wide-awakeness. She tried saying the multiplication table. That often worked, but this time she got completely through twelve times twelve. Toward morning she dozed off, finally going into a deep and exhausted sleep.

But it was not late when she woke up. She lay in the delicately carved mahogany bed, and the day seemed to press down upon her as though her misery were a deep pool of water. Her misery was a deep pool and she lay drowned in the bottom of it, her long dark hair spreading out about her, swirling in the gentle currents of water, mingling with strange underwater plants.

With a violent effort, she thrust aside her clinging misery, and got up. For a moment, when her foot caught on something, she didn't realize what was the matter, and it wasn't until she had dragged it out of bed and the bell fell to the floor with a clatter that she remembered what she had done the night before. Bending down, she untied the bathrobe cord from her ankle and from the bell, put the cord back through the loops on her bathrobe, put the bell away. When she had dressed, she went downstairs to the drugstore for her breakfast; to go into the kitchen and make coffee seemed an impossible exertion.

After a glass of orange juice and a cup of coffee, which she forced herself to swallow, she climbed back to her mutilated apartment, forgetting to lock the door behind her. She practiced until she was weary, then flung herself down on the couch. Her body felt as heavy as lead, her eyes like a cigarette hole burnt in a velvet curtain. She didn't sleep, but she didn't think either; she just lay there on the couch, wrapped in a cloud of unhappiness that was hardly feeling. She didn't hear the bell ring. She didn't realize that Manya had climbed up the stairs and pushed open the unlocked door, until she sensed that someone was standing by the couch.

Opening her eyes without moving, she saw Manya. Still she didn't move. Manya had seen her, so there was no use in pretending.

"Katya," Manya said, looking down at her, lying there like a puppy who had been run over, the small body so limp, the great dark eyes staring so pleadingly and with such pain that Manya sat down on the edge of the couch, took Katherine in her arms, and began rocking her back and forth.

Katherine began to cry. At first she cried quite quietly, then her sobs came more quickly, torn from deep inside her until they threatened to choke her. Manya sat rocking her back and forth, kissing her gently over and over again, making little, soothing, comforting noises.

The sobs quieted down as they had come. "I've made you all wet," Katherine said, "your beautiful dress."

"It doesn't matter. It will dry."

Katherine lay heavily in Manya's arms, her face pressed into the strong shoulder. Her voice came out low and muffled. "It was my fault. It wasn't his fault at all. I spent so much time at the piano. It wasn't fair to him. He didn't understand. He thought I cared more for my music than for him. But it's not true. I don't. I'd give it up. I'd never touch a piano again if only he'd love me, if only everything could be the way it was before."

"Then perhaps it's just as well it never can be," Manya said quietly. After a time Katherine got up and went into the kitchen. "I'll make you some tea," she said, splashing water into the kettle.

When she came back into the living room, she was almost calm.

"I was afraid I might find Felix here," Manya said.

"I sent him away last night," Katherine told her. "I told him I didn't want to see him again. I hurt him."

"Why did you do that?"

"I wanted to—to cut everything away . . . I don't think I like—Bohemianism."

Manya merely said, "I think your water's boiling."

When Katherine brought in the tea, Manya was examining the desk lamp. "I have an extra lamp shade," she said. "It's not a bad one. Better than nothing, at any rate. Come on up to the apartment this evening and get it. You can have one of my copper maple-sugar buckets for your coal and a few other things to fill in the holes. Your father's in an awful temper about this business. I think you'd better come to dinner."

"Must I?"

"I think you'd better."

"All right . . . Aunt Manya?"

"What, Katyusha?"

"Was it—was it with you and Father the way it is with Sarah and Pete?"

Manya waited a long time before she spoke. Then she said, "No, darling. I think it was very different."

"Oh. I just wondered."

When she had finished her cup of tea, Manya stood up and went to the door. "Practice another couple of hours, darling, and then come on up. Or would you rather come with me in a taxi now?"

"No. I'll stay here."

"Don't be late. No use making your father crosser than he is."

"I'll be on time."

"Until dinner, then, Kisienka, my baby."

"Yes. Good-bye."

She leaned over the banisters, watching Manya go down the long flights of stairs. Then she went back to the piano.

Summer came. Summer came early to the city. The leaves of the trees on Eleventh Street became gray and dry with dust. Heat lay in clouds over the buildings. Sometimes a thunderstorm would come. For the first moment, with the steam rising hot and strangely fragrant from the pavement, it would be cooler. Then the heat would sink down again with a slow sullen stupor.

After a time Katherine felt that she was neither happy nor unhappy, that all feeling was absorbed in the heat. She practiced constantly, often sitting at the piano only in her underclothes or completely naked, feeling—why do I do this, what does it matter, nothing matters—even while her fingers went diligently over and over an exercise.

Several baths a day. Not much to eat. Gallons of water to drink. Sometimes at night it was too hot to lie on the bed, and she tried to sleep on the bare floor. When Manya's play closed for the summer, she and Tom moved out to Connecticut. She phoned Katherine frequently, sometimes, but not often, managing to persuade her to come out for a week end.

One day early in August Albert Peytz gave Katherine her mother's records.

"I've decided," he said, "not to wait until I die, as I intend to live a good while longer and I think you're old enough now to have the records. But promise me you won't play them too much."

"I'll try not to."

"Are you all right, child?"

"I'm fine."

"Not unhappy?"

"No."

"Restless?"

"I guess so."

"Lonely?"

"Yes."

"I'm not working you too hard?"

"Heavens, no."

"You've made great progress this summer."

"Have I really?"

"You know you have. You've heard of Mrs. Egon Carmer?"

"Yes. Of course."

"You knew that, besides all she does here in town, she also sends several students abroad each year to study?"

"No. I didn't know that."

"Only one piano student, unfortunately. She prefers voices and violins. Well, child, I think you'd better try for one of her fellowships. The heat this summer has worn me out. I need to rest next winter. Even you, easy though you are to teach, are too much for me. I've entered you. You will go to Paris and study with your Justin. Would you like that?"

"Yes!"

"The audition is next week. I haven't told you before, because I didn't want you to get too upset about it. I see no reason why you shouldn't get the scholarship. I've spoken to Mrs. Carmer about you, and she's very interested. God knows, you are advanced beyond your years. You are not mere brittle technique. There is something there. This is the program. Everything we've been working on this summer. I think you can manage."

"Yes!"

Somehow, the heavy ceiling had been lifted off the heat. It was possible to breathe again. She went home and re-read

363

the letters she had received from Justin and Anne in the spring. Phoned Manya eagerly.

"Darling," Manya said, "don't count on it too much. Peytz is an old man, and he's always been overly cocksure about his pupils. He thinks that just because he's made up his mind about something it's bound to happen. I've met Mrs. Egon Carmer and I know those auditions. You'll be playing against dozens of young people who have had as much if not more training than you."

"I know, I understand," Katherine said. "But when Mr. Peytz makes up his mind about something it usually *does* happen."

Mr. Peytz was not allowed to go to the audition with her. She was to come back to his studio after it was over. Mrs. Carmer had promised to phone him as soon as the winning candidate had been decided upon.

On her way uptown something happened that effectively shattered Katherine's control. For the first time since the last night on Eleventh Street she saw Pete. He was walking on the other side of the street, and he didn't see her. He wore a soft blue shirt, open at the throat; his face looked tanned and healthy; his stride was easy and light; she thought he looked well and happy.

Standing stock-still on the sidewalk, with people surging hotly by on either side of her, she watched him. Her heart was beating like a bird against her breast. She clenched her hands to keep herself from running across the street to him, although she knew her body was incapable of stirring from that one particular spot of pavement. Even after he had disappeared around the corner, she stood there, until someone jostled her and she almost lost her balance. Automatically she started walking again.

When she became one of the group of nervous, excited students, she was able to forget Pete, to concentrate on her music, on going to Paris to study with Justin again. Most of these boys and girls, chattering feverishly, seemed to know each other; she knew no one and sat silently, her knees hunched up, waiting her turn, listening carefully to the other candidates. Her turn came near the end, and she played well. While she was playing, there was nothing but the music, except for one very small portion of her mind, quite separate from the rest, that was telling her, "Yes, Katherine, this is all right."

When she got back to Mr. Peytz's studio, he was not sitting in his usual chair but was pacing up and down nervously. "Well?" he demanded. "Well? How did you do?"

"I did all right," she said.

"Could you hear the others?"

"Yes."

"Well?"

"I was the best. There was only one other person who was possible. A boy. Very handsome. His technique was magnificent. Better than mine. Much better. But there wasn't anything else. It was completely empty."

Mr. Peytz nodded. "All right, sit down. Sit down," he said. "Stop standing around like a little black sheep. Sit down. Harold! Harold!"

Katherine sat down on the piano bench, her back to the piano, leaning her elbows on the keys with a soft discord. Harold came running in.

"Yes, Mr. Peytz? What can I do for you, Mr. Peytz?"

"Get the young lady a glass of sherry."

"Yes, Mr. Peytz. Right away, Mr. Peytz." He took a decanter out of one of the musty cupboards and poured Katherine a small glass.

She sipped it gratefully, feeling very strange and puzzled. Because, although Mr. Peytz was still walking nervously about the room, she could not keep her mind on the audition; she kept seeing Pete on the sunny side of the hot city street in his blue shirt with the open collar, his hair moist with the heat of the August day. Perhaps she was too sure of winning this fellowship. Perhaps she had too much confidence, and that was why her mind was free to torture itself with images of Pete Burns. But without question she had been the best.

The telephone rang. "Harold!" Mr. Peytz shouted. "God! Katherine, he'll never get there. You answer it."

Katherine went to the telephone. She thought she recognized Mrs. Carmer's arrogant voice asking for Mr. Peytz. With a "Just a moment, please," she held the phone out to him.

He came hurrying toward it; he jerked the receiver out of her hand. He stood listening, without saying a word. Still without a word he hung up. Off the back of the bookcase he swept the bust of Beethoven. It lay in fragments on the floor. His face became so red, his eyes so staring, that Katherine was frightened. When at last he could speak, he bellowed for Harold. But when Harold came running in, he said heavily, "No, I don't want you. Get out of my sight. Leave me alone."

Harold beat a hasty retreat. Katherine sat down on the piano bench and finished her sherry.

"The old witch," Mr. Peytz said, "the cream-faced loon, excrement of a sow!" He sat down heavily in his chair, and forgetting the heat, pulled his blanket over his knees.

"It's the boy," he said at last. "The pretty boy with the technique. She always did like a pretty boy. If you were only a boy, it would have been all right. Well, he'll pay for his prize. Possessive females are not the best patrons . . . I'm sorry, child. I'm unutterably sorry."

366

"I'm sorry, too," Katherine said. "I know you're terribly disappointed."

"My feelings are immaterial," Albert Peytz said, throwing off the blanket. "I've let you count on this. I thought it was what you needed to make you happy. I've—I've tried to help you," he went on with difficulty, "but I seem only to have hurt you. The last time I talked with your Aunt Manya, it seemed to me she thought I was responsible for the break-up with your young man."

All Katherine could say was, "Don't be silly. She doesn't think that at all. She's just angry in general because she thinks I've been hurt. How could you have been responsible? Don't be silly."

"Child," Albert Peytz said, and then, after a moment, "go home. Go home. Your next lesson is on Monday. Go to the country till then. Now good-bye. Tell that cretin Harold to come here."

And so she went to the country, and on the train two nuns sitting opposite her made her think of Sarah and her acquired superstitions. She thought that indeed she would have to learn to be very patient. It would not be easy. Three seats ahead of her sat a young man who looked exactly like Pete from the back, though sallow and unattractive when she saw his face, and she sat staring at the back of his head, pretending he was Pete. —It's like when you're little—she thought—and have a bruise and keep on pressing it to see if it still hurts even though you know it does.—

Manya met her at the station, sorry about the fellowship, tender and understanding. Tom, as usual when he was anxious about her, was irritable.

Sunday night, before Katherine went back to the city, Manya got out her guitar and swung it about her neck.

"Tom's off in the lodge, wrestling with a new suite for strings. Let's climb the mountain and watch the moon rise."

They climbed up through the cool, green evening. Katherine lay on her back on the flat rock, while Manya sat near her, playing the guitar and singing softly.

As Katherine lay on her back, looking up at the sky—Cassiopeia, Vega of the Lyre, Boötes, Andromeda, Capella, the soft path of the Milky Way—she remembered the last time she had been there, wrapped in an old fur coat of Manya's, lying there on the rock with Pete's arms around her.

After a while Manya put her guitar down and lay back on the rock. "The moon will be up soon," she said. "See that sort of radiance over the mountain."

"Um," Katherine nodded.

"Here comes the moon now, Katya. Look."

The moon seemed to spring up from behind the mountains, a great full white disc, and float loosely in the sky. The stars were suddenly dimmed like city stars.

"I remember once in Russia," Manya said, "soon after I'd lost my baby. I lay all night on a mass of straw in the bottom of a wagon going from Kharkov, where I had been playing all winter in the theater, to a very small village where I had friends. I remember how I felt, lying there in the darkness, my body inert on the straw, smelling the heaviness of old tobacco mingling with the straw and sweat and the cold dew of black nights. My hand felt so heavy I didn't think I'd ever lift it again. The driver was a dark shadow up on the box, his whip swinging in the air. I felt so terribly alone, there was no one left in the world but me, lying there, an inert mass in the night of stars pressing through thick trees above me. The wagon's creaking seemed the earth's slow turning on its rusty hinges, an old earth, round and bare from friction with the sky, like a pebble worn too smooth by waters turbidly flowing. And I felt that my soul, too, was bare and round from too much rubbing against life. Well! I was nineteen! So old. So very old. Shall we go down now?"

About halfway down the mountain Manya paused. "Katya."

"Yes, Aunt Manya."

"I think you'd better go back to Paris next winter. I'm going on the road with my play. Your father's going to be out in Chicago for a couple of months. I don't like the idea of your being in New York with no one to take care of you. If you're in Paris, Pauline and Charlot can find a place for you to stay near them. You can study with your Justin all winter. I'll come and get you in the summer, or we can wait and see what our plans are by then."

Katherine sat down suddenly on the nearest rock. Manya sat down, too. Around them the birches were white against the dark night. Katherine sat there, leaning against Manya, and cried. Her tears came easily, gently, like a soft early rain. She realized how much she wanted to go back to Paris, back to Justin.

She felt as though she had been in great pain, as though she had been lost in it, had ceased to be Katherine Forrester and become a part of pain. But now she was herself again. She was Katherine. And although the pain was still there, it no longer possessed her. No, she possessed it; it was part of her; she could enclose everything in the span of her mind and heart.

When she was ready for bed that night, she re-read Justin's letter. "I miss you," Justin said. "Katherine, if you ever betray me by becoming mediocre, if you ever dishonor your work . . ."

She folded the letter and stared out the window into the night, stared down the path where she had walked, years ago, with Julie.

"I won't betray you," she said. "I'm coming back. I'm coming home!"

She sailed early in September. Tom had already left for Chicago, but Manya came to see her off.

Katherine suddenly felt whole and alive again. "It's all so wonderful! It's so exciting! It's so exciting I can hardly bear it. Why am I so happy? Why is everything all right again?"

"Dearest," Manya said, and kissed her.

The siren wailed shrilly, restlessly. A steward went down the stairs and through the passage, beating his gong. Manya put out her cigarette and stood up. "I must go now." She took Katherine's hand in hers, and they left the cabin and went up on deck. Katherine leaned very close to Manya, who quickly put her arms about her, whispering, "God bless and keep you, my darling."

She felt the cool pressure of Manya's soft cheek against hers. Then there was the firm, light sound of Manya walking away. Katherine watched her hurry down the gangplank, turn as she reached the dock and wave a small white handkerchief. Katherine waved back. Under her feet she could feel the throb of engines. Slowly, quietly, the ship began to pull away.

She ran in and up to the sports deck, where there were only one or two other people. Manya, growing smaller and smaller, was still waving her handkerchief. Violently Katherine waved back, tears starting to her eyes.

After Manya had completely disappeared, when the shore was only a chain of blinking, beckoning lights, Katherine pulled up a deck chair and lay there, under the stars, under the wind, under the vastness of the universe, while land became lost in the September night, and water reached out, illimitable, mysterious, on all sides.